The Spirit Gene

Also by Mark Reynolds

A Journey with Strangers

Mark Reynolds

THE SPIRIT GENE

A journey beyond the fringes of science

This book is a work of fiction. Although certain aspects were inspired by actual events and living persons, the storyline was entirely the product of the author's imagination and should not be construed as real. Where public figures appear, the author hereby disavows and makes no representation regarding the authenticity or historical accuracy of events and dialogue attributed to them. In all other respects, any resemblance to persons living or dead is entirely coincidental.

Cover Art: *Front:* design © Mark A. Reynolds. *Back:* the Eagle Nebula's Pillars of Creation. Photo credit: NASA, ESA/Hubble and the Hubble Heritage Team.

First Edition.

ISBN: 978-0-692-15032-0

July, 2018

"Now faith is confidence in what we hope for and assurance about what we do not see. This is what the ancients were commended for."

Hebrews 11:1-2

PROLOGUE

"Transcendence"

11:45 AM. Monday, August 18TH, 1980
Indian Ocean, 1000 miles southeast of Madagascar

THE MANNEQUIN-LIKE BODY floated face up amidst the rolling waves. Clad in a white lab coat, with rigid outstretched arms and legs, only his clothing and long dark hair swayed rhythmically with the undercurrents. The formerly alive young scientist had an aquiline nose and prominent cheekbones, yet his face now held a frozen expression of astonishment. And his olive skin reflected a plastic-like sheen, with no signs of bloating or discoloration despite a merciless sun beating down from a cloudless sky.

Where might this strange floating body have come from? Few would have believed the answer, were it ever to be known. Commercial air traffic flew well to the north, and the last container ship to pass this way had been weeks before. Over 600 miles from the nearest island, it was just a tiny speck on a massive expanse of open water. Even satellites ignored this part of the world.

Darkness still covered the University of California's San Francisco campus, where the young man had been working alone in Professor Higgins' laboratory only moments before. He preferred working at night, when no-one else was around. His absence wouldn't be noticed for days.

Most of the other graduate students and staff who worked on that floor were now home sleeping soundly, except for two night owls who had chosen instead to head down to Clancy's, a popular local watering hole in the Sunset District. They sat by the window nursing their mugs, gazing out to a thick evening fog. Tiny droplets coalesced into larger ones on the outside window pane and then drizzled down the glass, one after another.

Brett Roberts, the taller of these two budding young scientists, had an agile distance runner build and a blonde curly mane. He thought the hairstyle made him look a bit like Roger Daltrey, lead singer from his favorite rock band *The Who*. The puka shell necklace reminded him of sunnier Southern California days. Sitting across the table from Roberts was his friend Owen Mudford, the cross-bred offspring of an all-American Iowa farm boy father and a native Hawaiian mother. Owen bore a strong resemblance to Mel Gibson in the movie *Mad Max*, except for the slant of his Polynesian eyes. An avid surfer, he also held a black belt in Karate.

The hazy blur of a clanging streetcar rumbled by.

"Last call!" shouted the barman from behind his counter. Roberts gestured to their empty pitcher. "C'mon, Mudford, your turn to buy."

Mudford grinned wryly, "You sure you're up for it?"

Roberts nodded. "Bring it on." It was dollar pitcher night, after all.

Mudford went up to the bar and paid for another round. He carried the brimming pitcher back to their table without spilling a drop and proceeded to top off their mugs. "There. You happy?"

Roberts took a pensive sip. "Thanks, Owen. By the way, have you managed to catch that new *Star Trek* movie?"

Mudford leaned forward with a bemused grin. "Whoa, that came out of nowhere. No man, I haven't seen it."

"Really, you should go. Pretty cool watching Kirk and his crew on the big screen, and the special effects were awesome. In fact, they filmed one of those scenes right here at UCSF, inside our molecular graphics laboratory."

"Huh. Didn't know you were a *Trekkie*."

"Yeah, guess I've always been fascinated by the concept of intergalactic space travel. Watching *Star Trek* made me believe it could one day become a reality. In fact, a good number of their futuristic gadgets already have."

Mudford had just taken a sip of beer and almost spit it out with his chuckle. "Brett Roberts, space explorer," he mocked.

"No really. Consider the amazing progress our space program has made over the past two decades. Neil Armstrong took man's first steps on the moon less than three years after *Star Trek* first aired on television. Bet we'll have men walking around on Mars within our lifetime. Warp drive might be a few centuries away. Then again, most people thought breaking the sound barrier would be impossible until Chuck Yeager managed to poke a hole through it back in '47. And now here we've got supersonic jets flying in excess of Mach-3."

"Hold on a minute, Brett. Where are we going with this?" Roberts had a tendency to ramble when he was tired, and both he and Mudford had just pulled another 14-hour shift in the lab.

"I was just getting to that," said Roberts. "Something about *Star Trek* has been puzzling me lately."

Mudford teased, "You mean how Captain Kirk always manages to get those alien chicks to fall for him?"

Roberts winced. "No, I've been wondering a lot about teleportation. You know, how Kirk and his crew would just step onto the transporter, magically get vaporized into sparkle dust, and then rematerialize on the surface of some unknown planet, which to me...."

Mudford cut in, "Okay, so what's your problem?"

"The movie version made teleportation seem almost real, you know? And perhaps it *will* be possible to teleport an object someday." Roberts shook his head. "Just doesn't seem possible to teleport a human being."

Mudford settled back in his chair, a bit more interested now. "Okay genius, why's that?"

"Well for one thing, it would violate the 'uncertainty principle' of quantum mechanics. You could never perfectly teleport an object without changing it in some unpredictable way...."

Mudford held up his free hand and made Roberts wait while he took a long pull from his mug. "Not so fast, my friend. What about the Einstein-Podolsky-Rosen paradox? You know, from Professor Richter's lecture last week?"

"Dude, I'm surprised you even remember those names," said Roberts.

Mudford nodded. "I read more about it after the lecture. Back in the 1930s, Albert Einstein and two other physicists published a thought experiment involving the entanglement of sub-atomic particles, and concluded that quantum mechanics could not fully describe it. Einstein referred to this phenomenon as *spooky action at a distance*. He later mused that there must be something missing in the wave equation, some variable yet to be discovered. So you can't fairly say that quantum mechanics disproves teleportation, at least not in its present form."

"Guess you've got me there," said Roberts. "But what about our memories? How could you possibly hold onto your sense of who you are?"

Mudford leaned back and folded his arms. "Consider what we've learned since Einstein's time about neurotransmitters and brain receptors. Our sensory perceptions are really just biochemical signaling processes, and we've got billions of neurons firing away inside our heads each moment. What was that expression Descartes once wrote, *I think therefore I am*? Maybe self-awareness is just an illusion."

"Well, what if something went wrong? Doesn't that bother you?"

Mudford waved dismissively. "Nah, I'd be willing to take my chances. Teleportation is such an awesome concept. Scientists will eventually figure it out. Perhaps someone already has…." His eyes darted across the room. "Hey, how'd you get over there?" He then glanced back to Roberts with mock surprise. "See? Here you are again. Feel any different?"

"Ha, ha." Roberts was just about to mount another challenge, something about mathematical concepts of infinity trumping empirical thought, when the barman shouted his final warning, "Closing time!"

Roberts sighed. "Damn, forgot they close early on Sunday. Looks like he's about to kick us out. Sorry I made you buy that second pitcher. Feel like chugging it?"

"I'm good." Owen pushed away and he began to rise. "By the way, it's supposed to be sunny tomorrow, at least according to *The Chronicle*. How about an early morning bike ride before heading back up to the lab?"

Roberts shook his head. "Wish I could, but I need to be in by 7 AM to change the fraction collector in the cold room for this enzyme I've been purifying."

"Suit yourself, bud. I'll probably be in around ten."

The lifeless body of Juan Virtanen would not be floating above the surface much longer. A great white shark had been patrolling the area on high alert for schools of pelagic fish to satisfy its ever present appetite. A handful of fuzzy morsels had fallen into the water about an hour before, formerly the lab mice that Virtanen had been experimenting with earlier that evening. Definitely not fish, but its primitive brain didn't care. In a predator's world, the ocean was simply food or not food. The shark sensed another disturbance in the water up above, and despite the body's lack of scent, it instinctively swam upward to explore the anomaly.

A massive dorsal fin broke the surface and the shark began to swirl around its prey while eyeing it hungrily. It surged forward and took a tentative nibble from one of the outstretched limbs, but the flesh was bloodless, unsatisfying, a most unexpected outcome. The shark quickly lost interest and swam away.

The fearsome predator returned a mere ten minutes later, having already forgotten his previous encounter with the body. And this time, with jaws raised high above the surface of the water, the shark chomped down fiercely and took the body down to the depths below.

Soon the surface was calm again, in every direction.

CHAPTER ONE

"The beginning"

Thursday, June 16th, 1977
University of Michigan, School of Pharmacy, Ann Arbor

THE SUN BEAMED DOWN through feathery wisps of clouds in an otherwise powder blue sky. Juan Virtanen stood alone amidst a sea of fellow classmates on the grassy lawn outside the Rackham Building, all of them smartly dressed in new graduation gowns with the distinctive olive green sash of their chosen major. The procession into the auditorium was about to begin. Students chatted away nervously in small groups nearby, but Virtanen was too preoccupied to share in their excitement. After five years of lectures, classwork and many long hours of studying, he was about to receive his bachelor's degree in pharmacy. He wished he could be happy for this day to finally arrive, but all he felt right then was troubled.

Juan's father and older sister had been unable to make the trip from northern Brazil. His sister Maria had explained over the phone that Father was simply not well enough to travel. She'd try to visit later that summer if Father's health improved, although she hadn't sounded hopeful about that possibility.

The Virtanen family had migrated to Brazil from their native Finland during the rubber boom era of the late 1800s. They had prospered in Manaus for a time, but eventually their bloodline admixed with the Portuguese and their numbers slowly dwindled. Juan would soon be the last of their line who still carried the name.

Juan was particularly disappointed that Maria could not be with him for today's commencement. He had questions about their mother that he desperately wanted to ask her.

His mother Luisa was an orphaned descendent of an indigenous tribe, brought by missionaries to the convent in Manaus and raised there since a young girl. For reasons that no one was willing to discuss, she ran away to a slum or *favela* upon reaching the age of fifteen. Juan's father rescued Luisa from those same streets some years later, although Juan knew few of the details. The two of them eventually married and had two young children in rapid succession.

Luisa strangely left them when Juan was barely three years old and his sister less than a year older. Sadly, he remembered little about his mother.

Juan's father never spoke about the drugs that had reclaimed his poor Luisa. What little Juan knew about her had come from the random gossip of neighbors. The once bright and beautiful Luisa had apparently been spotted in the favela a few times but eventually vanished without a trace.

Juan's father was too despondent from her loss to continue teaching at the University of Manaus, deciding instead to purchase a local bookstore where Juan and his sister were raised in an upstairs apartment. Juan left for boarding school at the age of ten and never looked back, which was his own way of putting his mother behind him.

Thoughts of his mother scarcely entered his mind until five days before, when he received a package from Brazil containing his mother's leather-bound journal, along with this handwritten note from Father:

> *Juan, I am sorry to have kept this journal from you for so many years. It appeared at our doorstep on the morning of your twelfth birthday. I hadn't known that your mother was still alive until I held it in my hands. As I read through the pages, I realized it was something you should not see until you were much older. You see, I was worried you may fall into similar depths if you were to read it at a younger age. But now my son, I know that you are strong. You will soon be receiving your pharmacy degree, and regardless of what you might do next, you have made me proud to be your father. So I bequeath this to you now, trusting you can forgive the wife and mother we both lost. I also hope it can provide a few answers to your many questions. By the way, your sister has already read through these pages, such as they are.*

The journal was filled with his mother's ramblings, lamentations about her struggles with drug addiction and her yearnings to find God, and on the final pages her scattered reasons for returning to the streets of the favela. She would go there to find herself; she would go there to punish herself; and perhaps she would get better… or not. Her indigenous past was mentioned in a number of different ways, but it was a lot like trying to follow a spiral that never actually connected. On the very last page, her musings abruptly ended thusly: *I must go back.*

Juan re-read his mother's journal a number of times over the days leading up to his commencement. The pages had almost consumed him.

On this morning of his graduation, shortly after Juan had shaved and dressed in the new suit that he now wore, he cracked the diary open once again. And this time, while flipping through the pages, he spotted a faint scribbling down one of the right-hand margins:

Juan, you must follow my past. It will help you to understand.

How had he missed that?

Juan's original plan had been to become a pharmacist. It was an honorable profession, but he no longer felt certain about that path. His mother's scribbled words had embedded themselves into his subconscious mind: *you must follow my past…*

He pressed his lips together and made a curt nod when the dean handed him his diploma, then followed the queue of recent graduates back down to their row, sitting together in unison as they'd been taught to do in practice. The rest of the ceremony was a muted background blur until he realized that he was once again standing outside in daylight, in the middle a mob of hugging classmates. Not wanting to draw much attention to himself, he tossed his cap into the air along with the others and then quickly ducked away when no one was looking, to exit the campus for his very last time. He unbuttoned his gown with one hand while clutching his newly minted diploma in the other as he walked up Thayer Street.

With his gown casually draped over one shoulder, Juan climbed the front steps of a fifties-era house that he had been renting along with four other students. The maple tree out front bore a fresh set of leaves; they rustled in the wind as he fumbled with his keys.

The house was empty now, his other housemates having already left for the summer. David, an engineering student who would be returning in the fall, had precisely cleaned his assigned section of the house including the dishes, although he'd left them in the drying rack for Juan to put away.

A stack of pizza boxes in the kitchen needed to be tossed as well. Eugene, now a second year medical student, had left his room in disarray, as it would remain until he too returned from summer break. The last two housemates were recent Michigan graduates and had already cleared out their respective rooms. Noting the trash they'd left behind, Juan surmised they'd likely forfeit their cleaning deposits.

The plan had been for Juan to rent out the unoccupied rooms while sending out applications for his first real job. As a fallback, there was always the pharmacy downtown where he'd interned over the past two summers. Eugene had agreed to take over the lease and Juan was now paying month to month.

But none of that seemed important at the moment. Juan loosened his tie, stepped into his room, and noted his mother's journal still there on the night stand where he'd left it. He glanced upward to the national flag of Brazil hanging above his bed, pausing a moment to admire the stars within its central blue orb, their respective positions matching the nighttime sky over Rio de Janeiro on the evening in 1889 when Brazil first became a republic. The gold rhombus and green background inspired an emotion that he hadn't felt in years.

Picking up his mother's journal, he re-read the note she'd obviously written for him in the margin. What could she have meant by this? There was only one way to find out. He packed a suitcase and boxed up the rest of his things.

The city of Manaus had been named for the indigenous Manaó tribes that still inhabited the region. It was once described as one of South America's gaudiest cities during the rubber boom era of the late 1880s, with outrageous displays of opulence ranging from expensive yachts to elaborate menageries. Due to its prominent location where the Rio Negro and the Rio Amazonas converged, Manaus had long been known as the undisputed heart of the Amazon, growing rapidly to become a regional powerhouse of trade and commerce. By the late 1970s it had matured into a diverse industrial city with over 450,000 inhabitants. Now the capital of the State of Amazonas, it was also a popular tourist destination for adventurers and anglers yearning for more exotic catch.

But being located 900 miles inland in a country with relatively few major highways, it was still best accessed by boat or plane. Juan had found the bumpy flight in from Caracas Peru to be an endurance test of nerves and fortitude.

He stepped down from the bus onto a tired-looking downtown street. The city center of Manaus had undergone decades of decline ever since the construction of the Free Port where most of the city's business and trade were now conducted. He picked up his suitcase and followed the familiar route of back streets and alleys until he found himself standing in front of his father's used book store. In days of better health Father could often be found there behind the counter, reading or passionately chatting with anyone who happened to drop in. But the bookstore now was closed and dusty. Juan released a long breath and opened the faded wooden door to the right of the shop entrance, the one leading upstairs to his family's apartment above the bookstore. He quietly climbed the stairs to avoid waking Father who would probably be napping.

Juan leaned his suitcase against the sidewall at the top of the landing and softly rapped on the door. It opened a crack and his sister's delicate fingers wrapped around to hold it in place while she peered out warily.

"Hello Maria."

She abruptly slammed the door. Disheartened at first, Juan then heard her fiddling with the chain lock. He waited patiently for her to open the door. "I didn't mean to startle you," he ventured, while studying his sister's careworn expression. Was she not pleased to see him?

"Juan! What a surprise," said Maria, a bit awkwardly.

Juan noted how pale his sister's skin was, concluding that she must rarely venture outside. He pulled her into an awkward embrace and softly pecked her cheek before stepping back. "How is Father?"

"Not well." Maria smiled bravely. "Come in and let's get you settled. Father should be up from his nap soon." She led him into the front sitting room and motioned for him to take the sofa. "Relax a moment while I go make us a fresh pot of coffee."

Amber light diffused through the dirty front windows, casting an ethereal glow onto the features of the room. This room seemed much smaller than Juan remembered, the entire apartment in fact. He heard Maria humming softly to herself. Good, he thought. She seemed pleased to have him home after all.

Then Juan heard the labored and uneven footsteps of his father coming down the hall from his back bedroom. Juan crossed his arms and rocked his shoulders back and forth to relieve the tension in his knotted muscles.

Senhor Virtanen made a noisy entrance and thumped his cane on the floor before leaning upon it with wobbly legs. He gave his son a stern appraisal. "Well, this is indeed a surprise. We hadn't expected you home this summer, my son."

Juan stood and offered his father the sofa. "Please Father, have a seat."

Senhor Virtanen shuffled into the room and defiantly took his reading chair by the window instead. "Well then, don't just stand there like an idiot. I'm perfectly fine, there's nothing to worry about."

He put a handkerchief to his mouth and coughed noisily into it before settling back in his chair. "Sit, sit, my son."

Juan slowly lowered himself back onto the sofa and leaned forward attentively with his elbows resting on his knees. He would wait for Father to begin.

"You've read your mother's diary."

Juan was briefly taken aback by how much his father had aged since the last time he saw him. The wrinkles had deepened around his eyes and his wild and unkempt hair was now white as snow. "Yes Father, I have."

"*Humpf*," Senhor Virtanen grunted. "I expected it might provide some closure about your mother, but apparently not. Well, then. What brings you home so unexpectedly?"

"It's good to see you too, Father," said Juan.

Senhor Virtanen grunted again, unwilling to concede the point.

"Actually, I would like to learn more about her indigenous origin. Having sent Mother's diary, I had hoped you might finally be willing to talk about her." Juan reminded himself to be patient. Father's expression suggested this subject was still quite unwelcome.

Maria returned with the coffee service and carefully lowered two steaming cups of the strong Brazilian brew onto each of their end tables. Juan could almost taste it already from the strong aroma but waited for Father to have the first sip. Senhor Virtanen unsteadily lifted the cup to his bearded lips and slurped noisily.

"Why does this still concern you?" the senior Virtanen asked.

"She scribbled something to me in her journal, Father. Surely you must have seen it too, down one of the margins? Something about following her past...."

Senhor Virtanen leaned forward. "Which was precisely why I withheld it from you for so many years."

"But why, father?"

"Your mother's journal is filled with meaningless riddles, my son. I've tried almost everything to solve them without success. I even hired a guide to search for her in the indigenous territories. But he never found a trace of her presence there. Nothing learned, only money wasted."

This was the first time Juan's father had ever mentioned the possibility of his mother returning to her own people. Although that nugget didn't surprise him.

Juan wanted to ask a few more questions, although he could see how difficult this discussion still was for Father. Mother's disappearance had torn a hole in his father's heart, one that would never heal. Something else appeared to be troubling Father as well. Juan made a mental note to ask Maria about that later.

The two of them resumed sipping their coffee and let the silence linger. Senhor Virtanen set his cup back down after a while, shut his eyes, and began snoring softly. Juan wondered how Father could nod off like that. Maria's strong coffee made him want to pace around the room. But he didn't dare disturb the old man, not right now. So he sat there and waited patiently with clenched teeth.

The wall clock ticked, ticked, ticked....

Senhor Virtanen suddenly began coughing, uncontrollably. He pulled a handkerchief from his pocket and pressed it to his mouth between desperate gasps for air. It was painful to watch, but Juan instinctively knew not to interfere. His father finally pulled the handkerchief away and folded it quickly before returning it to his pocket, but Juan had already spotted the bloody phlegm.

"Are you all right, Father?" Senhor Virtanen waved a hand to suggest that he was fine, but Juan could see it in his eyes, his father's acceptance of finality. Father had always been a heavy chain smoker, ever since his early teens. Juan suspected that it may be lung cancer, and upon glancing to Maria, her pained expression confirmed his suspicion. Attending to

Father's deteriorating health had been her full time job. Juan felt ashamed not to have appreciated her sacrifice until now.

"Father, perhaps I should take you to a hospital in America?" Juan tried to sound hopeful.

"No, my son, it is too late for that. I'm told I have but a few months left to live. We must both let go of things that cannot be changed."

Juan had caught his father's innuendo. "Father, please tell me. Which tribe did our mother come from?"

Senhor Virtanen grimaced. He should have destroyed Luisa's journal instead. May as well tell the boy. Juan would never stop asking otherwise. "The *Yanomami*," he uttered in a strained and throaty voice, intending for more words of admonishment to follow. Instead, Senhor Virtanen plunged into another coughing fit, this one more desperate than the one before.

Maria rushed over to assist him. When Father's coughing had mercifully subsided, she looked to her brother and said firmly, "Juan, I think Father has had enough for now." She helped him out of his chair and guided him back down the hall to his bedroom.

Juan paced around while waiting for his sister to return. He noticed a small circular picture frame on the end table next to his father's reading chair which must have been obscured by the coffee cup earlier. He bent over and picked it up.

It was a photo of his mother, her long black hair parted down the middle and tied loosely behind in a way that flattered her features. How beautiful she had once been with her elegant brown oval face and high cheekbones. And such captivating blue eyes, so out of place with the rest of her indigenous features, as though she had been expecting something magical to happen when the photo was taken. Juan understood why his father had kept this picture.

"Father wouldn't approve of you touching that."

Juan turned to see his sister standing there with arms crossed and a stern expression that reminded him of the nuns back in parochial school. He felt a bit embarrassed but wasn't quite sure why. "I've never seen this picture of our mother before."

Maria took it from him and carefully arranged it back on the end table. "I was cleaning out the storeroom downstairs a few months ago. Father always left it such a mess, but he hasn't been down there since his health began to fail. When I brought up one of the boxes to sort through he snatched it away, told me to leave him be and later carried it back downstairs all by himself. I noticed this picture of our mother the next morning. He won't even let me dust that table now."

Juan motioned for his sister to take the sofa but she refused and took the reading chair instead. Father's chair was hers to protect, evidently. She was his caregiver after all. Juan settled back on the sofa, leaned forward and waited for her to continue.

Maria said, "Father must have also found our mother's diary in that box. He allowed me to read it before sending it to you." She put a hand to her mouth, wishing she hadn't mentioned that.

Juan stared at his sister with a hurt expression, but said nothing.

"Please forgive me, Juan. Father forbade me from telling you, although apparently our mother wished you to have it. I have no idea why he withheld it from you for so many years."

Juan choked back his anger and nodded for Maria to continue.

"Mother told me stories about the Yanomami when I was a little girl. I can still remember them." Maria averted her gaze and stared absently out the dusty window while continuing the narrative. "Shortly after she left us, I asked Father about the Yanomami, but he became angry and sent me to my room without answering. I tried again when I was older, but this time he said that I should simply forget about the Yanomami, that it was the nuns who had raised our mother, not them. I never asked him again."

Juan remembered how Maria had once planned to become a nun herself. For some unspoken reason, she changed her mind after her first year as an initiate, although she never went on to marry. Juan couldn't recall his sister ever dating a man. Her dedication to Father now required her full attention anyway. Juan admired her for that. He'd always been much too restless to remain in one place for very long.

Maria continued, "When I was still an initiate back at the convent, I stumbled upon a file in Mother Superior's office. It said that our mother had been brought to them by Catholic missionaries working with the indigenous tribes in the northern mountains of Amazonas. According to their notes, our mother kept following them around the village and asking them questions about God, saying that she too could speak with God and wanted to learn more about Him. This was their justification for bringing our mother to the convent in Manaus. She must have been about five at the time. The nuns gave her the name Luisa and taught her how to read and write.

"I thought Sister Daniela might discipline me when she caught me with the file, but instead she softened and chose to tell me herself. She fondly remembered how bright our mother's spirit had been, how she spoke almost constantly with God. And especially her deep blue eyes. Sister Daniela kept commenting about how bright they were. The nuns believed it to be a miracle. They also hoped she would one day join their order as an initiate. Unfortunately, our mother's sweet nature changed in a bad way after reaching the age of puberty. She became increasingly disruptive and ill-tempered. Before the nuns or God could save her from her torment, she ran away. The nuns were badly shaken by this, I can still see it in our reverend mother's eyes.

"They searched the streets of the favelas for over two years but never managed to encounter anyone who knew her whereabouts. Then one day a miracle happened, for them anyway. Our father returned to the church with his Luisa, our mother, and asked for permission to marry her. For the nuns it was an answer to their prayers."

She pressed her lips together. "But the story did not end well, as you know. According to Sister Daniela, our mother's mental illness returned after bearing the two of us. And as we both know, she left our family soon after that. I still struggle to understand why!"

Maria turned to face the side wall as a tear began rolling down her cheek. Juan had long known about Mother's drug addiction. He could see from his sister's expression that she could no longer continue.

"Thanks for telling me," Juan uttered at last.

Maria nodded, "Will you be staying long?"

"Perhaps a few days…" Juan answered. "Do you think the nuns would be willing to tell us more?"

Maria released a heavy a sigh. "We could ask them tomorrow, I suppose. But you must be hungry and tired after such a long journey. Come with me and I will prepare something for you to eat."

They ate together at the kitchen table in silence. Juan tried to make Maria smile, but it was not forthcoming.

Seeing that Juan had finished, Maria carried their plates to the sink. "I'd like to go to my room now, if you don't mind."

Juan listened to the receding sounds of her footsteps down the hall, heard her open the first door to check on father, and then retire to her own bedroom for the evening, shutting the door with a soft click. He waited for Maria to fall asleep before heading downstairs to explore his father's book shop.

The dusty shelves hadn't seen customers in many months. Juan browsed down the aisles until he spotted a reference book about the indigenous tribes of the Amazon Rainforest. He carried it over to a badly worn reading chair behind the counter that reeked of stale tobacco, his father's preferred location when minding the shop. The springs protested with a loud squeak when he sat. He crossed one leg over the other and then cracked the book open, thumbing to the chapter about the Yanomami.

For thousands of years, the Yanomami had lived undisturbed in the rainforests and mountains of northern Brazil and southern Venezuela. The American anthropologist Napoleon Chagnon described them as an isolated people living in small villages who spoke their own unique language. They were notoriously known for their blow guns and poisoned darts, although mostly used for hunting despite the popular myths.

The Yanomami relied heavily on the rainforest for their food. They hunted wild pigs, monkeys, birds and rodents, as well as large insects. Caterpillars were considered a very desirable meal. They also practiced a primitive form of horticulture, moving on whenever the land no longer supported their crops. Most of the tribes lived communally in large huts or *shabonos*, supporting up to 150 people, which were built from tree trunks, vines, palm leaves, and other forest plants.

Juan was curious to learn about the hallucinogenic drugs that were used for their religious rituals. With his pharmaceutical background, he read with particular interest how *yopo* snuff was prepared by their local shaman. Dried seeds of the tree *Anadenanthera Peregrina* were ground to a fine powder and mixed with ash, as well as a drop or two of honey and other fragrant herbs to give the snuff a more pleasant scent. The final mixture was kept in a special gourd container that only the shaman was allowed to open. Juan knew the ash would provide an essential alkalinity to activate the most likely active ingredient, one he had learned about in pharmacy school, dimethyltryptamine.

It saddened him to read on about how contact with outsiders had disrupted the Yanomami. During the 1950s, Portuguese miners began to invade the Yanomami regions in search of gold. They brutalized the Yanomami women and forced the men into slavery to work the mines.

When the missionaries arrived, many of them of the Salesian Catholic order, the Yanomami villages accepted their presence at first as protection from the fearsome and murderous miners. The missionaries offered them safety, but they also imposed strict rules of discipline upon them, prohibiting their traditional ways of communal dwelling and requiring unattached men and women to live separately. They forbade the Yanomami from practicing polygamy and were especially scornful of the shamans.

Perhaps not surprisingly, many of them escaped into the hill country bordering Brazil and Venezuela to reclaim their independence.

Then in the early 1970s the Brazilian military decided to build a perimeter road into their northern territory. With no prior warning, the bulldozers plowed through a number of the Yanomami villages. Their inhabitants were wiped out by diseases from which they had no immunity. These diseases spread rapidly from one village to the next, decimating nearly forty percent of their population within the span of only five years.

Most of the remaining Yanomami tribes were now wary of outsiders.

Later that evening, Juan took in the familiarity of his childhood bedroom as he lay atop his single bed. His father had constructed a shelf ledge around the upper perimeter of the room when he was a little boy, about a meter down from the ceiling. Resting upon it were various memories from his childhood, wind up robots and space ships, plastic dinosaurs, model cars and tractors and various other knick-knacks, things that had once been important to him, although he couldn't remember why.

He smiled when he spotted the single volume Britannica Encyclopedia, given to Juan by his father on his eighth birthday. Juan had spent many hours lying on the floor of this very room while flipping through its pages.

Juan had always possessed a voracious appetite for reading, which eventually propelled him to the prestigious Colégio Bandeirantes in São Paulo, having received a fellowship to study there at the age of twelve.

He flashed back to that fateful moment, sitting at his desk in a crowded classroom with paddle fans spinning around noisily from above. The nuns paced vigilantly up and down the aisles in their heavy black habits as though immune to the heat. The rector stepped into the classroom and summoned Juan forward. Minutes later, while fidgeting nervously in the rector's office, Juan was asked if he would like to study in São Paulo. He eagerly embraced the news, having often found it difficult to relate to his fellow classmates.

He discovered his love for science a few years afterwards, at São Paulo's Centro Federal de Educação Tecnológica. And it was at the farmácia, located on the opposite corner of a busy street just beyond the campus, where Juan met his future mentor Senhor Rodriguez. Senhor Rodriguez gave Juan an opportunity to work behind the counter during the afternoon hours. He showed Juan how to formulate different medicines while explaining their properties. This was why Juan had decided to study pharmacy in America.

Juan remembered the day he returned home to tell Father that he'd been awarded a full scholarship to attend the University of Michigan, one that included room, board and travel expenses. All Father did was send him off with a firm pat on the back. He must have presumed the last of the Virtanen clan was leaving Brazil for good.

Juan had hoped his father would be pleased to see him now, and yet he seemed disappointed instead. What else could he have expected after sending Juan his mother's journal? Couldn't he understand Juan's yearning to learn more about where his mother came from?

It didn't matter. Mother's words had now come alive through her journal, and Maria had agreed to take him to the convent to speak with the nuns. Tomorrow, Juan would learn how to find his mother. Of that he felt certain.

Exhaustion began to subsume him. He pulled the bed sheet up to his chin and nestled his head into a feather pillow that his sister had made for him many years before. He closed his eyes.

He soon began to dream. While still a young boy, he found himself standing in the graduation robe he would wear years later to receive his pharmacy degree. The sleeves hung well past his fingers with the tails cascading down onto the bright green grassy field. His pharmacy classmates towered nearby. Juan tried desperately to shout out loud but no one seemed to notice his pre-pubescent body.

Then he glanced upward and spotted a faint ball of light hovering above the Rackham building, translucent and getting larger as it floated down to meet him, like Glenda's entrance in *The Wizard of Oz*. A fuzzy image gradually sharpened inside the orb until he recognized his mother, the face from the photo next to his father's chair in the sitting room. She beckoned him upward with her piercing blue eyes, her long dark hair flowing about her head as though weightless, or perhaps underwater. He couldn't quite hear what she was saying but the meaning was clear… *you must follow my past.*

Juan rose early the next morning and found breakfast waiting for him in the downstairs kitchen, along with a note from his sister encouraging him to eat while she attended once more on Father. He ate quickly, rinsed his dishes in the sink, and poured a second cup of coffee while awaiting Maria's return. While pondering his dream from the night before, Juan reached a fateful decision. He would travel to the Yamomami territory himself. There was no other way, he realized. Perhaps the nuns might be able to assist him through one of their missionary channels. If not, he would go it alone.

He heard Maria's deliberate footsteps and she entered the kitchen soon afterwards, now wearing a wide-brimmed hat. "Father ate a little but still needs to rest. He is most unhappy about us visiting the convent this morning and asked me to tell you so, which I now have done. But I know how stubborn you can be when your mind is set on something." From his sister's determined expression, Juan sensed her struggle to summon the courage for their brief outing. The kilometer stroll to the cathedral where they both had been baptized would take them through a sketchy part of town.

They descended the stairs to street level and entered the bright sunlight. Juan held Maria's hand protectively as they walked briskly past the street vendors hawking their wares along Rio Cinco de Septiembro. Her desperate grip told Juan how uncomfortable she was being out on these noisy and busy downtown streets. Juan appreciated his sister all the more for the effort. She was doing it for him, he realized.

It was a hot and humid morning and their clothes were already sticking to their skin when Juan spotted the familiar bridge, one they'd crossed over many times together as children. Maria's grip tightened once they had reached the opposite bank of the narrow inlet.

Juan said, "Relax, Sister. We are almost there."

"I'm uncomfortable being this far from our apartment," said Maria. "What if something happens to Father?"

"We'll be back within the hour, I promise."

They made a right and wound their way northward through a hardscrabble neighborhood to a grassy field near the water where the cathedral came into view. For Juan, the sight of its twin towers had always come as a pleasant surprise after emerging from these narrow and dirty streets. They appeared to glisten in the sunlight. Maria directed him over toward a queue of nuns just leaving mass and spoke to one of them in Portuguese. The woman nodded and led them into a walled courtyard behind the church.

At the opposite end of the courtyard was the 'convent' of Manaus, more of a dormitory really. Nuns of the Salesian order boarded here on temporary rotations to minister to the indigenous poor in the city's favelas or slums. These were desperate areas of extreme poverty where the city's more prosperous citizens dared not venture. Most of the nuns willingly returned to their mission churches in the indigenous territories within three to six months.

Maria led Juan into the convent and spoke softly to an initiate at the reception desk, who promptly stood and went to summon the Reverend Mother.

Sister Daniela looked to be somewhere in her late fifties with sad, intelligent eyes. "So good to see you, Maria. And you must be Juan. All grown up now I see." With graceful hand gestures, she beckoned them into her office and motioned for them to be seated.

After a brief exchange in Portuguese, Maria switched to English, "Thank you for agreeing to meet with us, Reverend Mother." Juan was grateful, having grown more accustomed to the language of his adopted country.

Sister Daniela turned her attention to Juan and studied him a moment. "How may I help you?"

"I'd like to ask a few questions about our mother," Juan began.

"I thought you might… well then, what is it you wish to know?

Juan paused a moment to collect his thoughts. "My mother kept a journal, it seems. Father mailed it to me in America recently. Evidently she wanted me to have it, although he kept it from me for many years. I have returned home to find out what it means. I presume you knew about her struggles, with…"

"Yes Juan, we knew. Your mother fell back into drug addiction shortly after you were born. Our aid workers reported spotting her on the streets of Cidade de Deus around that time, over fifteen kilometers northeast from here. How she managed to slip away like that undetected with you two small children at home, no-one knew. Your father would never speak of it. She returned to us once to confess her torment, how she required drugs that could only be found in the favelas to get closer to God. We encouraged your mother to stay the night and join us for matins the next morning, but she insisted that her place was with her family."

The Reverend Mother looked away, and Juan happened to notice her folded hands trembling as she recovered her composure. "Your mother disappeared soon afterwards. We knew this, because your father finally came around asking about her. We searched the streets of the favelas for months afterwards, hoping to find some trace of where she might have gone. But no one we encountered seemed to know. Unfortunately, there are certain areas where nuns are not permitted to enter, places with prostitution, drugs, and much violence."

Sister Daniela was deeply saddened by these memories, but she understood that Juan needed to hear them. "What else would you like to know?"

Juan leaned forward. "She wrote about her home tribe in her journal. The Yanomami, why are they important?"

Sister Daniela hesitated a moment before answering. "Your mother might have returned to them, of this we are not certain. About ten years ago, one of our missionaries reported overhearing the Yanomami speak about a spirit woman who had returned to them. We thought it could have been your mother, but our prayers remain unanswered."

"Might she still be alive?" Maria interrupted, every bit as surprised by Sister Daniela's admission as Juan was.

Sister Daniela sighed. "After so many years, it does not seem likely."

Juan reflected on his dream from the night before, his thoughts coalescing into an unfamiliar conviction that transcended his logical mind. His mother may indeed have died, although she was still trying to reach him. Of that he felt certain.

Maria mistook Juan's expression for disappointment. She reached over to grasp her brother's hand, and stood while encouraging him to do likewise. "Juan, we should leave now. Thank you for your time, Reverend Mother."

"I am sorry to be the bearer of such unfortunate news," said Sister Daniela. "We continue to pray for your mother's spirit." Then she spoke in Portuguese to Maria, "Will *you* return to us, Maria?"

Maria nodded, "Perhaps, when I am ready. But Father still needs me."

"Of course he does. Please know that you are always welcome here."

"As God wills it," said Maria. She pushed her hands against the armrests and began to rise.

"Wait!" Juan blurted out just as they were leaving. "The missionaries you mentioned, I'd still like to speak with one of them about the Yanomami. Do you think that might be possible? Please Sister, if I could only locate her village, I…" Juan's voice tapered off.

Sister Daniela studied him skeptically. She sighed, and then spoke to Maria in rapid Portuguese. Juan found their discourse a bit difficult to follow.

Maria recounted what they had just discussed. "A priest here at this parish might be able to assist you. Father Ernesto has a license from the government to enter the indigenous territories. He used to be a missionary, and still travels to the Yanomami villages occasionally to report back on their numbers and general health."

Juan couldn't believe his luck. He asked Sister Daniella excitedly, "When could I speak with Father Ernesto?"

Sister Daniela subtly crossed herself. "Come back tomorrow after morning mass. I will introduce you then."

Maria urged Juan to reconsider while they were crossing back over the bridge to the Central District, "Dear brother, I fear nothing good shall come from this."

But Juan could not be dissuaded. There were clues about Mother yet to be discovered, and it was up to him now to find them.

CHAPTER TWO

"Indigenous"

FATHER ERNESTO was a robust and vigorous priest in his mid-thirties, a broad-shouldered man of 180 centimeters in height who once played for Brazil's soccer team before deciding to become a priest. He then worked as a missionary in the indigenous areas before assuming his clerical duties in Manaus.

Sister Daniela made introductions and then switched back to Portuguese. The priest appeared to be stroking a phantom beard as she spoke, one that would soon be growing back. He turned to Juan once she had finished. "So you wish to visit a Yanomami village, yes?" Having spent time in America, Father Ernesto spoke much better English than Juan had presumed.

"Yes Father," said Juan, "you know the one I'm looking for?"

Father Ernesto stroked his chin once more. "Perhaps, although it will be difficult to reach them, an arduous trek of over five days through the rainforest. Are you willing to endure such a journey?"

"Most definitely, Father."

Father Ernesto tried to conceal his excitement, although he'd already made up his mind. From the look in his eyes, it was clearly time for another adventure. "In that case, we can leave in the morning. Go home, get a good night's sleep, and come back tomorrow with your belongings. I shall fetch you a backpack and other hiking necessities from our mission office here in Manaus."

"Thank you Father!" said Juan excitedly. Father Ernesto cautioned, "Best to thank me later."

Juan carried his suitcase back to the cathedral the next morning, this time ignoring the street vendors when he passed them by. Father Ernesto had been waiting in front of the church and directed him into the nave where an empty backpack was leaning against the side wall.

Father Ernesto gestured toward Juan's suitcase. "May I?" He zipped it open and pulled out a few essential items that Juan would need for their excursion into the rainforest. "The backpack is yours. With your permission, I shall donate your suitcase and the rest of your clothes to the poor. You won't be needing them where we are going."

"Um, okay…" Juan said after concluding that it would be a fair exchange for Father Ernesto's assistance.

That settled, Father Ernesto led Juan back to the rectory where the gear had been laid out for him on a folding table. Juan was pleased to see items of clothing that would be more suitable for the rainforest, including a wide brim bush hat and a pair of hiking boots that miraculously fit.

"How long did you say we'd be hiking in the rainforest?"

Father Ernesto replied, "It could be six days or more."

Juan packed up his gear, shouldered his pack, and followed Father Ernesto down to the street corner where an ancient-looking taxi cab waited with its engine roughly idling. The driver climbed out and popped the trunk to reveal a second, much heavier looking backpack that Juan presumed to be Father Ernesto's.

After slamming their squeaky doors back shut, Father Ernesto called up to the driver, *"Para o aeroporto, por favor."* The driver mashed down on the accelerator and the cab lurched forward into downtown traffic.

"Wait, what's the plan for today?" asked Juan, once he had recovered from his initial bewilderment.

"We must first fly to São Gabriel da Cachoeira, about 750 kilometers up the Rio Negro. You will find this preferable to traveling there by boat."

They drove north out of town to a small commuter airport. The cab driver deposited them next to a hanger on the opposite side of the tarmac where a Cessna 172 Skyhawk awaited with a rumpled looking mestizo pilot leaning against it. He pushed himself erect and paced unsteadily over to greet them. From the acetone smell of his breath, he must have been hitting the booze already.

"Shhow gear in back," he slurred.

Father Ernesto took the co-pilot's seat and motioned for Juan to take the back one. "I am trained to fly this plane, just in case." He whispered with a wink. The pilot climbed aboard and they all buckled in.

The plane took off noisily and droned above the Rio Negro in a northwesterly direction, a meandering black snake of a river winding its way through bright green grasslands and stunted Amazonian forest. The bright sun's shimmering reflections made it seem almost alive. Juan stared absently out the window and willed himself to trust his instincts.

Juan spotted a distinctive looking white-steeple church as they were approaching the landing strip, the only noteworthy feature of the small river town which was their initial destination. This particular Salesian Mission church served as a base of operations for Catholic missionaries working with the indigenous tribes. From there they traveled up the headwaters of the Rio Negro to establish their mission centers throughout the region. A number of villages had become receptive to their teachings, some even adopting Christianity. But of all tribes throughout the Amazon, the Yanomami were known to be particularly resistant to outsiders.

The pilot taxied over to the hanger, then set the brake, killed the engine, and abruptly slumped over in his seat. Just when Juan started to worry, he lifted his head and reached over to unlatch the door.

"I need a drink," the pilot muttered to himself as they climbed down from the plane.

After retrieving their backpacks, Father Ernesto led Juan to a dirt parking area behind the hangar where a dusty olive military jeep awaited, one with a canvas top and no side windows. The priest effortlessly hoisted his backpack into the rear compartment and gestured for Juan to do likewise.

They climbed aboard and Juan fastened his seat buckle while noticing that Father Ernesto had chosen to ignore his. "Not much traffic in the direction we are headed," explained the priest. He pressed the ignition button and the engine roared to life.

They drove out of town and turned onto a logging road that had only recently been cut through the rainforest. This route would one day join a network of other such freshly cut roads through the Amazon, and ultimately lead to massively unchecked deforestation, although that ecological nightmare was still decades in the making.

Father Ernesto's words were difficult to make out above the high-pitched whine of the all-terrain tires as they rolled along the hard packed washboard dirt road, further amplified by the tall stands of trees lining the roadway. Yet after frequent requests for the priest to repeat himself, Juan eventually gained new insights into the missionaries and the indigenous tribes they had come here to save.

"We saw it as our calling to bring the Gospel message to these uneducated indigenous tribes, although perhaps we went a bit too far in the early days," Father Ernesto said. "The first wave of Franciscan missionaries were forced out during an indigenous revolt that happened back in the late 1880s. Unfortunately, this led to decades of abuses by the rubber tree barons, and after that the illegal gold miners. Our missionaries then returned to offer protection, which many villages willingly accepted."

Father Ernesto continued, "Now there is a government agency chartered with protecting the indigenous people. We must first obtain their permission before entering the protected regions, although a few of the tribes have fled to the northern mountains to live as they always have done. It is much more difficult to reach these villages, and the routes can be quite dangerous. Our missionaries often go missing up there for months at a time, sometimes never to be found."

Juan found that news a bit unsettling, considering he'd been having second thoughts already about this journey.

Father Ernesto reached over and clapped Juan's shoulder while smiling reassuringly. "Do not worry my friend. God will protect us." Juan wished he could share the priest's confidence. Despite his Catholic upbringing, he'd never quite sorted out his willingness to believe. Yet here he was on an illogical pursuit to find his mother based on conviction alone.

The road ended and Father Ernesto killed the engine. "This is as far as the Jeep can take us, my friend. Now we hike."

They climbed out and shouldered their packs. Noticing Juan's confusion, Father Ernesto reached over to assist with the waist belt and strap adjustments. "*Solte*," said the priest, a Portuguese word for 'let's go'. He led them toward a gap in the trees and then disappeared. "Are you sure this is the way?" Juan asked warily as his eyes adjusted to the dimming light.

"I have been this way many times," the priest called back. "Come."

The damp air smelled pleasant and earthy, although the heat and humidity soon became difficult to bear. Juan's pores opened almost immediately and quickly drenched his clothes with sweat. He resented Father Ernesto's insistence about wearing a long-sleeved shirt and bandana tied around his neck for protection. But when the first cloud of biting mosquitos swarmed by, he changed his mind.

Juan's ears began to pick up distant sounds of birds calling for their mates, punctuated by the occasional *hwonk* of a monkey frog, which sounded a bit like air being let out of a clown's balloon. He spotted an overwhelming number of trees, palms, broad leafed plants and ferns unlike any he'd seen before, and recalled reading somewhere that the rainforest was estimated to contain over 40,000 different species, all of them competing for each and every available ray of sunlight.

The Kapok trees had enormous, buttress like root systems and towering trunks rising skyward to the top of the canopy. Another species he recognized were the Brazilian nut trees, similarly vertical but with cylindrical trunks supporting a starburst of branches.

A Walking Palm soon caught his attention, its trunk resting on a shoulder-high network of roots reaching outward for stability in the soggy earth. Common lore held that such trees were capable of sprouting new roots toward the sunlight and shedding withered roots behind as they slowly migrated their way toward more favorable locations.

A flock of squawking green parrots flapped by and settled onto a bromeliad sprouting from a nearby tree trunk. Juan found this all quite fascinating, although he also found it increasingly difficult to keep up with Father Ernesto, who seemed to draw energy from almost every step. The priest eventually became aware of his companion's labored steps and called a brief halt. They took off their packs and rested against a downed tree trunk.

Noticing Juan's clammy complexion, the priest removed a water bottle from his side pouch and passed it over. "You should be drinking more water, my friend." Juan took a few tentative sips, but the tepid well water tasted bad. "Keep going," urged Father Ernesto. Juan reluctantly complied and began to feel his energy returning.

"Thanks," said Juan. Father Ernesto grinned. "Better now, I see. Are you ready to continue?"

"Yes, I think so."

"Solte. But please remember to take more frequent sips of water."

Father Ernesto led them onward at a more manageable pace until late afternoon. With darkness falling quickly, he suggested they find a place to make camp. After a bit of scouting around, he located a nearby stream and called Juan over. They shed their packs and rested a moment.

"The bank seems dry enough," said the priest, "and this fast running water should be safe to drink." He organized their cooking gear and set about preparing a meal of steamed rice with black beans. They finished it off with mugs of strong sweetened coffee and rolled out their blankets. Although there was insufficient room to pitch a tent, Father Ernesto still used the poles to support a mosquito net above them.

The sporadic animal sounds were difficult to ignore after dark, although the temperature had mercifully dropped to a more tolerable level. Juan rested his arms against his chest and focused on his breathing, about to nod off when a howler monkey startled him back awake. *"What was that?"* Juan whispered.

"You shall soon get used to such noises," said Father Ernesto, who shifted to his side and began to snore.

Juan rocked in the sand to make depressions for his tired and aching body. While doing so, he glanced upward to a riot of stars now becoming visible through tattered holes in the darkened canopy. So beautiful, he mused. He closed his eyes and made an effort to quiet his active mind, although he found this difficult after reflecting on what he'd learned about his mother from Sister Daniella. His pharmacy training had exposed him to a wide variety of neuropsychiatric drugs that could potentially be used for treating her symptoms, if indeed she were still alive. Perhaps this was the reason for his journey.

A fat drop of dew fell from an overhanging branch and splattered against Juan's face, startling him awake. He opened his eyes and realized that the mosquito net had already been stowed away. Father Ernesto sat cross-legged while minding a steaming pot of porridge on his little backpacking stove, with a freshly made pot of coffee on the ground next to him. He smiled when he saw Juan approaching, poured a second cup and handed it up to him. "Thank you," said Juan after taking his first sip. The strong brew quickly revived him.

They repacked their provisions and shouldered their packs to resume their journey. The trail became increasingly difficult to navigate and Juan found that he needed to observe Father Ernesto's footing before finding his own. He guessed they were headed in a northeasterly direction from the few light beams filtering down. Father Ernesto occasionally used his machete to hack through the foliage. This went on for over two hours.

Eventually they reached the mouth of a narrow canyon extending eastward for a distance of about five kilometers. A mountain stream cut through its entire length, according to Father Ernesto's map.

"We shall head this way." The priest pointed to a well-trod path following the water. "But we must be careful. Tribes living nearby are known to be unfriendly. Keep a close watch for any signs of movement from above."

Juan continued glancing nervously to the ridge lines in a state of hyper awareness, fearful of spotting a blow gun at any moment, which caused him to trip a number of times as he followed after the priest.

Upon hearing yet another stumble, Father Ernesto spun around and palmed Juan's shoulders to steady him. "Do not worry, Juan. Animals do not come down to this stream until after nightfall. The indigenous people know this. We should not encounter their hunters during the day, although I prefer to get to higher ground before the sun sets."

This provided sufficient motivation for Juan to pick up the pace. The trail gradually rose upward and eventually returned them to the relative safety of the trees. They stopped briefly for lunch next to a waterfall and continued upward through moderately hilly terrain. Once above the tree line, Father Ernesto called a quick halt, grabbed a bush hat from his pack and pulled it down low. "You should wear yours also, my friend. The sun's rays can be quite strong at this altitude."

After cresting the ridge, they descended into the next valley and hiked down toward a winding green river, about thirty meters across. With dusk falling quickly, Father Ernesto held up a hand when they reached the bank. "Hold a moment, Juan."

Juan followed his gaze to a pair of empty canoes pulled up on the opposite side.

Father Ernesto murmured, "That must be a search party for one of the logging companies. They won't bother us, so long as we mind our own business. We shall make camp on this side of the river, but we must be gone by morning."

While laying out their bed rolls, Father Ernesto noticed a small campfire flickering across the river. "Those men have returned." He stood and called over to them in Portuguese. After receiving a reply, he called over a second time.

"What?" Juan asked impatiently.

"As I suspected, they are surveying this area. I asked if they could verify the location of a Yanomami village we are seeking."

"Are we close?"

"According to their report, we have about another day's journey."

"Oh," Juan reacted with slumping shoulders.

"Unfortunately, they were not able to answer my second question."

"What was that?"

"Whether the route is still safe to travel. They have not been up that way since the last dry season."

Hiking got increasingly difficult on the third day as they followed the winding trail toward a distant plateau. They rested briefly at the top. Father Ernesto pointed to a tall barren peak about fifteen kilometers to the north. "There is Pico da Neblina, the tallest mountain in Brazil."

Juan studied the route with resignation, not quite up for another endurance test. "Will we be heading up that way?"

"Hopefully not, unless the tribe we are seeking has moved on." He unfolded his map and pointed. "The village should be about here, to the east of us." Juan looked in that direction and noticed more hilly terrain, from the contours. Noticing his discouragement, the priest added, "You are going to miss this trip when it is over, my friend. Boa, vamos!"

Juan focused on the rugged trail ahead as they navigated over roots, rocks and narrow streams. After several hours of this grinding monotony, they eventually reached the edge of a swampy meadow. "We must make our way across," said the priest. Their boots sank into the muddy turf with almost every step. Father Ernesto called a halt after locating a rocky patch of ground on the opposite side, gaging that Juan could no longer continue.

They made camp and gathered wood for a small campfire. Later after dinner, Juan quietly sipped his coffee while watching a full moon rise above the tree line. The caffeine seemed to help, although his body still ached all over. Father Ernesto patted Juan's shoulder in his now familiar way. "I think we should call it a day."

Juan smiled bleakly. "Probably a good idea. How much farther tomorrow to the Yanomami village?"

"We should reach it by mid-day."

Encouraged by this news, Juan crawled beneath his blanket and soon fell fast asleep.

They reached a shallow and fast moving river late the next morning. Father Ernesto shrugged off his pack and removed his boots and socks. "We must traverse this river," he explained. "Remove your boots and use the laces to tie them to the back of your pack, like so."

After fording the river, they pulled their boots back on and located a trail leading into the canopy. Juan's eyes had barely adjusted to the dimming light when they emerged into a bright and grassy clearing. Father Ernesto held up his arm again. "Wait here a moment."

Juan couldn't believe his eyes. The Yanomami village consisted of a rectangular log house, about thirty meters in length by ten meters wide, with a dozen or more circular thatched huts surrounding it. Scantily clad brown-skinned people squatted around in clusters. One of them had apparently spotted the intruders. He rose and slowly approached.

Juan wisely heeded Father Ernesto's advice and stood perfectly still.

The little man wore a leather breechclout with a wooden stick pierced through the nape of his nose. His jet black hair was cropped in a severe bowl cut, his face streaked with zig-zag tattoos. He stopped two meters away and eyed the intruders warily.

After an uncomfortable silence, the Yanomami man spoke to Father Ernesto in a poor rendition of Portuguese that Juan found almost incomprehensible. Then he turned his attention to Juan and gave him a sage nod of familiarity. Juan found this a bit disturbing, having never seen the little man before. Their soon-to-be interpreter returned to Father Ernesto and gave further instructions.

"He says we may enter his village," said Father Ernesto.

The Yanomami led them to one of the perimeter huts and grunted. "This hut shall be ours for the night," Father Ernesto explained. "I suggest we stow our packs inside."

The octagonal shaped hut contained a pair of hammocks strung over a hard dirt floor. Father Ernesto climbed into the lower one and pulled his bush hat down over his face. "The Yanomami take their siesta during the heat of the day. We should do the same." He quickly nodded off.

Impatient for answers about his mother, Juan found sleep elusive. Or so he thought.

Father Ernesto shook Juan back awake two hours later. "The Yanomami are ready to meet with us now."

Heat radiated quickly from the rocky soil after dusk had fallen, especially at that altitude. Juan ducked outside into noticeably cooler air and caught his first whiff of a savory aroma. He turned in that direction and spotted an iron pot simmering just above a cooking fire. A woman tending the fire had been watching him intently. She ladled out two generous portions of the tribe's evening meal and carried them over. Father Ernesto bent down and graciously accepted one of the steaming gourd bowls. He nodded for Juan to follow his example.

Juan detected the scent of wild licorice as he brought the bowl to his lips and took his first tentative slurp. He found the piping hot stew to be surprisingly delicious, definitely preferable to another plate of Father Ernesto's beans and rice. It contained purple colored tubers that reminded him of turnips, only sweeter, some green vegetable that tasted like a cross between broccoli and asparagus, and chunks of gamey meat that were easy to chew. Juan quickly emptied his bowl and handed it back to the woman with a genuine smile.

Young boys played down by the river after dinner, chasing each other around with sticks while engaging in mock battle. The men ignored this commotion while passing around a long-necked pipe. The stench of wild tobacco soon permeated the air. They chatted amongst themselves in a strange sounding language.

The Yanomami interpreter came over and invited Juan and Father Ernesto to join the circle of elders. He seemed proud of this assignment, as though it elevated his importance in some way.

Father Ernesto relayed a message through their diminutive interpreter. The elders grunted in response, and based on their stern expressions, the answer was no.

Juan grabbed Father Ernesto's arm and whispered, "What did you just ask them?"

"To send their children to our mission school in a neighboring valley. I shall come back another time and try again."

"Could you please ask them about my mother?" Juan asked evenly, no longer able to contain his impatience.

"Yes, yes of course." Father Ernesto turned and relayed the question via their interpreter, who promptly rose and left the circle.

"Where's he going?" asked Juan. "To fetch the shaman," muttered the priest.

Juan tried not to stare when their interpreter returned with the shaman shuffling behind him. The wild-eyed little man looked extremely thin with streaks of charcoal crisscrossing his ribcage, and his face was caked with tar pitch. He wore a narrow woven breechclout, an elaborate bone necklace and a head wreath made from white bird feathers.

The shaman urged Juan to remain seated while they made eye contact. After a long and painful moment, the shaman mercifully turned and spoke to their interpreter, who then relayed the message to Father Ernesto, along with a few extra words of his own apparently.

"The shaman knows who you are. He also knew your mother."

"Knew?"

"Yes, I am sorry Juan," said Father Ernesto. "The shaman says your mother is dead."

Juan's eyes widened in anguish. The priest wrapped his arm around Juan in an effort to console him. "According to our friend here, the Yanomami revered your mother as a living saint. There is much sadness that she no longer lives among them."

The shaman spoke again through their interpreter. Father Ernesto paused a moment before translating. "The shaman is prepared to administer the ritual. He claims this can point the way to your mother. Juan, if you decide to follow the shaman, it is not something I can be a part of. Do you understand?"

"Father, I've come all this way…."

Father Ernesto stood up and pensively kicked a pebble around with the toe of his boot. Clearly, he did not approve. After a while, he squatted back down and studied Juan as the shaman had done. "But I must warn you. The spirit world can be a hostile place for living souls. There are evil, deceptive places that must never be entered. Are you certain that this what you want?"

Juan answered without hesitation. "This is what my mother would have wanted. I am certain of that. How could I say no?"

Father Ernesto lowered his head. "Then go if you must."

Juan stood and nodded that he was ready. He followed the shaman back to the spirit hut and ducked inside through the portal. Unable to stand fully erect, Juan noticed a hole in the ceiling and went over to investigate. Stars were just appearing in the darkening sky. The shaman tapped Juan's shoulder and pointed toward a wooden plank along the side wall. Finally realizing that he should sit, Juan lowered himself down and hugged his knees. He took a deep breath, exhaled slowly, and nodded for the shaman to proceed.

Satisfied, the shaman moved into a slow and rhythmic dance, hopping from heel to toe on alternate feet while uttering a disturbingly melodic tune, which sounded to Juan both hopeful and dreadful. His mystical chanting almost lulled Juan to sleep, until it stopped abruptly. Juan opened his eyes to see the shaman now standing before a makeshift altar near the back end of the spirit shelter.

The shaman picked up a long hollow tube with colorful bird feathers hanging down from one end. Juan feared it might be a blow gun until the shaman reached into a small gourd bowl and withdrew a pinch of something brown and powdery, presumably *yopo*. The shaman tamped this substance into the feathered end of the tube, held it out ceremoniously with both hands, and resumed his sing-song melody. Then slowly and purposefully, he carried the blow pipe over to Juan.

He directed the blow pipe toward Juan's face and willed him to accept. Juan wasn't quite sure what to do, so he simply closed his eyes, and soon felt something pressing gently against his nostril. This was it, he thought, no turning back.

The tingling blast came suddenly and quickly penetrated Juan's sinuses. His eyes began watering uncontrollably and he tried to open them but couldn't focus, his surroundings nothing but a hazy blur. At first he feared the shaman might have just puffed a poison dart up his nose instead, although he could feel no obstruction after probing gently with his fingers. By then his face had gone completely numb. At least the burning sensation was gone.

With his heart pounding wildly inside his chest, Juan clenched his teeth and suffered through a brief episode of nausea. A powerfully itchy sensation erupted from behind his eyeballs and he desperately tried to rub it away but no longer had control of his body. Then a pulsating hum sounded from deep inside his skull. Getting louder by the second, it beckoned him to follow.

A ball of light flashed by and hovered just beyond the edge of his awareness, bright as the sun but with no heat radiating from its surface. Juan instinctively ventured over to have a closer look, when suddenly a rainbow beam of light reached out and sucked him into the orb like a vacuum cleaner. He felt weightless now, surrounded by multi-dimensional crystals too numerous to name, each one emitting a uniquely different hue of color from deep within. They whispered *"take this!"* in rapid succession. So many different options, if only he could grasp their meaning....

Juan saw himself as merely a bystander in this vibrant display of visual energy, completely unable to control the light beams as they darted hither and yon. Forcing that vantage away with a swipe of his mind, he hearkened back to random thoughts from his youth, brightly colored scenes with vivid textures, and all of them happening much too quickly. Powerless to control these either, he let go of the images and watched them shimmer and slowly fade away.

Only then did he spot the familiar glowing orb with his mother inside. She seemed to be calling to him. He reached out urgently, desperate for the touch of her delicate hands, but the harder he tried, the more distant she became. *"No!"* he shouted into the void.

Juan slowly regained awareness of his breathing, the weight of his body, and two warm hands resting gently on his shoulders. He opened his eyes and realized that the shaman had been there the whole time. Relieved at first, he slowly realized that he had failed to reach his mother. The dread of losing her again was almost unbearable. Tears welled up and slid down his cheeks, a welcome distraction because he knew they were real.

The shaman's grip tightened as he willed Juan to stand. Juan followed the little man out of the hut and back to the elders, who were now seated in a circle around the fire pit. Father Ernesto looked up to Juan with a somber expression and shifted over for Juan to sit next to him. The shaman uttered something inaudible to their interpreter before shuffling back to his dwelling.

Juan could hardly wait for Father Ernesto to translate the shaman's words. "Well?" he asked urgently.

"The shaman says that you are not a *seer*. He also wants you to know that he is sorry."

"What the heck is that supposed to mean?" Juan had considered using a stronger word but chose not to. Father Ernesto would not have approved, and he had no desire to provoke him just then. So he stared into the crackling embers and waited.

Father Ernesto reached over and shook Juan gently, to make sure he was okay. "Juan, if truth is what you seek, you must put your faith in God." Seeing this wasn't helping, he wisely added, "I am sorry about your mother."

Juan wept softly at the remembrance of his mother, although still not convinced about the shaman's words. And after a while, he raised his head. "Thank you, Father." Fully spent, he decided to leave the matter for another day. "Think I'll head back to our hut now."

Father Ernesto returned a few minutes later, and within moments began snoring as usual from the hammock below. Juan had finally learned to ignore this distraction, although he continued to find sleep elusive. He kept replaying his failed *yopo* experience again and again in his mind. What could have possibly gone wrong? There must have been the reason for his mother's scribbled note to him in her journal, of that he felt certain. He wondered….

CHAPTER THREE

"The path of science"

THE DOWNHILL TREK back to the military Jeep took less than three days. They loaded up their packs and wearily climbed aboard. Father Ernesto turned the ignition key and broke into a toothy grin when the engine finally fired to life. "Beats hiking, yes?" he announced proudly. Juan nodded and couldn't suppress a grin. The priest's scraggly beard seemed to suite him. "Sure does, Father."

"Ah, such a relief," said Father Ernesto. "I was starting to wonder if you had forgotten how to speak." He maneuvered the Jeep around and shifted through the gears. "Then perhaps I should share something with you now. You see, I too had hoped your mother might be still alive."

The priest's admission surprised Juan. "Have you ever seen her with them, Father? The Yanomami, I mean."

"Not with my own eyes," replied Father Ernesto, "although I have heard stories about her, from other missionaries who work in that region."

Juan asked urgently, "And how did they describe her?"

"People from the villages claimed she could speak directly with God, as she had been known to do back in our convent. We had hoped she might somehow benefit our cause. Unfortunately, she was most unwilling to meet with us."

Father Ernesto wrenched the wheel to avoid a rough patch in the road. "As I mentioned before, some of the Yanomami villages have become more receptive to our presence, others not so much. We encourage them to send their children to our mission schools. Sadly, they often refuse."

Juan remembered Father Ernesto's disappointment following their meeting with the elders. "Like the tribe we just visited?"

The priest heaved a sigh. "The younger man who translated for us once studied in one of our mission schools, although these days he seems more interested in his status among the elders." He reached down for his canteen and took a swig before passing it over. "I suppose we should not blame him. Our church was too unbending in the early days. So many rules they could not understand. Sadly, it may take a very long time to regain their trust."

Juan wanted to challenge the priest, but kept his tongue. The Yanomami were clearly not ignorant people. Why else would his mother have returned to them? "Think I'll take a brief nap, if you don't mind. Didn't manage to sleep much last night." Juan pulled down his hat and tilted the seat back. Despite the bumps and jolts, he quickly nodded off.

Father Ernesto shrugged off Juan's not so subtle rebuff and settled into the drive. Alone with his thoughts, he began to ponder where God might be leading him. No clear answer came to mind, yet he still felt a powerful conviction to his calling. God's ways were not human ways. The important thing was to have faith.

Darkness had fallen by the time they reached São Gabriel da Cachoeira. Father Ernesto pulled the Jeep to a merciful stop next to the airstrip and shut off the engine. With Juan still sleeping soundly, he popped his own seat back and closed his eyes.

The priest awoke to the dim light of dawn, his usual time. He gave his passenger a gentle nudge. Juan snapped up and recognized where he was. "Whoa, how long was I out?" he asked incredulously. "Over twelve hours. So now, are you ready to head back to civilization? Our plane awaits."

They retrieved their packs and walked out to the Skyhawk to find their pilot clear eyed and sober. "My wife, she take me back," he announced proudly with a mostly toothless grin.

The Skyhawk's engine whined with increasing pitch as it accelerated down the runway to liftoff velocity. Once airborne, the pilot banked into a tight left-hand turn and leveled off on a southeastern heading above the shimmering Rio Negro. Juan took advantage of his time aloft to reflect on what he'd learned about his mother during this fateful trip, her struggles with drug addiction and ultimate return to her ancestral tribe. Apparently she had regained her ability to speak with God. How might this have been possible? Juan couldn't fully grasp the implications, yet something about his failed *yopo* experience still captured his imagination. Perhaps it triggered a switch of some kind. And there may even be a physiological explanation. He would simply need to learn more about this mysterious plant extract.

Juan knew what his next move should be when the bustling port of Manaus reappeared. He smiled to himself as the Skyhawk descended.

The pilot made a near perfect landing and taxied over to the hanger. Juan and Father Ernesto stepped down to the tarmac and retrieved their backpacks from the side compartment.

"Thank you, my friend," said Father Ernesto to the pilot.

"It is you I should thank, Padre. You have brought me luck." The pilot embraced them both and shook their hands for good measure.

They took a cab back to the church and said their final goodbyes. "Keep the backpack, Juan. You may need it again one day." Juan grinned, remembering that he no longer had a suitcase. They embraced and stepped back, eyeing each other with welling emotion.

"I pray that you find closure from the loss of your mother," said the priest.

"Thank you, Father Ernesto, for everything. You've helped me learn what I needed to know," Juan lied.

"I am happy to hear that. Well then, Godspeed to you, my friend."

Juan shouldered his pack and hiked back over the bridge. He wondered how to express what he had learned to his father and sister. Maria awaited him with open arms at the top of the landing, having heard Juan's footsteps coming up the stairs. She stepped back and studied his eyes. "Oh Juan, I am so sorry."

"Our mother is gone, dear Sister."

Maria nodded and tried to look disappointed, although she had known this all along. "Come. Father has been waiting to speak with you."

Maria led Juan into the front room to find their father seated in his favorite chair. He was clean shaven for once, with his hair brushed even, although his condition had apparently worsened. Juan sensed from the look in his eyes that Father knew this as well.

Senhor Virtanen cleared his throat.

"Welcome back, my son. I trust you have satisfied your curiosity?"

"Our mother is dead, Father. It shouldn't have come as much of a surprise, I suppose. But it was important for me to find out for myself."

Senhor Virtanen's eyes softened as he struggled for consoling words. But they wouldn't come. He coughed a few times and then promptly regained his composure. "Well then, I presume you are ready to return to America."

"Yes, Father. Although I no longer wish to become a pharmacist."

"What? After such excellent schooling? What shall you do?" Virtanen senior erupted into another fit of coughing and Maria rushed over to assist. Juan waited for Father to recover and then approached. Kneeling down, he spoke softly, "Father, I have decided to enroll now in graduate school. I want to become a scientist."

Juan rose early the next morning and quickly dressed himself. Stepping outside, he walked toward the corner market where a pay phone was mounted on the outside wall. After fumbling in his wallet for a slip of paper, he picked up the receiver and dialed the operator, intending to charge the long distance call to his father's account. He gave her the number, and after a brief moment of static, heard a ring tone on the other end.

"Hello?" Professor Higgins answered in his familiar British accent.

Juan had taken a pharmaceutical chemistry course taught by Professor Higgins while he was on sabbatical at the University of Michigan. A renowned expert in neuro-transmitters, he had recently returned to the University of California at San Francisco, where his laboratory was designing new drugs to treat various psychiatric disorders.

"Professor Higgins! It's Juan Virtanen, remember me?"

"Of course! What a pleasure to hear your voice, Virtanen. But where are you? There's a fair amount of static on the line."

"I'm visiting my family in Brazil at the moment."

"Then I presume you've just graduated. Congratulations, my boy!"

"Actually, that's why I'm calling," said Juan. "I've decided to enroll in graduate school and continue on to earn my PhD. Guess I'd rather be a scientist. Do you think your department might consider my application?"

"We'd be happy to have you, I'm sure." Professor Higgins was pleased with the thought of attracting such a promising student. "Although I'm fairly certain you're past the deadline for fall admission," he added.

"Oh…" Juan muttered dejectedly into the phone.

"Not to worry, my boy. I may be able to pull a few strings and get you admitted for winter quarter. Assuming they accept your application, perhaps you might be interested in working in my laboratory as an intern until then. I could offer you a small stipend."

Juan beamed. "That would be wonderful!"

"Well then, send me the application and I'll run it by our admissions committee."

Juan thanked Professor Higgins profusely. He felt even more excited after hanging up the phone.

The acceptance letter arrived less than three weeks later, along with a congratulatory note from Professor Higgins.

That settled, Juan decided to use his remaining time in Brazil to prepare for his next academic adventure.

Pontifical Catholic University
São Paulo, Brazil

Juan returned to São Paulo after saying hasty goodbyes to his family, where he now resided in a back corner study carrel on the second floor of the Medical Sciences library. After many long days of intensive research, he had just begun to summarize his copious notes on various plants extracts that were used by the indigenous Amazonian tribes for their hallucinogenic rituals.

The common active ingredient was a molecule called dimethyltryptamine, or DMT. Its discovery had been credited to a Brazilian chemist and microbiologist named Oswaldo Gonçalves de Lima, who first extracted a substance with hallucinogenic properties from the root bark of the plant *Mimosa tenuiflora*. American chemists solved its chemical structure in 1959 and speculated that its amino acid precursor might be L-tryptophan. But Juan was mainly interested in the plant species *Anadenanthera Peregrina* which was used by the Yanomami shamans to produce their *yopo* snuff. As he suspected, the seeds from this plant contained DMT at relatively high concentrations.

Juan was intrigued by the published evidence suggesting that DMT might also be present endogenously in humans. In an article dating from 1965, the German researchers Franzen and Gross claimed to have isolated DMT from human blood and urine samples. But their methods were seriously challenged and later discredited in subsequent publications. Nonetheless, Juan became convinced that DMT must be a naturally occurring neurotransmitter.

Studies on the psychotropic effects of DMT fascinated him even more. The Hungarian neurochemist Dr. Stephen Szára was the first to study the effects of DMT in healthy human volunteers back in the mid-1950s. He later chose to make DMT the focus of his work at the US National Institutes of Health. His original proposal to study LSD had been denied on grounds of national security, presumably to prevent the powerful hallucinogen from falling into the hands of the Soviets. DMT was much shorter acting, with episodes lasting fifteen minutes or less, so he argued that it should be a relatively safe alternative.

The more Juan read about DMT, the more convinced he became that it was not at all like LSD, a longer acting drug which produced a more complex variety of hallucinogenic effects. Most subjects recounted their DMT experiences as having been spiritual or supernatural in nature. Many imagined they had been communicating with angels. Some described encounters with diminutive humanoid beings such as trolls or elves, and still others believed they had been communicating with alien life forms from distant galaxies. Such accounts suggested that DMT might be targeting more specific regions inside the brain.

And with that realization, Juan concluded that *yopo* must be the reason for his mother's scribbled note to him in her journal. She expected it to help him communicate with her in the spirit world. That note down the margin had been an afterthought, he realized. A final entry. She must have known she was dying. Then why had it failed?

Juan couldn't stop thinking about the scientific implications. What might DMT be doing inside the human brain? Could it possibly open a portal to spiritual awareness? Juan now considered it his destiny to find out. He began to jot notes for his doctoral research proposal.

Most subjects reported fleeting experiences while under the influence of DMT, too brief to fully grasp their meaning. That must be the key, Juan realized. Perhaps he could prolong the effect by synthesizing a more potent derivative of DMT, one with a tighter binding affinity for whatever brain receptor DMT might bind to. This would perhaps give him more time to reconnect with his mother….

"Juan Virtanen, is that you? Getting older, I see. What brings you back to São Paulo? The last I remember, you left to study in America and become a pharmacist."

Alfredo Ruiz had been one of Juan's secondary school classmates. Juan had never particularly liked Ruiz. "Good to see you, Ruiz. How long has it been?"

"About five years, I suppose. But of course you knew that. So, what brings you here to our humble campus? I thought it wasn't good enough for you?" The Pontifical Catholic University had been Juan's back-up option before receiving his acceptance letter to the University of Michigan.

"I'm just here for the summer to visit my family after receiving my pharmacy degree. Now I've decided to become a scientist instead. I'll be returning to the States in two weeks' time to start graduate school."

"Well then, I presume you have come to our prestigious library for inspiration?"

"Something like that. What about you? I thought you were planning to go on to medical school."

"Indeed, I have," he announced proudly. "It's a joint MD-PhD program here at the university. So you see, I shall become both a doctor *and* a scientist. My plan is to study the nuances of the human brain, what makes some of us exceptional and others not so much, like you for instance. The field has been waiting for someone like me."

Juan bit his lip and decided to say nothing further. He had always found Ruiz to be a bit of a narcissist. "Good luck with that," he muttered without making eye contact, then returned to his notes and waited for Ruiz to get the message and leave.

CHAPTER FOUR

"Disentanglement"

University of California, San Francisco, CA

NIGHTTIME had become Juan Virtanen's only friend, although he never did have many to begin with. He preferred the solitude while working in Professor Higgins' laboratory, having found it increasingly difficult to interact with his other lab mates during daytime hours. They kept on asking why he seemed so distant, wanting to know if he was alright. Well of course he was, which was precisely why he avoided them now.

Earning the ability to work independently in the laboratory required considerable training and effort, although for Virtanen it had been easier than most. First were the mandatory graduate level courses in physical chemistry, synthetic organic chemistry, and advanced medicinal chemistry. He found these classes particularly enjoyable. Then came courses on drug metabolism and pharmacology that helped him understand how drugs were broken down in the body to be excreted. Last were courses on human physiology that were co-taught with the UCSF medical school. It amused Juan how neurotic the medical students could be. He had bested them all on every one of the exams.

An academic epiphany occurred to him during one of his biophysics classes, where he learned how to apply the principles of quantum mechanics to problems of biological significance, for example the use of spectrophotometric techniques to probe molecular interactions. The close interrelationships between matter and energy intrigued him, and this got him thinking about neurochemical signaling processes. Perhaps his hypothesis about DMT-triggered brainwaves opening a door to spiritual awareness wasn't that far-fetched after all.

Concurrent with his classes were the much-dreaded cumulative exams. First year graduate students were required to take one of these every month until they passed ten in all. Each exam contained multi-step problems that might touch on any area of physical chemistry, organic chemistry, or biochemistry, and often required a seamless mastery of each of these disciplines to get the right answer. They usually addressed some novel area of research for which it was impossible to study. Graduate students were expected to think for themselves, to apply their academic knowledge to problems they might encounter one day in their own research. They had until spring quarter of their second year to fulfill this requirement, otherwise they would be dismissed. One failed exam was a reason worry; not passing two or more in a row could be a disaster.

Virtanen passed ten such exams in only eleven tries, although he was still disappointed with his performance.

Students were also expected to find a professor to sponsor their research project by the end of their first academic year. Again Juan was ahead of the game, having already secured Professor Higgins' endorsement before beginning his course work.

But the final hurdle was to present and defend his project orally to an advisory panel. The panel's job was to decide whether or not the project would be worthy of a Ph.D. degree. If approved, the candidate could go on to complete their work and write up the results for their doctoral dissertation. If denied, they would need to find a different project and come back to defend again. Or they could suspend their candidacy and leave the department having already met the requirements for a master's degree.

Juan's oral exam turned out to be a bit more challenging than he anticipated. He began by introducing the disputed research findings of the German chemists Franzen and Gross and their claim to have isolated DMT from human blood and urine specimens. He discussed the work of Julius Axelrod who had discovered the enzyme N-methyltransferase in rabbit lung tissue, and then sketched out the proposed mechanism for how the amino acid tryptamine could be converted to DMT. He drew the chemical structure of DMT on the chalk board and that of serotonin next to it and pointed out their structural similarities.

Then he described the spiritual euphoria that most subjects reported while under the influence of DMT. Assuming DMT was indeed a naturally occurring neurotransmitter, Juan hypothesized that its abnormal secretion may be responsible for a variety of neuro-psychoses.

The panel asked a number of difficult questions along the way to challenge his understanding, for example, questions about other known neurotransmitters and how they had been characterized. They seemed dubious that Juan could possibly make headway on such an ambitious project. Beads of sweat were dripping down his temples by the end of this four-hour grilling, despite a cold February rain pelting the windows.

Professor Higgins waited patiently in the hallway during Juan's oral exam. Juan stepped out and timidly shut the door behind him. His face was drawn and he appeared to be physically exhausted, almost like he'd just finished running a marathon.

"How did it go, my boy?" Professor Higgins asked urgently.

Juan took a deep breath and released it slowly. "Not well, I'm afraid."

"Perhaps they thought your project was too ambitious?"

"That might be putting it a bit lightly," said Juan.

Professor Higgins was confidentially aware of numerous studies that the CIA secretly conducted on human subjects during the Cold War. His security clearance was not widely known, although he had shared a few personal observations with Juan.

"It doesn't surprise me…." Professor Higgins paused a moment to reflect. "I presume their main objection was the lack of experimental evidence supporting your hypothesis?"

"Of course," said Juan dejectedly. "But when I described the various types of DMT derivatives I was planning to synthesize, they seemed to agree that such compounds might be of interest to drug companies for further investigation."

"Excellent," said Professor Higgins. "A basic research project. I think they may have bought that."

Professor Nelson opened the door and invited them both inside to hear the panel's decision.

Virtanen's dissertation project was accepted under the provision that any animal experiments first be approved by UCSF's Institutional Animal Care and Use Committee. Juan agreed to submit the protocols, although he had no intention of following them to the letter.

11:00 PM. Sunday, August 17th, 1980

It had taken him months of trial and error to perfect the methods needed for testing his chemical derivatives of DMT. First he injected them into rats and recorded their behaviors, although it was difficult to tell exactly what they were experiencing. For this reason, Virtanen eventually began using himself as a test subject, at least with the more interesting compounds based on his initial observations with the rats. First he'd snort a tiny amount up his nose when no one else was around. Then he'd later jot down experiences in his personal journal, which always seemed to remind him of his mother.

Occasionally he'd experience a peaceful, 'top of the world' euphoria. Other times he remembered feeling fearful or anxious, and the ensuing nausea could sometimes last for hours, or even days. He needed to maintain his strength in order to continue with these experiments. So he decided to implement a countermeasure. He would wait 24 hours after dosing the rats, then sacrifice the animals and examine them for signs of liver toxicity before snorting the compound.

This precaution had served him well up to now, and he felt certain that he was closing in on the right molecule, could sense it with every fiber of his being. The effects had been lasting a bit longer, and incrementally more similar to what he remembered from his *yopo* experience, although he failed to notice how increasingly delusional he was becoming as well, a consequence of his frequent self-experimentation.

Juan prepared a solution of his latest DMT compound and placed the vial into a cardboard box along with other items he would need for dosing the rats. He carried it down the hall and through a connecting corridor into the Biochemistry wing, then he punched a keypad to enter the vivarium.

The animal lab in the recently constructed Biochemistry wing now served as a core facility for all of Medical Sciences. The 500 square foot vivarium contained rows of vertically stacked cages housing the various strains of mice and rodents being used for a variety of different disease models. Juan preferred Sprague-Dawley rats since their natural behaviors were well-documented in the scientific literature.

Juan walked over to a lab bench along the side wall and arranged his experiment. He snapped on a fresh pair of latex gloves and used a glass syringe to withdraw fifty microliters of solution from the vial. Then he turned to one of the cages labeled "Higgins lab" and reached in to retrieve his latest victim. While holding its tiny paws back with his gloved fingers, he carefully pierced the rat's tail vein and injected the solution. That done, he gently lowered the animal into an observation box and repeated the process until he had dosed five of them in all.

He stepped back and watched them intently.

The rats continued to probe the Plexiglas walls with their inquisitive noses, but gradually their movements began to slow. After a while, they each raised their heads as if trying to hear something, and remained that way several minutes before resuming their normal behaviors.

The compound seemed safe enough. Juan pondered whether he should wait the usual 24 hours and then surgically remove their livers to test for toxicity. No, they seemed perfectly fine. Perhaps he'd let them live this time. He pulled off his gloves and tossed them into a biohazard waste container as he exited the vivarium.

Back in the Higgins lab, Juan unlocked the drawer beneath his workstation and pulled out the sample vial. He had only synthesized a small batch of this particular DMT derivative and estimated about 100 milligrams remaining in the vial. The wall clock read 11:30 PM. No activity across the hall. Brett Roberts must have finally gone home, typically the last of the other graduate students to leave in the evening. It was now or never. He reached for a stainless steel micro-spatula, inserted its diamond-shaped tip into the vial and withdrew a tiny amount of the white crystalline substance.

"Okay, here goes…" he whispered to himself. He carefully raised the spatula tip up to his right nostril and took a powerful sniff, then pinched his nose to coax the substance into his nasal membranes. He had done this many times before. He watched the clock and waited… five minutes, ten….

Nothing seemed to be happening. Hugely disappointed, Juan returned the vial to a box in his drawer and locked it, then straightened his lab bench and prepared to leave. Tomorrow he'd begin synthesizing the next DMT analog in this particular series of design modifications. He had already sketched out the reaction scheme in his lab notebook.

Unfortunately, fate had other plans for Juan Virtanen. Back in the vivarium, his recently injected rats had begun to flicker in and out intermittently as if each under its own tiny strobe light. And then, one by one, they vanished in bright flashes of illumination. Soon the observation cage was empty.

Juan was just about to remove his lab coat when he experienced a loud and discordant shriek from inside his skull. He clutched his ears but couldn't make it stop. Then he felt an intense burning sensation in his feet, like standing bare-footed on searing hot coals. Looking down in disbelief, he watched them emanate a strange, pulsating bioluminescence, faster and faster until... *they were gone!* He appeared to be levitating above the floor with no feet at all, or shins for that matter. At least the searing pain was gone. He almost wished it would return.

The compound must be interacting with his systemic nerve receptors in some unfortunate way, accompanied by this strange hallucination now moving up his legs… and reaching his torso, fascinating… wait, this could not be good. Panic took over and he focused on his wildly beating heart in a desperate struggle to hold on to the belief that he was still alive.

Juan Virtanen's body suddenly vanished in a blinding flash of disseminated energy, his molecules having already begun to reassemble on the polar opposite side of the world. His life force went elsewhere, unfortunately.

7:49 AM. Tuesday Morning, March 30TH, 1993
Thomas J. Watson Research Center, Yorktown Heights, NY

Archibald Stevens headed IBM's Advanced Physics Division, a savvy administrator and British ex-pat with a Ph.D. from Oxford. His team had contributed over 200 patents to IBM's impressive intellectual property arsenal. He unlocked the door to his cluttered office and began to remove his coat when the phone started ringing. "Good lord, I only just arrived." He also spotted a stack of phone messages on his chair. "Bollocks! Can't I have a moment's peace around here before starting my day?"

He shifted stacks of paper around on his desk until he uncovered the phone. "Stevens speaking."

"Doctor Stevens? Jim Murphy here from the *New York Times*, science section."

"Yes, yes, how can I help you?"

"Well I'd like to ask you a few questions about that teleportation paper your team published yesterday, the one in *Physics Review Letters*? We think it could be very important...."

"Yes of course. That's our job, you know."

"I promise not to take up too much of your time...." The reporter used his shoulder to cradle the receiver and reached for a notepad while trying to locate a pen.

Stevens settled back in his chair and turned his gaze to the blustery weather outside. Damn, his coffee was already getting cold. "What's your first question?"

"If I'm understanding this correctly, your guys supposedly came up a solution for teleportation. Is that right?"

"Dear man, it was merely a theoretical paper. Our ability to teleport even the simplest of objects is still decades away, possibly even centuries."

"But you think it could one day become a reality?"

"I wouldn't go that far. There are quite a number of technical challenges yet to be overcome. But yes, we do think our argument supports the *theoretical* possibility."

"Perhaps you could explain this to me in lay terms, hopefully in a way my readers could understand?"

"Oh, alright, I'll do my best. You see, my team simply applied an elusive principle of quantum mechanics known as the Einstein-Podolsky-Rosen effect...."

"Um, would you mind spelling that?"

Stevens released a controlled breath. This man was getting a bit irritating. He glanced at his watch. "E-i-n-... oh, Heaven's sake – the reference is in the paper!"

"Yes, you're right, my apologies."

"Just write down what I say as best you can and try not to further interrupt. I have a meeting in five minutes."

"Sure Doctor Stevens, please go ahead."

"It means that we don't actually need to know the precise relationship of every individual atom inside an object before initiating the process of teleportation. Instead, one could extract just a portion of its qualities and send that on whilst simultaneously sending a second portion to a registry. Once that first portion has been received at the distant location, the information stored in the registry can then be used to reassemble the object. This process would actually require a large number of repetitive steps depending on the complexity of the object, but once completed it should indeed result in an exact copy. However, the original object must necessarily be destroyed by the end of the transfer process. The same object cannot exist simultaneously in two different places, you see?"

The reporter had been scribbling frantically and his pen just ran out of ink. "Yes, I think I've got it. May I quote you in the article?"

"Simply for stating that teleportation is *theoretically* possible, nothing more mind you. Good day, Mister Murphy."

"Well thank you so much for your time, Doctor Stevens! Oh yes, one more thing…."

Dr. Stevens had already hung up the phone.

1:52 AM. Monday Morning, September 15ᵀᴴ, 2025
People's Republic of China

The most secretive branch of China's computer surveillance program resides deep within the bowels of the Ministry of National Defense building in downtown Beijing. Its subterranean mission falls under the direct control of the Paramount Leader, his economic advisor and two ministers of the Central Military Commission, trusted men all who were handpicked by him alone. Each cyber cell has compartmentalized tasks with information flowing only upward through the chain of command. The game is global economic domination, and unbeknownst to the rest of the world, China is winning.

However, the Paramount Leader is never satisfied with the pace of progress. Inspired by the early theoretical papers on quantum computing, China continues to invest heavily in such technologies, as it has done for the past three decades. Unlike conventional silicon computers which manipulate bits of information in 0's and 1's, China's new prototypes are capable of processing *qubits* of information possessing multi-dimensional degrees of freedom.

The theory seemed simple enough in the early days, although finding a means of manipulating these *qubits* turned out to be exceptionally difficult. Unlike conventional digital switches, *Qubits* cannot simply be turned on and off, nor can they be interrogated directly without destroying their inherent properties. Despite these obstacles, China's quantum physicists first demonstrated a method of "hyper-entanglement" back in the 1990's to harness them, and had been perfecting this technological advance ever since.

A third generation quantum computer now hums away in an adjacent room of this top secret facility, seven stories below ground. The amber-walled room is restricted to a handful of the program's most trusted computer geeks, and always under the direct supervision of their military handlers. The Supreme Leader has them monitored 24/7, even while asleep in their heavily guarded dormitory. They are never permitted to leave the complex.

In the next room is the control center, in the middle of which stands a large holographic projection monitor that can be manipulated by hand movements and gestures. A rectangular array of workstations surrounds it supporting the more traditional LCD monitors. The quantum geeks prefer this backup redundancy because the projection monitor is known to be *Chū wèntí*, or glitchy.

Fluorescent lights are dimmed at this hour, offering just enough illumination for the 360 degree surveillance cameras to record any signs of movement, although the security guard in charge of monitoring them upstairs has been struggling to stay awake. He pushes away and heads to the kitchen to make himself a hot cup of green tea.

Less than a minute later, one of the LCD monitors in the control room flickers to life in solid blue illumination, and an MS-DOS cursor appears at the top left-hand corner.

At last! The spirit's sentience exudes, who still stubbornly considers himself to be Juan Virtanen. He has bypassed the sophisticated firewall by summoning an ancient operating system from the 1980's. MS-DOS, the only computer language it had known as a living person.

Although the spirit entity continues to struggle with this trans-dimensional connection, and the buttons of the keyboard are all labeled with Chinese characters, it manages to type "H-E-L-L-O_W-O-R-L-D" next to the cursor, the first executable command any computer programmer would use. Once the spirit has entered this command by activating the keyboard, a graphical user interface appears on the screen:

The spirit realizes that it has finally achieved the ability to interact with a physical entity, although apparently non-human. Ever since leaving his physical body, the spirit has constantly been probing the boundaries of eternal darkness. Occasionally it senses a flicker of physical resonance, but nothing more. Until now.

Recognizing this to be some sort of search engine, the spirit entity manages to type the letters "Y-A-N-O-M-A-M-I" from the keyboard into the rectangular window and then hits 'Enter'. This query summons up tens of thousands of pages worth of digital copy. While no longer constrained by physical thought processes, the spirit entity is likewise unable to sort through this copious text, so it types "G-E-N-E-T-I-C_D-I-F-F-E-R-E-N-C-E-S" and hits 'Enter' again.

How surprising that such information exists! The genomic sequences of indigenous tribespeople throughout the Amazon have now been studied and published, hundreds of them in fact, using a new technology called next-generation sequencing. The first such study was published in the year 2012. How could this be? Time must be fluid, the spirit realizes.

The spirit then adds the term "B-R-A-I-N_R-E-C-E-P-T-O-R" to the query, hoping to identify mutations that might help explain their unique ability to contact the spirit world under the influence of DMT. Where had that notion come from? No matter, what it learns next turns out to be even more surprising. Many of these genomes were found to possess a common mutation in one particular gene, a mutation present in less than 0.25% of the general population, at least according to one of the published studies. Unfortunately, the samples for that study had been collected from indigenous peoples throughout the Amazon region, with no specification as to which regions they came from. The spirit entity has no way of determining which samples might have come from Yanomami tribes.

But wait… the spirit now has access to the genome sequences of over 50 million individuals, most of them secretly hacked from the servers of sequencing centers throughout the world. It begins to query the portal for the names of other individuals who possessed this mutation, people the spirit may have known when still alive.

At last it obtains a hit, from a human wellness center in San Diego California, a subject by the name of Brett Roberts who had donated his DNA sample for this particular study. The spirit entity types another query and stumbles onto his LinkedIn profile. Although somewhat older in the photo, the image of this man is most definitely recognizable. Yes, a scientist who had graduated from UC San Francisco and later worked for a biotech company in San Diego. This must be him!

The spirit begins to wonder whether it might be possible to reenter a former time and make contact with this Brett Roberts. Emboldened by its most recent portal encounter, or perhaps even enlightened by the experience, the spirit entity is determined to make such an attempt.

With an extreme exertion of ethereal will, the spirit entity returns to the place and time where it had ultimately left its physical body. It hovers about, finding the laboratory essentially the same as when it had left its body. But wait! Someone has evidently 'borrowed' the liquid handling pipettes from Juan Virtanen's workstation, *his workstation!*

The spirit hovers over to a former colleague Troy Simpson's work area and finds the pipettes. *Damn him!* Simpson's lab notebook lies open on the bench as well, another protocol violation. And look, the door to the laboratory has been left open. Perhaps the janitor had forgotten to lock it after emptying the trash bins. But wait… the spirit entity then glances down to Simpson's lab notebook and notices the date, which would have been two days after its final memory as a living person.

Back in real time, and finally, on the eleventh ding, Brett Roberts exited the elevator and made a left to return to his laboratory. He checked his watch. Yep, the organic chemistry reaction he'd left cooking since mid-afternoon should be about ready for another reagent addition. He disliked returning to the lab so late at night, although he would have lost a day if he'd waited until the next morning. As his mentor Professor Nelson often would say, science never sleeps.

Spotting the Higgins lab door left open across the hall, he decided to poke his head in. "Anybody there?" Hmm, no-one apparently. Although something felt odd inside the dimly lit lab, creepy even. Perhaps he was just tired. But it was against safety policy to leave these lab doors open when unoccupied. The janitor must have forgotten to lock it after emptying the trash bins. Roberts pulled it shut and then stepped across the hall to enter the Nelson lab.

How could he not sense my presence?! Having failed to connect with Roberts, Virtanen's spirit lingers inside the Higgins lab until the first rays of daylight. No longer able to hold its position in physical space, the spirit entity must return to its unworldly state of perpetual darkness.

But just before yielding to the inevitable, it senses several faint glimmers of resonance in the vicinity, perhaps from other living persons – mediums, psychics, healers and the like. Emboldened by this realization, it resolves to return another night and attempt to communicate with Roberts through one of them.

CHAPTER FIVE

"Delivery"

**10 PM. Sunday, September 7th, 1980
San Francisco, California**

IT WAS DARK AS DEATH on the hilly streets of China Town with yet another dense fog rolling in. Outside the Wai Fat grocery store, the sidewalk displays of colorful Asian produce had been tucked away in the shadows behind a locked metal grate. No-one strolling down the sidewalk at that hour would have noticed an old man puttering away behind the counter of his herbal medicine shop next door.

The Grand China Herb Company had been family owned and operated since the late-1850s. Always an essential part of China Town's cultural fabric, it had also become a popular tourist attraction during daytime hours. Chow-Yun Wang was its current proprietor. Hanging on the wall behind him were framed pictures of various celebrities who had visited his shop over the past three decades. Mr. Wang obviously enjoyed being photographed with such famous people, although it was also evident how he had aged over the years. Now in his early sixties with his hair dyed an unnatural shade of black, it was becoming increasingly difficult for Mr. Wang to climb the ladder behind his counter, to reach the upper shelves where his most expensive Chinese medicines were stored. His son generally assisted him with such tasks, although Mr. Wang had sent Hung home early that evening. He had an order to fill that needed to be handled with utmost confidentiality.

Mr. Wang kept a select assortment of herbal extracts from other parts of the world in a locked drawer beneath the counter, reserved for special customers whose names were known only to him.

A dream had come to Mr. Wang the night before, embedding itself in his mind with quite specific instructions. He'd never been contacted in quite such a way before, although being the spiritually-minded person he was, Mr. Wang would follow these instructions to the letter. The mysteries of the universe were not all his to question.

He glanced out the window to the dimly lit street to be certain that his actions would continue to be unobserved. Satisfied, Mr. Wang knelt down and unlocked the drawer to retrieve one of the hand blown glass vials. He studied the label to verify its contents before setting it down on the counter above. Then with the aid of a wooden spatula, he measured out precisely one gram of the amber powder, then carefully tapped it into a plain white envelope. The Chinese characters he drew on the front of the envelope were quite different from those on the bottle. Again, he paid no mind to the reason behind this. Although it was difficult for him not to wonder about the cursive writing he then scribbled on the back. The pen moved as if under its own volition, the style clearly not his own. Satisfied that he had completed the task, he shuffled down to the other end of the counter and picked up the phone.

"Son, come back to pharmacy. I have important delivery you take for me."

Twenty minutes later, Hung Wang pulled up with his scooter and knocked gently on the door. His father opened it a crack and handed his son the envelope.

"I want you deliver right away, my son. Here is address," said Mr. Wang as he then handed his son a folded slip of paper. Hung's eyebrows raised involuntarily as he read through his father's detailed instructions.

"But Father, surely the building will be locked at this time of night."

"I know you find a way, my son." Mr. Wang knew about his son's association with the Wah Ching. He was not proud of Hung's gang involvement; however there were certain skills he'd learned that would be necessary for tonight's assignment.

The scooter put-putted away and quickly disappeared into the chilly downtown fog. Hung gave it full throttle to coax the tiny engine up Hayes Street hill, and ignored the next two stoplights while coasting back down with increasing speed.

Approaching Steiner Street, he slowed to a stop and turned his head to briefly admire the city's famous Painted ladies up the hill to his right, then made a left and another right on Fell Street. The fog began to thin as he continued westward along the northern edge of the Panhandle, although the wind still felt icy against his face. He let go of the gas handle just long enough to pull up his scarf before throttling on.

Hung wondered about his father's instructions as he approached the eastern edge of Golden Gate Park. Such a strange request, but certainly not the first time he'd been sent out on such errands. Making a left on Stanyan and then another right on Parnassus, he coaxed the little scooter's 80 cc engine up the next steep grade at full throttle until he reached the Medical Center at the top.

Glancing around for an unobvious place to park his scooter, he decided to leave it behind a tree at the corner of Hillway. Then he crept back through the shadows until he found himself standing directly opposite the Medical Sciences building. Making an effort to conceal himself against the glass clock tower outside the student union, he waited there patiently for the night janitor to arrive.

Hung glanced over to the beige high-rise structure of tile and glass, one of a cluster of high-rise buildings comprising the medical campus. To the left was UCSF hospital with its brightly lit Emergency Entrance less than fifty yards away. Stair-stepping down the hill to its right were the older clinical sciences and dental college buildings, dating back to the early 1950s.

But all was quiet at this hour.

Hung huddled against the clock tower in an effort to shield himself from a bracing wind blowing in from the Pacific Ocean. He checked his wristwatch and estimated that the janitor should be arriving within the hour, having cased the building several times in the past. Medical supplies were a prized commodity on the black market.

Fortunately, it didn't take long for Hung to spot the man coming up the hill from the Judah Street direction. He hustled across Parnassus without being seen, hid behind some bushes next to the stairway, took a quick few breaths, and waited.

After hearing the metallic clanking sound of the janitor's keys opening the door, Hung counted to five before scrambling up the steps, just in time to stop the door from slamming back shut with the toe of his boot. He froze and waited for the janitor to disappear into the back hallway, then crept into the lobby and listened for the sound of the elevator doors closing before making a left at the end.

The elevator rose unnervingly slowly. He watched the numbers advancing on the metal panel overhead until the elevator had stopped on the 9th floor and counted to sixty before summoning it back down.

With Hung now inside, and finally stopping at the eleventh ding, he cautiously poked his head out with his ears on hyper alert for sounds of human activity. Satisfied, he padded down the hallway and stopped in front of door number 1152, Professor Nelson's laboratory. He picked the lock and tentatively surveyed the lab before shutting the door behind him with a muted click.

Hung was relieved to find the lab unoccupied at this hour, although not exactly peaceful inside with the two fume hoods in the opposite front corners sucking air up their exhaust, and vacuum pumps beneath the lab benches thumping rhythmically like Clydesdales trotting along a distant path.

A long rectangular work bench ran down the center of the lab, with open shelves bisecting it and an industrial lab sink at each end. Two additional lab benches ran along each side wall. The more hazardous chemicals were stored in the cabinets mounted above them behind sliding glass doors.

Hung made his way around to the back of the lab while admiring the various experiments in progress, each one an intricate assembly of glassware, stir plates and sensors all held in place by screw clamps connected to tall vertical metal rods. Chemical reactions bubbled away inside their vessels in colors ranging from ochre to crimson. Some of them reminded Hung of the hand blown glassware his father would use to prepare his herbal extracts and distillates.

The three untidy desk carrels along the back wall were cluttered with tall stacks of paper, lab notebooks and binders. The dirty panel windows behind them looked out to a modern looking high-rise less than thirty yards away. Not much of a view, thought Hung. He took care not to touch anything and left the envelope on the seat of the middle chair, just as his father had instructed. Then he quietly left the lab and checked to make sure the door was locked. Spotting the janitor now polishing the floor at the end of the hallway to his right, the direction where the elevators were located, he deftly turned and walked silently down the opposite way. He would take the stairway down eleven flights to the street exit. Caution had saved him more than once.

Hung finally relaxed when he saw his scooter still parked behind the tree at the corner. Its tiny engine whinnied back to life after several kicks of the starter peddle but screamed in protest while he coasted down Parnassus without using the brakes. He gave it some gas at the bottom and made his way back to the foggy streets and anonymity of China Town.

6:20 AM. Monday, September 8TH, 1980

The loud metallic rumble came suddenly when a streetcar emerged from the early morning San Francisco fog. Brett Roberts groaned inwardly. He'd finally trained himself to sleep through such street noises, although not today for some reason. He heard loud sparks spitting out from a pole atop the lead car as it struggled to draw power from an overhead electric cable. Then came the wrenching screech of steel wheels against the rails when the two-car Muni train pulled to stop at the corner of Carl and Cole.

Roberts glanced over to the clock radio on his night stand to check the time. No sense trying to fall back asleep. The first run of the N Judah line had just come and gone, but another would follow in less than fifteen minutes. He swung his legs out from beneath the warm covers, tentatively probed the chilly floor with the balls of his feet, and then padded over to the bay windows behind his drum set to check the weather outside. Using his palm to rub a circle of condensation away from the glass, he peered down and caught a final glimpse of the tail car disappearing into the tunnel running beneath Buena Vista Park. Morning commuters were already heading back to their business jobs downtown.

Then he heard the shuffling sound of his roommate Patrick O'Reilly rushing down the hall to stake his claim to their unit's only bathroom. "Shit, I've waited too long." O'Reilly feigned exercise and did pretty much everything in slow motion, unlike Roberts who ran almost daily. Despite their differences, the two of them had been close friends since their freshman year of college. Both were now just entering their third year of graduate school at UC San Francisco.

O'Reilly had learned about this apartment the previous fall by scanning the obituaries. Most of the scratched and badly worn furniture was willingly left behind by a landlord whose father had lived there for over fifty years. There was plenty more of it stored down in the garage, which gave O'Reilly the idea of converting the front living room into a second bedroom. He 'graciously' offered this room to Roberts, although Roberts wasn't so sure he'd gotten the better end of the deal.

The coal burning fireplace directly opposite his bed hadn't been used since the 1930's. Roberts studied his face in the antique mirror while running a brush through his shoulder-length wavy blond hair. O'Reilly would be a while. Checking his watch, he decided that shaving could wait another day. Roberts dressed in a worn pair of jeans and pullover sweater and reluctantly pulled his hiking boots back on, still soggy from walking home through a rainstorm the previous afternoon.

Roberts clomped noisily down the wood panel staircase and forced open the rain warped street level door to enter the morning chill. A strong gust almost pushed him sideways as he turned to face the wind. Such quickly changing weather patterns no longer surprised him. At least the fog had blown inland, nothing but clear blue sky above, for now. He zipped up his jacket and thrust his hands into his pockets as he made his way up Carl Street, then made a left on Stanyan for a brief reprieve from the wind.

The way up Parnassus from that direction would be a much steeper grade, but there was a crumpet shop on the next corner that had recently opened. He smiled at the pretty girl behind the counter while she toasted his freshly baked crumpet and then dabbed on generous portions of butter and cream cheese.

Roberts was just finishing off the last bite and licking his fingers when he reached the top of the hill, where the wind hit him again with a vengeance. He leaned into it and focused on closing the gap between himself and the Medical Sciences Building, then climbed the steps and struggled to pull the glass door back shut behind him to silence its howling.

This particular plot of land at the base of Mount Sutro had been annexed by the UC Regents during the late 1870's. They envisioned an affiliation of medical colleges spanning the disciplines of medicine, pharmacy, and dentistry. A hundred years later, the sprawling high-rise campus now surrounded a treeless grass courtyard barely wide enough for a spirited game of Frisbee. UCSF wasn't much of a campus in the Ivy

League sense, although it did happen to overlook Golden Gate Park, a runner's paradise for Roberts.

The Medical Sciences building supported the post-graduate departments of biophysics, biochemistry, and pharmaceutical chemistry. The combined classrooms and overlapping curricula encouraged students to interact and explore ideas outside of their respective disciplines. Roberts and O'Reilly had enrolled at UCSF to learn more about the underlying molecular causes of human diseases, and hopefully go on to promising careers in the biomedical industry.

Roberts practically lived in the lab these days, ever since completing his required coursework and passing his cumulative exams. But the only part he didn't like was waiting for these damned elevators to arrive. He stared absently at the bulletin board until he noticed that Herb Boyer would be giving a seminar on gene-splicing that Thursday. Dr. Boyer had co-founded a biotechnology company in South San Francisco and was now rumored to be a molecular millionaire, although he maintained a research lab at UCSF and lectured infrequently. Boyer still preferred wearing jeans and a T-shirt despite his impressive net worth. Roberts admired him for that and made a mental note to attend Boyer's seminar.

He released a sigh when the bell finally announced the elevator's arrival. He rode it up to the eleventh floor and made a left down the hallway. Standing before the entrance to the Nelson lab, he fished out a key from his pocket and unlocked the door. A familiar pungent odor wafted out. The constant stench of organo-phosphorus chemicals required some getting used to.

The Nelson group studied enzyme mechanisms and how they processed biomolecules such as nucleotide triphosphates, a hot new area of drug discovery. This involved the synthesis of isotopically labeled analogs and used a relatively new technology called nuclear magnetic resonance spectroscopy to interrogate their atomic distances when bound to the enzyme.

He walked to his desk carrel facing the back wall and shrugged out of his jacket, draped it over his chair and gazed out the hazy windows to the Biochemistry wing directly across. Their labs may be more modern, he mused, but they also stank of sulfides, chemicals that were used to stabilize proteins.

Roberts ignored the piles of spectrophotometer printouts on his desk that were waiting to be analyzed. Nah, they could easily wait another day, like this stubble on his face. He grinned while rubbing it. Reaching for his lab coat, he spotted a strange-looking envelope on the seat of his chair, with a pair of Chinese characters written on it in bold strokes.

How odd... he'd been the last to leave the lab the night before... and the janitors hadn't yet emptied the waste bins that morning. Tiny hairs bristled on the back of his neck; he had no idea why.

Roberts remembered the enzyme he was purifying in the cold room and decided to worry about this later. Time to go change the fraction collector before it eluted from the column, otherwise his precious enzyme might spill out onto the floor.

He didn't return to inspect the envelope until two hours later. Still thinking it must have been intended for someone else, he flipped it over and his eyebrows rose when he saw the writing on the back.

"Owen will know what to do."

Roberts wondered, could this another one of Owen's practical jokes? If so, he didn't find it all that funny. Determined to find out, he locked the door behind him and strode purposefully down the hall to the Anderson lab, where he found Mudford busy setting up a chemical reaction in one of the fume hoods.

Owen Mudford was a Navy brat from Honolulu, so named after the destroyer his father had been serving on when Owen was born. His mother was a local Island girl whom Mudford Senior had fallen madly in love with and eventually won over. After giving birth to Owen, she went on to bear four more children, all boys. Owen's aloha family helped explain his carefree nature and unique blend of facial features, with keen blue eyes and a full head of brown hair cut just below the ears. He also had an exceptional knack for chemistry, which had earned him a Regent's fellowship to attend UCSF after earning his Bachelor's degree from the University of Hawaii.

"Hey Owen, I've got something I need to show you."

"Hang on a sec," said Mudford. He inserted a glass syringe through a septum into a round bottom flask containing his stirring reaction mixture and slowly added the catalyst, drop by drop. The solution turned a bright purple, then suddenly began to bubble and boil. "Whoa, hold on."

Mudford added crushed ice to the water bath in an effort to control the reaction temperature.

"Take your time," said Roberts. He turned to gaze out the lab's back panel windows, one of the benefits of working in the Anderson lab. They looked northward over the city and offered an impressive view on even the worst of days. Today was somewhere in between. With another thick fog rolling in, Roberts could barely make out the peaks of the expansion towers where the Golden Gate Bridge should be.

Mudford finally stepped away from the fume hood and removed his goggles and chemically resistant rubber gloves. "Okay, what have you got?"

Roberts showed him the envelope. "Any idea where this came from?"

Mudford accepted the envelope with a quizzical look, noting the Chinese characters on the front. "What the? Where'd you get this?"

"You're telling me you don't know?"

"Nope. Never seen it before."

Roberts studied Mudford's face as his friend flipped the envelope over and read the writing on the back. "Hey Brett, this looks like Virtanen's handwriting."

Roberts was even more dubious now. Juan Virtanen had gone missing over three weeks before. Detectives were still coming around asking questions, but no-one seemed to have any clues. Not surprising really, considering the reclusive fourth year student worked mostly nights in Professor Higgins' laboratory.

"I thought you told the cops you didn't know anything," said Roberts.

"Believe me Brett, I have absolutely no idea what might have happened to the dude."

"So how come he mentions your name?"

"Beats the shit out of me," said Mudford. He held the envelope to his ear and shook it, then tore off a corner and peeked inside. "Tell you what. Let me run a few tests on this stuff in the analytical lab. I'll get back to you later tonight. That cool with you, Brett?"

Roberts had a pretty good idea now what the envelope might contain, having observed the reaction schemes sketched on the Higgins lab chalkboard across the hall, structures of molecules similar to hallucinogenic drugs such as psilocybin and LSD. He suspected that

Virtanen may have been testing them on himself, and possibly OD'd. "You sure you don't know anything about this?"

"Honest, Brett."

Roberts studied Mudford's eyes once more and caught no sign of impishness or malintent. But it still didn't make sense. How could this envelope have wound up on his chair? He decided to give Mudford a bit of free rein. "Well, you should probably be careful with that."

Mudford spotted Patrick O'Reilly shuffling into the lab and he slid the envelope into an inner pocket of his lab coat.

"Hey guys," said O'Reilly as he passed them by and made his way to the back section of the lab where his work bench was located. His shoes were untied and he looked a bit dazed at the moment. Roberts figured his roommate must be pondering why yet another one of his experiments had failed. O'Reilly was not exactly a promising synthetic organic chemist, and few would have predicted he'd one day become a world-renowned expert in computer-assisted drug design, an emerging new field being pioneered at UCSF.

Mudford patted his lab coat pocket and whispered to Roberts, "Check back with me later." He put his gloves and safety goggles back on and returned to the fume hood to resume his work.

Roberts said somewhat unnecessarily but loud enough for O'Reilly to hear, "Well, I need to get back to the lab. See you guys later."

After inspecting the reaction mixture, Mudford replaced the water bath with a glasscol heating mantle. It would now need to reflux overnight, so he went to fetch his jacket and backpack from his cubicle. On a hunch, he decided to take the BART train over to the UC Berkeley campus. Their libraries were much more comprehensive, and Owen Mudford had some detective work to do.

Mudford crossed Parnassus and passed through the Student Union to take an elevator down to Irving Street. He stepped out into the same crosswind that Roberts had battled earlier and ducked into the bus stop shelter to await the N-Judah's arrival. His timing couldn't have been better despite the late morning hour, with the olive green street car rapidly approaching as if aided by the wind.

It pulled to a stop with a screech and the conductor reached for the lever to open the door. Mudford climbed aboard, inserted a quarter into the money box and accepted a transfer slip from the conductor as he passed him by. He chose an unoccupied bench seat near the back, in no mood to be social just then. All he could think about was Juan Virtanen, how reclusive the dude was, where he might have run off to, and why the envelope?

The 50's-era streetcar lurched forward and rolled noisily down the track with the conductor clanging the bell repeatedly as they made their way through the Cole Valley and Church Street neighborhoods. It then connected to a common rail that ran northeast through the middle of Market Street all the way to the Embarcadero. Mudford pulled the rope at the Van Ness stop and exited the streetcar to make his way over to the BART entrance, a light rail service connecting the San Francisco Peninsula with a network of East Bay communities.

He descended into the tunnel and walked briskly past a homeless fellow belting out a pretty decent rendition of a Bob Dylan song while strumming away on his beat up guitar. It didn't seem to matter that the old guy had no teeth. Mudford could never understand Dylan's lyrics anyway.

Unlike the aging streetcar that Mudford had recently stepped down from, the BART train cars had a sleek exterior of polished stainless steel with carpeted aisles and padded seats. The song *Tainted Love* by a band called Soft Cell would later remind him of the "boop-boop" sound the BART train made as it pulled to a stop.

The whooshing sound deepened as the BART train descended beneath the San Francisco Bay. Mudford's ears popped several times during this subterranean transit. He stared absently out the window and watched the tunnel lights flash by until the train began its ascent back up to sea level. The pitch increased, his ears popped again, and then it was daylight.

It was a surprisingly windless and sunny afternoon on the East Bay. Mudford rode the escalator up to street level and shielded his eyes from the blinding sunlight as he stepped onto the sidewalk at Shattuck Avenue. The musky and pungently-sweet smell of incense announced the pending arrival of yet another Hare Krishna parade. Then came the sandal-clad faithfuls processing down the road in their yogi pants or saris trimmed with colorful Harinam Chadars. They chanted away rhythmically with some beating on drums and others clanging their bronze finger cymbals together in accompaniment. Many of the men (and some of the women) had shaved their heads to demonstrate their devotion, including a number of students still experimenting with their new found freedom away from their parents.

This was not an atypical sight for the funky downtown Berkeley neighborhood that wrapped around the western and southern borders of the UC campus. Once a mecca for the peace movement back in the 1960s, it continued to champion tolerance and freedom of expression, a wildly eclectic place where weirdness was the expected normalcy.

Mudford weaved his way through the crowd until he reached the corner of University Avenue, where he made a right and headed east toward the main campus entrance. He followed a shaded path through mature Eucalyptus trees and breathed deeply, enjoying their crisp menthol scent. When he got to Campanile Way, he made a left and followed that route onward through the center of campus. He glanced briefly upward to admire Sather Tower, a distinctive landmark that could easily be spotted from the San Francisco side whenever the fog was on hiatus.

He entered the Bancroft Library, showed his student badge to the lady behind the front desk and made his way to the anthropology section where he located an unoccupied study carrel along the back wall. Then he unzipped his backpack, took out a notepad, and began to review the notes he had made during his commute across the bay.

Mudford recalled overhearing Virtanen mutter something about his mother being descended from an indigenous tribe back in Brazil. This happened shortly before Virtanen stopped working days in the lab, around the time when his weird streak shifted into overdrive. He kept repeating the word 'Yanomami' over and over again, as though it had become his new mantra. Mudford suspected that this might explain whatever was inside the envelope. Now he wanted to learn more about the hallucinogenic plant extracts that were used by the indigenous tribes for their religious ceremonies.

First he browsed through the Botany section and read about the *ayahuasca* drink, the most commonly used hallucinogen throughout the Amazon region. Its main ingredient was extracted from the vine *Banisteriopsis caapi*, although not particularly hallucinogenic when consumed by itself. But when cooked together with any of three compañeros, or companion plants, a much more potent drink resulted. The compañeros contained an active compound now known to be dimethyltryptamine or DMT, whereas the vine extract contained an inhibitor that prevented stomach enzymes from metabolizing the drug before it could hit the bloodstream. Fascinating how such potions were perfected throughout the Amazon region, hundreds if not thousands of years before, by illiterate tribes who shared no common language.

The Yanomami discovered a completely different way to get DMT into the bloodstream. Mudford plowed through several articles about the *yopo* snuff their shamans would use to contact the spirit world. They puffed it through a blow tube into the nose of the recipient. For the Yanomami, this represented a passage of energy from one being to another. They believed it gave them special powers to defeat their enemies.

The essential ingredient for *yopo* was extracted from the plant *Anadenanthera peregrine*, which only the shamans were permitted to cultivate according to long-standing tradition. Not surprisingly, the seeds of this plant also contained massive amounts of DMT.

After exhausting all the books he could find on the subject, he left the Bankroft Library and followed the gravel path over to the nearby Moffitt Library. This building housed an extensive collection of chemistry and biochemistry journals. Mudford wanted to find out whether *yopo* extracts had ever been characterized, and was pleased to find quite a number of published articles on the subject, including one containing a detailed analytical protocol. He carried the bound journal over to a Xerox machine and photocopied the pages containing the protocol and representative chromatograms. Then he returned to his study carrel and prepared to return to the foggy side of the bay.

Mudford savored the sunshine as he walked back through the UC Berkeley campus, until an ominous looking fellow approached him unexpectedly. The guy wore a medium brimmed leather hat pulled down low. "Need some bud?" he muttered.

"What? No man, I'm good."

Mudford continued walking but the drug dealer persisted while keeping pace. "You a student here?"

"Not really." "You sure look like one. Where you headed?"

"Back to San Francisco," Mudford stupidly replied. He bit his lip.

"So you're a graduate student then, over at UCSF I'm guessing. I bet you're one of them chemistry majors. Am I right?" The pusher wasn't actually psychic. He'd been stalking Mudford for over an hour.

"What's it to you?"

"Yeah, that's what I thought. Well here kid, let me ask you something…."

Mudford shrugged off the thought of his recent conversation as he rode the elevator back to the 11th floor of Medical Sciences. The Anderson group possessed their own analytical lab for characterizing the break-down products of drug metabolism. Mudford reviewed the pages he'd copied from the library while mentally checking through the procedure he'd follow to confirm his hypothesis. After placing a sheet of weighing paper on the scale, he tapped out a small portion of powder from the envelope, about a tenth of a gram. He carefully transferred the substance to a glass vial and added a half-milliliter of 0.1 molar aqueous sodium hydroxide, followed by a half milliliter of chloroform, knowing this would neutralize any DMT that might be present and extract it into the immiscible chloroform layer. The water soluble components would remain in the aqueous phase. He capped and shook the vial and then set it down on the lab bench to allow the two layers to separate. Using a glass syringe, he withdrew a small volume of liquid from the bottom chloroform layer and injected it into the gas chromatograph.

Mudford studied the chromatogram as it rolled out of the machine. Each peak corresponded to a different molecule depending on its size and other physical properties. There it was, a peak at the precise location where DMT should be, according to the chromatogram that he had photocopied from the UC Berkeley library.

And having just completed his own work for the day, Roberts headed down the hall and noticed that the door to Professor Anderson's analytical lab had been left partially open. He poked his head in and found Mudford busily working away, presumably on whatever was inside the envelope. "Hey Owen, thought you might be in here. How's it going?"

Mudford feigned surprise when he saw Roberts with his backpack. Brett almost never left the lab before dark. "Dude, you're actually leaving? Slacker! But hey, I just might be on to something here. Need to run a few more tests though. How about you come by my place tonight around 8 and I'll fill you in."

"You bet," said Roberts. "And thanks, by the way. I really appreciate your help on this."

"Yeah, well, let's see if I'm right first."

Roberts exited the Medical Sciences building and drew inspiration from the late afternoon sunshine, a rare treat for that time of year. With over an hour of daylight remaining, it seemed like a perfect opportunity for a run in Golden Gate Park. He walked down Parnassus, made a left on Willard Street and passed by Mudford's place, a purple three-story Victorian house where Mudford shared a flat on the second level with two other UCSF students. Their unit had its own private courtyard, ideally suited for growing marijuana plants. The courtyard also had a ladder leading up to the roof. They'd cart up their beach chairs to enjoy the panoramic view whenever the weather allowed. But not today. Mudford was still working, although Roberts didn't feel the least bit guilty about playing hooky.

Continuing on, he took a right on Carl Street and fast-walked back to his own apartment, took the stairs two at a time and quickly changed into running clothes before heading back out. He left his key in the mailbox and trotted down Stanyan at an easy pace to loosen his muscles.

The park's eastern entrance faced Haight Street, the nexus of the Summer of Love back in 1967. He headed toward a pedestrian tunnel that ran beneath Kezar Drive, its ceiling decorated with artificial stalactites that dated back to the 1894 World's Fair, many of them now crumbled and broken after decades of neglect.

Roberts lengthened his stride after passing through the tunnel and continued along the path through a grassy field bordered by century old trees of oak, magnolia, eucalyptus and pine. To the far left was Children's Park with its century old merry-go-round, elaborate climbing structures and concrete hill slides.

He took the right hand fork and skirted around Sharon Meadow in the direction of Hippie Hill, with the distant sound of drumbeats getting louder and louder. Clusters of eclectically dressed people sat cross-legged up the rise, bohemian types and sixties-style hippie types and plaid-shirted backcountry types. Percussionists filled the park benches at the bottom of the hill, all pounding rhythmically on hand drums of various shapes and sizes. Today's ad-hoc jam session sounded a bit livelier than usual. Roberts almost stopped to ask if he could borrow a drum and join in, but then changed his mind.

He continued running up around the tennis courts, and crossed over a maintenance road toward a dirt trail leading into the trees. This would take him down to a secluded area known as Lily Pond, one of his favorite places. He loved the simple act of running along this path. Large fern trees cast late-afternoon shadows on the lily pads while ducks swam slowly by. It was peaceful here, a place where the city seemed far away, a horticultural masterpiece that few tourists knew about.

He continued back up to John F. Kennedy Drive and deftly dodged a roller skater speeding down the concrete sidewalk. This particular section would be blocked off to traffic on Sundays, where skaters could practice their dance moves to the accompaniment of loud disco music blaring from their boom boxes.

Roberts ran on up from there to the music concourse, which sat within a large rectangular section of the park also known as the museum district. The music concourse was bordered by the De Young Museum to the north and the Academy of Sciences to the south. Fronting the western edge was Speckles Temple of Music, where Sunday afternoon concerts were usually performed free of charge. This concrete and plaster 'temple' resembled something out of Greek Mythology with its matching ionic columned porticos extending to the left and right of the band shell.

Roberts took a left-hand stairway that bordered the Japanese Tea Garden and continued up from there to Stowe Lake. He slowed to a jog and continued around the path while observing the swans paddling gracefully by on the water. On weekends this place would be loaded with people in their rented rowboats and paddle boats splashing this way and that. Picnickers crowded its grassy perimeter, and parking anywhere nearby could be next to impossible. But all was quiet today, the surface of the water almost glassy except for occasional ripples made by the swans.

Wishing he could stay a bit longer to enjoy this peaceful moment, Roberts remembered that it was his turn to fix dinner back at the apartment. He wanted to set a good example for his roommate to follow, so began trotting down the entrance road, and then made his way back across Chrissy Meadow toward an exit gate. Once there, he turned east on Lincoln and picked up the pace at a brisk clip for home.

<h1 style="text-align:center">CHAPTER SIX</h1>

"Interpreting the message"

O'REILLY WASHED THE DISHES while Roberts showered and changed back into warmer clothes, having noticed it getting blustery again outside after glancing out the window. Time to head back out to Mudford's place, he reckoned. His cheeks were icy and his fingers felt numb by the time he got there.

Mudford called down from the top of the stairs. "Dude, you look pretty damned frosty. Why don't you wait in the front room while I make us a nice hot pot of tea?" Roberts blew onto his fingers in an effort to thaw them while rubbing his hands together. "Think I'll take you up on that." He hung his coat on a rack at the top of the landing and settled into a worn leather sofa. Mudford's front room was filled with dark antique furniture that had come with the flat. Another light rain began to splatter against the front bay windows. Roberts watched the droplets coalesce and then streak down the glass, which gave him a brief sense of déjà vu.

Mudford came into the room carrying a teapot in one hand and two Chinese tea cups in the other. He beckoned Roberts over to the dining table near the left-hand wall, and then pulled out a chair from the opposite side and lit a sandalwood candle before pouring the tea. The two pleasant aromas soon filled the air.

Roberts breathed in through his nostrils and tried to relax. Not quite working, unfortunately. He studied Mudford's face, again sensing no hint of subterfuge. He leaned forward, "Well?"

Mudford slid the envelope across the table. "First off, I've figured out what these two Chinese characters mean," he pointed. "The first signifies *God* or *Deity*, and the second one stands for *Medicine*. Ever been to that herbal pharmacy on Washington Street in China town?"

"No, but I'll take your word for it," said Roberts. "And how do you explain the words on the back? You said it looked like Virtanen's writing. We haven't seen him in weeks, right?"

"Look man, I've got no clue where Virtanen might have off to. Hardly ever saw the dude these past few months."

Roberts was actually starting to believe him. Almost. "And I have no idea how this envelope wound up on my chair," he said evenly. "I locked the door to the lab when I left last night, and I'm pretty damned sure I was the first one in this morning. Frankly, the whole thing is freaking me out right now."

Mudford settled back in his chair. "Yeah, I get that. Look, I swear I don't know what may have happened to Virtanen. But I do know now what's inside this envelope."

"Thought you might," said Roberts. "Okay, so how'd you figure it out?" Roberts figured he'd indulge his friend a bit, knowing how much he loved explaining things.

Mudford grinned. "I began thinking about Virtanen being from Brazil, and then I figured this could be one of those hallucinogenic plant extracts, you know? Those indigenous tribes in the Amazon have been using this stuff in their religious ceremonies for thousands of years. It just seemed like the kind of thing Virtanen would be into. You did know he was synthesizing tryptamine analogs, right?"

"I figured that from the chemical reaction schemes that were sketched on the chalkboard inside the Higgins lab," Roberts admitted. "They've never been that fastidious about erasing it, although they're supposed to keep their lab notebooks locked up at night."

"Yeah, and Virtanen once asked me to co-sign his lab notebook, which was how I also recognized his handwriting. Guess he thought he'd discovered something that might need to be patented. Okay, so now the second clue. I once overheard him muttering something about his mother being from an indigenous rainforest tribe called the *Yanomami*. When I asked him about it he said it wasn't any of my business and turned back to his experiment. I never mentioned it again, didn't want to piss him off."

Roberts started tapping his fingers pinky to thumb and back again on the table. "So you think the stuff inside this envelope might have come from one of those indigenous tribes in the Amazon?"

Mudford said, "Well yes, as a matter of fact. So following up on my idea about the Yanomami, I went over to UC Berkeley this afternoon to access their libraries. First I read up on the compositions of various hallucinogenic plant extracts used throughout the Amazon. The Yanomami tribes throughout the hill county in northern Brazil and neighboring Venezuela use a substance called *yopo*. It's some pretty heavy stuff, apparently. Contains massive quantities of DMT. Okay, so with that in mind I took the envelope into the analytical lab, weighed some out and extracted the basic compounds to run through the gas chromatograph. As I suspected, one of those compounds turned out to be DMT, a whopping peak as a matter of fact. But that's not all. I also found a couple of published analytical studies on *yopo* in the journal *Toxicology*."

Roberts was impressed by how quickly Mudford had managed to figure this out. This also explained what he was doing inside the analytical lab that afternoon.

"Okay, let me see if I've got this. You're telling me the powder inside this envelope is a substance called *yopo*, a hallucinogen used by Yanomami shamans for their spirit rituals?"

"Yep. The chromatograms are a perfect match."

"Well, what are we supposed to *do* with it, exactly?" Roberts wasn't quite sure he wanted to hear the answer.

"I think we should try it out," said Mudford.

"Are you kidding? No way!" Roberts shook his head firmly. "How do you know we won't get brain damage?"

"Don't be such a pussy. Like I said, indigenous tribes throughout the Amazon have been snorting this stuff since the Stone Age. Come on, aren't you the least bit curious?" Mudford went on to describe more about how such hallucinogens were prepared. Like Mudford, Roberts found this part fascinating, to consider how such disparate tribes had all discovered different ways to get buzzed on DMT.

"But that thing you mentioned about *yopo*, how they deliver it through a blow tube... you're not planning on snorting this stuff yourself, are you?"

"Maybe," said Mudford with a mischievous grin. "Just to see what happens. We'll be fine, you'll see. I've done this before."

"Yeah, so I've heard." Roberts shook his head, not at all certain he was thinking clearly. He re-read the writing on the back of the envelope. *Owen will know what to do...* was he actually expected to go through with this? Roberts sighed with slumped shoulders. "When?"

"What do you mean?" Mudford snapped back.

"Well I'm not doing it tonight, that's for sure. Look, I'm right in the middle of an experiment that needs to be completed by Friday morning. I promised to write up the report and give it to Professor Nelson before he heads off to a conference. And he's been hinting about covering my stipend after my Regent's Fellowship runs out. I can't risk screwing that up."

"Alright then, Saturday."

Roberts had a sinking sense of inevitability. "I suppose Saturday could work. But you've got to promise me something, Owen. One of us tries it while the other guy watches, just to make sure nothing bad happens. And neither of us leaves the room until the effects are gone. Promise?"

Mudford wasn't all that worried. "Yeah, whatever." He folded the corner down on the envelope and went back to his room to stash it away in a top dresser drawer. Upon returning, he reminded Roberts unnecessarily, "So you're in then. On Saturday we do this?"

"I said okay, didn't I?"

"Yeah, yeah. Good luck with your experiment."

Roberts felt like a man with too many commitments as he walked back to his own apartment under a light drizzle. He also had band practice that Friday afternoon, which meant that he'd need to finish his experiment on Thursday and write up his report the next morning. Their band leader Pete Slater wrote most of the songs and could get real agitated if anyone was late, even though they were really just a bunch of amateur musicians from UCSF who mostly played parties for free. Roberts had been late several times already. He didn't dare risk being late again. Pete might kick him out of the band, and playing music was Brett's only true escape.

There was only one way to get it all done, and that would mean working extra-long shifts in the lab, possibly even an all-nighter. The next several days were going to be intense. Roberts would have to finish purifying his enzyme and have everything ready for the NMR experiments by Wednesday afternoon at the latest.

His research project involved a new class of enzymes called tyrosine kinases, already known to be involved in a number of disease processes. Understanding how such enzymes worked was needed for designing more effective drugs, and UCSF had pioneered a novel approach for characterizing their binding sites. The method involved the use of nuclear magnetic resonance spectroscopy, or NMR, which essentially used pulses of radiofrequency energy to interrogate atoms inside a protein after first subjecting them to a high magnetic field. By analyzing the data, the distances between atoms could be calculated, and then by connecting a large number of such distances together, the three-dimensional structure of the binding site could be deduced. Roberts found it fascinating how radiofrequency energy could be used to interrogate atoms, which caused him to wonder about the interdependencies between matter and energy. Perhaps teleportation wasn't so far-fetched after all, he mused.

Roberts had actually managed to complete his experiments by Thursday afternoon, having pulled an all-nighter in the NMR lab. His brain was fried, his body exhausted, and he felt like a zombie walking back down Parnassus.

He willed himself up the stairs and unlocked the door to find his roommate watching television in their sparsely furnished front den. Brett's 13-inch black and white TV rested atop a folding tray table, and O'Reilly had taken the room's only proper chair, so Roberts dragged over a banana-yellow bean bag to join him.

"What's happening, Patrick?"

"Not much Brett, just watching this new comedy I stumbled on a couple weeks ago. Whoa, you look trashed." O'Reilly returned to his show without further comment, and very little sympathy.

The program was about an alien from another planet, one played by a local comedian who still did occasional standup at a few select clubs around the city. Roberts remembered seeing him perform once in Golden Gate Park. The guy was hilarious. One couldn't watch him without laughing hysterically, although Roberts found that difficult on an empty stomach. "Hey Patrick, isn't it supposed to be your turn to make dinner?"

"Already done, my friend. They're in the fridge." Roberts hoisted himself out of the beanbag and went around the counter to their tiny kitchen nook to investigate. He opened the door to see that O'Reilly had thoughtfully prepared a plate of sandwiches, sliced diagonally and neatly stacked on top of each other.

"Dude, seriously?" said Roberts.

O'Reilly said, "Sorry, man, I didn't have much time. In fact, I need to head back up to campus right after this show."

"Really? I haven't seen you in the lab much lately."

"Yeah, I've been meaning to tell you. I decided to switch advisors. Now I'm working for Professor Richter."

"Isn't he in the Biophysics department?"

"He has a joint appointment with Pharm Chem," said O'Reilly.

Roberts asked, "Does that mean you'll need to come up with a new research proposal?"

"Not according to my advisory committee," said O'Reilly. "I'll be working on the same drug problem, only using computers instead. Look, I've got time scheduled in the molecular graphics laboratory starting at 5 PM." Turning back to the TV, he added, "Sorry man. I'll make dinner again tomorrow night, maybe spaghetti this time. Deal?"

Roberts decided not to answer. He took a few sandwich halves from the plate and grabbed his last can of Budweiser to wash them down.

Roberts got jolted awake from a dreamless slumber when the last streetcar of the evening came clanging by and screeched to a stop at the corner of Carl and Cole. He opened his eyes and found himself still slumped in the bean bag with an empty beer at his side. He rubbed his sore neck, massaged his temples, and checked his watch. Not quite 9 PM… he should probably stay awake for a while before heading off to bed.

He spun the TV knob to see if anything worthy was on, stopping on a UHF channel that featured all-night science fiction movies. Next up was *The Time Machine*, the 1960 movie version of H.G. Wells' classic novel. A perfect distraction. Too bad he was out of beer, he could really use another to take the edge off his headache. He hoisted himself out of the bean bag and went to his room to see if he had any cash left in his wallet. Just a couple bucks, although he'd be picking up his next monthly stipend check from the UCSF accounting office tomorrow. Time for a mini-splurge.

Roberts fetched his coat and stepped out into the blustery evening chill to make his way down to the Ramona Market on Cole Street. It was a tiny little neighborhood convenience store and the prices were higher, but he knew it would be open at this hour. He nodded to Mustafa behind the counter and ignored the dusty shelves of mostly-expired canned goods while making his way to the back of the store where the display refrigerator was located. The six-pack of Budweiser was a luxury he could only afford about twice a month. O'Reilly preferred expensive dark chocolate whenever he had a little money left over. To each his own, thought Roberts. He carted the beers back to the counter and placed them next to the cash register for Mustafa to ring up.

"How's it going, Mister Brett?" Mustafa asked with surprising enthusiasm. He spoke with a throaty accent and it sounded more like "gho-eeeng". His family had owned the Ramona Market for the past eight years, having emigrated from Iran in the early 1970s.

Mustafa evidently hoped to strike up a conversation, must be bored-out-of-his-mind at this hour, but Roberts was eager to get back to his apartment before the movie started. He made a mental note to come back Sunday afternoon and chat a bit longer with Mustafa. The football game would probably be playing on his TV set behind the counter, always a great time to drop in. Mustafa was proud of his adopted city and he loved the 49ers. Roberts really liked the guy.

"I'm good Mustafa, how about you?" He forked over the last two bills from his wallet and pocketed the change. "Listen, I need to get back, okay? Sorry."

"No problem my friend, we talk more next time. Cold night, no?"

"Always." Roberts tucked the paper bag under his arm and exited the store.

Minutes later, he cracked open another beer and turned on the TV set to find the show already in progress. The main character played by Rod Taylor had just invited three of his colleagues into the parlor room for a drink to celebrate the dawn of the next millennium. It was December 31st, 1899, a few moments before midnight.

First he introduced the concept of time travel, describing time as "the fourth dimension". Then he produced his tiny prototype, about the size of toy sleigh with little lights on the control panel and an intricately painted bronze dish in the back. He claimed it could generate a time vortex and went on to demonstrate by placing a cigar inside and pulling the lever. The lights began to flash and the bronze dish began to spin. The three stodgy English gentlemen stared back in disbelief as the cigar mysteriously disappeared and reappeared when their host reversed the lever, convinced that it must be another one of his clever parlor tricks. They finished their drinks and wished him goodnight.

But after they had left, the main character went to another room and unveiled his life-sized machine. Roberts enjoyed watching the man use his time machine to travel back and forth through the ages, although the apocalyptic theme seemed a bit obvious. Mankind would eventually destroy itself without learning from the mistakes of history.

He also found it amusing to imagine how such a bogus-looking contraption could possibly work. The story was set in Victorian England after all. H.G. Wells wrote his novel back in 1885, still the age of Newtonian physics. This was so pre-Gene Roddenberry.

That got Roberts thinking about his discussion with Mudford a while back over a pitcher of beer at Clancy's. The Einstein-Podolsky-Rosen effect....

He continued to wonder about it as he lay in bed. Perhaps Einstein was on to something with his universal field theorem. He had been working on a mathematical proof right up to his death. Physicists were still trying to solve Einstein's equations. Perhaps one day....

Roberts was horrified to wake up the next morning and find it already past 7 AM. He must have forgotten to switch on his alarm clock the night before. But upon hearing O'Reilly still snoring softly through the wall, he decided to take a quick shower before pulling on his last clean pair of jeans and a sweatshirt. Then he went to the kitchen to prepare a toasted muffin with peanut butter before rushing out the door.

Crunching the numbers turned out to be less time-consuming than Roberts had anticipated. He slipped his report under Professor Nelson's door, and by 3 PM had disassembled his drum set and loaded it into the back of his Honda Civic. He floored the car's tiny engine to give it a running head start before climbing up Shrader Street. Pete's flat was the only one big enough for the four of them to practice in, although his neighbors would protest mightily if they weren't finished by dinner time.

The band started jamming, a free-flowing blues number. Roberts loved this part about practice, when he could hit away however he liked and crash his cymbals without drawing much attention to himself.

Just as they were getting loose, Pete called a halt and announced that he written a new song, a rock ballad that turned out to be exceptionally difficult. Roberts was noticeably challenged by the unpredictable changes.

Pete yelled "Stop!" and rudely asked Roberts what the fuck he was playing.

"Sorry man, guess I'm having a difficult time with this piece." Roberts sensed Pete's temper rising.

Pete hit him with his usual barrage of insults before finally lowering his voice. He took a controlled breath and then said, "Let me try to explain. Have you ever had a breakup with a girl that hurt so bad you could hardly breathe?"

"Oh yeah, that I have."

"Okay, so maybe you needed to get away for a while, go find an open meadow somewhere and just lie there in the grass while gazing up to the sky for answers. Are you feeling it Brett?"

"Yeah, I think so."

"Well *that's* how I felt the day I wrote this song back in Davis. So now answer another question for me Brett, ever felt like God might be listening?" Pete asked.

Roberts pondered his answer while the other bandmates looked away and fidgeted. "Yeah, I think so."

"Well, *play* it like that!" Pete emphasized the word 'play' like it was the eleventh commandment. Then he went back and picked up his guitar, stepped to the microphone and said almost kindly, "Alright guys, one more time from the beginning."

The band tightened up after that, almost like they'd been playing this song together their entire lives. Feeding off each other's rhythms was intoxicating. They let the moment linger after striking their final chord.

"Thanks everyone. Maybe we'll record it next time."

That was as close to a compliment as Pete ever came up with.

Roberts walked over to thank him as the band was packing up. "Don't mention it," said Pete. With that, he turned away. Practice was over, obviously.

Back in his room with the drum kit reassembled, Roberts grabbed his sticks and began to practice Pete's song. He heard a loud and persistent knocking at the door a few minutes later, getting louder and angrier until he finally stopped playing. He opened the door and was startled to find Zelda glaring at him, one of two lesbians who shared the back apartment on his floor. She appeared to be the dominant one in their relationship, with a butch haircut, muscular build and tattooed arms. He rarely spoke to either of them and they kept mostly to themselves.

Roberts couldn't help but notice Zelda's girlfriend Cindy standing there in the back doorway, pretty hard to miss in her string bikini with a large yellow snake draped over her shoulders that was coiling itself around one of her arms. Finding this disturbingly erotic, Roberts mustered the good sense to look away. O'Reilly had warned him about these two, said they practiced Wiccan rituals on Fridays by candlelight. Roberts had no idea how or why O'Reilly knew this.

Zelda poked her fleshy finger into Brett's bony chest and said, "Keep it down bub or we'll call the cops."

"Um, okay, sorry about that." Roberts backed away and closed the door before Zelda could resume her rant. After a long uncomfortable moment, he heard her stomp back to her own apartment and slam the door behind her. He exhaled slowly and decided to change into his running clothes. Drum practice was over, obviously.

Seeing it was getting dark, he altered his route and trotted down Judah toward the ocean. It would be about an eight-mile loop but relatively flat. He gradually lengthened his stride and then settled into an even pace.

The Sunset district was the last part of the city to rebuild after San Francisco's devastating earthquake of 1906. Its boxy two-story houses lacked the grandeur of their Victorian predecessors, although many were brightly painted with carved wooden trim. Lights began switching on from behind the upper floor picture windows, illuminating cozy living rooms and dining rooms, and families now sitting down to dinner.

Roberts heard the familiar sounds of waves collapsing and cascading along the shoreline as he approached the coastal highway. He crossed over and continued north along the seawall, his reward for having come this far. He loved watching the flashes of iridescent foam as the waves spilled down into the dark churning water. Such magical moments reminded him that he was alive. Upon reaching the next streetlight, Roberts reluctantly crossed back over and make a right on Lincoln, a main boulevard skirting the southern edge of Golden Gate Park. He opened his stride and pumped his arms, completing the run in well under an hour.

CHAPTER SEVEN
"Connections"

BRETT ROBERTS SLEPT A FULL NINE HOURS that night and awoke the next morning feeling surprisingly stress-free, although a bit sore from his run the night before. The sun was shining, it was Saturday, and he was feeling great to be alive. Until he remembered about the envelope.

So today was the day. He wondered if there might still be a way to talk Mudford out of this. *Owen will know what to do…* yeah, right. He shuddered at the thought of snorting whatever that stuff might be up his nose.

Roberts pulled on a pair of sweat pants, opened his bedroom door and was surprised to find O'Reilly making breakfast in the kitchenette, stirring up a medley of scrambled eggs with shredded cheddar cheese, diced onion and chives.

"Sorry man, I know I promised to make dinner last night, but I got back late and didn't want to wake you. Figured I'd make us some breakfast."

"O'Reilly, you have no idea how great that smells right now."

"Yeah, well have a seat." Roberts pulled a stool up to the counter while O'Reilly spooned a steaming pile of eggs onto his plate. "We're out of bacon but I made toast."

Roberts felt much better after a few hungry swallows. "All is forgiven."

O'Reilly said, "You seem a bit out of sorts. Something bugging you?"

Roberts was surprised that O'Reilly had actually managed to notice. He wasn't exactly the touchy-feely type. "I'm okay, I guess. Been working longer hours than usual, you know?"

"Yeah, I can relate to that," said O'Reilly between bites. He began to clear the dishes away. "So, you planning to take the day off or what?"

"Probably head out for a bike ride with Owen," Roberts ad-libbed. This was what would usually do on their rare Saturdays off. "Hey, want to come along?" He hoped O'Reilly might say yes.

"Thanks anyway. Nobody's signed up for the molecular graphics lab today. I should have it all to myself." O'Reilly wasn't into cycling back then, although that would miraculously change after he graduated. "Tell you what, how'd you like to hit the I-Beam later this evening? There's a new wave band playing tonight."

"Now that sounds like a great idea." Then he recalled Ruth mentioning how much she liked new wave. "Would you mind if I invited Ruth along?"

Ruth Simpson was a first-year graduate student from Kansas, a slender, confident brunette with beautiful green eyes. Roberts had been struggling for weeks to come up with an excuse to ask her out, although the jury was still out on Brett as far as Ruth was concerned.

"The more the merrier," said O'Reilly. "I should be home around six."

Roberts took a long hot shower after O'Reilly had left. He luxuriated under the spray and gave it time to relieve his aching muscles while watching the steam rise.

The phone rang and Roberts tried to ignore it. But after about the twelfth ring, he shut off the faucet and reached for a towel to dry off. Still ringing… he wrapped the towel around his waist and padded out to their wall phone in the kitchenette.

It was Mudford. "Didn't wake you, did I?"

Roberts answered, "I was in the shower, although I presume that was your intention."

Mudford laughed, "Ha! Guess you got me. Listen my brother, how about you and I go out for a bike ride first before we do that other thing? We could head over the Golden Gate Bridge and have us an early lunch in Sausalito."

"I was hoping you might say that," said Roberts. "Probably should do some stretching first, though. Must have run a bit too far last evening."

"Well, come on over then. I'll teach you some yoga moves," said Mudford.

Roberts needed a moment to think, still hoping he could come up with a way to dissuade Mudford about that *other thing.* "Think I'll pass on that, but I should be over with my bike in about 30 minutes."

Brett called Ruth next and was pleased with her response about coming along to the I-Beam later that night. Perhaps this wouldn't be such a bad day after all.

It was a crisp and clear morning, perfect weather for such a ride. They peddled northward through the Presidio until they reached Chrissy Field and caught their first glimpse of the Golden Gate Bridge towering over the mouth of the bay. Roberts followed Mudford up a bike path to the pedestrian entrance where they made their way onto the bridge free of charge.

A strong crosswind made it challenging to round the first tower while steering clear of the handrail that served as their only protection from the whitecaps below. But it got easier while peddling over the span, and Roberts couldn't help but glance repeatedly over his shoulder to the stunning view of Alcatraz Island rising out of the deep blue water. He spotted Coit Tower, a distinctive white column atop Telegraph Hill that still dominated the 1980 San Francisco skyline. Sailboats were cutting back and forth through the whitecaps with their sails tightly sheeted and masts tilted sideways.

The wind mercifully subsided after they rounded the second tower. Although he wasn't usually afraid of such heights, Roberts found himself more than a bit relieved when they reached the exit ramp that would take them beneath the bridge to the opposite side and from there down to solid ground. With the massive Golden Gate now briefly overhead, Roberts glanced upward and contemplated the webbed netting that spanned its entire length. A jumper would need to leap out quite far to avoid it, although that knowledge never seemed to console him as he rode up above.

The bike path emptied onto More Road where they followed the signs to the waterfront and coasted downhill, faster and faster until they saw the yacht harbor with stopped traffic just ahead. Mudford gripped his handbrakes and Roberts did the same to avoid an otherwise fateful collision.

Mudford led them into the village and they coasted to a stop in front of a deli on 2nd Street. Roberts grabbed a couple of cold bottled waters and a loaf of French bread while Mudford went over to the butcher counter for some sliced salami and a wedge of cheese. They pooled their money at the counter to pay.

Remounting their bikes, they rode down to a small park near the water and sat cross-legged on the grass while eating their lunch. Out on the water, a small craft sailing regatta appeared to be just wrapping up. As each of the Laser class 14-footers rounded the final buoy, it tacked downwind and darted off toward Tiburon. Downtown San Francisco made a striking backdrop from this vantage across the deep blue water. Roberts shut his eyes and leaned back on his elbows to enjoy the sunshine, but he knew it wouldn't last. He had put off the inevitable long enough, might as well get it over with.

"Okay Owen, I think I'm ready to head back."

"Yeah?" Mudford smiled and stuffed the remnants of their lunch inside his backpack. "Let's ride."

They peddled back over the bridge at a more leisurely cadence to savor the view, this time from the ocean-facing side. A gargantuan shipping tanker passed slowly beneath them, laden with truck-sized cargo containers stacked high above the gunwale.

Seeing Fort Point beneath them with the tollgates approaching, they took the exit ramp, crossed back under the bridge to the bike path, and coasted down to the Presidio with another rush of acceleration.

They raced each other through Golden Gate Park and soon found themselves peddling back up Willard Street. Mudford unlocked the door and they carried their bikes up the stairway to his second level flat. They leaned them against a side wall at the top of the landing.

Mudford caught Roberts glancing out to the courtyard.

Roberts said, "Hey Owen, how about we take a couple beach chairs up to the rooftop? The sun's still out."

"Not today," said Mudford. He knew Roberts was stalling. "Come on, my brother. Let's go find out what *yopo* feels like." He gave Roberts a firm pat on the shoulder and led him down the hall to their drug den behind the kitchen.

The tiny room had a single window of frosted glass in the far back corner, mostly obscured by a thriving Creeping Charlie plant that hung there from a macramé sling, one that Mudford's girlfriend had crocheted for him the previous fall. Its tendrils had already conquered the upper shelf ledge running the perimeter of the room. The modest furnishings included an over-sized wicker hanging chair in the opposite back corner, a mocha-colored futon along the front side wall, and a beat up coffee table supporting a bong and various other smoking devices. A thumbtacked poster from Pink Floyd's *Dark Side of the Moon* album completed the decor. The purpose of this room was obviously for getting stoned.

Mudford selected one of the pipes and pulled out a drawer revealing the envelope with its ominous Chinese characters: *God Drug.* He settled into the hanging chair and motioned for Roberts to take the futon. "I read somewhere you can also smoke this stuff. You ready?"

Roberts held up a hand, "You first."

Mudford's eyes narrowed as he drew his mouth into a nasty grin. "Pussy…" he taunted again.

"No really. I'll go next, I promise."

"Okay then, here goes." Mudford lifted the flap and peered inside. "Should be enough for about a couple hits." He carefully tapped a measure of the pale brown powder into the bowl of his pipe. That done, he settled back in his chair and got ready to light up. He put the pipe to his lips, flicked the lighter a few times until it lit and took a long drag. He held it in a few moments and exhaled slowly while closing his eyes.

Roberts watched him anxiously to see what would happen. Mudford's breathing gradually slowed and deepened, but then it got faster and his shoulders lifted involuntarily as though something had startled him. He settled back in his chair as a blissful expression took over his face. His breathing slowed again to a more peaceful rhythm. Then his head began moving from side to side like a race car driver anticipating the turns. REM initiated behind his eyelids and his mouth drew into a dopey grin. He seemed to be enjoying his mental roller coaster ride. That last part went on for at least five minutes.

Roberts was relieved when Mudford finally came back around. He slowly opened his eyes and leaned forward, shook his head a couple times and then smiled at Roberts.

"Well, how was it?" Roberts could barely contain himself.

"It was nice… vivid colors and crystalline patterns and fractals of light, a pretty decent ride I guess. But it faded all too quickly, just when things were about to get interesting, sort of like a psychedelic bungee jump that's over before you realize what just happened. Frankly, I much prefer mushrooms. The trip lasts longer."

Roberts had often noted Mudford's exceptional ability to tolerate drugs. He could do complex math problems while smoking a joint, and he popped caffeine pills like they were candy. So despite Mudford's lackadaisical assessment just now, Roberts was still wary.

"Okay Brett, your turn. Let's find out what Virtanen supposedly wanted you to experience." He tapped the rest of the powder into the bowl and handed the pipe over to Roberts, along with the lighter.

Roberts tentatively raised the pipe to his lips and struck the lighter repeatedly until it flamed. The smoke he inhaled was not exactly unpleasant, more of an icy caress inside his lungs, although it did sting a little when he exhaled. The substance had evidently been ground together with fragrant herbs to make it more pleasant.

Mudford said, "Now take another hit and hold it in a bit longer this time." Roberts did as instructed, and felt his body sinking back into the incredibly comfortable futon.

His body began to feel like it was being squeezed through a greased tube of increasingly narrow dimensions. The tube finally released its slimy grip, spitting him into a place of utter darkness and unbearable silence. Roberts felt weightless, like he was floating in space….

The next twelve minutes inside his mind seemed like lifetimes.

Roberts spotted a bright orange flower spinning off in the distance, and it appeared to notice him as well, expanding and morphing into some sort of membrane as it drew closer…. He felt compelled to poke his finger through it… and upon doing so, it immediately sucked him into a room filled with iridescent crystals of all different shapes and sizes, their light emanating from unknown dimensions yet to be discovered…. The sounds of horned instruments emerged from a great distance away, barely audible at first but getting louder by the second, high and low, deep and resonant, louder still... and stopped abruptly. Then strange, disembodied voices began shouting *"Come this way! No, over here!"* one after the other, a cacophony of taunts ... until they mercifully gave up and scattered. Had he won? A brief calm ensued, but not for long.

A ball of light zipped by with radiant flames like the sun. It paused at the end of its trajectory and ricocheted back, then hovered there before him. The flames withdrew and an image emerged inside the orb. Roberts recognized the aquiline nose and olive skin, the long jet black hair still parted down the middle but now flowing freely about the face as if unburdened by gravity, and those Beatle glasses he had always worn. The face bore an expression of immense satisfaction.

"Juan Virtanen?" Roberts ventured.

Hello, Roberts. You have come at last, as I knew you would.

"Why have you summoned me here?" Brett's mind was having none of this, yet he knew it was true. *"What do you want?"*

To connect with you, obviously. I need your help.

"I have no intention of helping you, Virtanen!"

Oh but you will, in time.

The ball of light slowly faded away and then vanished.

Roberts sensed that his mind was about to enter a state of incredulous rage, but the emotion faded quickly as he became aware of his breathing and the weight of his body resting on the futon. He touched his fingertips together. Yes, they were still there. He opened his eyes.

Mudford pulled his hands away from Brett's shoulders and knelt back with his lips pressed tightly together. Had Mudford been shaking him just then? "Whoa, dude. You seemed pretty out there for a while."

Roberts sat up and took a deep breath, then exhaled slowly.

"That's better. How you feeling, buddy?"

Roberts nodded while smiling meekly. "Okay, I guess."

Mudford blew out a breath of his own. "That's a relief. So... how was it?" Roberts' *yopo* experience must have been nothing like his.

"It wasn't too bad at the beginning. But then I got sucked into this image of Virtanen. It felt like he was trying to mind fuck me. Sounds crass, I know, but I can't really explain it any other way."

Roberts described everything he could remember, starting with the orange flower pinwheel.

Mudford looked dubious. "You sure it was Virtanen?"

"There's no way I could have imagined it Owen, not like that. It must have something to do with the *yopo*."

Mudford returned to the hanging chair, sat and folded his arms. "Well, I still find it hard to believe. You're telling me Virtanen actually died and found a way to communicate from the spirit world? Just doesn't make any sense. Look man, I think you'd better shake this one off."

"Yeah, maybe you're right..." then Roberts looked at his watch. "Shit, I promised O'Reilly I'd meet him back at the apartment. You feel like coming along with us to the I-Beam tonight?"

"You know I can't stand that new wave shit. I'll put on a *Jimi Hendrix* album and chill here for a while.... But *you* should definitely go. Might help you shake this thing off."

"Okay, thanks Owen. And about what just happened ...."

"It *never* happened. I'll toss that envelope into the furnace down in the basement just as soon as you leave."

"Good idea. See you later." Roberts hoisted his bike over his shoulder and carefully made his way back down the stairs. Feeling a bit more like himself by the time he reached the sidewalk, he straddled it and peddled back down Carl Street.

The line for the I-Beam had already reached the McDonald's parking lot, a half block down from the concert venue, when they arrived at the corner of Haight Street and Stanyan. Roberts checked his watch. The I-Beam wasn't scheduled to open for another thirty minutes.

"You guys want something to eat?" Ruth asked. She was wearing her Dorothy costume from *The Wizard of Oz*, one she'd made for a Halloween party back in college, having taken Brett literally when he described how people dressed for these I-Beam events. Roberts had spray painted his hair gold for the occasion. He bought it on sale from a costume store downtown after last year's Halloween and the label said it was supposed wash out with a good shampooing, or so he hoped. O'Reilly figured his faded tie-dye T-shirt was enough but really didn't care.

Brett glanced down to Ruth's ruby slippers and grinned as she clicked them together three times.

"Guess I could do with a Big Mac and coke. How about you Patrick?"

"Yeah, likewise," said O'Reilly.

They each handed Ruth a couple bucks from their wallets.

Brett watched her walk away, thinking that Ruth made a great looking Dorothy. She might be a keeper, if he could just figure out a way to catch her.

"Who's playing tonight?" Roberts turned and asked O'Reilly after Ruth had disappeared from view.

The I-Beam catered mostly to the gay community, but tonight was a special live engagement and all were welcome.

"A new band called *Romeo Void*," said O'Reilly. Their breakthrough single had been playing almost nonstop on FM radio for the past several weeks.

Brett's mental tape deck began playing the song in his head and it got to the part where the sultry voiced lead singer belted out *"I might like you better if we slept together"*, over and over against a baritone sax accompaniment.

Just when the line began to move, Ruth returned carrying a cardboard tray of cokes in one hand and a bag of burgers in the other. Brett helped her distribute the burgers and drinks. "Thanks Ruth, you're a saint. I'll take care of the cover charge and get us a round of drinks once we're inside."

O'Reilly added, "We'd better hurry. No food past the door." He'd already polished off half his burger.

Roberts spotted a number of other people dressed in costume as they shuffled along. Ruth didn't look so out of place after all, and he began to regret not dressing up more himself.

The heavily tattooed bouncer wore a tank top despite the evening chill. He held out his hand as they approached the entrance. Roberts pulled out his wallet and glanced over to O'Reilly, whose response was, "Thanks buddy. I'll make sure buy us a round of drinks once we get inside."

The music became progressively louder as they queued up the stairway, its thumping bass rhythm causing the side walls to vibrate. Roberts admired the various band posters tacked up above the handrail. Quite a number of well-known punk and new wave bands had played here.

Ruth reflexively covered her ears once they reached the upper landing. Brett handed her a pair of earplugs and inserted another pair into his own.

"GOT ANY MORE OF THOSE?" shouted O'Reilly.

"WHAT? Brett teased before handing over his last pair.

They passed by a game room where a group of twenty-something gay men were playing a spirited game of pool, dressed in tight-fitting T-shirts with neon colored slacks. Most of them sported dark eyeliner. A pimple-faced kid in the back corner with spiked red hair and a black leather jacket was wildly tapping the levers of a pinball machine.

His body jerked back and forth as he wrestled the ball.

Roberts tried not to stare as they funneled out with the crowd into the main hall. He was beginning to feel a bit out of place.

"Let's dance!" Ruth grabbed Brett's arm and yanked him out onto the dance floor. O'Reilly joined them and started dancing with no one in particular. They soon found themselves surrounded by a sea of writhing humanity, gays and straights and lesbians and cross dressers all wildly dancing to the DJ's pulsating mixes that magically blended from one song to the next. Colorful spotlights swirled overhead and strobe lights flashed on and off, making their fluid movements seem like stop-animation.

Nearly an hour later, the DJ switched off and the lights came on for a brief intermission. Brett turned to Ruth, "Want a beer?"

"Sure!" Ruth nodded.

"Me too!" nodded O'Reilly.

"Okay, but you're buying the next round," said Brett. Good thing for O'Reilly, the lights dimmed just as Roberts was weaving his way back through the crowd with the uncapped bottles of brew.

Spotlights hit the stage with the club's iconic emblazoned I-Beam hanging from above. With the audience crowding forward, the band members walked out to loud hoots and whistles. The drummer struck the beat, the base player joined in, and the sax player began to wail. Everyone cheered when the lead singer stepped up and reached for the microphone. This was it, their hit song from the radio! Her sexy vibe took over the room as she vamped around the stage in her crimson red gown. The song had come alive. "Yeah!" Brett shouted. They danced in place amidst the tightly packed crowd of sweaty bodies.

After a 90-minute set and two encores, the lights finally came back on for good. The audience mustered several rounds of screaming and rhythmic clapping to summon one more song, but to no avail.

"That was fun!" said Ruth as they stepped back out into the moist and chilly evening air. "But my feet are going to make me pay for this tomorrow."

A light rain must have fallen. Puddles on the sidewalk reflected the rippling images of amber streetlamps from above.

Roberts spotted a circle of homeless people out in front of the Bowling Alley across the street, huddled around a makeshift fire of burning candles and rubbing their hands together for warmth. He wished he had a buck or two left in his walled to walk over and hand to them. Trying not to stare, he turned his attention to the shops lining Haight Street. The used record store had a fresh coat of paint, chartreuse maybe; Roberts had always been a bit Red-Green colorblind. A head shop two doors down had a riot of colorful glass bongs on display. A popular vegan market was dark at this hour. And half-way down the street on the opposite side, a giant and shapely pair of mannequin legs in fishnet stockings kicked out from the second story window of a kinky lingerie shop.

"Feel like walking down to *Kiss my Sweet* for some hot chocolate?" asked O'Reilly. The coffee and desert shop at the corner of Haight and Ashbury had a growing line of patrons out the door.

"You still got any money? I'm broke," Roberts whispered into O'Reilly's ear, who seemed a bit less enthusiastic after that.

Ruth rescued an awkward moment by taking both their arms. "Come on guys, we should probably head back before it starts raining again."

O'Reilly said his goodbyes when they rounded the Carl Street corner and Roberts continued on to escort Ruth back to her to her place.

"Thanks for coming along, Ruth."

"Well thanks for inviting me, it was fun!" After a few paces, Ruth added, "You know Brett, it was good to see you loosen up a bit."

"What's that supposed to mean?"

Ruth persisted, despite Brett's feigned puppy dog expression. "No, really. You've seemed so preoccupied lately. Is something wrong?"

Was it that obvious? "Just the usual lab stress, I suppose. This project I'm working on is turning out to be a lot harder than I imagined. Sometimes I wonder if I'll ever finish."

Ruth gently touched Brett's shoulder to reassure him and he instinctively put his arm around her. He felt a tingle of warmth despite the cold as they walked on through a threatening drizzle.

They stopped in front of Ruth's house on Second Avenue, a grand two-story Victorian being rented by the room to students who preferred living near to the UCSF campus. Roberts stood awkwardly with his hands in his pockets.

Ruth stepped forward and gave him a quick peck on the cheek. "Tell you what. How'd you like to come to church with me in in the morning? I usually go to Saint Anne's. You know, the one in the Sunset District?"

This question really caught Roberts off guard. He hadn't gone to church much since college. Going along with Ruth did seem like a good idea. But instead he punted. "How about next Sunday? I've got another big experiment planned for tomorrow."

"You're on!" Ruth smiled.

The drizzle transformed into full on downpour while Roberts headed back down Carl Street. His thoughts turned inward once more and he shuddered involuntarily. What had happened to him that afternoon? Had he actually been communicating with the spirit of Juan Virtanen? Or was it just some figment of his imagination, a Technicolor hallucination brought on by the *yopo*? He thrust his hands in his pockets and quickened the pace.

Later in his room, Roberts shed his wet clothes and changed into dry boxer shorts and a T-shirt. He stood by the side wall with his fingers gently touching the light switch, hesitant to shut it off and walk the five steps in darkness to his bed. He felt tiny hairs bristling on his forearms and gently rubbed them to smoothen out the goose bumps while his eyes darted about the room. He hadn't felt this unnerved since a young boy. Nothing out of place, everything as it should be. *Okay....*

Roberts switched off the light and went straight for his bed. He quickly slipped between the sheets and pulled the blanket up to his chin.

Despite his best efforts to relax and breathe slowly, a black veil of dread descended upon him, unstoppable. The walls of the room began to close in around him, until he imagined himself lying inside a coffin. His heart began to race and he felt a tingling sensation deep in his chest.

Could this be some sort of DMT flashback? If so, he desperately wanted it to stop. He slipped out of bed and quickly went over to switch the light back on. The walls were as they had always been. He knelt to look under his bed, feeling a bit silly afterward. Nothing but dust.... He switched the light off once more, climbed back into bed, and willed himself to think of something pleasant.

He started thinking about Ruth, yeah that was better, her smile when she said goodbye. And the look in her eyes. They seemed... hopeful. Brett's thoughts gradually quieted and his breathing slowed.

Virtanen came to him in a dream later that night, the first of many such dreams. Roberts didn't remember much of it the next day, but the dread of Virtanen's image had attached itself to his subconscious mind like a thin layer of black sticky tar. It had spoken to him again, of that Roberts felt certain, and there was something else, something it wanted him to do.

The first streetcar of the N-Judah line didn't run until a luxurious eight o'clock on Sundays. Roberts awoke to a bright beam of sunlight shining against his face. Thankful to have fallen back asleep after such a fitful night, he jumped out of bed and rushed down the hall to beat O'Reilly to the shower.

Unknown to Roberts, O'Reilly had already gone down to the *Other Café* for coffee. Located at the corner Carl Street and Cole, it served up a tasty bistro-style menu for breakfast and lunch. Their omelets and deli sandwiches were almost to die for, although Roberts and O'Reilly couldn't afford to eat there very often. But the best part about *The Other* was their nighttime entertainment, when the café was transformed into a bohemian style nightclub. Monday was Comedy Night and it only cost a dollar to get in.

O'Reilly sat at a window table reading the Datebook, more popularly known as the pink section in the Sunday edition of the San Francisco Chronicle. This was his go-to source of information for bands and movies playing around town. Each review contained a cartoon of a little man in the upper left corner. If the little man was sleeping, the show was a dog. If he sat there blankly, it should probably be avoided. A clapping little man meant the show was definitely worth watching. But O'Reilly only cared about the ones where the little man was standing on his chair bent forward and clapping enthusiastically. The little man was almost never wrong. Hmm... *The Clash* would be playing at the Warfield in about three weeks. He wondered if there might still be tickets available.

With the sunny weather outside, O'Reilly considered taking a Muni bus up to Marina Green to test fly his new fighter kite. But first he wanted to finish reading the comics. Noticing his cup empty, he went to the service counter to have it refilled, decaf this time.

"Who's the comedian tomorrow night" O'Reilly asked the pretty brunette behind the counter. He thought the headband went nicely with her fifties style red polka dot dress.

"It's supposed to be a surprise," she said.

"Still a dollar to get in?"

"Yep. Can't say anything more, but really, you should come." She gave him a quick wink.

MONDAY, September 15th, 1980

The line outside *The Other* seemed a bit longer than usual that night. Roberts and O'Reilly paid their dollar cover at the door and wove through the audience until they spotted an empty table near the back.

The lights dimmed and the owner of the club stepped up to the microphone. He waved his hands to quiet the noisy crowd, and said, "Ladies and Gentlemen, tonight's entertainer is a comedian with roots right here in San Francisco. Let's give him a nice round of applause."

The crowd hooted with glee when the comedian ran onstage. He had shag cut brown hair and wore a red striped T-shirt with baggy pants and suspenders. Many had seen him perform before at other venues around town, although his routine was never the same.

It took him several minutes to quiet the room. "Settle down, people, settle down," he said, and told his first joke.

His skits ran an unpredictable gamut, from the short and competitive existence of a sperm swimming up the birth canal, to a space ship of aliens landing in a field of marijuana plants and accidentally setting it on fire, only to forget why they came and head back unsteadily for home, a hilarious roller-coaster ride of non-stop absurdity. About an hour into the set, he suddenly stopped and asked if anyone had a question. He crossed his arms and waited patiently with a wry smile for the audience to catch their breath from laughing so hard.

Someone finally shouted out. "Do you think God gets stoned?" That one elicited a few nervous chuckles.

He answered almost humbly but with just enough edge, "Well I don't know about that, but if God truly did create man in His image, I'm pretty sure there must be something to it, know what I mean?" Then he shielded his eyes from the spotlight and scanned the audience for someone to pick on.

"You there sir!" He pointed. "What was the first of Christ's miracles to be recorded in the Bible?"

The man answered tentatively, "Um, turning water into wine?"

"Yes! Praise Jesus!" He threw his head back and waved hallelujah with both arms raised. Then he leaned into the microphone and said, "Now I expect some of you must have read the *Book of Revelation?* The Bible people! Come on, you know what I'm talking about. Yes? Was that some kind of psychedelic trip or what? God communicates in mysterious ways, I know."

Pleased to see a number of people smiling and nodding from their tables, he took on the personae of a charismatic televangelist preacher and gestured wildly about the stage while acting out scenes of the apocalypse. This went on for close to twenty minutes. The audience laughed so hard their stomach muscles were cramping when it was over.

He mercifully stopped, bent down to a table near the stage and kindly asked the guy sitting there, "Hey buddy, you mind if I borrow that beer?" The guy nodded so he quaffed it down and stepped back to the microphone. "Thank you, kind sir. Waitress, please get this table another round of drinks on me." Then he continued, "Ben Franklin once said that *beer is proof God loves us and wants us to be happy.* He's right you know, and I personally don't think God minds us getting stoned once in a while. But addiction can be a dangerous thing. And friends, *cocaine* is God's way of telling us when we've been making too much money."

The comedian seemed fleetingly serious for a moment, but then broke into in an impish grin and shouted out, "Thank you, and good night!" He bowed and quietly left the stage when the spotlight faded to black. The audience clapped rhythmically, louder and louder in an effort to bring him back onstage, until the house lights came on and stayed that way.

Roberts and O'Reilly stepped out into the chilly evening air and fast-walked the short distance back to their apartment. Neither of them had bothered to bring a jacket.

"Hey Brett, I noticed in the Pink Section this morning that *The Clash* will be playing at the Warfield three weeks from now. Want to go?"

Roberts shook his head while fumbling with the keys to their apartment. "There's no way we could afford tickets without cutting back on food until then."

"We shouldn't have to, Brett. I just learned about a way for us to make some extra cash."

Roberts presumed there must be a catch, but then again, he was getting a bit tired of being broke all the time. So he finally relented. "Okay, Patrick, I'm listening."

O'Reilly's idea was to volunteer at the drug study unit on the twelfth floor of Medical Sciences. The drugs they studied had already been approved by the FDA, although now they were testing them in different kinds of formulations, tablets and capsules and elixirs that would supposedly make them slower or faster acting. Graduate students were popular guinea pigs for these types of studies since most of them worked on the adjacent floors. If they agreed to participate after signing a consent form, they would be dosed for five days each week while subjecting themselves to frequent blood-testing throughout the day. For that they would be paid in the neighborhood of $300 - $700 after completing a three week study. The actual amount depended on the drug's potential side-effects. They could quit at any time and receive a partial payment. All this was spelled out in the study agreement.

Theophylline was up next, a natural stimulant found in coffee and tea. The purified drug was used pharmaceutically for treating asthmatic symptoms. O'Reilly had spotted the flyer on a bulletin board in the downstairs lobby, next to the glacially slow elevators. Roberts reluctantly agreed to do the study after O'Reilly's persistent badgering. $400 bucks for a three-week study was a lot of money.

They weren't allowed to drink coffee or tea over the duration of the study, or consume anything with chocolate. O'Reilly grimaced, being a devoted chocolate freak. Roberts figured he could do without coffee, although he worried about being keyed up on theophylline for days on end. "Would it be okay to smoke pot?" he asked. The study coordinator consulted the protocol and reluctantly agreed.

Mudford gave Roberts a few buds to take home that evening and a hit or two before bedtime turned out to be essential for falling asleep. It had another benefit as well. Brett's dreams weren't troubled over the duration of the study, at least what little of them he remembered the next morning.

That Friday afternoon, band practice lasted a bit longer than usual. Inspired by a paying gig they had coming up in two weeks, a private party down in Pacific Heights, their instrumentals and vocals seemed tighter than ever. Pete didn't stop once to complain about Brett's timing, which flowed from his sticks like never before. They'd even recorded Pete's new song. It only took two takes to meet his exacting standards. The song was playing on Pete's tape deck while Roberts disassembled his drum set.

Pete came over to assist. "Hey Brett, I think your playing is almost where it needs to be, but it would sound even better if you got yourself another crash cymbal. What do you think?"

"Funny you should ask. I should have some extra money coming in about three weeks. From a drug study that O'Reilly and I volunteered for."

"What's it on?" Pete asked.

"Theophylline." Roberts answered.

"Huh. Maybe that helps you play better."

"Well, don't get your hopes up. I can't imagine how asthmatic patients take this stuff every day."

Pete grinned. "Just kidding… anyway, take a look at this, maybe you'll find something." He handed over a weekly music rag from a record store on Haight Street. The back section had personal ads for used instruments and stage equipment. "I got that microphone stand from an ad in last week's edition," he pointed. "Go ahead, keep the magazine."

Back in his apartment, Roberts thumbed through the magazine until a three-line ad caught his attention. A 10-piece Tama drum set was being offered for only $500, an insanely cheap price for such a professional grade kit. The money from the drug study wouldn't be enough, but then again he could probably resell it for a lot more than what they were asking.

He almost hung up after the seventh ring.

A woman finally answered. "Hello?" she said with a velvety voice.

"Hello ma'am, I'm hoping I have the right number. Are you the person with the Tama drum set for sale?"

"Oh, yes! May I ask your name?"

"It's Brett, ma'am."

"Hello Brett, and you really don't need to call me that, ma'am I mean… so you saw my ad?"

"Yes, that's why I called."

"Wonderful. It used to belong to my ex-boyfriend, but he took off one day and abandoned it. Haven't heard from him in over six months. The darned thing's just been collecting dust."

"Gosh, I'm sorry."

"That's alright, certainly not your fault. Would you like to stop by and take a look at it? I can't really describe it over the phone. My house is in Marin, first exit north of the bridge."

Roberts suspected the woman had no idea what the drum set was worth. He didn't feel right about that, but felt compelled to make the drive anyway. Maybe she'd be willing to sell him one of the cymbals. "I could probably make it up there around seven this evening, if that works for you?"

"Oh yes, Brett. Please come. I'm looking forward to meeting you." She gave him the address and he wrote it down.

Roberts coaxed his little Honda Civic up a winding and steep grade lined with split-level homes overlooking Tiburon Bay. He spotted a lighted entryway with a number matching the address and pulled over, shut off the lights and killed the engine. *Okay, here goes.* Stepping out, he crunched along a gravel path bordered by exotic-looking shrubbery and Asian sculpture until he found himself standing before a solid oak doorway with an intricately carved "Tree of Life' design. He took a deep breath, reached for the button, and waited for the resonant chimes to announce his arrival.

The door cracked open a few inches and a strikingly beautiful woman eyes peered out, with captivating green. She looked to be somewhere in her mid-thirties and reminded Roberts of Judy Collins, so much so that he began to wonder if it might actually be her.

The woman gave Roberts a quick appraisal and then met his eyes with a welcoming smile.

"So nice of you to come, Brett. Please call me Vivian."

It was the same velvety voice he had heard over the phone. The door opened the rest of the way and she waved him inside with a graceful hand.

"Please come in" she beckoned.

Vivian led Roberts into a large open room that offered a spectacular view of the bay. Clusters of musical instruments and microphones lined the side walls with a mixing board in the back left corner. The only other furnishings appeared to be a square mahogany coffee table near the center of the room along with an assortment of large Persian cushions scattered about. The plush cream colored carpet made him want to take his shoes off.

Vivian noticed his hesitation. "You can leave them by the door in the foyer if you like."

Roberts returned to find her seated at the coffee table with another cushion waiting for him on the opposite side. Once they had settled in, she leaned forward intimately. "I haven't had anyone over in a while. Hope you don't mind the mess."

"I hadn't really noticed," Roberts replied. Vivian's gaze made him a bit uncomfortable. "So, about the drum kit…."

"We'll get to that in a minute." She studied his eyes. "You seem troubled, Brett. What's wrong?"

The question surprised him. "Um, I'm fine. So…."

"Well, you don't look fine to me." She closed her eyes, breathed in slowly, and exhaled. "Yes, you do have a strong aura... but I sense something has been troubling you lately." She opened them again and looked at Roberts with a hint of concern.

Was it that obvious? Thought Roberts.

"Tell you what. Let's go downstairs and have a look at that drum set. Then we can come back here to discuss your problem. Would you like a glass of wine?"

Vivian left the room before he could answer. Roberts heard the pop of an uncorked bottle and wondered if he should leave before she came back. He glanced over to his shoes.

Too late. She had already returned with two glasses of chardonnay and handed one over to Roberts. "Come, follow me."

Vivian led him down a spiral staircase and into a foam walled recording room. The display of drums before him was magnificent, something Keith Moon or Carl Palmer might play onstage.

Roberts said, "Wow. It's beautiful, but much more than I can handle right now. Our band doesn't get that many paying gigs. We can't afford to rent a van to haul our stuff around, and there's no way I could cram all this into my Honda Civic. Playing music is more of a hobby for us, really. We're all graduate students at UC San Francisco, so…."

"Now that doesn't surprise me, you being a graduate student I mean. You're obviously quite an intelligent young man."

Roberts couldn't tell if she was teasing or not, but he did feel compelled to advise her about the price. "Thanks for the compliment. But listen, I think this drum set may be worth a lot more than what you're asking."

"Really? I had no idea."

Roberts persisted, "Well, I think you should probably pull the ad and get it appraised first. Anyway, I do have a 5-piece set already, just nowhere near as nice as this one. Guess all I really need right now is another crash cymbal. Sorry for wasting your time on this."

She stroked her hair while considering. "Hmm, maybe you're right. Perhaps I really should get that thing appraised. Tell you what. Give me a call back on Sunday. If it hasn't sold it by then, you can have one of those cymbals, stand and all."

"Really? Alright then, it's a deal." Roberts felt much better with that out of the way.

They returned to the upstairs room and began with small talk. Vivian refilled their glasses and asked Roberts about his graduate project. He could already feel the ethanol kicking in. Such a relief after speeding on theophylline over the past few days.

"Brett, I think it's wonderful how committed you are to your work."

Warming up to Vivian, Roberts decided to go ahead and ask her. "You said something about me having a 'strong aura', what did you mean?"

"Oh Brett, I think you know. It's a special gift that some of us have." She reached across the table, palms up. "Here, give me your hands." Roberts tentatively rested his hands on top of hers. She massaged them gently with her thumbs for reassurance. "Now close your eyes, and just breathe…."

Roberts felt peaceful and relaxed, almost like his body was floating above the cushion, that is until Vivian released her grip and he recovered his awareness of gravity. "Whoa, what just happened there?"

"I was reading you, Brett." she said matter-of-factly.

"Reading what?"

"Your spirit, silly. I thought you knew that already. But something is definitely troubling you. Would you like to talk about it?"

Roberts suddenly felt an urge to tell her about the envelope and his experience with *yopo*, and before he could stop himself, it was done. "I still have no idea how or why this happened."

She smiled, knowingly. "You were lucky, Brett."

"Oh really, why is that?"

"Because your friend Owen was there with you. It's important to have an earth partner the first time you attempt to contact the spirit world. Otherwise, you might not be able to find your way back. But tell me more about this vision you described, was it of someone you recognized?"

Roberts began to suspect that meeting Vivian wasn't some random occurrence. "Perhaps... how did you know to ask?"

"As I told you before, this is one of my special gifts. You have a similar ability, you know? Although you probably aren't aware of it yet."

"You're right about that last part anyway. I don't have a clue what's going on."

"Yet I sense there may be more to your story."

Roberts figured he may as well go ahead and spill the rest of it. He walked her through the details of Virtanen's mysterious disappearance, what resembled Juan's writing on the back of the envelope that had been mysteriously left for him, and his disturbing dreams afterwards.

"I see," she responded with a low and breathy voice. "Well then. What do you think this friend of yours might have wanted?"

"Juan Virtanen was not exactly my friend. I barely knew him, really."

"Well, he must certainly have had a reason for contacting you."

"Look Vivian, I really don't get what you're saying. But whatever might be happening, I simply want it to stop. Do you think you can help me?"

"Hmm, perhaps my Spirit Voice would know."

"Hold on a moment, now I'm really lost. Your 'spirit voice'?"

"She speaks to me sometimes. I'll try contacting her tonight."

Roberts suspected that Vivian might be toying with him, and saw this as a good opportunity to excuse himself. "Thanks, I guess. Look, I should probably get going."

She followed the handsome young man to the door, waited for him to pull his shoes back on, and then gently kissed his cheek. "It's been a pleasure talking with you, Brett. Please be careful driving home. And oh, don't forget to call me back about the drum set. I should also have an answer for you from my Spirit Voice by then."

When Roberts had gone, Vivian pulled out a drawer to retrieve her Ouija board. She arranged it on the table and removed a pendulum from the box, one she'd made from a woven silk cord with a quartz crystal tied to the end. She patiently held it over the Ouija Board and whispered softly, "Luisa, are you there?" The crystal began to rotate in a circle, and then hovered above the word "YES", as if defying gravity.

CHAPTER EIGHT
"Beyond the senses"

7 AM. September 20th, 1980

ROBERTS AWOKE to the pleasant realization that another Saturday had finally arrived, with bright sunlight streaming in through the front Bay windows. What a beautiful day! Desperately in need of a break from the lab, he strode out to the wall phone and dialed Mudford's number.

"Hey there, bud. I was just about to give you a call myself," said Mudford. "Got a little something special for us to try today. How'd you like to take a drive up to Mount Tamalpais with me?"

"I presume you mean, how would *I* like to drive us there?"

"Hey man, you're the one with the car."

It did sound like a good idea. "Think I'd like that, actually." He checked his watch. "Assuming my car starts, I should be over in about twenty minutes. Be waiting outside, okay?" He quickly made sandwiches and stuffed them into a day pack along with a bargain bag of raisins and two cycling bottles that he filled from the tap.

Mudford was there at the curb when Roberts pulled up in his yellow Honda Civic. Roberts rolled down the passenger window and hollered out, "I presume whatever you had in mind for today must be inside that brown paper bag you're holding."

Mudford's shit-eating grin pretty much said it all. "Get in," said Roberts.

They drove north across the Golden Gate Bridge, continued on US 101 until they reached the Shoreline Highway exit, and followed it westward through Tamalpais Valley to the Panoramic Highway. Roberts clutched and shifted repeatedly to coax his little car up the windingly steep grade.   He passed the first entrance sign for Muir Woods, and continued on until he reached a picnic area near the top of Mount Tamalpais, where he pulled into an empty parking lot and shut off the engine. They appeared to have the place all to themselves, which fit perfectly with Mudford's plan, yet to be revealed.

They exited the car and looked down to rolling hills of dry grass textured with groves of Douglas fir and California oak. Large granite boulders were scattered about, remnants of an ancient ice age that had passed through this area.

The view from atop Mount Tamalpais was supposed to be incredible, so they hiked on up and gazed out to a panoramic view of shimmering Pacific Ocean. "Whoa, this was definitely worth the drive," said Roberts. "Yeah," Mudford agreed. He pointed to a winding dirt trail on the downward slope. "That leads all the way down to Muir Beach. Want to give it a try?"

Roberts imagined them hiking back up from the bottom. "I don't know, Mudford, looks pretty steep."

"Okay, lazy ass. Let's head back to the parking lot. I remember seeing a sign for a trail loop that runs around here."

Twenty minutes later, they reached a field of dry grass with a flat topped boulder off to one side. Mudford said, "That looks like a perfect spot. Want to eat something first?

"Before what?" Roberts asked dubiously.

"Before this," Mudford held up the crumpled brown paper bag that he'd been carrying along in his back pocket.

"Shoot, Mudford. I'm not so sure I'm up for another one of your psychedelic adventures."

"C'mon Brett, you're not having second thoughts on me again, are you?" Mudford reached into the bag and pulled out a pair of triangularly-wrapped aluminum foil pouches. He presented one to Roberts before tearing the other one open. Roberts recognized the button caps and stems… magic mushrooms. *Oh shit.*

"You didn't…." Roberts sighed.

"Oh yes I did," said Mudford matter-of-factly. "I figured this would be a good place for the two of us to try them out. They each contain a gram of 'shrooms, weighed them out myself, should keep us buzzed for about a couple hours. C'mon man, don't let me do this alone."

Roberts watched as Mudford popped the 'shrooms into his mouth, chewed a few times and then washed them down with a swallow of water. "Ahh," he exhaled. "Okay man, your turn."

Why did Roberts feel so compelled to do this? Mudford sure seemed keen for him to try them. Before he could change his mind, Roberts tore open the other pouch and popped the contents into his mouth, then chewed and swallowed as Mudford had done.

They sat cross-legged on the boulder and waited for the psilocybin to meander its way into their bloodstreams. About fifteen minutes later, the textures of the surrounding landscape began to shimmer and the colors become much more vibrant.

Roberts looked around and back to Mudford who nodded in agreement with another quite obnoxious shit-eating grin. The field of grass began to emit a golden radiance, one he hadn't noticed before, every blade and stalk unique in its own way, zooming in and out, almost like looking at them through a magnifying glass. He turned his attention to a grove of trees and watched them swaying back and forth, soaking up the sunlight with delightful glee. Their branches had come alive! Mudford walked over and appeared to be talking to the trees. After what seemed like hours, although it was only minutes, he returned with an armful of sticks that had fallen to the ground, and plopped them down near where Roberts was sitting.

"You planning on building a fire?" Roberts feared the worst.

"Nah, watch this." Mudford picked up one of the sticks and hurled it back toward the pine grove. It made a WHOOP-Whoop-whoop sound while flying through the air, which reminded Roberts of a helicopter scene from the movie *Apocalypse Now.*

"Yeaoow!" Roberts responded quite loudly. He wondered if anyone else had heard him.

Mudford bent down for another stick and handed it to Roberts. "Want to try it?" Roberts rose up off the rock and tossed the stick into the air with all his energy... WHOOP-Whoop-whoop, it went. "Whoa, that sounded so cool!" He settled back onto the rock, still feeling a bit unsteady. Mudford hurled a few more but eventually got tired and went back over to talk to the pine trees. The conversation they were having appeared to be quite interesting, although Roberts wasn't ready to leave the safety of his rock.

Roberts heard a distant rumble and then fissures began to open and close again all around him, *an earthquake!* Roberts instinctively knew he'd be safe so long as he remained right here on this boulder. The granite rock told him so. He patted it for reassurance and closed his eyes. Colors began to burst and swirl inside his mind, like looking through a giant kaleidoscope that never stopped turning.

Mudford happened to notice Brett's deteriorating state of consciousness, so he returned to the rock and gently shook his friend back to the present, a kindness that Roberts greatly appreciated. Roberts opened his eyes to find Mudford standing there. *How the heck did he manage to make his way back across this meadow?* Roberts shook his head and willed himself to focus again on his surroundings, which had pretty much returned to normal by that time.

"Come on Brett, we need to get you up. Let's hike some more."

They marched single file along a winding dirt path that led them around giant boulders with a different eye popping vista just beyond, into pine groves and back out into sunlight, down into ravines and up over hills, a constant stream of movement.

Mudford finally called a halt. "Do you recognize this trail, Brett? I'm not exactly sure where we are."

"No way, dude. I was following you." Glimmers of doubt began to emerge at the edges of Brett's awareness, something he desperately wanted to hold on to. "So you're saying we're lost?"

Mudford broke into a Cheshire cat smile with gleaming teeth. "No need to worry. We'll just back-track until we recognize something."

Roberts didn't quite share Mudford's confidence. "You sure, man?"

"Heck yeah. Come on, let's go."

Roberts followed along while Mudford muttered to himself about distances and angles and landmarks and how long they had been traveling this way and that. Roberts couldn't quite understand what he was saying, so he firmly grabbed Mudford by the arm and turned him around. "*What?!*" shouted Roberts. For some reason, they both found this hysterical.

"Sorry man," said Mudford after catching his breath. "I made sure to study a topo map of this area before we left this morning. And if my bearings are correct, your car should be just around that next hill."

Mudford picked up the pace and Roberts followed with growing anticipation. They rounded the hill and lo behold, there it was! Brett's bright little yellow car in the distance. Both of them howled like coyotes.

But they were no longer alone, evidently. A faded-green VW bus was also now parked in the lot, with a rusting roof and paisley side curtains. As they drew nearer, they spotted its former occupants up on the ridge, sitting in a half circle beneath the shade of a large oak tree and facing the ocean, waiting for sunset.

Roberts and Mudford instinctively hiked up toward them, curious to find out if they were real.

The barefoot young man in the center had long blond hair, with purple mirrored sunglasses obscuring much of his face. And he sat perfectly still. He was dressed in a straw-colored pirate shirt, a blue denim vest, and red velvet pants that were a bit too bright for Roberts and Mudford to deal with just then. "Welcome," said the man without moving his head, his gaze focused intently on the pending sunset.

Sitting to either side of him were two amazingly attractive women, a blond with equally long straight hair and a brunette with hers trussed up in a beehive. The blond sat cross-legged in a hand-sewn yellow dress, with a wide golden belt cinched around her narrow waist, and pink sandals that suited her perfectly. The leggy brunette wore a white mini-skirt with her knees swept to one side, and brightly beaded moccasins.

Next to the blond woman was muscular looking guy, somewhere in his mid-thirties, with curly brown hair and a matching bushy beard. He wore pale blue bell-bottom jeans and a brown serape, nothing more. And next to the brunette was a thin young man with a clean-shaven head, wearing a salmon colored robe with a mustard sash, perhaps a Buddhist monk.

"Enjoying the view?" Purple Sunglasses spoke at last. He glanced toward Roberts and Mudford. "You dudes are tripping too right now, aren't you?"

"You've got us there," answered Roberts, still not quite sure if he was talking to real people.

"Join us, man," said Purple Sunglasses. "We're about to witness a beautiful sunset." They had been passing a bouquet of flowers between them. "Here man, smell these," said the muscular guy at the end when Roberts and Mudford both squatted down next to him. The blond woman picked up a bamboo flute and began to play it softly.

The sky exploded in a rainbow of colors as the bright orange ball slowly sank into the horizon, one of the most spectacularly brilliant sunsets that Roberts had ever experienced. His body felt increasingly relaxed with each passing breath. Mudford glanced toward his friend and smiled knowingly. He felt that way too.

The golden hues gradually deepened, transitioning from burnt orange to dark red and then deep violet. Roberts began to hear the distant sound of angels singing and shook his head in disbelief.

"You're hearing them too right now, aren't you?" Purple Sunglasses commented without moving his head.

"Yeah, I think so," Roberts agreed. And for a fleeting moment, it seemed like heaven was almost within his grasp. Until the music stopped, and then there was silence.

They sat quietly and continued to watch the horizon. Stars began to appear.

With darkness quickly falling, Mudford reached over and firmly shook Brett's arm. "You good to drive, brother?"

Roberts drew a deep breath and let it out slowly. "Yeah, partner, let's ride."

They said goodbye to the hippies and hiked back down the hill to the Brett's Honda Civic, which was no longer a beacon of yellow to his relief.

He didn't remember the sandwiches in his backpack until he got back to the apartment, now warm and soggy and most unappealing. So he heated up a can of tomato soup and decided to call it a day.

Roberts opened his eyes to another bright and sunny morning. *Three days in a row, must be a record.* He groggily stretched himself awake, feeling right with the world and eager to start another day. His first experience with mushrooms hadn't been all that bad, definitely an attitude adjustment, and one for the better actually, although he wasn't sure he'd be willing to try them again.

Then he remembered today was Sunday.

"Shit!" he hissed after noticing the time, almost half past 8. He'd promised to meet Ruth in front of Saint Anne's church for 9 o'clock mass. Better hurry.

Roberts dressed quickly, remembered to shave, and dashed out the door. With a mile still to cover, he fast-walked and checked his wrist watch repeatedly for reassurance.

Saint Anne of the Sunset Church had been rebuilt in a Romanesque-revival architecture following the 1906 earthquake. Located at the corner of Judah and 14th Street, its uneven twin towers made a majestic silhouette against the darkening coastal sky at sunset, an often photographed scene.

Roberts crossed 10th Street and started jogging when he heard the first chime of the bell tower.

Ruth had been standing outside for over ten minutes already. *Darn that Brett Roberts, if he weren't so good-looking...* then she caught a glimpse of him rushing around the corner.

Roberts tried to apologize between breaths, "I'm sorry Ruth... I got here... as fast as I could." He tried to appear calm despite the trepidation he was feeling inside. This would be his first Catholic mass. He glanced up to the rosy red church and briefly admired the ivory frieze sculpture adorning its front entrance, with eighty figurines depicting various scenes from the Bible narrative.

Ruth couldn't suppress a grin. "I was beginning to think you'd forgotten. You ready? " She offered him her arm.

They rushed up the steps and accepted a bulletin from an usher as they passed through the narthex. The sanctuary had rose stucco walls, ivory column archways and a massive dome ceiling rising above the nave. Colorful beams of light streamed through the intricate stained glass windows.

Older parishioners smiled and nodded to acknowledge the handsome young couple as they made their way up the center aisle. Glancing around, Roberts estimated that they must be the only two worshipers younger than fifty that morning.

Ruth gently tugged Brett's arm and guided him toward an available pew near the front facing the pulpit. She briefly genuflected before stepping into their row and then flipped down the kneeler. Uncertain what to do, Brett remained seated and looked to the altar. He noticed a beam of sunlight shining down from an oculus in the dome ceiling above, just now illuminating a golden cross on the altar. What perfect timing, it seemed. Then he studied the ivory statues of Mary and Jesus mounted in alcoves to either side. Brett felt grateful to be here. He shut his eyes and briefly uttered a silent prayer of thanks.

Ruth finished praying and crossed herself before settling back.

"The interior of this church is amazing," Brett whispered. "Yes it is," Ruth whispered back without turning her head, although Brett noticed her smile this time. He slid closer to her without thinking, and to his relief she responded by gently resting her hand on his knee.

Pipe organ music began playing from the back balcony. All rose to sing the opening hymn as the priest strode purposefully forward with two little altar boys in tow. Ruth held up the hymnal and they both joined in. How had Brett forgotten what this felt like? The simple act singing in church. And Ruth had a surprisingly beautiful voice

The priest reached the altar and turned around to sing with the congregation during the final verse. When the music stopped, he made the sign of the cross to begin mass in the name of the Father, Son, and Holy Spirit.

To Brett's surprise, the liturgy turned out to be remarkably similar to the one he'd grown up with in his Lutheran church back home. He began to feel a sense of belonging, one he'd sorely missed.

After two brief scripture passages read by members of the congregation, the priest stepped to the pulpit and read the day's Gospel lesson. A passage from the Book of John, the one where Jesus told His disciples that He would soon be going to His Father to prepare a place for them. Roberts shuddered inwardly after hearing the words "a place for you". His mind began to wonder. *What about Virtanen?*

He regained his sense of where he was when the congregation rose to recite the Apostle's creed. Most of the words were familiar to Brett, but when the sacrament of Eucharist began, Ruth whispered for Brett to remain in the pew since he wasn't Catholic. Although disappointed, he flipped down the kneeler when the rest of his row had left and began to pray. He wanted his prayer to come from the heart, not the usual rote "Our Father" he still occasionally recited before falling asleep. When the words finally came, he regained a long forgotten sense that God might actually be listening. He let go of his anxiety, if only for a moment, and the answer that replaced it was simple. *Have faith.*

The congregation sang a closing hymn, received their final benediction, and began to queue back outside. Stepping out into the late-morning sunshine, Brett thanked Ruth emphatically for inviting him along. Then he ventured, "Care to stop somewhere for coffee?"

"I'd like that!" Ruth broke into a smile. She felt more comfortable with him now for some reason. Perhaps inviting Brett to church hadn't been such a lame idea after all.

They chose a sidewalk table outside Moe's diner and ordered cappuccinos. "So, did you enjoy the service?" asked Ruth.

Brett's eyes twinkled for the briefest of moments. "Oh yes, very much."

"Good, then I'm glad we did this. You know, I was just beginning to worry about you…."

"Me too. Wait… what was that last thing you said?"

"There's that look again. What's bothering you, Brett? Please tell me."

Brett wasn't quite sure how to answer. "I don't know. I suppose it might have something to do with Juan Virtanen."

Ruth hadn't expected that response. "That was terrible, although he disappeared over a month ago. Why, have you seen him?"

"No, not exactly." Although reluctant to disclose his *yopo* experience, Roberts proceeded to tell Ruth about the dream he had afterward. And why not? He'd already shared this information with a total stranger.

Ruth set down her cup and studied Brett's eyes with growing of concern. "Maybe you've been working too hard lately…."

"I'm fine, Ruth, honest."

"Okay… but please let me know if it happens again. Dreams like that can be sometimes reflect deeper issues you may be dealing with."

"Probably nothing to worry about," said Brett. He shook it off, paid the check, and walked Ruth back to her apartment.

"Thanks again. I enjoy spending time with you, Ruth."

She stepped forward and gave Brett a quick peck on the cheek. Brett wasn't quite sure how to respond, so he simply stood there and grinned. Ruth found this amusing. She smiled, and said, "Tell you what. How'd you like to come back by for dinner next Friday? I could make a pot roast."

"Yeah, that'd be great." Brett replied, after regaining his composure. "Not much of a cook myself, but I could take you out to dinner sometime afterwards to repay you. I know a great place in China Town."

"Sounds like a deal," she chuckled. So, see you around?"

Roberts reflected on his church experience that morning while walking back to his own apartment, having caught something new in the words of the Gospel message. Jesus was describing His Father's house as a place of *many rooms.*

He wondered. If not all spirits go to Heaven, where might they then reside? Roberts wasn't so sure he believed in Purgatory, although neither could he accept death as an ultimate end. While pondering this quandary, he eventually reached the unmistakable conclusion that Juan Virtanen's spirit must be lost somewhere. Roberts again shuddered at the thought.

Upon reaching the corner of Stanyan, he decided to make a right and head back up to the lab. The rigor of planning another experiment would be a welcome distraction.

When he reached Parnassus, a bright produce display caught his attention on the opposite corner, outside the Sunshine Market. This reminded him that he and O'Reilly were almost out of food.

An attractive young woman walked out with a basket of vegetables and began restocking the shelves. She was tall, at least five foot eleven, with long auburn hair and hazel eyes. Roberts had noticed her a few times before.

"Awesome weather," he ventured.

She nodded enthusiastically, "It sure is! Can I help you with something?"

"Well it's my turn to make dinner tonight, and your produce display caught my eye so I thought I'd come over to investigate. By the way, any meat on sale today?"

She pressed her lips together. "I suppose you could check with the butcher inside. I'm vegetarian myself."

"Really?" *That must have sounded a bit lame…* he thought.

"Oh yes," she said. "Animal fats clog your arteries, you know. Not only is this bad for your heart, it cuts off circulation to other parts of the body. This can prevent your brain from functioning properly, achieving higher states of consciousness for example."

Roberts kicked himself for his lack of social awareness. This was San Francisco, after all. "I'd like to hear more, if you don't mind sharing."

She smiled. "You know the Tassajara Bakery, the one on Cole Street?" Roberts nodded. "They've got a Zen center up in Marin, where they grow their own food, and bake their own bread. In fact, we get a lot of our produce from there. I worked in their fields last summer, and it really opened my eyes." She went on to describe a few of her meditation experiences, until the manager poked his head out and nodded for her to get back to work.

Roberts glanced toward the produce bins. "You've got some great looking vegetables today. Maybe I'll make sure to pick out a few things later on my way home. Anyway, I'd better be going. I was just on my way up to the lab to plan my next experiment. What's your name, by the way?"

She hesitated a moment. "It's Zena," she answered coolly.

"Hey Zena! Mine's Brett, Brett Roberts."

"Nice to meet you… guess I'll see you around." Zena turned away and resumed arranging her produce.

While hiking up Parnassus, Roberts wondered why Zena had disengaged so abruptly. Perhaps she didn't like academic types. Yeah, probably considered them too left-brained to get her mystical personality. If she only knew what he'd been dealing with lately, tormented by the spirit of someone he barely had known.

Roberts decided to let it go once he entered the Medical Sciences building, determined to focus on his experiment for the rest of the afternoon. But he remembered something while riding the elevator up to the eleventh floor, how Juan Virtanen always used to keep his lab notebooks locked up in a drawer next to his desk. He wondered if they were still there….

While fumbling with the keys to the Nelson lab, Roberts noticed that the door to the Higgins lab across the hall had been left open a crack. He peered inside and saw that a drawer next to Virtanen's desk had been jimmied open. He walked toward it and looked down. As he'd suspected, the notebooks were gone. Cops must have taken them. Oh well, time to plan his next experiment.

Dusk had fallen when Roberts exited the Medical Science building and stepped down to the curb. He looked westward for a moment to observe the final rays of sunset, with crimson hues surrendering to violet. Saint

Anne's twin church towers rose majestically above the darkening skyline. He made a mental note to pay closer attention to sunsets from then on.

Roberts checked his watch and realized that the Sunshine Market would be closing shortly. He made it there just as the manager was wheeling in the produce carts. "I'd like to purchase... some of those vegetables... if it's not too late," said Roberts between breaths for the second time that day. The manager forced a smile and stepped aside. "Please be my guest, but make it quick," he said. Roberts grabbed a small paper bag and filled it with handfuls of yellow summer squash, fresh green beans, and a red bell pepper. He went inside to pay. Zena had already clocked out, unfortunately.

He unlocked the downstairs entrance to his apartment and pondered what to make for dinner while climbing the steps. Hmm... they still had a can of tomato sauce and some pasta in the cupboard, along with a few spices... maybe he could steam the veggies and make spaghetti.

Roberts was in the middle of seasoning the sauce and stirring it on the stove when he heard the door unlatch. He glanced up to the wall clock. Right on time, he grinned. O'Reilly was almost never late for dinner, especially when it was Brett's turn to cook.

O'Reilly rinsed his plate in the sink and announced that he needed to return to the computer lab. Roberts remembered his promise to call Vivian shortly after his roommate's departure. Finding the music magazine still on the floor next to his drum set, he flipped to the ad he had circled and carried it back to the wall phone next to the kitchen.

Vivian answered after about the tenth ring. "Hello?" she said. It sounded as though she'd just run up from downstairs.

"It's Brett Roberts, remember me? You wanted me to call you back about the drum set."

Vivian cupped her hand over the phone. Roberts heard muffled voices until she uncovered again. "Sorry Brett, the drum set is no longer available. My boyfriend came back yesterday. Apparently he's no longer my ex, although I'm still making him earn his forgiveness."

"That's okay, I understand. But what about that other topic we discussed?"

"Oh yes, of course. I did manage to ask my Spirit Voice about you."

"And? What did this 'Spirit Voice' of yours have to say?"

"She might know this other spirit who has been taunting you. It could have been her son Juan, although she has no idea what his intentions may be. Luisa was unable to make contact with him herself during our session."

"That's it?" said Roberts after realizing she had stopped talking.

"Oh yes, one more thing. She asked me to tell you she is sorry."

"But… what am I supposed to *do*?"

"Don't worry, sweetie. Everything happens for a reason. Anyway, it was nice meeting you the other day. I enjoyed our conversation. Goodbye, Brett." Vivian hung up the phone with a click.

Luisa Virtanen had always shared a spiritual bond with her daughter, ever since Maria first started kicking inside her womb. Her son was different, unfortunately. *Perhaps when he is older*, she kept promising herself, although Juan had been too young to know for certain when she made the painful decision to leave her family. How difficult that choice had been, but what else could she do? It had been the only way she could free herself from the trappings of drug addiction.

This was why she snuck back into Manaus years later to leave Juan her personal journal. She hoped it might encourage him to find her when he was older. Luisa desperately yearned to teach Juan how to communicate spiritually, assuming he too shared Maria's special gift. Alas, she died soon afterward.

After leaving her physical body, Luisa's spirit made numerous attempts to communicate with her son Juan back on earth, although never successfully, not even that fateful moment when the shaman interceded on her behalf. Luisa's metaphysical heart wept for her son that day.

Now comes this new revelation from her earth medium. Maria had never mentioned Juan's passing, even though she and Luisa still communicated almost daily. Luisa fears that her son may be lost forever.

But wait! Juan's spirit has somehow managed to connect with another living soul back on Earth. For what purpose, she wonders?

Luisa is temporarily at a loss for what to do, until an idea begins to form. Yes, perhaps she can use this Brett Roberts as an intermediary to communicate with her son! She will try to reach him, although based on her earth medium's inquiries, the young man may be a bit lost himself.

CHAPTER NINE

"The pusher"

1:05 AM. Wednesday, October 1ˢᵗ, 1980

THE PUSHER STRODE PURPOSEFULLY through the chilly mist down Telegraph Avenue. He had a new drug to sell, one he intended to peddle soon on the streets of downtown Berkeley. But he wanted to test it on someone first, just to make sure the dose was okay. He never touched the stuff himself, hence his reason for peering into the darkened alleyways at this ungodly hour. Eventually he spotted a pair of badly worn tennis shoes sticking out from one end of a battered refrigerator box.

He cautiously approached the poor fellow, knelt down and looked inside to inspect his next victim, a young man sleeping soundly beneath a soiled wool blanket. The poor guy's face was filthy, his long blond hair badly matted, and he smelled like he hadn't bathed in weeks. Could be some drugged out hippie, or possibly an ex-student who'd washed out of college and didn't want to tell his parents.... So sad, but then again, these kids were a big part of his business. Most of them were desperately addicted to drugs and would try just about anything.

"Hey buddy, can I interest you in a little blow?"

"Hmmm?" The young man raised his head and attempted to focus on his new found benefactor, although his mind was still recovering from a drug-induced fog.

"It's okay there.... Here, try some of this," said the pusher while holding out a tiny glass vial. He used a tiny metal spoon to withdraw a portion of the white crystalline powder, then bent down and held it just beneath the nostril of his first test subject. The kid snorted it up greedily, just as he'd expected, but seconds later began to writhe in obvious pain. What happened next was strange beyond belief.

The young man's skin began to emit some sort of faint green bioluminescence. And then, slowly, his body began to rise. Was he actually be levitating now beneath that blanket? The pusher rubbed his eyes and blinked a few times, relieved to find him back on solid ground where he belonged. But wait… the young man appeared to have stopped breathing. The pusher slowly knelt down and put a finger beneath his nostrils just to make sure… *"Shit!"* he hissed. An overdose, obviously. He was about to turn away when he decided to give the body a kick with the toe of his boot, stunned to find such abrupt resistance, as though rigor mortis had already set in.

The pusher hurried away from the scene and didn't look back. He had no idea that the young man's drug-riddled brain was too fried already to react to the drug in the same manner that had resulted in Juan Virtanen's unfortunate demise. He simply presumed the drug must be too potent in its current form.

So he did what he would usually do under such circumstances. Upon returning to his kitchen lab a few blocks away, the pusher reached for a bottle of ketamine, used a mortar and pestle to crush the pills, and cut his new designer drug with an equal amount of the resulting powder. That ought to do it, he thought to himself. Should he test this again on another victim? *Nah.* Money was money.

Saturday, October 4th, 1980

The Warfield auditorium had originally served as a prominent downtown vaudeville theater back in the 1920s. After decades of decline, the rock promoter Bill Graham finally recognized its potential, restored the grand dame to her former glory, and then booked Bob Dylan to play there for a two week run. The place has been rocking ever since.

Patrick O'Reilly was the lucky ninth caller to win a pair of tickets for tonight's performance. That happened three days ago, around lunch time, while he was listening to KSAN on the radio back at their apartment. He was just making a sandwich when he caught the announcement for free tickets to see *The Clash* in concert that Saturday night. He took a MUNI bus downtown the very next day to pick them up.

Brett Roberts had gladly come along, and couldn't believe how close they were to the stage once they'd taken their seats in the middle of the second row. Neither of them had been inside The Warfield before, and seeing a concert there was definitely on their bucket list. Roberts glanced upward to the high arched ceiling, marveling at the decorative wood panels all trimmed in gold. The mural just above the orchestra section featured heavenly matadors cavorting through the clouds with their senoritas, and he had no idea what to make of that.

Most of those seated nearby were sporting hair spiked and dyed blue, pink and red, with safety-pin piercings through cheeks, earlobes and eyebrows. Black eye shadow seemed quite popular as well. Some of them had dressed up as characters right out of the *Rocky Horror Picture Show*. Roberts felt obtrusively out of place.

Loud cheers and whistles erupted from the audience when *The Clash* finally came on stage. Dispensing with formalities, the band picked up their instruments and blasted into their first song at over 140 decibels of non-stop, undecipherable noise. Brett's ears were shot by the end of *"Should I Stay or Should I Go?"* He turned to find O'Reilly hunkered down in his seat, and clutching his own ears in obvious pain.

Roberts bent down and shook O'Reilly's shoulder to get his attention. "Want to split?" he yelled. "Hell yes!" O'Reilly shouted back, although neither of them could really hear the other above the ear-splitting noise.

They rushed out to the lobby and felt a bit relieved to find other concert goers standing around and debating amongst themselves whether or not they should go back inside. A lean and heavily tattooed kid with spiked hair said "Fuck it!" and did just that, while others started heading for the exit doors. Roberts and O'Reilly decided to join them. With their ears still ringing, they made a beeline for the nearest MUNI stop.

Roberts was glad to be home two hours later, back in their sparsely furnished yet cozy little apartment. He and O'Reilly were now watching the late evening news when a reporter came on standing outside the Warfield. Wondering what that might be about, Roberts reached over and turned up the volume to hear what the man was saying.

"Police have now identified the bodies as those of Robert Spratt, age 19, and James Gilligan, age 20, both of Berkeley. They were discovered inside this concert hall behind me about an hour ago...."

"Holy cow!" shouted O'Reilly.

"The place was awful damned loud, but seriously?"

"Good thing we left when we did."

"No kidding," said Roberts with a decisive nod.

The reporter didn't have much additional information, drug over dose, apparently. Autopsies were pending.

"Well, think I'll turn in," said Roberts. "You about done watching?"

"Yeah, let's call it a day," said O'Reilly. "Feel like flying our fighter kites on Marina Green tomorrow afternoon?"

"You're on, my friend," said Roberts. He reached over to shut off the TV.

The pusher also had been watching the newscast that evening. He recognized those two guys on the screen, the same ones he'd sold to two nights before. *Well shit*, he thought. Remembering what had happened to that kid in the alleyway, he rounded up the remaining baggies and systematically tore each one open to empty their contents into the toilet with a flush of finality. Then he burned the empty wrappers in an oil drum out back and swore he'd never do business with that UCSF kid again. As far as the pusher was concerned, this new "designer drug" never happened.

Roberts went over to Mudford's place the following Friday night. They were sitting in the front room, listening to Jimi Hendrix on the stereo. Mudford had just poured them each a mug of his sudsy homebrew.

"Dude, this beer is excellent."

"Yeah, I get the barley malt from a brewing shop down in the Mission district. It's not the safest neighborhood to be walking around in, but the guy who runs the place sure knows his stuff."

"How much does it cost to brew a batch?" Roberts asked.

"Probably a lot less than you spend on Budweiser," Mudford teased.

Then came a loud and persistent knocking on the downstairs door. Roberts rushed to the window and looked down to see a squad car with red lights flashing. "Owen, it's the cops."

"Shit!" Mudford rushed out to the courtyard with a blanket to conceal his pot plants, hoping they wouldn't be noticed.

All the while, the banging continued. "Open the door, police!"

Mudford poked his head back in with a harried expression. "Hey Brett, better go down and see what they want. See if you can stall them while I stash away all the drug paraphernalia."

Roberts cracked open the door and politely asked what the problem was. "Are you Owen Mudford?" "No, sir, I'm a friend of his." "Please step aside, sir." Roberts slowly led the two cops up the stairs in an effort to buy a bit more time, but they brushed past him at the top of the landing. Mudford had now returned and was seated at the dining table with a surprised and innocent look on his face.

"Owen Mudford?" the cop asked sternly.

Mudford nodded warily while struggling to maintain his composure.

"Please step around the table with your hands above your head… now put them behind your back." The first cop covered Mudford while the second one cuffed him from behind with two metallic clicks.

"Owen Fletcher Mudford, you are hereby charged as an accessory to the distribution and sale of an illegal drug, one already linked to several deaths in the area that we know of…."

"Wait, there must be some mistake, I…."

"…You have a right to remain silent. Anything you say can and will be used against you in a court of law." Each cop took an elbow and roughly escorted Mudford down to the stairway.

"But I haven't done anything!"

Roberts looked down from the upstairs window and stood there shaking as he watched the cops load Mudford into their squad car and drive away. This was definitely not good. But what should he do? After pacing a while, he eventually realized there was no use waiting around. Mudford's roommates were both off on a backpacking trip in the Sierras. So he carried the beer mugs back to the kitchen, rinsed them out in the sink, and returned to the front room to retrieve his coat.

Roberts rode a streetcar to the downtown precinct the next morning. He signed in, showed his driver's license at the front desk and was told to have a seat.

After an hour of waiting, a deputy finally stepped out and instructed Roberts to follow. Roberts was led into a visiting room with a row of stalls facing a two-way mirror.

"Take that one," the deputy pointed to an empty stall. Roberts tried to see through the mirrored glass but couldn't. He soon heard shuffling and chains rattling on the other side of the glass. Then a light clicked on to reveal his friend Mudford, desperate and scared in his bright orange jumper. Mudford reached for the phone and gestured for Roberts to do the same.

"It wasn't my fault!" Mudford appeared to be fighting back tears.

"*What* wasn't your fault? What the hell happened, Owen?"

Mudford leaned toward the glass and waved Roberts closer from the opposite side. "Look Brett, if I tell you something, you've got to keep it to yourself." "Owen, whatever you're into, I'm not sure I want to be involved...." "Just listen, okay?"

Roberts kept the phone to his ear and leaned back while nodding for Mudford to continue. He was his friend after all.

"Remember how Virtanen used to keep his lab notebooks in a locked drawer by his desk?"

"Yeah, I checked it out the other day. The drawer had been jimmied open and Virtanen's notebooks were gone. I presumed the detectives must have taken them." Brett's eyes widened in astonishment. "It was you, wasn't it? Seriously? Owen, what have you done?!"

"I didn't think it would be a big deal. See, I met this chemist over in the East Bay who specializes in designer drugs that technically fly underneath the DEA's jurisdiction, or so he told me. He asked if I had any good ideas. I wanted to blow him off, but considering what Juan Virtanen had been working on, some new series of DMT analogs, I figured the guy might be interested. The guy offered me five hundred bucks for Virtanen's notebooks. Look Brett, I needed the money. Virtanen clearly had no further use for them."

"Dammit Owen, how could you do something like this!"

"Believe me Brett, I wish I hadn't. Just please promise me you won't say anything. Seriously, get a lawyer if you have to. You had nothing to do with any of this. Got it?"

Mudford hung up before Roberts could answer. He was pissed with himself for having told his friend about the notebooks. He hadn't fully thought through the consequences. Now he needed to minimize the damage.

Mudford stood and called for the guard.

His father wanted to hire an expensive lawyer and was planning to fly out from Hawaii for the trial. Unfortunately, Owen had already decided to plead guilty and couldn't be dissuaded.

The arraignment was held the following morning, with only Roberts in the public seating area to support his friend. Roberts presumed that Mudford and his court appointed attorney must have reached some sort of plea deal, but the sentence left him shocked and mortified. He couldn't have possibly imagined a worse outcome for his friend. Considering deaths were involved in the drug trafficking charges that Mudfurd was facing, his offense was classified as a 2nd degree felony.

Owen Mudford was sentenced to 10 years in prison at San Quentin. He was later released on good behavior after serving only five.

Monday, February 21ST, 1983
UCSF Medical Sciences Center, Eleventh Floor

Over four years had passed since Brett Roberts and Patrick O'Reilly first began their graduate studies. O'Reilly was now in the process of writing up his dissertation, having developed a computer graphics program that enabled the design of an entirely new class of serotonin receptor inhibitors. Not to be outdone, Brett Roberts completed his final lab experiments in record time, all of them with remarkably successful outcomes.

It took less than six weeks for Roberts to write up his dissertation, although much of it was still in draft form. His remaining challenge was to find the money for a professional typist. He had no desire to enroll in another drug study, and the prospect of typing it himself seemed oppressively daunting. Keying it into their lab's Apple II computer would be easier, although dot matrix printers of the day weren't capable of generating documents of sufficient quality to meet the UC Library's exacting standards.

Terry Strickland was a graduate student in Professor Johnson's group. He loved tinkering with instruments in the lab, although he was showing no signs of progress on his research project after five-plus years. He poked his head into Professor Nelson's laboratory. "Hey Brett, I have an idea."

Roberts leaned back in his desk chair and stretched with a yawn. "Okay, I'm listening."

Strickland continued, "I think I've figured out a way to interface an IBM Selectric typewriter with that computer of yours. I could plug a digital interface card into the back."

Roberts checked his watch and saw that it was after midnight. He yawned again. "Let me sleep on it, Terry. I'll let you know tomorrow."

Terry already had it working by the time Roberts arrived the next morning. There was a slight problem though, two of them actually. First, the digital link only went in one direction, meaning there would be no way to verify the typewriter had received the correct signal. A few errors per page should be expected. Second, the typewriter could only process one sheet of paper at a time. Roberts would need to proofread each page and make the necessary corrections before scrolling it out of the typewriter and loading another sheet of paper.

"Well, what do you think?" asked Terry.

Roberts hesitated, "Man, I don't know. Seems like a lot of mindless babysitting. But I guess I'll give it a try."

Roberts tried out a few pages after Terry left. It seemed to work okay, although he estimated that it would probably take him about 15 hours to type out the entire dissertation. So Roberts did what he would usually do before starting such an endeavor. He went out for a run, perhaps his last hurrah in Golden Gate Park.

2:55 AM. Wednesday, February 23rd, 1983

Roberts checked his watch and grimaced. Sure enough, he'd been at it for over 15 hours, 16 now and counting. With ten pages left to go, he inserted another sheet of paper into the Selectric, and was about to hit return on the computer when the neon ceiling lights began to flicker. He pushed his chair away and went over to flip the wall switch a few times. That seemed to do the trick, but suddenly, the Selectric resumed its typing before he could return to the computer.

"Crap! Damned thing must be broken," he muttered to himself. Expecting to find gibberish on the page, Roberts looked down and couldn't believe his eyes:

`You've completed your dissertation now, I see.`

Roberts felt tingling goosebumps. *No way should this be happening.* He shouted out loud, "Virtanen! What do you want?!" and felt a bit silly afterwards.

The Selectric started typing again.

```
To congratulate you.
```

Holy shit! Roberts shook his head in disbelief. Then he got an odd predilection to play along. "Juan… did you die?"

```
Not exactly.
```

"What the hell is that supposed to mean?"

```
It simply means I've left my body without a way
back.
```

Roberts spoke this time in a louder and firmer voice, "So where are you, *exactly?*" He'd emphasized that last word to convey his frustration.

```
I seem to be alone in the spirit world.  Others
residing here are unable to communicate with me,
nor I with them.
```

So he'd been right about Virtanen. *Okay, time to get to the bottom of this.* "Look, Virtanen…" He stopped when the Selectric resumed its typing. Roberts hadn't realized that Virtanen could also read his thoughts.

```
But I have found a way to communicate with a few
mortal souls.  You in particular, my friend.
```

Roberts was angry now despite his bewilderment. He shouted, *"Dammit Virtanen, what do you want from me?"* A long silence followed. Roberts sighed, thinking it was over. But then….

```
I want you to help me find out why this happened.
```

"I don't think so, Virtanen."

```
Your yopo experience.  It was different from your
friend's.  Yes?
```

"How did…?"

```
Find out why.
```

The page spit out of the typewriter and settled like a feather to the floor.

Brett's mind reeled with perplexities, even after he had recovered from his initial shock. Follow the path of science? What could Virtanen have possibly meant by that? Then he recalled a debate that he and Mudford were having a few years back over a pitcher of beer at Clancy's. Mudford seemed to think that human consciousness is essentially an illusion, resulting from complex webs of neurons firing at ultra-high frequencies.

Roberts couldn't accept that. There must be more to life, an infinitely spiritual dimension that people like Mudford were either unwilling, or perhaps unable to grasp. What might explain the latter, if indeed it were true? Could it have something to do with subtle differences in brain biochemistry?

He firmly shook his head. No, he would *not* go down that rabbit hole. Virtanen would simply need to find someone else to play the puppet, whatever his intentions might be. But the more Roberts thought about it, the more intrigued he became. Herb Boyer's lecture had inspired him to imagine such possibilities. A new era of biotechnology was emerging, one promising to unlock the genetic mysteries of human biology.

Monday, October 21ˢᵗ, 1985
San Quentin

The inmate shuffled through the second to last door and was instructed to spread his legs while the guard removed his shackles. He was given a plastic bag containing his original street clothes and waved over to a screen in the corner where he could change. After shedding his orange prison jumper and leaving it behind on the floor, the inmate stepped back around to be processed for discharge.

"Owen Mudford, please sign this form." The guard handed him a clipboard and pointed to the place where he should scribble his name.

"Okay inmate, consider yourself officially discharged. You're free to go." The guard nodded toward the final portal to the outside world. "And please don't come back," he added with a condescending grin.

"Thank you, sir." Mudford squinted as he stepped out into the hazy sunlight.

Jack Bradley was leaning against the outside prison wall. "Well, hello there, stranger! Come on over here and give your cousin a hug." He wrapped his arms around Mudford in a hearty embrace.

Mudford had ultimately decided to ask his cousin Jack to meet him for today's release. He wasn't quite ready to face Brett Roberts outside of prison. Which was probably a good thing, he now realized.

After completing his PhD, Roberts had accepted a post-doctoral fellowship from a prestigious university back east, to learn the latest techniques in genetic engineering while maintaining a long-distance relationship with Ruth until she too finished graduate school. They were recently married in her home town of Kansas, just three months shy of Mudford's release from prison. Roberts sent a letter shortly afterward to announce their union. It contained a photo of Ruth in her wedding dress, holding out her bound dissertation with a beaming smile. Mudford dearly wished he could have been there. The more he thought about it, the more terrible he felt about what had happened before. He shook it off after stepping away from Cousin Jack, and promised to give the two of them a call once he got back on his feet.

Jack Bradley had done quite well for himself in a round-about way. He was booking acts at the Whisky a Go-Go in Hollywood during the late 1960s when an international rock promoter took a liking to him and decided to give him a job. Jack turned out to have an exceptional knack for stroking egos and negotiating deals. He spun out his own promotion company with the old man's blessing, aggressively building his brand with bands like David Bowie and Roxy Music and Queen. Bradley Productions even managed the west coast leg of the 1974 Rolling Stones World Tour. Jack projected the hyperkinetic look and persona of Lou Reed, one of his favorite performers, and few would have predicted he'd retire at the age of fifty with a net worth exceeding $50 million dollars.

Cousin Jack now spent most of his time surfing, although he still dabbled in the local music scene whenever the mood caught his fancy. He owned an ocean view home on the cliffs of Point Loma and had been more than happy to lend Mudford a spare room until he got back on his feet.

Mudford managed to complete his master's degree while serving time at San Quentin, having already met the course requirements at UCSF. A portion of his dissertation was even published in a leading scientific journal. Despite his ex-felon status, the advanced degree eventually helped him land a job at a seaweed processing company in San Diego. KelpCo extracted agar from seaweed and processed it for use in cosmetics and industrial applications. He quickly worked his way up to lab manager with his own team of formulation chemists. This wasn't exactly his dream job, certainly not what he had been hoping for while still a graduate student at UCSF. But it was something he was good at and that was enough.

Mudford signed a lease on a tiny studio apartment in Ocean Beach once he had saved enough money for the deposit. He appreciated its proximity to the ocean, having rediscovered his love of surfing in recent months. He also enjoyed hanging out in the funky bars and restaurants along Bacon Street.

He even met a girl the following summer, a ridiculously attractive Swedish blond transfer student who happened to be studying international relations at Point Loma Nazarene University. They were both waiting for waves one sunny afternoon and easily struck up a conversation. Elsa's student visa was about to expire. She couldn't bear the thought of leaving, and Mudford had a charming personality, she thought. She invited him over for dinner that night, and one thing led to another.

Elsa moved into Mudford's apartment two short and passionately combustible weeks later.

CHAPTER TEN

"Genome"

Friday afternoon, September 17TH, 1999
Miami Beach, Florida

THE GENOME SEQUENCING AND ANALYSIS CONFERENCE was now a must attend-event for the international genomics community, and the Fontainebleau Hotel had solidified its reputation as the preferred venue. People came to GSAC to hear about the latest discoveries, presented and debated by many of the brightest scientific minds in the field. Major announcements called for lavish parties afterwards, often followed by drunken scientists splashing around in the pool until the wee hours of the dawn. The coastal Florida sunshine wasn't bad either.

The Fontainebleau had been built in the 1950s with a neo-baroque architecture of sexy curves that still felt uniquely cool and modern. The fifteen-story high-rise resort and conference center faced the ocean in a graceful arc, and a two-story ribbon of luxury suites opened directly onto the beach. These buildings had the color and texture of bleached white coral, and together made a sweepingly beautiful composition of form and function. Every window was strategically designed to draw the eye outside. Nestled within the arc was a rock waterfall, swimming pool with private cabanas and over five hundred lounge chairs for sunbathing. The grounds also included tropical gardens, a croquet lawn, even a couple of putting greens for the more energetic guests.

The top buzz this year was the anticipated completion of the Human Genome Project, the first comprehensive sequence of an entire human genome, our very DNA, the stuff that makes us who we are, also known as the *genetic code of life*. It had been a massive undertaking. The twenty-two diploid chromosomes plus the sex chromosomes X and Y contain over 3 billion nucleotide bases. If one were to stretch out the individual strands of DNA from a single cell and lay them all out end to end, they would span a distance of almost 2 meters. The cell packages them inside a nucleus less than 10 microns in diameter, or less than ten *millionth* of a meter, a truly amazing feat of biology.

The idea for sequencing the human genome stemmed from the DNA-to-RNA-to-Protein discoveries of the 1960s. Knowledge of a gene sequence enabled scientists to deduce the corresponding amino acid sequence, a first step toward understanding whatever protein it might code for. It also allowed scientists to clone and express different genes of interest. Applying the principles of molecular biology, the protein's function could then be studied systematically in the laboratory.

The scale of the Human Genome Project was not unlike landing a man on the moon. By 1999, it comprised 20 universities and research centers from around the world, consuming over 3 billion dollars of research funding. Administering this consortium required a political will of iron to distribute and coordinate the various efforts. Launched in 1990 under the leadership of the Nobel laureate James Watson, co-discoverer of the structure of DNA, the torch soon passed to Francis Collins, a devout Christian and brilliant scientist in his own right who first discovered the gene for cystic fibrosis. With Collins at the helm, the sequences of several individual chromosomes were rapidly nearing completion. Over 750 million base pairs of genetic sequence had already been made publicly available, or roughly one-quarter of the entire human genome.

J. Craig Venter, a maverick scientist from the National Institutes of Health, still believed the public effort was moving much too slowly. To the surprise of many in the genomic community, he secured private funding to develop a new "shotgun sequencing" process, which he claimed would be capable of sequencing an entire human genome at a fraction of the cost. His method involved breaking the genome into lots of tiny bits and then sequencing the individual fragments. Stitching all those sequences back together was a bit like matching enormous strings of dominos. This required powerful new computers with software yet to be developed. Few believed the approach could be used successfully to assemble a human chromosome.

Venter's new company Celera Genomics had been in full operation for less than three months. Few scientists outside the company believed their new approach could be used successfully for something as complicated as a human chromosome. Nevertheless, rumors were flying that Venter was planning a major announcement at this year's GSAC conference. Celera representatives had been handing out free T-shirts to conference attendees, with the image of a fruit fly on the back shoulder and a circular graphic on the front depicting the fully annotated fly genome.

The common fruit fly, scientific name *drosophila melanogaster*, was the first living organism ever chosen for studies of genetic inheritance. Even high school students were familiar with such experiments, having crossed-bred different strains to understand how traits such as eye color and antennae length were passed on to their offspring.

A session on the fly genome was on the schedule for Sunday afternoon. The program featured several scientists from Celera, including Venter himself. Had they actually done it? This was no small boast, considering the fly genome had been estimated to contain approximately 140 million base pairs of genetic information.

Celera wasn't the first commercial venture to enter this space, however. Several other high-throughput sequencing companies had been in operation since the early 1990s, although rather than sequence the genome directly, they had chosen to focus instead on messenger RNA, the genetic material responsible for making proteins. Their strategy was to systematically compare mRNA sequences from normal and diseased tissues to identify new protein targets for drug discovery. They had also pioneered a revolutionary business model for generating revenue, charging huge sums of money to subscribe to their proprietary databases. Most of the major pharmaceutical companies were already on board.

Brett Roberts now worked for Spectrum Genomics, among the top two RNA sequencing companies, and was attending his second GSAC conference here in Miami. Having arrived a day early, he was excited to hear what other sequencing labs were up to, and also a bit nervous about the presentation he was scheduled to give during one of the workshop sessions on Saturday.

He sat by the pool and tried to relax while sipping his tall and frosty Piña Colada through a straw. On the lounge chair next to him was Westfield Westfield, his close friend and colleague. Both worked in Spectrum's Microarray Division.

Westfield was an eclectic audiophile and a devoted Dead Head who mostly wore jeans and T-shirts to work from concerts he'd attended. He wore his ginger hair pulled back in a ponytail and sported a scraggly goatee. But poolside, his pasty white skin was the first thing most people noticed.

Westfield asked in a low voice, "What do you think Venter might have to say on Sunday?"

"I think the fly genome was just a teaser," Roberts answered. "Rumor has it they've already begun sequencing human DNA."

"I doubt the public consortium will be happy to hear that," said Eric.

Roberts glanced over and noticed Eric's skin getting pink already. "Dude, you should probably put a shirt on."

Eric reached down into his conference bag and unwrapped a T-shirt from its plastic sleeve. He pulled it over his head and thrust his arms through it.

Roberts grimaced when he recognized the circular graphic. "Really?"

"Hey man, it was free," said Eric.

"Well if Celera's announcement has anything to do with that T-shirt, it'll definitely heat things up a bit, that's for sure."

Roberts ratcheted up his lounge chair, took a long sip from his straw, and adjusted his Ray Bans while watching Mindy climb out of the pool. She worked on Eric's team back at Spectrum and was excited to be attending her first GSAC conference. Both of them considered her strictly off-limits, but the way she looked in a bikini made it difficult to avert their gaze.

Westfield reached over to nudge Brett's arm and gave him a wry smile when their eyes finally met. "On a different note, how'd you like to join us at Mangos this evening?"

Roberts had intended to review his slides that evening, although Mangos was supposedly quite a scene. Located in the heart of South Beach, it featured salsa music with lots of drinking and dancing. "I should probably go. But Eric, you've got to promise me something…."

"Don't worry, Brett. I'll make sure your sorry ass is back by eleven at the latest. You have my word, alright?"

Westfield had been known to bend his word on occasion, especially when drinking was involved. But Roberts decided to trust him anyway. They were in Miami Beach after all, a rare opportunity to unwind.

Walking into Mangos was a lot like entering a theme park version of a tropical rainforest. With a wrap-around balcony over the dance floor, and a trio of sparsely dressed Latin dancers on the circular stage below, the energy was highly contagious. Bartenders worked furiously behind the stage while off-duty dancers peddled their test tube racks of colorful alcoholic elixirs for two bucks a shot.

Eric bought a couple of the test tubes and handed one to Roberts. "Bottom's up dude!" Against his better judgment, Roberts knocked it back and handed the empty tube to the amazingly seductive waitress.

"Would you like another?" she shouted above the salsa music in her Cuban accent.

"Maybe later!" Roberts waved her off with a smile. Then he reached over to get Eric's attention, who happened to be eying another one of the waitresses. "C'mon, buddy. Let's check this place out."

They wove through the crowd and made their way to the back dance floor, where they found Mindy now dressed in a flowered wrap skirt with a matching halter top. She had seen their approach and rushed over to give them each a hug.

"Hey, guys! Want to dance?"

Mindy was one of Eric's most productive lab technicians, but she could also be a bit of trouble after a few drinks. Having no desire to encourage Mindy, Roberts raised his hands in surrender. "We're good for now."

"Alright then, have fun being wallflowers!" Undeterred, Mindy sauntered over to a stunningly handsome Latin guy with a sleeveless white T-shirt and guns for arms. She extended her arm and he led her onto the dance floor without hesitation. Roberts had to admit, Mindy's dance moves were pretty amazing.

"Want another drink?" Westfield shouted. Roberts nodded while moving rhythmically with the music. That second drink led to a third, and as was typical of Mango's, they soon lost track of time.

Roberts checked his watch and saw it was close to midnight. "Shit! Eric, we have to go."

"C'mon, man!" Westfield whined. "We're in *Miami*." Westfield always hated it when Roberts put the hammer down, but his friend had a point this time. The first scientific session started at 9 AM the next morning. "Oh alright, guess I'm done. But we should probably take the boardwalk back up to the hotel, sober up a bit before we hit the hay."

Roberts slapped Eric's shoulder, a bit sluggishly. "Probably a good idea."

Mindy broke away from her partner long enough to say goodbye. "Good luck with your talk tomorrow, Brett!"

"Thanks, Mindy…" said Roberts, although Mindy had already returned to the dance floor.

"Let's get out of here before I order another drink," said Eric.

They walked north along the boardwalk with a cool ocean breeze and a full moon rising just above the horizon, casting a cone of silver rippling reflections on the water. Roberts felt almost sober by the time they reached the hotel, although his head didn't hit the pillow until after 1 AM.

The wife of a wealthy German businessman hadn't slept well that night. They were vacationing in one of the hotel's cabanas along the beach, but the loud pool party had kept her awake most of the night. Now in her mid-forties, her waistline had expanded somewhat but she didn't care. This was Miami Beach after all. So she slid out of bed and put on the skimpy bikini she'd purchased the day before from that trendy boutique shop down on South Beach. She shut the door behind her as quietly as she could to avoid waking her snoring husband, and walked out onto the sand under a cloudless sky to lay out her beach towel and do some sunbathing. She undid her top and put a pair of sand dollars over her eyes.

Bright sunlight beamed straight through Brett's hotel window around that time, and as could be expected, his head was throbbing. How many of those test tubes had he quaffed the night before? He seemed to recall having only two….

He peered at the digital alarm clock on his night stand as it clicked over to 7 AM. *Still early,* he realized, and pulled a pillow over his head. Intent on falling back asleep, he then remembered the talk he was scheduled to present later that morning. He hadn't reviewed his slides the night before. Better do it now.

"*Shit,*" he hissed, and then wrestled his hands free from the knotted sheets to massage his temples.

Roberts forced himself out of bed, caught his balance, and stumbled over to the bathroom to pop a couple of much needed aspirin. He then went over to a cherry wood desk near the window and booted up his laptop. While the operating system was loading, he went over to the coffee service and tried to focus. Pouch here, get water from sink….

Coffee cup in hand, but not quite ready to face his presentation, he stepped over to the window and peered down to the beach. It surprised him to see a woman sunbathing at this hour. She also happened to be topless… afraid she might see him staring down at her from up on the tenth floor, Roberts quickly turned away.

More fully awake now, he settled into the chair at his desk and began to review the slides for his presentation. His topic was on gene homology, the nucleotide sequence similarities between genes coding for proteins that performed similar biological functions – for example the tyrosine kinase enzymes he'd studied in graduate school.

Two hours later, Roberts stood nervously before an audience of over five hundred scientists who shared the same interest. *You can do this,* he told himself. He took a breath, clicked on his first slide, and spoke his first words into the microphone. Nervousness slipped away as he surveyed his attentive audience.

Saturday's evening bash was hosted by Spectrum Genomics, New Orleans style. Showgirls handed out colorful plastic beads to the scientists as they entered the main hall, now transformed into "Bourbon Street" complete with bar-front facades.

Mindy spotted Roberts in the crowd and hopped over to put a string of beads around his neck. "I thought your talk was wonderful, Brett. Congratulations!"

Mindy seemed half buzzed already, thought Roberts. "Thanks, Mindy!" He smiled and politely excused himself to go find a beer. Mindy shrugged and glanced around for another victim to flirt with.

Roberts joined the queue at the bar and recognized a familiar face. Conrad Wilkins, Spectrum's director of business development, had negotiated contracts with over a dozen pharmaceutical companies already that year. "How's it going, Conrad?" Roberts shouted.

Wilkins waved hello. "Hey Brett! Want a hurricane? I'm buying."

Drinks were free of course, although Roberts appreciated the gesture. "No thanks! Think I'll stick with beer tonight."

Conrad motioned Roberts over to join him. "Probably a good idea," he teased. "Great talk this morning, by the way. Tell you what. I've got meeting lined up next Friday in Palo Alto with another team of pharmaceutical executives. Think you'd mind driving over to join us? That microarray study of yours could help close the deal."

"Sure!" Roberts was always happy to showcase the microarray division, although the drive across the Dumbarton Bridge to Spectrum's Palo Alto campus would cost him an extra hour of bumper-to-bumper morning traffic. Fortunately he didn't have to make that drive every day. East Bay traffic was bad enough.

The music stopped and a spotlight hit the stage at the end of "Bourbon Street". Jeremy Watts stepped up to the microphone, the president and chief scientific officer of Spectrum Genomics. The son of a California state congressman, he was well known for his oratory talents.

"Hello everyone," he said. "And thanks for coming out for our little party this evening." This evoked hoots and whistles and he waited for the crowd to quiet back down before continuing.

"As you know, we are nearing the completion of a lofty goal that was once considered insurmountable. The sequencing of our human genome, the genetic instructions that make us who we are. For the past nine years this task has engaged the collective talents of thousands of scientists, engineers and computer experts from across the globe. The public consortium is now on track to complete a working draft by the end of next year."

He paused for effect. The crowd knew what was coming. "And as you will learn more about tomorrow, we now have a private company claiming they can get it done even sooner. I'm sure we all wish them well."

Watts endured the jeers and boos that followed before continuing. "However this all comes together, we still face the daunting task of translating the genomic sequence into biologically meaningful information. Where to begin?"

The hall went quiet. He had their attention. "At Spectrum Genomics, as most of you know, we've chosen to bypass the genome and focus instead on *messenger RNA*. Over the past six years, we've sequenced mRNA libraries from hundreds of different tissues. Our bioinformatics team now estimates the total number of genes to be around 120,000."

'Genes' were now generally understood to encode for messenger RNA, which in turn served as templates for protein synthesis. In 1909, the Danish botanist Wilhelm Johannsen coined the term gen (or "gene", in English) to describe the fundamental units of inheritance that were originally discovered 40 years earlier by a famous German Monk named Gregor Mendel. The word derives from the Greek word genos, meaning birth.

Watts continued, "But we still have little idea what the vast majority of these genes are actually doing inside our bodies. Understanding their function will require decades of research, and new tools are needed to accelerate the pace. That's why at Spectrum, we've invested in a new microarray technology that can...."

Hearing the word "microarray" made Roberts and Westfield want to cheer, but they didn't dare interrupt their president's oratory.

"...Profiling gene expression is just the first step to an eventual answer, however. Disease-associated genes will then need to be cloned and expressed into proteins for further study. Such efforts will be driving new technical innovations for decades to come. But one thing should be clear to us now. We are about to enter a new era of genomic medicine. I think that deserves a good party, don't you?"

Loud cheers erupted and the jazz band struck up a rounding chorus of "When the Saints Go Marching In".

Roberts had a good beer buzz on as he rode the elevator back up to his hotel room. His president's speech that evening made him feel part of something important, to be working in an area of science that would ultimately make a difference in human healthcare.

He unlocked the door and noticed that he'd forgotten to turn off his laptop. The screen saver played a continuous slide show from his family's Yosemite vacation that summer. He went over and pressed down the off button, more than once, but nothing happened. Pictures of his sons Michael and Thomas kept sweeping by on the monitor. He tried unplugging it but couldn't seem to yank the cord out of the wall.

Then the room went dark.

He glanced out the window. No signs of lightning, although a dark brooding cloud was eclipsing the moon. He went over and flipped the light switch a few times to no avail.

The computer went to blue screen, and then text began sweeping by in 24 point font.

You have chosen the right path.

Shit! It was Virtanen again, the first time in over 16 years. "I don't see how that's any concern of yours, Virtanen. What do you want?" Roberts felt silly to be speaking the words out loud.

It's almost time for the next stage of your journey.

"Please leave me alone!"

She will soon come to you, a prominent scientist.

"What?"

Listen to her.

The slide show resumed on his computer, although the lights were still out. Roberts felt his way to the bathroom and splashed cold water on his face. Finally the lights came back on. He had difficulty sleeping that night.

Roberts awoke the next morning at a more comfortable hour, with the rising sun no longer blazing through his hotel window and no scientific sessions scheduled until 1 PM that afternoon. He decided to go for a run along the boardwalk before breakfast and then check out the Science and Technology Exhibit Hall. It showcased the wares of over 150 biotech companies, all of them vying for a piece of the genome pie.

The commercial sequencing companies had secured the most prominent booth locations near the center of the hall, each one marketing their proprietary databases and software to pharmaceutical executives in attendance. Other companies peddled their latest advances in robotics and instrumentation designed to make the sequencing process faster, cheaper and easier. The smaller companies had hired "booth babes" to attract scientists to their fringe locations, which made Roberts feel a bit like he was attending an auto show.

The Main Hall was filled to capacity by half-past noon, with Jazz fusion music playing softly in the background. Many in attendance had chosen to wear their fly genome T-shirts for the pending announcement. The music stopped at five minutes before the hour and the lights began to dim.

The crowd began clapping rhythmically in anticipation. This was the moment they'd all been waiting for, almost like being at a rock concert. Gerald Rubin stepped up the podium, waved the tightly packed crowd to silence, and made a few introductory comments to open the session.

First up was Celera's head of operations, who presented an overview of their "shotgun sequencing" process. Over 300 of the latest model automated DNA sequencers had been purchased for the effort. Collectively, they were capable of sequencing over 10 million base pairs per hour. A cluster network of Compaq AlphServer computers had been harnessed to analyze the data.

As anticipated, Celera's head of bioinformatics unveiled their fully annotated fly genome. He walked through numerous examples of genes that had been sequenced, along with their mapped locations along the fly genome's four pairs of chromosomes. Few had expected such a preponderance of data, which proved convincingly that Venter's "shotgun sequencing" process actually worked. Loud clapping erupted at the end of his presentation, particularly among the fly genome scientists in the audience.

Craig Venter had the honor of speaking last. He began by calmly stating that Celera was now on track to complete the sequence an entire human genome by the following spring. Venter paused for effect and his body language said it all. This announcement struck the bow of the public consortium like a cannon ball.

But what really shocked the audience was Venter's estimate for the total number of genes encoded within our human genome. Having already completed their analysis for chromosome 21, Celera's bioinformatics team now predicted the number to be somewhere around 25,000 genes. At the time, it was difficult to comprehend how a human being could function with such a limited number of genetic instructions.

A lesser surprise was Venter's announcement that Celera was planning to commercialize the availability of their proprietary genome sequence. He concluded there and opened for questions.

The first and most obvious question was who had donated their DNA for this effort. Venter acknowledged that it was a blend of genomic DNA isolated from five different individuals spanning a range of age, sex and ethnicity, although he wouldn't be more specific. Each donor had signed an informed consent form and their identity was to be kept strictly confidential. What he didn't say but would later admit was that one of those donors happened to be himself. This juicy tidbit was known only by three of his most trusted colleagues inside the Celera organization.

Westfield leaned toward Roberts as they were funneling out of the hall, and whispered, "How the heck did Venter manage to raise all that money?"

"Must have promised his investors the keys to the kingdom," said Roberts.

"Yeah well, I wish them luck. Regardless of how many genes we have, it'll take decades to translate all that sequencing data into biologically meaningful information."

"You got that right, my friend."

CHAPTER ELEVEN

"Countdown to the Next Millennium"

Wednesday, September 22th, 1999
Spectrum Genomics Microarray Facility, Fremont, CA

MICROARRAYS WERE HOT, the latest rage for identifying novel gene targets for new drug discovery. Pharmaceutical companies were interested, and Spectrum's stock price had been trading at an all-time high.

Spectrum's microarrays contained 10,000 tiny dots of genetic material printed robotically onto a chemically treated glass microscope slide. Each dot represented a different gene identified by the Palo Alto sequencing division. A typical experiment would compare two different tissue samples, for example a tumor that had been surgically removed *versus* the benign tissue immediately surrounding it. RNA was first extracted from the two tissue samples and each labeled with a different florescent dye before applying them to the microarray. Any fluorescently labeled RNA molecules that recognized their corresponding gene dot would bind there through a process called complementary base-pairing. The slide was then scanned with a laser to quantify the relative amounts of fluorescence at each gene dot. This made it possible to focus on disease-associated genes that would most likely respond to therapeutic intervention.

Leading cancer centers from around the country were now shipping their samples to Spectrum be analyzed. The microarray division's staff of scientific experts worked closely with the investigators to help them interpret the results, and hopefully report their findings in peer-reviewed journals. Such publications were important for attracting new customers.

Brett Roberts was presently studying the results of one such microarray experiment on his computer monitor. His office looked out to a lovely rose garden with a bubbling water fountain in its center, although he typically ignored the view unless he happened to be on a conference call.

The patients who donated their tumor samples for this particular study had all been diagnosed with an aggressive form of brain cancer called glioblastoma. They were participating in an early phase clinical trial for a newly developed cancer drug that had shown promising results in animal models. Unfortunately, less than 5% of these patients showed any significant improvement in disease-free survival, although a few of them were still alive and cancer free 18 months later.

Roberts was keen to understand why. The data pointed to a novel gene expressed predominantly in the brain, possibly a membrane receptor based on its sequence homology to other known proteins. He wondered whether any of the patients who had responded to the drug might also possess a mutation in this particular gene. *Hmm…* the only way to confirm his hypothesis would be to obtain blood samples from the few surviving patients for DNA sequencing.

He picked up the phone, about to dial the lead investigator, when he got interrupted by a loud and persistent knocking. Roberts couldn't pretend not to hear it from behind his glass panel wall.

The woman outside his office wore a stern expression which reminded Roberts of a librarian he'd known back in college, that same sourpuss look when the students were making too much noise. She knocked even louder once they'd made eye contact.

Roberts clicked 'save' on the computer screen and walked around his desk to open the door. "Can I help you?" He made an effort to be polite, despite the noisy intrusion.

The harried-looking woman barged right past him while slamming the door shut behind her and took an empty chair without introductions. "Sit," she commanded. "There's something we need to discuss."

Roberts settled back into his own chair behind the desk. "Um, who are you?"

"Your company recently signed me on as a part-time consultant. And I'm also a tenured professor at Stanford University, in their department of Neurophysiology."

"In that case, I'm glad you stopped by. I happen to be working on a brain cancer study at the moment, and…."

"Yes, I know. That's why Jeremy sent me over here to speak with you." Roberts leaned forward and gave the woman his full attention when he realized that she was on a first name basis with Spectrum's president and CSO.

"Excuse me. I didn't get your name?"

"It's Feinstein. Professor Janet Feinstein."

"Well then, it's a pleasure to meet you Dr. Feinstein. So, how can I help you?" His skin tingled with the recollection of Virtanen's admonition, *a prominent scientist....*

Over the next half hour, Janet Feinstein described the research she was conducting in the area of brain dementia, specifically Alzheimer's disease. In fact, her laboratory had recently provided a number of autopsy tissue samples to Spectrum's RNA sequencing group over in Palo Alto.

Roberts realized that those sequences must already be in Spectrum's database.

"So here's where you come in, Dr. Roberts." Roberts didn't like the way she had just used his professional title. Clearly, she wanted something from him.

"I understand that your team has the ability to manufacture custom microarrays," she continued.

"Yes, of course. It's just a matter of accessing the clones for those genes from our sequencing facility in Palo Alto and having someone drive them over."

Roberts pointed to the glass-walled Class I clean room on the other side of the building. A dozen or so technicians were now hustling around amongst the robotic workstations, tending the various processes of microarray production. They all wore disposable lab coats and powder blue hair nets. Even the tiniest amount of dust or human dander that happened to fall onto a microarray could render it useless.

"Excellent. I'll call your sequencing group in Palo Alto and tell them which genes we're interested in." She stood up to leave.

"Great, thanks. It was a pleasure talking to you...." Roberts stopped on that beat after noticing that Janet Feinstein had already left. He waited a moment to make sure she wasn't coming back, then went down to Westfield's office to fill him in. Westfield was in charge of microarray development, which meant that any new projects like this required his approval.

"I see you've met Professor Feinstein," Westfield said.

"Then I'm assuming she also stopped by your office."

"Indeed she did, wanted to know about our production schedule over the next several weeks. When she told me why, I suggested she discuss her idea with you first. So you caved, apparently?"

"Didn't seem like the type of person who'd take 'no' for an answer. Matter of fact, she didn't even wait for one."

Westfield folded his arms and leaned back, with an amused expression.

"Also, she claimed that Jeremy Watts had sent her over."

"Hope you're planning to check that out."

"Don't I always?"

Roberts returned to his office and got Stuart Avery on the phone, Spectrum's Vice-President of Research and Development over at the Sequencing Division in Palo Alto. They were just wrapping up when Roberts spotted his wife and two little tow-haired boys approaching his office. Although delighted to see them, he waved for Ruth to hold a moment when they reached his office. His older son Thomas started making faces against the glass.

"…Yes Stuart, I'll get right on that." Avery abruptly ended the call with a brief admonition. The microarray division needed to generate more publishable data over the coming months. Watts wanted to escalate the "buzz factor" to maintain their lead in the genomics community. It also helped drive market adoption for their new proprietary gene expression database. Roberts should give Professor Feinstein whatever she needed.

"Thanks Doctor Avery. I'll make sure Feinstein's project gets top priority…" but he'd already hung up. Time was money in the genomics industry. Ruth smiled wryly when Brett waved them in. Thomas and Michael burst into his office and ran over to play with the microarray hardware and other mementos on his bookshelf.

"Sorry dear…." Brett felt bad for making her wait.

"What's this one Daddy?" Thomas interrupted.

"That's a prototype of the microarray print-head we use in our production facility."

"What's a prototype?"

Before Brett could answer, Thomas picked up plastic laminated microarray and asked what *that* was.

"That's a genomic chip, son. It's something we can use to learn about the special instructions inside our bodies."

"Um, we have special instructions? What are those?"

"Yes, Thomas. They help our bodies work properly."

Michael wanted to see but, Thomas held it up above his reach. "Genomics chip! Can I have one?"

Brett's senior lab technician Anthony poked his head into the office to announce that he'd finished scanning the microarray slides from that day's experiment. "The results should be compiled and ready for viewing in another five to ten minutes."

"Fantastic." Brett waved him in to introduce his family. "Anthony, I'd like you to meet my wife Ruth and our boys Thomas and Michael."

"Nice to finally meet you Mrs. Roberts. Oh sorry, I meant *Dr.* Roberts!"

Ruth graciously accepted the misstep. It happened to her all the time when Brett was around. "That's quite alright, Anthony. I've been looking forward to meeting you as well. My husband speaks highly of your talents in the laboratory."

Anthony felt himself blushing. He turned and bent down to Thomas. "What have you got there, little man?"

"Genomics chip!" Thomas held it up proudly. "Can I have one?"

Anthony looked up for approval and Brett nodded.   He turned back and whispered conspiratorially to Thomas. "Let me go see if I can find one for you, okay?"

"Okay!" Thomas smiled proudly.

Anthony left and Ruth explained that school had let out early that day. She'd been out shopping with the boys when Thomas realized they were near Daddy's work and wanted to visit. Their oldest son had an autistic spectrum disorder, although he also possessed a phenomenal memory that extended to locations and directions.

After getting married, Ruth and Brett had both focused on their respective careers before deciding to have children seven years later. The movie *Rain Man* had helped foster social awareness of Thomas's disorder, although that hadn't made it much easier to deal with his special needs. Finding daycare for an autistic child had turned out to be a considerable challenge, and things got increasingly difficult after Thomas entered grade school. Ruth eventually decided to quit her job at the Lawrence Livermore

National Laboratory, a major sacrifice that she was still learning to deal with. Brett's tendency to work long hours hadn't helped. They often missed dinner together as a family, although Brett always tried to make it home in time to read the boys a quick story before tucking them into bed.

Brett sensed his wife was feeling a bit guilty about showing up unannounced. "Hey, it's really great to see you guys!"

He walked around the desk and hugged his wife in plain view of his coworkers. The boys joined in of course, this was fun for them. They held the embrace for a while. It was enough. And this time, Ruth's smile was genuine.

"I'll try to leave the office by five." This was a significant commitment, considering how brutal traffic could be up the 680 Interstate during rush hour.

Anthony returned with a little black box at precisely that moment. He knelt down and opened it for Thomas to see what was inside. Nestled within the notch of a purple sponge insert was one of their glass microarrays, fresh from production. The tiny little gene dots could still be seen with the naked eye when held up to the light, since they hadn't yet been fixed onto the surface. It even had an "official" looking barcode sticker. Anthony put the slide back in the box, clicked it shut and handed it to Thomas.

"Thanks!" Thomas said happily.

"You are most welcome, little man."

"Thomas, let your brother Michael hold it, okay?" said Brett.

Noticing Brett's dilemma, Anthony rushed back to the lab and returned with another box just like Thomas's. He handed this one to Michael, who opened it cautiously to find a little flip-cap plastic tube inside. "These are called 'Eppendorf' tubes. We perform our genomic reactions inside," said Anthony. Michael beamed. "Thanks!" he said.

Brett mouthed "thank you". Anthony grinned, and then said, "Well, I should probably get back to my experiment. A pleasure meeting you, Dr. Roberts. You too, boys," he added.

Jeremy Watts was scheduled to give an open lecture at Stanford the following Thursday evening. His talk was entitled "Science and Spirituality in the Age of Human Genomics." Roberts had noticed the flyer tacked up on a bulletin board outside the Chemistry Library at UC Berkeley. Watts made no secret of his professed Christianity, although it surprised Roberts that his company's president would step out on such a polarizing topic within the science community.

Ruth encouraged Brett to go after hearing about the lecture topic. "Take good notes. I'd like hear about it later," she'd said.

Roberts left work early that afternoon, and nearly two hours of bumper-to-bumper traffic later, he finally located a parking space on a quiet residential side street several blocks away from the Stanford campus.

He noticed the 'For Sale' sign on the front lawn as he was backing into the space. This seemed like an omen, considering Stuart Avery had been hinting about moving his research team over to the Palo Alto campus "at some point". After setting the parking brake, Roberts climbed out to grab one of the brochures clipped to the sign post. It was small, 1950's-era three-bedroom home, about 1300 square feet of floor space on less than a tenth of an acre lot, and the asking price was over $900,000. Moving his family over to the Peninsula to be closer to Spectrum's main offices was not looking too promising. Perhaps he'd just buy a new car to make the commute easier, one with a decent stereo system this time.

Roberts entered the auditorium with 15 minutes to spare and spotted a few empty seats near the front. He made his way down the aisle while surveying the eclectic mix of students, professors, and people from the surrounding community who had all come to hear tonight's lecture. The chatter seemed a bit livelier than usual, with everyone wondering what the president of a genomics company might have to say about this particular topic. Doctor Watts came on stage to polite applause.

He began his lecture with a question. "Are science and spirituality compatible?" Watts glanced around to see if anyone wanted to raise their hand. No one did.

"I know that many of us find this question a difficult one to answer. Our rational minds tell us that the physical universe is all there is, that we alone are in charge of our own destiny. Although you may be interested to know that many brilliant scientists throughout history were also notable theologians. "Here's a quote from Blaise Pascal, a seventeenth century

French mathematician and physicist credited with inventing one of the first mechanical calculators."

> *"The immortality of the soul is a matter which is of so great consequence to us and which touches us so profoundly that we must have lost all feeling to be indifferent about it."*
> ... *Blaise Pascal (1623-1662)*

"And here's another one from Isaac Newton, the father of modern calculus and one of the most prolific minds of his day."

> *"This most beautiful system of the sun, planets, and comets could only proceed from the counsel and dominion of an intelligent and powerful Being. And if the fixed stars are the centers of other like systems, these, being formed by the likewise counsel, must be all subject to the dominion of One."*
> ... *Sir Isaac Newton (1643-1727)*

"So why is it that we now find this question such a difficult one? Let's take a step back and consider it from an evolutionary perspective."

He clicked through a few more slides while narrating the history of biogenesis. "As most of you know, Earth's first 500 billion years were inhospitable to life. As it began to cool, almost 4 billion years ago, the first living single-cell organisms emerged within the relatively short span of a hundred million years. The chemistry of evolution would select deoxyribonucleic acid polymers, or DNA, as the primary information source. Living organisms were self-replicating, of course by definition. Even the simplest bacteria required hundreds of genes to survive and perform this process – hundreds of thousands if not millions of nucleotide bases. How did all this come about? Is it reasonable for us to contemplate why?" He clicked to a classic illustration of evolution from fish to walking reptile to primate to man.

"We are quite rapidly approaching a transformational event in human history, the decoding of our human genome, with over 3 billion nucleotide bases. Scientists have labored over this task for almost ten years. With the Human Genome Project nearing its completion, we are about to enter a new era of genomic medicine.

"Then what about evolution? Through this genomic sequencing effort, we now have convincing proof that we humans are in fact descended from our primate ancestors." He clicked to a slide illustrating the structural similarities between human and ape chromosomes. "For example, the arrangement of genes within our Chromosome 2 tells us that it must have originated from the fusion of two separate chromosomes that are present in modern gorillas and orangutans.

"So our genomes do in fact contain evidence supporting the theory of evolution. But does this prove the physical universe is all there is, that it is solely responsible for everything we see and touch and experience?"

He clicked to another slide, this one a photo of a child in a grassy field blowing on a dandelion.

"It has become popular to think that evolution somehow justifies atheism. But how can we prove or disprove God when we limit our thinking to what only we ourselves can measure? I'm sure the scientists in the audience can appreciate that the more we learn, the more aware we become of what we still do not know.

"One simply *believes* that since evolution actually happened, God must therefore not exist. That in itself is a faith statement. Wouldn't you agree?"

His final slide was a quote from Billy Graham, from a publicly broadcasted interview with David Frost back in 1997:

> *"I don't think that there's any conflict at all between science today and the Scriptures. I think that we have misinterpreted the Scriptures many times and we've tried to make the Scriptures say things they weren't meant to say, I think that we have made a mistake by thinking the Bible is a scientific book. The Bible is not a book of science. The Bible is a book of Redemption, and of course I accept the Creation story. I believe that God did create the universe. I believe that God created man, and whether it came by an evolutionary process and at a certain point He took this person or being and made him a living soul or not, does not change the fact that God did create man. ... Whichever way God did it makes no difference as to what man is and man's relationship to God."*

The lights came back on to scattered applause.

Roberts overheard mostly negative comments about the lecture while making his way out of the auditorium. Why, he wondered? He reflected on the topic during his long drive back to Pleasanton.

The boys were already in bed and sleeping peacefully by the time he got home. Brett kissed each one softly on the forehead before heading back downstairs to join Ruth at the kitchen table. She'd reheated a plate of chicken tortellini casserole for him.

Brett poured himself a glass of Chardonnay, topped off Ruth's, and took his first bite. "Delicious as always."

"Michael asked for it again. In fact, he helped me prepare it this time. So, how was Dr. Watt's lecture?"

Brett took a sip of wine and savored it while flashing back through the lecture in his mind. Then he said, "I found it inspirational, although apparently I was in the minority. Most folks walking out seemed to think it was bunk."

Ruth took a sip herself, set down the glass, and settled back with her hands folded on the table. "Okay I'm ready. Please tell me about it."

Brett recounted Dr. Watt's lecture without referring to his notes, having committed most of it to memory. "I think he made a number of valid points, especially the one about how choosing not to believe in God is itself a faith statement."

"Well, I find it interesting that he spoke about how early scientists were also theologians."

Brett said, "Yeah, but most scientists today seem to think that evolution has all the answers."

"And I really liked the Billy Graham quote," Ruth added.

"Me too, especially coming from a supposed fundamentalist."

The IT guys at Spectrum Genomics were fully preoccupied with the "Y2K threat" as the year 1999 drew to a close. Computer operating systems hadn't yet accounted for the extra digits needed to date stamp their outputs, which could potentially cause massive computer failures world-wide come January 1st. They'd been working frantically throughout the past 90 days to insulate Spectrum's computer servers from the pending crash. Spectrum's executives were now claiming that everything was in order, although a remote possibility of a crash still existed once the clocks had ticked over to the next millennium.

Brett and Ruth attended a party that New Year's Eve hosted by Patrick O'Reilly at his recently purchased hilltop estate in Oakland Hills.

The field of computer-assisted drug design had proven an ideal career move for O'Reilly. He was recruited straight out of graduate school by a major pharmaceutical company on the East Coast, where he hired a team of software engineers to expand on the programs he created in graduate school. Five years later, he returned to the Bay Area to start his first company. He was now on his second start-up, having raised over $140 million dollars of venture capital.

O'Reilly discovered a passion for windsurfing after returning to the Bay Area and lost 40 pounds to "go faster". The sport also introduced him to a strikingly beautiful blond who proved to be exceptionally intelligent. They'd recently married.

Most of the other guests were actually employees of O'Reilly's new company, many a bit quirky and all of them exceptionally brilliant. The highlight of the evening thus far had been experiments with grapes inside O'Reilly's microwave, a particularly engaging activity after a glass or two of wine. A single grape was sliced partially through, leaving a small piece of skin connecting the two halves, and then placed inside the microwave with the flesh facing upwards. Turning on the microwave for a few seconds resulted in a brilliant flash of electrical energy rising up from their surfaces. Other kinds of fruit were experimented on next, however none of them produced a similar effect. O'Reilly's head of software engineering came up with the most plausible explanation, that the diameters of the two tethered grape halves must closely match the wavelength of microwaves bouncing off their surfaces, causing them to interfere with each other and produce the effect.

With the clock approaching midnight, the guests moved to the outdoor deck and gazed down to a panoramic view of the bay while awaiting the coming millennium. O'Reilly's new wife Judith handed out party hats and then stood next to him with her arm affectionately around his waist. Brett thought they made a nice pair.

Ruth came over with a pair of Champaign glasses and handed one to Brett. She looked stunning in her royal blue evening dress. He wrapped an arm around his own wife and pulled her close. "I love you, dear," he whispered. Ruth gently kissed his cheek and then smiled. "Me too," she said.

The countdown began and Brett glanced over to the San Francisco skyline, wondering if the twinkling lights would all go dark after midnight. *"Ten! Nine! Eight! Seven..."*

Fireworks erupted simultaneously from multiple barges scattered around the bay, one the most spectacular displays that Roberts had ever seen. Then noticing the lights still on in the high-rises of San Francisco, he realized the Y2K doomsayers had been wrong.

That brief moment somehow reminded Brett of the movie *The Time Machine*. Reflecting on the technical advances he had witnessed already in his lifetime, he wondered what the next millennium might have in store.

CHAPTER TWELVE

"Science Yoda"

Monday, January 17th, 2000
Spectrum Genomics Microarray Facility

COMPUTER PROCESSES had more or less returned to normal by the second week in January. Thoroughly absorbed in microarray data from the previous day's run, now graphically displayed on his computer screen, Roberts was startled by the sound of a loud and throaty motorcycle pulling into the front parking lot. The rider revved it a few times before killing the engine. Several minutes later, a tall and powerful looking man strode confidently down the hall. Roberts turned to see the man standing outside his office. He wore faded blue jeans and a grey T-shirt emblazoned with a Norton Motorcycles logo, with black military boots and a brown bomber jacket to compliment the badass personae he was channeling. His exceptionally large head was bald and tanned except for a sidewall of prematurely grey hair tied back in a ponytail.

The man opened the door before Roberts could wave him in.

"You must be Roberts," he said, then pulled up a chair and rested his boots on top of Brett's desk.

"Um, Yes, and you are…"

"Calvin Schwarzkopf." He smiled confidently, revealing an impressive set of perfectly white teeth.

Roberts recognized the name. The man was a legend in the genomics community, having founded a company that had helped revolutionize the field of automated DNA sequencing. Most major sequencing labs were now using his instruments and hardware.

Roberts also knew the guy was a molecular millionaire, having sold his company to a much larger conglomerate the year before.

"It's a pleasure to meet you, Dr. Schwarzkopf.

"Call me Cal, if you like. 'The chairman' sent me over," he said matter-of-factly. This was Schwarzkopf's preferred nickname for Jeremy Watts, president and co-founder of Spectrum Genomics.

He flashed Roberts another one of his game show host smiles. The man was apparently taking over and there was nothing Roberts could do to stop him.

"I thought you retired, heard you'd bought a ranch in the Sierras."

"Yeah, my wife and kids are up there now. But I'm not built for retirement, kid. Never was, and never will be. Anyway, your chairman hired me on as a consultant, asked me to come over here and see what I could do with the place."

He swung his boots back down to the floor and readied himself to stand. "By the way, where's my office? The chairman said I could have the one your division's former president vacated after the acquisition."

The ex-Stanford professor who had founded Brett's microarray division left shortly after selling it to Spectrum Genomics, which was soon followed by the installation of the new Spectrum Genomics sign out front. Roberts and Westfield were left in charge of microarray operations, although Roberts now suspected that Spectrum's president might be thinking about going in a different direction. Maybe with 'Cal' at the helm.

It didn't take long for Schwarzkopf to familiarize himself with the inner workings of the microarray facility. He spent most of his mornings interviewing lab technicians, bioinformatics specialists, and even the production personnel. And most afternoons he was in Westfield's office analyzing the volumes of microarray data that had been logged over the previous twelve months. Schwarzkopf was already convinced that significant process improvements would need to be made.

The corner office was now littered with the guts of vintage motorcycle engines that Schwarzkopf seemed to always be restoring. Spectrum's president had approved this eccentric hobby to keep him on site whenever an engineer might need his advice or assistance. Quite a number of engineers from Spectrum's sequencing facility in Palo Alto had transferred over to assist Schwarzkopf, who they considered inspirational beyond measure. With little automation left to perfect on the sequencing floor, they were more than eager to hammer out a better microarray process.

Cal was adept at massaging their eccentric egos. He presented them each with a T-shirt to commemorate their transfer to "the dark side", emblazoned with a customized <u>M</u>icroarray <u>A</u>dvanced <u>D</u>esign and <u>D</u>evelopment <u>G</u>roup logo on the front, or MADDOG for short. Schwarzkopf's newly deputized engineers had an annoying habit of growling at the beginning of every group meeting.

Roberts and Eric's teams had wisely elected to join the effort. Together they made incremental modifications to every step of microarray production, including major upgrades in automation for printing the microarrays.

Within the span of just four weeks, the analytical performance of the microarrays had already been dramatically improved.

Schwarzkopf called a meeting in the 'fish bowl' to review the data, a conference room built in middle of the facility with tall glass panel side walls. The MADDOG engineers were already seated around the back part of the conference table when the Roberts and Westfield teams arrived, no doubt basking in the glory of their extraordinary automation improvements. Schwarzkopf arrived late, making his typically dramatic entrance and pulled a chair away from the table so he could stretch his legs. "Who wants to go first?"

The MADDOG engineers showed videos of their upgraded liquid handling robots and microarray print heads in action. Robert's group gave a tag team Power Point presentation describing their improved process for amplifying and labeling the extracted RNA with florescent dyes. Westfield's group showed gene expression data demonstrating the improved analytical performance of the microarrays. The results were actually much better than any had anticipated. All three teams broke into a unifying round of applause when Schwarzkopf switched back on the lights.

Schwarzkopf waited until he had everyone's attention. "Ladies, Gentlemen, and Dogs." He paused a moment to give the engineers a chance to growl. Then he continued, "Through your collective efforts, we now possess the most accurate and precise microarrays in the industry. Remember folks, we all did this together as a team. I think you deserve to give yourselves another hand."

After those gathered had quieted down once more, Schwarzkopf smiled and glanced around the room, nodding to each one of them in turn for appropriate recognition. Then came his surprise announcement.

"In recognition for all your hard work, I'd like to invite you all up to my humble little ranch house in the mountains for the weekend. That'll be just a little over two weeks from today, so consider yourselves forewarned. Food and drinks will be provided, among other things...." His Cheshire smile hinted that there may be more than booze involved.

Roberts walked down to Westfield's office a half hour later. Inspired by Schwarzkopf's recent data review, Westfield was now busy reviewing his microarray validation experiments in much finer detail.

"Dude, the reproducibility of this data is incredible," said Westfield. "Here, take a look at this." He turned around his computer monitor for Roberts to see the x-y precision plot he'd just generated.

Westfield stroked his bearded chin. "Most of our commercial microarrays appear to be okay, but we should probably start re-manufacturing our custom arrays."

Roberts winced when he realized that the results from Janet Feinstein's most recent experiments might not be as precise as they should have been. "Feinstein will probably be pissed once she learns about these improvements in our printing process. Think we could bump up the Brain Array as a high priority?"

"I'll alert my team. If all goes well, we should be able to get Version 2 in production by the middle of next week."

"Thanks, buddy. Feinstein will probably still be pissed, but at least I can tell her we're on it." As Roberts spoke these words, he realized that Westfield was no longer listening. "What's on your mind Eric?"

Westfield swiveled away from the window and returned his attention to Roberts. After a brief hesitation, shrugged sheepishly. "Tell you what. Wendy's away on a business trip. How'd you like to come by my place after work tomorrow to listen to some music? I could barbeque a couple of fresh sword fish steaks on the grill." He paused again before continuing. "Actually, there's something else I'd like to talk you about, considering you're the only guy I know who's still happily married. You think Ruth would be okay with you sacrificing your Friday night for a friend?"

Roberts figured it might have to do with Wendy. "I'll ask Ruth."

Roberts tested out his new cell phone while driving through Niles Canyon. It surprised him to hear the call going through considering the spotty reception that was typical along that route.

"Hey Ruth, how was your day?"

"Hello dear! The boys and I had a nice day. I took them to the playground after school. Thomas still plays mostly by himself, although Michael seems to have made a few friends. Where are you?"

"Still in Niles canyon. How's the reception?"

"Pretty good for a change. What's so important that it couldn't wait until you got home?"

"Remember we talked about going out to dinner tomorrow night?"

"Of course. I've already got a sitter lined up." *This had better be good,* she was probably thinking.

"Eric invited me over…."

"You? Not us?"

"He wants to talk to me about Wendy. I think he's planning on asking her to marry him. Would you mind?"

"Wow, that's exciting! No, I don't mind in that case. But you'll have to make it up to me," she teased.

"Tell you what, how about I call the Blue Dolphin right after this and make reservations for Saturday night?"

"You're on."

This was going to cost him. The Blue Dolphin was one of the more expensive restaurants in downtown Pleasanton, although it also happened to be one of Ruth's favorites, with an exotic menu of Veracruz themed Mexican dishes and an abundant selection of rare tequilas. He figured he'd wait until after that dinner to mention Schwarzkopf's party up in the Sierra foothills. Spouses and significant others had not been invited. "And don't worry about the dishes tonight, I'll do them when I get home." He was probably going to need those extra brownie points.

Eric Westfield lived in the upscale bedroom community of Lafayette, which was located about seven miles east of downtown Berkeley. Most of Eric's neighbors were UC professors and similarly educated professionals. He'd managed the down payment by exercising his stock options from a previous biotech company that went public shortly after he joined.

Roberts felt a bit odd about not having Ruth along. Ruth and Wendy had become close friends. He pulled into the driveway and shut off the engine. Must be nice living on two incomes with no kids to support, he mused. He heard jazz fusion music playing from inside, getting louder as he approached the front door, and wisely chose to use the door chime instead of knocking.

Westfield unlatched the door and opened it with his shoe while supporting two glasses of Pinot Gris. He handed one to Roberts. "Come on in, Brett. Really appreciate you coming by."

"Thanks for inviting me." Roberts noted that Eric's face looked a bit drawn.

Westfield led them to the back room and motioned for Roberts to take a seat on the sofa while he went out to start the grill, leaving the sliding glass door open so they could talk. Roberts admired the music console along the side wall while he listened to the music. He couldn't imagine how much those stereo components must have cost, and the twin Bose tower speakers in each corner sounded incredible. Westfield had also amassed a considerable music library, with hundreds of vinyl albums and CDs lining the shelves.

Westfield hollered in, "Hope Ruth didn't mind you coming solo tonight."

"I told her I thought you might want to talk about asking Wendy to marry you, hope that was okay."

Westfield didn't answer right away. But then he said, "Sorry about getting your hopes up."

"Not having second thoughts, are you? C'mon, man. You two are perfect for each other." From the awkward silence that followed, Roberts immediately surmised that he'd said the wrong thing.

"Wendy left a voice message from the airport this afternoon." Westfield sounded upset.

"Hold on, mind if I join you out there?" said Roberts.

"Sure man, if you like."

Roberts stepped out to the patio and rubbed his hands together. "A bit chilly out here, don't you think?"

"You'll get used to it. Here, take this scraper and clean off the grill. I'll be back in a minute." Westfield went back to the kitchen and returned with a butcher wrapped package from the fish market. Roberts stood by while Westfield dropped two swordfish steaks onto the grill and jiggled them with his spatula. They began to sizzle. He took another sip of wine while Westfield flipped them over and dabbed on a basting of melted garlic butter. A delicious smell soon wafted up from the grill.

Roberts was curious what the problem with Wendy might be, although clearly Westfield wasn't quite ready to talk about it. He decided to change the subject.

"Schwarzkopf seemed to hint that there might be drugs at the party. Any idea what he meant exactly?"

"Yeah, I've got a pretty good idea. Schwarzkopf's certainly been known to drop acid on occasion."

"How'd you know that?"

"Cal used to be one of Ken Kesey's Merry Pranksters. He told me once."

"Seriously?" Roberts remembered reading Kesey's book *The Electric Kool-Aid Acid Test* back in college. Those Kool-Aid laced acid trips were legendary. But he needed to ask, "You planning on trying it?"

"No man, I've got way too much on my mind right now to go tripping off like that."

Roberts felt relieved. "I hoped you might say that. I'm not sure I could handle it either."

"Really, why's that?" asked Eric. He flipped the fish once more and added a final basting.

"I'll tell you after dinner."

"Fair enough."

Eric's swordfish steaks were cooked to perfection like always. He carried the platter over to the patio table and returned to the kitchen for place settings and serving bowls of fresh asparagus and brown rice. "Oh yeah, one more thing." He went back for the bottle of Pinot Gris and refreshed Brett's glass before settling in.

"Thanks. Hey, it's really nice outside right now." Stars were just beginning to emerge from the darkening sky, more bright and numerous than Roberts had seen in quite a while.

"Told you you'd get used to it." Westfield reached out with his glass. "Cheers, my friend." They clinked glasses. "Thanks, buddy. Hope things are okay with you and Wendy."

They took a few bites and enjoyed a comfortable silence until Roberts finally yielded to his mounting curiosity. "Okay, what gives?"

"You go first...."

"Um, what was that again?"

"Cal hinted there may be drugs at the party, and you were about to tell me why that bothers you. C'mon, man, let's hear it."

Roberts struggled to find the right words. He'd never discussed his DMT experience anyone except Mudford, not even his wife.

"I tried a drug called *yopo* once back in graduate school, a short-lived but surprisingly powerful hallucinogen. Gave me recurrent nightmares for years. I've also tried mushrooms, and even though they seemed okay, I'm just wary of LSD for some reason. So there you have it. Look, I'd rather not talk about this anymore, at least not right now." He shivered involuntarily and willed Virtanen's image to fade back into the recesses of his mind.

"Fair enough." Westfield swallowed his last bite of swordfish and washed it down with another sip of wine. He set the glass back down and blew out slowly. "Okay, guess it's my turn now, so here goes. Wendy called to tell me she's moving out. Seems she's fallen for some guy she's been traveling around with for work."

"*What?* You two seemed so right together."

"Yeah, well apparently she's more into those GQ types."

Roberts could tell even by starlight how much it pained his friend to be having this discussion. "Eric, I'm so sorry."

Westfield picked up the plates and started to carry them back to the kitchen but Roberts refused. "Give me those, I'll clean up. Go relax and find us another CD to listen to."

Roberts grinned when he heard the familiar intro to Pink Floyd's *Dark Side of the Moon*, an excellent choice. He called out from the kitchen for Westfield to turn up the volume. After rinsing the last piece of kitchenware and placing it in the drying rack next to the sink, he returned to the living room and took a seat next to Westfield on the leather sofa facing the speakers. Westfield poured two glasses of a freshly uncorked bottle of Merlot and handed one to Roberts.

They listened to the entire album, front to back, without another word.

Later the following week, Schwarzkopf figured it might be a good idea to check on Westfield. The kid had been acting a bit distant lately, keeping mostly to himself. He poked his head into Westfield's office with his usual bluster. "How's it going, Eric? You've seemed a lot quieter than usual lately, and for you that's saying something."

Westfield looked up and waved him in to have a seat. Schwarzkopf could be a bull in a china shop sometimes, although the guy did seem to genuinely care about people he worked with. Westfield decided to give him the short version.

Schwarzkopf responded with, "Man, I'm really sorry to hear that. I can imagine how you must be feeling right now, having gone through a couple wives myself already. But trust me, you'll soon find yourself in a much better place. Just takes time. Tell you what, how'd you like come by my boat and have dinner tonight? I've got a mooring over in Redwood City."

Docktown Marina was a by-the-month slip rental along Redwood Creek, a meandering slough about four miles south of the San Mateo Bridge. Westfield wasn't exactly sure he was in the right place until he spotted Schwarzkopf's 1953 Norton Manx parked over by the marina building. Pristine and gleaming in the setting sunlight, the Norton looked out of place with the unkempt jumble of houseboats and dilapidated powerboats tied up along the quarter mile stretch of wooden dock.

Nothing elegant about this place, thought Westfield as he stepped down onto the cracked asphalt. He followed Schwarzkopf's hastily scribbled directions and counted four slips down to an aging cabin cruiser, about forty five feet long with *Proud Mary* painted across the stern in fading black letters and a blue plastic tarp draped over the front cabin. The roof leaked, apparently. He checked his map to make sure he had the right slip.

"Hello?" Westfield called down.

Schwarzkopf poked his head out the companionway and beamed when he spotted Eric.

"Permission to come aboard?" Westfield hoped he knew what he was doing. How well did he actually know this guy? Schwarzkopf climbed up and batted the dust off the bench seats before waving Westfield aboard.

"How about a beer?" Without waiting for an answer, Schwarzkopf nimbly climbed back down to the galley and popped open a couple of cold ones before handing one up to Westfield. "How'd you like your steak?"

Westfield could hear them sizzling already. "Medium rare would be great."

"Coming right up," Schwarzkopf hollered up from the galley and quickly flipped each steak over with a crackling sear. Then he added, "How do you like my place? Not much of a boat, but the rent's cheap."

"No man, I mean, this is really nice." Westfield looked across the channel to a dredged inlet where a new housing project was under construction.

"You about done with that beer?" Schwarzkopf hollered up.

Westfield passed down the empty, surprised that he'd polished it off already. Minutes later, Schwarzkopf handed up two steaming platters with the steaks and sides of rice and coleslaw. "Careful man, they're hot." He returned topside with silverware and napkins in one hand and a couple more beers in the other.

Schwarzkopf settled onto the opposite bench with his plate in his lap. "Bon appetite!" He began carving up his steak.

Westfield took another sip of beer. "Thanks Cal. It's peaceful out here on the water."

"Yeah, you almost can't hear the traffic back there on Highway 101, most nights anyway. So talk to me Westfield. How are you feeling?"

"Well I guess I feel betrayed, angry, hurt… did I say angry?"

"Like I said, I can definitely relate to that. But you know what? Sometimes you need to say fuck it and move on. How long were you and Wendy together anyway?"

"Couple a years, I guess." Westfield took another sip of beer to buy time, then finished it off.

"Want another one?"

"Um no, I think I'm good now."

"How about some pot, then? Come on man, it'll do you good." Westfield didn't consider long before nodding yes. It did sound like a good idea…. A cool salt breeze wafted in from the bay. Then a fog horn sounded off in the distance. Stars began appearing in the nighttime sky.

Schwarzkopf fumbled in a drawer down in the galley until he found the cassette tape he wanted to play. He popped it into the deck and then cranked up the volume. It happened to be one of Westfield's favorite

Grateful Dead albums. Schwarzkopf climbed back up the ladder, now clutching a baggie of pot in one hand and a can of salted cashews in the other, just in case.

The cashews were almost gone by the time they had finished the joint. Schwarzkopf flicked the stub overboard and decided it was time to break the peaceful silence. "Have you had a chance yet to see *The Matrix*?" Schwarzkopf was more than eager to describe the plot after Westfield shook his head no.

The movie was a futuristic adventure about human beings who had been plugged into a mainframe computer since the day they were born. Everything they experienced entered their minds through a fiber optic cable connected to the back of their skulls, which made them believe they were living in a three-dimensional universe, when actually their physical bodies were suspended in some sort of oxygenated bio-fluid, each one inside their own egg-shaped pod, with tiers upon tiers of these pods surrounding the mainframe.

But some of them had actually managed to disconnect themselves from the mainframe and escape. They now lived underground and were plotting to destroy the mainframe and free the others. The movie was intended to convey a sense of purpose, of striving for free will, even if it meant the loss of safety and comfort.

Schwarzkopf continued, "Kinda makes you wonder what human consciousness is all about, huh? What it means to be alive?"

"Guess I'll have to see the movie," Westfield answered matter-of-factly. He was too stoned at the moment to fathom this puzzle, although he made a mental note to revisit it later. Schwarzkopf had indeed asked an interesting question.

"Well, looks like the fog's about to roll back in," said Schwarzkopf. He lit another joint and took another hit before handing it over to Westfield. "Here buddy, better enjoy them stars up above, they'll be gone soon."

They gazed up to the stars for a long while without speaking, and sure enough, the fog eventually rolled in and hid them from view.

"Thanks Cal, guess I needed this little break from reality."

"Feeling better?"

"Maybe just a little."

"Listen Eric, feel free to stop back by here any time. Always happy to listen. But there's one thing I want you to take away with you."

"What's that?" asked Westfield.

Schwarzkopf reached over and slapped Westfield's thigh, hard. "Ow!" said Westfield.

Cal said, "Feel that? We humans are capable of interacting with the world in so many unpredictable ways. We are *not* part of the matrix, don't let anyone make you think differently. Hell, we're all unique in our own way. Believe in yourself Eric, I do."

This was the last thing Westfield had expected to hear from Schwarzkopf. It was also something he felt he could use. What had happened with Wendy would not define him. He pushed himself up off the seat and waited to regain his balance before climbing out of the boat.

Westfield and Roberts rumbled noisily east on Interstate 580 the following Saturday morning. They had just begun their descent into the Central Valley, on their way to Schwarzkopf's place in the Sierra foothills. Westfield's 1969 Volvo sedan had over 360,000 miles on it and was still truckin' despite its dented exterior. He'd owned it since college and had recently equipped it with one the finest sound systems that money could buy. Being an eclectic audiophile, he couldn't have survived his daily commute without his tunes. For today's drive he'd loaded the 6-CD changer in his trunk with an assortment of Grateful Dead albums.

Westfield seemed intent on driving so Roberts amused himself by looking out the window and counting the cows scattered about the rolling hills of freshly sprouted spring grass. He figured that Westfield didn't want to talk about Wendy. The wound was probably still too fresh. He came home from work last Monday and all her stuff was gone. She hadn't even left a note. Then the song *Casey Jones* came on and Westfield cranked up the volume. He started tapping away on the steering wheel. Roberts thought he might have just caught the first hint of a smile from his friend.

Westfield finally spoke. "You know what? I'm done feeling sorry for myself."

"Good to hear. You sure you're okay?"

"Yeah, I've decided to let it go. We weren't all that compatible anyway. She kept trying to make me get a haircut and wear nicer clothes. Never really liked my music. Guess I'd rather just let it go."

"Schwarzkopf's party might be a welcome distraction, in that case. Ruth even thought it was a good idea. Says I've been working too hard lately."

"Now that's funny," Westfield grinned. "You've always been like that."

"Yeah, I know." Roberts started slapping the dashboard like a drum in time with the music.

"Nothing like the Dead to liven your mood, eh?" said Westfield. "Why don't you reach into that cooler on the back seat and grab us each a beer?"

"Coming right up, my friend."

The deck clicked over to the next CD, Grateful Dead's last album *Terrapin Station*, as they left the sprawling inland port of Stockton behind and continued east on Highway 4.

Westfield figured it was time. "But there is something else I'd like to share with you, if you're up for it. That *yopo* experience you mentioned got me curious about DMT, the active ingredient. Thought I'd do a bit of background research on that. Ever heard about a psychiatrist named Dr. Rick Strassman?" He glanced right to see if Roberts was interested.

"No, but I expect I'm about to."

"You okay with that?"

"Sure man, go ahead."

Westfield glanced around to make sure no other cars were nearby and quickly took a sip of beer. "Alright then. So this guy ran a controlled clinical study on the effects of DMT back in the early 1990s. This was the first time DMT had ever been investigated systematically in a hospital environment. Over the span of five years, his team at the University of New Mexico administered over 400 doses of DMT to 60 human volunteers."

"You mean they actually got away with that?"

"Yep. IRB approved protocol, informed consent, the whole shebang. Most of the subjects described remarkably similar sensations of leaving their physical body while under the influence of DMT. More than half of them reported visiting some sort of spiritual or divine realm, like being inside a white and fluffy cloud with trumpets playing off in the distance, or choirs singing wordlessly. Some described unusual encounters with elf-like beings, while others seemed convinced they'd been talking with angels. A few even believed they'd actually experienced God Himself. Any of those visions sound familiar, Brett?"

Roberts turned the sound knob down on the stereo so he could think. "Perhaps in some respects, at first anyway, but then my mind suddenly got hijacked, like I'd completely lost control."

Westfield gripped the wheel. *Oops.* "That's right, you mentioned something about nightmares. Sorry Brett, I probably shouldn't have brought this up."

"That's okay," said Roberts. "What else did you learn?"

Westfield continued, "According to some of the studies I've read, there may be a biological explanation for the effects of DMT. It's only two enzymatic reaction steps away from the amino acid precursor tryptophan. Endogenous levels of DMT have been detected in human urine, blood, and cerebrospinal fluid. A recent study even supported the idea that DMT may be a natural neurotransmitter. Still interested?"

"Sure, why not," said Roberts.

"Okay, back to Strassman. He wrote a bunch of essays afterward about the metaphysical implications of his DMT findings. Some of his ideas are pretty out there, but check this out. His thesis is that DMT may be secreted by the pineal gland, an organ inside the brain that becomes fully functional on the forty-ninth day of fetal development. According to the Tibetan Book of the Dead, this also corresponds to the number of days it would take for the soul of a dead person to reincarnate. Makes you wonder, doesn't it?"

Roberts was beginning to feel like a recovered alcoholic who'd just fallen off the wagon. No, best to let it go. "I don't know, man." He shook his head and reached down to turn the stereo back up.

Westfield decided to focus on driving as they began their winding ascent into the Sierra Foothills, which was perfectly fine with Roberts. They passed a sign marking the historic mining town of Whisky and followed the directions on Schwarzkopf's invitation by making a right onto a gravel road that led up to the top. The Volvo's tires crunched upward until they reached an overlook with a spectacular view of the town.

Schwarzkopf's current wife had wisely left with the kids to visit her mother in Chico that weekend. Their "humble little ranch" at the top of the bluff had two ranch style wings spanning a tall octagonal structure with twelve-foot high glass panel windows front and back and a vaulted ceiling above. Schwarzkopf's family obviously resided in the two-story wing to the left. The right wing appeared to house an array of guest rooms.

As they drew nearer, Roberts also realized that the central structure was actually a conference room, with rows of chairs for about 50 people and a tall projection screen facing the valley. *Not a bad place for a scientific retreat,* he thought to himself.

Cal and several other members of the MADDOG crew were lounging in beach chairs to the right side of the gateway entrance.

Roberts rolled down the window, "Quite a place you've got here, Cal." Schwarzkopf flashed one of his signature white-toothed smiles and handed up a bottle of Courvoisier, waited for each of them to have a swig, and then pointed to a makeshift parking lot over by the Tiki hut, a recent construction project that appeared amusingly out of place.

As expected, the guest rooms took up most of the right-hand wing. Each room featured a pair of bunk beds along the side walls and a set of reading desk/dresser bureau consoles along the front wall beneath panel windows looking out to a panoramic view of the valley. Sleeping arrangements had been pre-assigned, although they would not necessarily be adhered to, especially among the younger scientists hoping for hookups later that night.

Roberts and Westfield had a room to themselves, being in management after all. They unpacked their things, then exited a side door and followed the sign-marked path through a stand of blue-green pine trees. This led them to a green meadow along the bluff with colorful tables set up for the evening fiesta and stacks of beach chairs for the guests to use and take home afterwards, each bearing a customized Spectrum Genomics logo for the Microarray Division. Roberts and Westfield headed to one of the ice chests and grabbed a cold Dos Equis to sip on while they mingled.

Most of their co-workers appeared to be mixing well after the past month's intensive improvement effort. Brett's senior technician Anthony was talking with Rita from Westfield's team. Evidently he'd finally gotten the nerve, and they seemed to be hitting it off despite their five-year age difference. Anthony had joined the company straight out of Stanford with a Bachelor's degree in human genetics, whereas Rita had completed a medical degree and a year of residency before deciding she much preferred lab work. Several of the MADDOG engineers appeared to be vying for Sasha's attention, a shy and voluptuous visiting scientist from Jordan. Someone had started a rumor that she'd be belly dancing later on. Mindy was drop dead gorgeous as always.

Two members of the production team started tossing a Frisbee back and forth and Roberts and Westfield went over to join them. Gradually the circle expanded with multiple Frisbees flying around. Mindy ran over and mischievously snatched the one before Roberts could catch it. "Hey!" he said. She giggled and tossed it back across.

The final rays of sunlight disappeared into a radiant display of red spectrum hues. Schwarzkopf returned wearing a serape and sombrero. He hollered out in a lousy Mexican accent, "Buenas noches, *mis compadres! Y bien venidos* a *mi casa!* We have got a fine evening planned *jou*, so everybody better have a good time. *Vamos amigos!* Let's party!"

A trio of mariachi musicians emerged from the pine trees and started to play. Then a team of food servers in white uniforms marched out to the buffet tables. Almost in unison, they lifted the lids to reveal a medley of Mexican dishes, sizzling steak and chicken fajitas, pork carnitas, Chile Verde, even Red Snapper Veracruz. A pair of brown-skinned Oaxaca women began pressing and grilling fresh tortillas at the end of each line and handed them out still hot and steaming.

When the mariachi musicians had quietly left the scene, with the guests now satiated and leaning back in their beach chairs on the cool wet grass, Schwarzkopf decided it was time. He hoisted himself out of his chair, carried it over to a fire pit near the edge of the bluff, and struck a match to light the bonfire. Partiers noticed the flames rising and began carting their own chairs over to join Schwarzkopf. When they had settled in a circle around the crackling fire, one of the MADDOG engineers swung a guitar to his knee and strummed the first few familiar chords to a Neil Young classic, *Needle and the Damage Done.* Drunken revelers joined in at the chorus.

How appropriate, thought Roberts, who tried to sing along but couldn't quite hit the high notes. Then he remembered a hand drum he'd brought along that was still in the trunk of Westfield's Volvo. "Hey Eric, can I borrow your keys?" He returned to rejoin the circle and softly kept rhythm with his drum between his knees. After a dozen or more such 60s rock ballads, ending with *Can't Find My Way Home* by Blind Faith, the guitarist stopped playing and everyone quieted down. Schwarzkopf chose the moment to produce a plastic bag with sugar cubes inside and whispered just loud enough to be heard above the crackling fire, "Any of you beautiful people fancy a drop of acid?" Having caught their attention, he added, "Not to worry, I diluted down the dose. Shouldn't last more than an hour."

About half of the younger revelers reached out to accept one of the cubes and pop it into their mouths. Westfield and Roberts demurred.

"Sorry Cal, not tonight," said Westfield.

"Me neither, Cal," said Roberts. "Not sure I could handle it." He fought to regain his composure after this admission.

Schwarzkopf understood Westfield's answer, but Roberts had peaked his curiosity. "What makes you say that, Brett?"

"It's nothing, really." Roberts said.

Schwarzkopf nodded, sensing he'd struck a nerve. "Come on kid, enlighten me."

Roberts hesitated. "Okay, so I tried something called *yopo* once back in graduate school. Didn't like it at all, bum trip I guess."

Schwarzkopf slapped his knee. "*Ayahuasca!* I've tried that shit a few times myself. Indigenous tribes throughout the Amazon rainforest all use similar plant extracts containing DMT to communicate with the spirit world, but all I ever got out of it was a sense of utter weirdness. One time I experienced a bunch of munchkin-like fellers jumping in and out, couldn't figure out what the hell they wanted. Pretty amazing what the brain can do on hallucinogens, don't you think?"

"I guess, but I'm not keen on trying it again."

Schwarzkopf studied Roberts intently. The kid seemed rattled. *Hmm*, he wondered. Roberts had recently completed a large study with Janet Feinstein on brain signaling pathways. *Yeah, that must be it.* He too was on a quest to understand the workings of the human mind, and also a bit afraid of what he might learn once he got there, evidently.

Cal set down the bag of sugar cubes and fingered for a joint inside his shirt pocket. He casually positioned it in the corner of his mouth and struck a wooden match to light up. After taking a long drag, he passed the joint over to Westfield and returned his attention to Roberts. "It sent you out there somewhere, didn't it Brett? The spirit world, maybe? I'll bet that spirit stuff bothers you."

"Not really," Roberts lied. "Just wasn't able to control the experience."

Schwarzkopf could easily tell from Brett's veiled expression that he'd been right, but decided to let it go. "Well for me the high was more like a wild-ass bungee mind jump. Just when you're about to lose your shit, you get yanked back to reality."

Roberts settled back in his chair and feigned disinterest. He accepted the joint from Westfield as a distraction.

But Schwarzkopf persisted, "It doesn't mean our conscious mind is always in control. Although personally, I find what's happening in our subconscious mind to be a lot more interesting."

Schwarzkopf studied Roberts some more. The way Brett rubbed his hands together was a dead giveaway. He'd file that away for future consideration.

"Go ahead and keep that joint. I'd better go check on the others and make sure nobody wanders off until they've stopped tripping."

Cal hoisted himself up and gave them each a bow. "Have a good time, gentlemen, and enjoy the rest of your night."

Roberts heard ankle bells and turned in that direction to see Sasha approaching, now dressed in her belly dancing costume. He surmised from her uneven gait that Sasha may have had one drink too many, although she regained her balance once she started dancing. Mindy went over to join her and soon both were writhing sexily to the rhythm of Sasha's hand chimes. The MADDOG engineers were attracted back to the fire pit like moths, but Sasha tired quickly and called it a night. People began returning to their rooms. Roberts spotted Anthony walking back with Rita. *Good for them*, he thought to himself.

With just the two of them left to tend the dying embers, Roberts glanced upward and froze in amazement as he began to study the majestic band of the Milky Way splayed across the sky, its stars glistening like finely powdered diamonds. He imagined himself as just a micro speck on a tiny little planet, in a galaxy surrounded by super novae and black holes....

Westfield shook his arm and said, "Dude, you about ready to hit the hay?"

Roberts released a long sigh and readied himself to stand. "Yeah, probably a good idea."

Luisa could almost reach Roberts during such brief moments as this one now, when his earthly mind was almost open. She also sensed the young man's gift of spiritual resonance, although clearly still unaware of his ability. Which brought her back to her original question: *how had my son managed to connect with this Brett Roberts?*

CHAPTER THIRTEEN

"Yoda must die"

JANET FEINSTEIN had actually demanded a complete re-design of the Brain Microarray. Her post-docs had scoured the literature to identify newly discovered genes of potential importance to brain biochemistry. These included genes associated neuronal differentiation, signal transduction across synapses, and other proteins thought to be essential for growth and metabolism. They even identified a handful of genes thought to be associated with dementia and Alzheimer's disease.

Feinstein's lab had also perfected a method for culturing stem cells in a petri dish and coaxing them to differentiate into neurons. They would stimulate them with a tiny electrode and measure their response using an instrument capable of detecting extremely low levels of electromagnetic wave emissions. RNA was then extracted to query their gene expression patterns. A control plate of neurons was similarly extracted, having not undergone electronic stimulation. The resulting genetic material was shipped on dry ice to Spectrum's microarray facility for analysis.

Roberts sat at his desk and stared at a recently generated heat map showing which genes were differentially expressed during one of Feinstein's experiments. Spots corresponding to genes that had been stimulated by the electrode were colored in red or yellow, whereas lesser expressing genes had colors ranging from green to pale blue. He leaned back in his chair while considering the implications.

Hmm, thought Roberts, such an approach could also be used to elucidate gene expression patterns while under the stimulation of DMT. He wondered, but then he shook his head. Why was he so obsessed with this topic? *Okay, that's enough,* Roberts struggled to convince himself.

He clicked out of the data window on his screen and then opened another file containing gene expression data from children with osteosarcomas.

Saturday, May 6th, 2000
Whiskey, California

It was a crisp Saturday morning, with the fresh smell of wet pine needles in the air after last night's rainstorm. Schwarzkopf had allegedly taken the weekend off to spend time with his family at the ranch house, although the real reason was now resting on its kickstand in the Quonset hut along with his other motorcycles. He'd just reconnected the fuel line to his newly restored 1942 Indian Scout. Such a beauty. Schwarzkopf had searched for months to find the replacement parts to rebuild this engine. He stepped back to admire his work. Yeah, time for a test drive. He strapped on his skid helmet and straddled the beast, stomped down hard on the starter peddle and waited for the idle to even while the cylinder head heated up. He eased it down the gravel road to the highway and then leaned forward and cranked the throttle with extreme acceleration, hugging the turns with the wind against his face.

Two days later, Professor Feinstein stopped by Brett's office unannounced to pay him a compliment, something she almost never did. "Dr. Roberts, your Version 2 Brain Array has been performing beautifully. The gene expression results from our last week's experiments were particularly spectacular."

"Wow. Thanks, Professor Feinstein."

She said, "You may call me Janet," and smiled for maybe the first time ever afterwards.

The phone started ringing and Roberts answered. It was Schwarzkopf's wife, calling from their ranch home in Whiskey. Brett's expression darkened as he listened to the news.

"What?" Feinstein asked urgently once he'd hung up the phone.

"Schwarzkopf had a tragic motorcycle accident over the weekend. Evidently his prognosis is not good."

Janet's eyes teared up almost immediately. "My God! How bad is it?"

"Severed his spinal cord. The doctors doubt he'll ever walk again. He also suffered massive internal injuries."

"Sorry, I have to go." Feinstein rose abruptly and dashed out of Brett's office. She seemed truly shaken.

Roberts hadn't known until just that moment that Feinstein and Schwarzkopf were close. The two of them had collaborated on numerous research projects over the years, many of them designed to probe human brain function at the molecular level. They also shared a certain renegade tendency to cut corners when planning their experiments.

Roberts was likewise unaware of their most recent collaboration, and wouldn't suspect until later that it had been focused on brain activity around the time of death. In fact, the tissue samples that Feinstein sent over the previous week had come from brain surgery patients who had expired only moments before.

Schwarzkopf's condition continued to worsen over the weeks that followed. A specialized medical staff was dispatched to his ranch home in Whiskey to attend to him 24/7. They'd recently increased his morphine dosage to alleviate the pain.

Now leaderless, the MADDOG team showed up later and later each day, sometimes not at all. Many had wisely chosen to exercise their company stock options once it hit $200 a share. Most of them now drove expensive sports cars. One had recently purchased a new Ferrari Testarossa.

Roberts picked up the phone and dialed Schwarzkopf's wife to ask how he was doing. A nurse answered, but then handed the phone over to Mrs. Schwarzkopf after Roberts introduced himself.

"Hello Brett, so nice of you to call."

"I was just wondering about Cal, hope you don't mind."

"Not at all. Here, he says he'd like to talk with you."

Roberts heard a wrenching groan of anguish and then a rustling noise with the phone. Schwarzkopf struggled to clear his throat, his voice a gravelly whisper. "Hello there, Roberts."

"Hello Cal. Hope I haven't called at a bad time."

"No, glad you called. They just needed to prop my head up so I could talk. By the way, how's that new Brain Microarray been working for you? Janet still happy with the data?"

"She said the latest results have been spectacular, her words exactly."

A long pause followed. Roberts was about to hang up when Schwarzkopf spoke again in a stronger voice. "That's great to hear. You guys have all done a fantastic job, you and Westfield especially."

"Thanks, Cal. That means a lot coming from you."

Schwarzkopf continued, "Yeah, yeah, but listen Roberts. Those MADDOG engineers need a tight hand at the wheel, and it doesn't look like I'll be coming back to work any time soon. I'd like them to report to you and Westfield in the interim. Discuss that with Westfield and merge them into your teams."

"Cal, I don't think that will be necessary..." but there was a click on the other end of the line, and then silence.

On Sunday morning, Schwarzkopf's wife contacted a handful of his closest and dearest friends to give them a dire update. Schwarzkopf's doctor didn't think he'd make it through the night. Janet Feinstein wept softly after hanging up the phone.

What happened next had been carefully orchestrated by Schwarzkopf against Feinstein's strong objections. A nurse had videotaped Schwarzkopf's informed consent to the procedure, and after viewing it, Feinstein grudgingly agreed to participate.

She summoned her team to load up the medical van and they sped off through the Central Valley without running the siren, not wanting to draw more attention to their mission than absolutely necessary, and arrived at Schwarzkopf's ranch in the Sierra foothills around 2 PM.

The chairs had been removed from the conference center, being the only room large enough to accommodate the portable operating suite. Feinstein's team was now there waiting patiently in surgical scrubs for her to give the signal. She snapped on a fresh pair of latex gloves and nodded for the orderly to wheel in Schwarzkopf's gurney. His morphine drip had been reduced to a sub-optimal dose so he'd remain conscious during the procedure.

One nurse hooked up the leads for recording Schwarzkopf's vital signs while another shaved the sides of his head. Feinstein stood by and watched their hurried preparations, unable to conceal her worry behind the face shield.

She reached for his hand. "Are you ready, Cal?"

Cal managed to smile despite the obvious pain he was experiencing. "This may be my last rodeo, but I'm not going down without a fight." It was his best attempt at humor, all things considered, and a struggle for Feinstein not to cry again.

"Cal, are you sure you still want to go through with this?" She was serious now.

He could only make a slight nod but the determination in his eyes was unmistakable. "What we're doing is important, old girl. It's bigger than you and me. You know that."

Dr. Feinstein took a moment to collect herself before nodding for the neurosurgeon to go ahead with the procedure. He began to attach the head ring, first by numbing the four areas where the pins would be tightened. This done, he nodded for the radiologist to perform a CT scan. Then the neurosurgeon made a tiny incision in the scalp and drilled a small hole through the skull, stopping just when it had exited the bone. He inserted a thin biopsy needle into the brain and carefully adjusted its depth with a thumb screw.

"Are you ready, Cal?" Dr. Feinstein whispered. He blinked his eyes.

With that, the neurosurgeon used the syringe to suck out a tiny biopsy core of brain tissue and transferred it to a plastic tube which was immediately plunged into a cryo dish of liquid nitrogen. After it had been snap frozen, the specimen was transferred to a Styrofoam cooler of crushed dry ice. He reinserted the needle and dialed it to a depth just beneath the first core.

Now the waiting began. As Schwarzkopf had dictated in the protocol, the morphine drip was replaced with a naloxone solution, one that would neutralize its analgesic effect. It increased his pain dramatically and his heart rate spiked abruptly on the monitor, and then gradually began to slow. Schwarzkopf's breathing became progressively more erratic after that. He'd given strict instructions not to be intubated during this procedure.

Feinstein could no longer look at him directly and turned to watch the monitor. The pulse slowed ever further, pausing intermittently for seconds at a time. Then came a solid beep from the monitor. Schwarzkopf's passionate heart had finally stopped beating.

The EMT monitor continued measuring brainwave activity for about thirty seconds after Schwarzkopf's heart had stopped beating. Dr. Feinstein nodded for the neurosurgeon to take a second biopsy core. Then, after disconnecting the head clamp and with a nurse's assistance, he withdrew five milliliters of cerebral spinal fluid from Schwarzkopf's spine, just below the fourth vertebra. According to Schwarzkopf's instructions, Dr. Feinstein was planning to have this sample tested for DMT.

After snap-freezing the samples and handing the cooler to Dr. Feinstein, the nurse returned to remove the IV from her recently deceased patient. Only then did Schwarzkopf's wife allow herself to weep softly. Her husband was one of the bravest men she had ever known, a man fiercely devoted to scientific discovery. He had paid an ultimate price. She gently caressed his cheek before turning away. A minimal crew would remain to attend to the body.

Feinstein's team loaded up the van and made it back to Palo Alto in a little over four hours. When they arrived at the campus, Dr. Feinstein carried the specimen cooler up to her lab, transferred the tubes to a specially labeled box and placed it on a shelf in the -80°C freezer. Now it was her turn to cry.

Dr. Feinstein barged into Brett's office the next day and placed a Styrofoam cooler on his desk. Her somber expression struck him instantly.

"What's this about?" Roberts ventured.

After an uncharacteristic moment to compose herself, Feinstein spoke softly, "He wanted you to analyze these biopsy samples as soon as possible. They're from his brain."

Brett's skin tingled. "You have got to be kidding."

"I'm afraid not. Calvin passed away last night. This experiment was his idea. He wanted to help satisfy your curiosity about DMT."

This cannot be happening, thought Roberts. "But...."

"You owe it to him now." She patted the Styrofoam cooler and then left without another word.

Four hours later, Anthony poked his head into Brett's office with bad news. "Sorry boss, I wasn't able to extract enough RNA from those tissue samples to run a microarray experiment."

Roberts felt relieved, but not entirely. "What would you suggest?"

"We could try that new RNA amplification procedure." Anthony had developed this method a few months earlier as a side project. It was an enzymatic process that replicated each RNA strand about 50 times without changing their relative copy distributions. Anthony had proven this using a dilution series of RNA extracted from normal brain tissue. But they hadn't yet tried it out on patient samples. This would be the first such attempt.

"How confident are you that it can work?"

"As confident as I usually am, Dr. Roberts." Anthony only used Brett's title when he was trying to make a point.

They really had no other choice. "Alright, please go ahead."

They were lucky. The procedure yielded a sufficient quantity of amplified RNA for a second microarray experiment if the first one failed. Roberts instructed Anthony to store the remainder of each sample in the freezer, just in case.

Schwarzkopf's ceremony of remembrance was held at his ranch on Saturday, outdoors on the meadow overlooking his favorite view. He had asked for his body to be cremated, with his ashes to be scattered at sea immediately following the ceremony. A helicopter was standing by.

Janet Feinstein's most recent study was published with expedited review in the *Journal of Molecular Biology*. Brett Roberts had been listed as a co-author on that submission, his first and last shared byline with Janet. This study reported for the first time that certain genes become activated around the time of death. Although considered a curiosity at the time, the paper would eventually become widely cited in the scientific literature.

Feinstein wanted to include a sub-analysis of the data obtained from Schwarzkopf's tissue and CSF samples, although the reviewers rejected these claims as inconclusive. But Roberts was convinced, and his awareness of that experiment would haunt him for years to come.

On June 26th, 2000, President Clinton held a press conference with Francis Collins and J. Craig Venter to jointly announce the pending completion of the human genome project. It seemed a fitting compromise, considering their respective teams were both nearing the finish line. The sequencing effort was almost over, although a final draft of the human genome wouldn't be published until three years later.

Dignitaries in attendance included representatives from most of the developed countries around the world, with a satellite link for commentary by those unable to attend in person. President Clinton addressed the assembled audience:

"The moment we are here to witness was brought about through brilliant and painstaking work of scientists all over the world, including many men and women here today. It was not even 50 years ago that a young Englishman named Crick and a brash even younger American named Watson, first discovered the elegant structure of our genetic code. "Dr. Watson, the way you announced your discovery in the journal Nature, was one of the great understatements of all time. This structure has novel features, which are of considerable biological interest." (Laughter) Thank you, sir. (Applause)

"How far we have come since that day. In the intervening years, we have pooled the combined wisdom of biology, chemistry, physics, engineering, mathematics and computer science; tapped the great strengths and insights of the public and private sectors. More than 1,000 researchers across six nations have revealed nearly all 3 billion letters of our miraculous genetic code. I congratulate all of you on this stunning and humbling achievement.

"Today's announcement represents more than just an epic-making triumph of science and reason. After all, when Galileo discovered he could use the tools of mathematics and mechanics to understand the motion of celestial bodies, he felt, in the words of one eminent researcher, "that he had learned the language in which God created the universe."

"Today, we are learning the language in which God created life. We are gaining ever more awe for the complexity, the beauty, the wonder of God's most divine and sacred gift. With this profound new knowledge, humankind is on the verge of gaining immense, new power to heal. Genome science will have a real impact on all our lives -- and even more, on the lives of our children. It will revolutionize the diagnosis, prevention and treatment of most, if not all, human diseases."

A new era of human genomics had only just begun. The publicly funded sequence was stored on terabyte servers at UC Santa Cruz, and made freely available to researchers worldwide over the internet.

Computer programmers at UCSC's Center for Biomolecular Science and Engineering had also developed specialized software for querying the data, likewise freely available for download over the internet. Understanding the human genome had now become an *in-silico* exercise of scientific discovery.

Bioinformatics scientists from Spectrum's Palo Alto offices had been working frantically to align their proprietary messenger RNA gene sequences onto the reference genome from Santa Cruz. To the great surprise of many, only two percent of the genome was found to be responsible for mRNA synthesis. No one had a clue what the rest of the genome might be for. Some had already taken to calling it "junk DNA".

Yet having now sequenced genetic material from hundreds of individuals, they were able to make two key observations. The first was that single nucleotide differences in the genes were sometimes noted when comparing the same mRNA sequence from multiple individuals. Sometimes these mutations would code for an entirely different amino acid, for example CAU (histidine) versus CAA (glutamine), meaning that people having that mutation would also have a single amino acid difference in their corresponding protein.

People were walking around on the planet with subtle differences in the compositions of their enzymes, membrane receptors and other proteins, single amino acid substitutions that could potentially alter their function. Scientists speculated that this could help explain why some responded differently to certain types of drugs.

The second observation was only made possible after the reference genome sequence had become available. Spectrum's data analysts began to notice that multiple mRNA sequences could be aligned to the exact same reference gene location on the chromosome. The explanation turned out to be a process called "RNA splicing".

Genes on the chromosome are actually partitioned into segments called "exons" and "introns". It is the "exons" that are responsible for "messenger RNA" sequence or mRNA, the template from which proteins are synthesized. When the chromosome is first transcribed into RNA, the initial copy is termed "pre-messenger RNA", containing a string of "exons" and "introns" all connected together as a continuous strand. Then, according to a complicated splicing process, sort of like scissors and tape, the "intron" segments get spliced out and the "exon' segments get pasted back together. The final mRNA molecule is then secreted out of the cell's nucleus to be translated into proteins.

This process might sound extremely complicated, and indeed it is. But it essentially means that a single "gene" region on the chromosome is capable of producing multiple different mRNA copies, each one having a different number of exons from that particular gene. Some mRNAs could contain most or all of these exons, whereas others might have one or more of them skipped. Think of it like this: if the exons were labeled A, B, C, D, E, and F, then some of the mRNAs might read like ABCDEF, or ACDEF, or ABDEF, and so on. The proteins made from each of these different mRNA copies can have slightly different biological functions. It's a bit like removing some of the keys from a piano and compressing it into a smaller keyboard. No two such keyboards would play exactly the same.

Armed with a new appreciation for RNA splicing, Roberts finally noticed a deficiency in the design of their Version 2 Brain Microarray. He called a team meeting in the fish bowl to discuss his idea.

"People, our current microarrays simply aren't capable of discriminating between these highly related mRNA splice variants. If we want to know exactly which membrane receptor is involved in a particular signaling process, we're going to have to do better. Any thoughts on this?"

After a pregnant pause, one of his chemists suggested the idea of using synthetic oligonucleotides. Newly designed DNA synthesizers were capable of producing them on demand, typically up to about 60 nucleotides in length.

Roberts pretended he hadn't already thought of that. "Yes, that could work. We could combine them to target specific exons within each mRNA splice variant."

Over the next half hour they discussed the logistics of the idea. A 400 gene microarray would require about 2000 oligonucleotides to be designed, synthesized and purified. The MADDOG engineers thought they could program their pipetting robots to perform the various reagent handling steps, although some of the proposed work-flow had never been tried before. Any mix-ups between all these different tubes of oligonucleotide reagents would be a disaster. Anthony proposed a novel barcoding scheme to keep track of them all once they had been dispensed into specially designed 96-well vessels called 'micro-plates'. The project was projected to take about 2-3 months, with an estimated cost of about $500,000 dollars.

Jeremy Watts enthusiastically approved the project. "Do great science and make sure to get something published, agreed?" He'd already hung up before Roberts could answer. Unfortunately, Roberts was getting used to these abrupt phone endings.

Two bioinformatics specialists from Palo Alto were tasked with designing the oligonucleotides. The new custom microarray would target 400 different mRNA splice variants corresponding to membrane receptor genes of known or suspected importance in brain signaling processes.

Westfield was assigned the task of selecting which genes would be included on the new microarray. He poked his head into Roberts's office. "Hey Brett, I bet your newly designed microarray would have done a much better job elucidating which genes were still firing right after Schwarzkopf died."

Roberts swiveled in his chair to face the exterior window. "Yeah, I know.

CHAPTER FOURTEEN

"A premature dawn"

Wednesday, September 13th, 2000

Fontainebleau Hotel, Miami

THE 12TH INTERNATIONAL GSAC MEETING was almost entirely dedicated to the completion of the human genome sequencing effort. That summer's joint press announcement had been broadcast live to a world-wide audience, with extensive media coverage to follow. A composite photo of Francis Collins and Craig Venter had even made the July cover of *Time Magazine*.

Tuesday's panel discussion on ethical considerations for genome sequencing had fostered lively debate, however the afternoon session on Wednesday was the one everyone had been waiting for. It had been simply titled "The Human Genome".

The 5,000 seat auditorium was filled beyond capacity by half past noon with late-comers standing on tiptoe outside the doorways. Venter's signature jazz fusion music could barely be heard above the rumbling murmurs, but the lights eventually dimmed and the crowd quickly hushed to silence.

The session began with presentations from key contributors to the public sequencing effort, followed by three presenters from Celera. Gene mapping along the chromosomes was discussed along with their potential clinical implications, for example children with Down's syndrome who possessed an extra copy of Chromosome 21. The historical implications of this pivotal moment in genome biology was impossible to ignore, and palpable for those in attendance.

And once again, Craig Venter topped off the program. The lights came back on to standing applause, although most of the attendees were speechless as they funneled their way out of the auditorium. The daunting task of translating all this data into biologically meaningful information had only just begun.

Celera had sent out invitations for an after party that night at the Perez Art Museum on Biscayne Bay. Venter intended to help everyone forget the previous year's New Orleans style bash that had been hosted by Spectrum Genomics. He'd reserved the entire museum and surrounding gardens for Celera's soiree, which would supposedly be a bit more "polished" than in previous years. The invitations had specified cocktail attire. Members of the media and other various public dignitaries were also invited, many of whom flew in specifically for this occasion.

Roberts and Westfield exited the lobby just as the first flight of buses were departing for the Celera event, so they joined an expanding queue of guests to wait for the next group of buses to arrive. Roberts leaned toward Westfield and murmured for only him to hear, "So what did you think of Celera's gene-mapping presentations this afternoon?"

Noticing that Westfield had been eyeballing a stunning brunette just ahead of them, Roberts tapped him again on the shoulder. "Eric?"

"Huh? Oh, sorry Brett. It's a bit like discovering the Rosetta Stone, as far as I'm concerned. We still need to figure out what all those words mean, or genes in this case. Still plenty of work ahead for us journeyman scientists."

"Insightful as always, my friend." Roberts began to feel a bit more validated, until he happened to overhear a brief conversation two Brits were having a short distance away.

"We've finally gotten to the bottom of it, haven't we? The code of life I mean. Not much room left for God these days."

"Quite right. How could anyone continue to believe in that Creation nonsense when we now have all this scientific evidence to the contrary? Simple-minded twits, I say."

The buses returned and they boarded. Fifteen minutes later, Roberts and Westfield stepped down and followed the excited guests into the courtyard. They were each handed a glass of champagne as they entered the museum. A classical jazz band played softly in the back corner while waiters in white tuxedos milled about with their trays of hors d'oeuvres.

Roberts was wearing his best oxford shirt with a navy blue tie. He hadn't dressed like this since his job interview at Spectrum three years before. Westfield, on the other hand, was wearing a button down tie dye shirt and a Jerry Garcia tie in protest. He'd already received a number of compliments on his chosen attire.

"He's over there." Westfield pointed out Venter, who was dressed in pressed khakis and a cream-colored golf shirt bearing the Celera logo, no tie. He seemed more interested in observing the crowd than talking with anyone in particular. Noting Venter's casual attire, Roberts promptly unbuttoned his collar and loosened his tie. Westfield grinned and made a mock courtly bow.

The head waiter eventually stepped up to the band microphone and announced that dinner was ready out in the back gardens. The guests were each offered their choice of chardonnay or merlot as they walked out into the humid evening air.

Strings of white lights spiraled up the palm trees and colored flood lamps illuminated the gardens, creating a lively atmosphere for the guests to mill around. Table stations had been set up with different varieties of world cuisine. Guests were urged to sample different dishes and mingle. Distant colleagues bumped into each other and began exchanging pleasantries.

The jazz band had re-stationed itself on the museum's back porch and was playing a medley of John Coltrane songs throughout the dinner. Trays of desserts were then passed around, and finally Venter stepped up to a microphone and waved his arms to get the attention of the guests.

His comments were on point, polite, even gracious at times, surprising some who knew him best. First he systematically thanked other prominent scientists in attendance, asking each one in turn to be recognized with a brief round of applause. Francis Collins was the last of them to be recognized. His applause lasted several minutes. Venter stood by and gave Collins his due with a look of strained composure.

Once the guests had quieted down, Venter stepped back up to the microphone and began to share his personal vision for the future of genomic medicine. For him, finding new cures for debilitating diseases was a short-sighted endeavor. Scientists should dedicate themselves to preventing disease altogether. By applying the power of genome technology, human beings would ultimately learn how to live longer, healthier and more productive lives.

Roberts stared blankly out the window during the bus ride back to their hotel. Venter's lofty ideas seemed logical enough. But the conviction in his voice had troubled Roberts, as though science had become the new god. Something felt terribly wrong about this, which reminded Roberts of an encounter he'd had a few months earlier while waiting for a plane at San Francisco Airport. Roberts had spoken briefly to an aging Bavarian gentleman standing next to him, and realizing the man spoke no English, he decided to try out his rusty German. When the man asked about his profession, Roberts did his best to describe the field of human genomics. This angered the man for some reason, and he held out a fist and shook it firmly. *"Du musst nicht klonen!"*

You must not clone....

Virtanen chose that night to revisit Brett's dreams, presumably to remind him of their metaphysical association. Although annoyed, Roberts found the encounter less alarming than in years past. Sometimes one needed to experience an uncomfortable moment to appreciate the possibility that science may not have all the answers.

Tuesday, November 28th 2000
Spectrum Genomics Microarray Facility, East Bay

The shipments of oligonucleotide reagents for Brett's new custom Brain Array had finally arrived. Following up on Anthony's idea, his assay development team systematically diluted and processed the reagents for printing onto specially treated microscope slides. All they needed now was a window in the production schedule to print their new microarrays.

Roberts waited for the night shift to arrive before walking over to ask their production manager for a favor. "Hey Miguel, do you think you could fit a custom print run into your schedule tonight?"

Miguel studied his clipboard and then firmly shook his head. "Sorry, Dr. Roberts. Pfizer has a big job on back order. We'll be printing those arrays all night."

"Come on, man. Couldn't you squeeze in just 10 slides? That wouldn't take more than an hour."

Miguel sighed with resignation. Dr. Roberts has recommended him for this job, after all. "Alright, but that's all I can do for you right now."

"Thanks buddy. I'll repay you with a bottle of Don Julio."

The performance of Brett's newly designed custom Brain Array had to be validated before it could be used with actual patient samples. For this purpose, they used RNA extracts from the brain tissue of cadavers. Such reference materials were purchased from medical supply companies catering to the biotech community. Only two unused slides remained, although the validation data looked extremely promising.

Roberts walked into the lab, asked Anthony to come to his office, and then said, "Let's go ahead and proceed with that experiment we talked about." Roberts had never mentioned to Janet Feinstein that their procedure for processing Schwarzkopf's tissue extracts had produced sufficient RNA for a second run, or more importantly that they still had those two tubes stored away in a -70 °C freezer.

"You sure we're ready, Brett? We've barely got enough material left for a single run."

Roberts couldn't suppress a grin when he realized that Anthony had just called him by his first name. "The validation data looks incredible. So yeah, I think we're as ready as we'll ever be."

The microarray results were available on his computer screen the following morning, all pointing to a novel membrane receptor gene designated 'SIGMAR-1'. His heart began to beat a bit faster. A considerable spike in DMT had been detected in Schwarzkopf's cerebral spinal fluid right after he died, although that data was never published. Might this be the gene? Roberts typed it into the SwisProt search engine to learn what might be known about its function. Unfortunately, relatively few studies had been published with this particular gene. Although it did appear to share considerable sequence homology with the more widely studied serotonin receptor gene.

Should he confess to Janet Feinstein that he'd conducted this experiment without her permission? Somehow, this felt like a really bad idea. And anyway, it would be better to wait until more of these new microarrays could be printed. Additional experiments would be necessary to verify this new finding.

Unfortunately, Brett's print job suffered numerous delays. Spectrum's stock had been trading at an all-time high, and there was a big push for revenue to justify the valuation. Roberts kept asking Miguel about the schedule, until Stuart Avery finally called and instructed him to stop. "Sorry Brett, you'll simply have to wait until next year. We really need to finish the year strong financially."

When January finally came and went, Roberts inquired again about the print schedule and received bad news. He dialed Avery's number. "Hey Stuart, I just learned from our production manager that my microarray job was cancelled. What's up?"

"I'm the one who cancelled that print job, Roberts. In fact, all internal research projects have been suspended until further notice."

Roberts pleaded, "But Watts wants to see a publication coming from this effort. That was his condition for funding the project."

"Look, Roberts. Watts is now busy with a new business venture. He's made me responsible for the microarray business, and I'm afraid I must say no. Revenue is key to our survival. That's all our shareholders seem to care about these days."

"But…." True to form, Avery clicked off before Roberts could finish his sentence.

On a Saturday in June, Roberts got up early and went downstairs to make breakfast for the boys. He carried a tray up for Ruth along with a section of the newspaper folded over to the daily crossword puzzle.

"Thanks dear, it's nice to get a break."

"Tell you what, how about we pack up the car and drive out to Santa Cruz for the day?"

"You sure you're up for it? You've been battling traffic all week."

"I know, but we haven't done much together as a family lately. Come on, it'll be fun!"

The winding drive up and down Highway 17 took much longer than expected. Roberts got increasingly frustrated while trying to locate a parking space near the board walk. He exhaled with relief after stepping out of the car and breathed in the pleasant salt air. *Ahh*…. Roberts had always felt drawn to the ocean, and today was no exception.

The boys rode the rollercoaster and then enjoyed hot dogs and ice cream. After a quick trip to the restroom to wash their faces and hands, the Roberts family took the stairs down to the beach and spread out a blanket to enjoy the late afternoon sunshine. The boys began constructing a sand castle and filled its "moat" with sea water from their plastic buckets.

"You know Ruth, things haven't been the same since Jeremy Watts stepped down as CEO of Spectrum."

Ruth shifted to face him. "Does this mean you're finally ready to talk about it?"

"Watts always encouraged us to do good science and publish our findings." Roberts blew out his renewed frustration. "Those days are over, apparently. Stuart Avery's in charge now, and all he seems to care about is revenue."

"Well, you are a publicly traded company."

"I know, but I may have stumbled on something important. If I could only complete my experiments." Roberts stared at the ocean and started to brood.

Ruth gently touched his shoulder, and said, "Tell me about it." At times like this, she knew it was best to listen.

Roberts began describing what he'd been working on. It was now known that the same gene could produce a variety of different proteins, depending on which exons were spliced into the final messenger RNA sequence. His new microarray was designed to discriminate between these different splice variants.

Ruth asked a number of challenging questions along the way, some of which Brett hadn't even considered yet. Her husband had a tendency to leap forward in his thought process and fill in the details later, whereas Ruth was more of a "connect all the dots" type of person. It was times like this that made Brett realize how lucky he was to have Ruth for his wife and partner. She also happened to be his closest friend.

"There's something else I've been meaning to talk to you about."

"What's that?" Ruth asked, pleased to have managed to stump her husband a few times about the workings of his new microarray.

"You know that paper I published last summer with Janet Feinstein?"

Ruth nodded and crossed her arms, wondering where this might be going.

"Two of the tissue samples used for that study had been donated by Calvin Schwarzkopf. Biopsies were taken from his brain shortly before and right after he died."

Ruth's jaw dropped. "And you never thought to mention this before?"

Brett's head lowered and his shoulders slumped. "The most interesting findings from that particular experiment never made it into the final paper, mainly because our commercial arrays weren't capable of discriminating between the splice variants of certain genes involved in signal transduction."

Ruth understood what Brett was referring to, a family of membrane receptors that were responsible for the effects of epinephrine, serotonin and other such neurotransmitters.

Brett continued, "Anyway, we decided to re-test the remnants of Schwarzkopf's amplified RNA using this new microarray design. Ruth, the expression data was so much cleaner, so much more precise. We only need to run a few more experiments to verify our findings. Unfortunately, the production crew has been much too busy lately to fit in another print job." He paused to gather himself, "And I just learned yesterday that Avery has decided to shut down our project."

Ruth waited to be sure he was finished, and then said, "Well Brett, you just might have to let it go."

Brett sighed, "Maybe you're right." He turned his attention to the horizon. "Hey, look! The sun's about to set. Come over here, boys."

They each tucked one under their arm and watched the sun sink slowly into the sea.

"God made that sunset just for us," said Thomas.

"I think you're right, Thomas," said Ruth while nuzzling him close.

Brett gave his other son a scrunch. "See it Michael?"

"Yeah!"

September 11TH, 2001

The morning rush into downtown Manhattan was nearly over. Office workers had just begun to settle into their usual daily grind, blissfully unaware of the horrors that lay ahead. American Airlines Flight 11 crashed into the North Tower of the World Trade Center at precisely 8:46 AM, instantly killing everyone on board along with hundreds of people inside the building. Then something even more unexpected happened. United Airlines Flight 175 crashed into the South Tower at 9:06 AM. Both towers began to slowly and noisily fall into piles of twisted iron beams and concrete rubble, and by 5:20 PM they were gone. People watched in horror as these events were broadcast live to a world-wide audience. A total of 2,753 people ultimately died in that tragedy, including hundreds of the emergency responders.

Stock trading was halted and the Dow Jones Average dropped 684 points in less than three hours after the markets reopened two days later. The mild recession that had begun earlier that spring was now in free fall. Over 1.75 million people in the United States would lose their jobs by the end of 2001.

The 13th Annual GSAC meeting was postponed and relocated to San Diego later that year. With their stock price still dropping like a stone, Spectrum Genomics sent just a handful of employees. And in early November, Jeremy Watts made the difficult decision to close Spectrum's microarray facility. Brett Roberts was laid off for the first time in his young professional career.

Monday, February 18th, 2002
Pleasanton, California

Owen Mudford felt a bit worried after clicking off the phone and figured he'd try Brett's home number next. He hadn't spoken with Ruth in a while anyway.

"Hello Owen! How are you?"

"Things are good with me, Ruth. Still a lab manager down at the kelp processing plant. It's not exactly drug discovery, although I've got a team of ten people reporting to me now. But the real reason I called is to announce that Elsa's expecting a baby. She just passed her first trimester."

"Oh Owen, that's wonderful!"

"Yeah, something about turning 36 must have changed her mind about having kids. Guess she figured it was now or never. I just tried calling Brett to give him the news but apparently his office number's been disconnected. Everything okay?"

Ruth paused a moment, and then said, "Brett's in his home office upstairs right now. Let me get him."

Mudford could hear her climbing the stairs. Ruth handed the phone to Brett after whispering who it was.

"Owen! How the heck are you?"

"Doing fine, I must say. Hey, I tried calling your office number to let you know that Elsa's expecting a baby."

"Wow, that's fantastic news! Sorry to put a damper on it, but I got laid off a couple months back. The entire microarray division was shut down."

"Bummer, I was afraid of that. Seems like there've been tons of layoffs lately. So sorry to hear you were impacted, my friend."

"Yeah, I've been meaning to give you a call, although finding another job has kept me pretty busy lately."

"No worries, I understand. Any leads?"

"Several, actually. One of them happens to be in the San Diego area. Seems they're interested in starting up a new program focused on cancer diagnostics."

"Man, it would be great to have you and Ruth close by. Your boys would love our beaches here; water's a lot warmer too. Be sure to let me know beforehand if you come down for an interview. And don't forget to bring your wetsuit. We'll paddle on out and do us some serious waves after you're done."

"Now that sounds like a plan." Brett quickly checked his watch. "Listen, I'm expecting another call in about five minutes…."

Mudford told one of his typically crass jokes before ending the call.

The outplacement agency had strongly emphasized the importance of networking for landing his next job. Taking this to heart, Roberts decided to email Jeremy Watts and ask for his advice. Watts promptly sent an email reply asking Roberts for his mobile number.

Not wishing to seem too anxious, Roberts let it ring a few times before clicking on the phone. "Brett Roberts."

"Hello Brett, Jeremy here. The consultants we hired to oversee the layoffs advised us not to initiate contact with ex-employees, but since you're the one who reached out to me, what's on your mind?"

Roberts already knew from talking to Westfield that shuttering their microarray division had been the board's decision, and definitely not Dr. Watts. Westfield was among the lucky few to be transferred over to Palo Alto, although his daily commute was supposedly brutal.

"Well, Dr. Watts, I've received several calls from headhunters looking to fill positions in the diagnostics industry, and was wondering if you'd be willing to share your thoughts on such opportunities."

"Happy to Brett, but please feel free to call me Jeremy. How about we meet for breakfast tomorrow in Palo Alto, say around 8 o'clock? Hope you won't mind the commute, got another meeting at 10 in Menlo Park."

Roberts was feeling better already. "Sure, no problem. Where would you like to meet?"

"How 'bout we meet at Spectrum and I drive from there?"

"Thanks Dr. Watts, I mean Jeremy. I'm looking forward to it."

"Me too, Brett." Watts clicked off the call.

Roberts left home before 6 AM to beat the first wave of morning traffic. He drove into Spectrum's main parking lot and spotted his former CEO standing outside the front entrance in his signature blue jeans, with a red polo shirt and brown corduroy sport jacket. Watts walked over to meet Brett's car as he was pulling into one of the visitor spaces.

"How was traffic coming over the bridge?"

"Don't ask."

"Sorry about that. You ready?"

Roberts followed Watts around to the back of the building where his Jaguar had been parked near the executive entrance.

Watts left the top down and they drove toward downtown Palo Alto under a cloudless sky. Roberts felt reenergized with the wind against his face. Less than five minutes later, they pulled into a diagonally lined parking space right in front of Flapjacks, a popular Silicon Valley gathering place for breakfast meetings.

They discussed the future of human genomics over breakfast.

"I think the field of cancer diagnostics would be an excellent fit for you, Brett. Especially considering your knack for assay development. What was the name of that company you mentioned in San Diego?"

Roberts pretended not to enjoy the compliment. "BioProbe. They've already launched several products."

Watts rubbed his beard. "Hmm, I might know their CEO. Let me make a few calls after I get back to the office." He checked his watch, waved for the waitress, and left a twenty on the table as they were leaving.

Back in the Jaguar, Roberts got up the nerve to ask an unrelated question, one he'd wanted to ask for quite some time. "Can I ask you something, Jeremy?" It still felt a bit odd for them to be on a first name basis.

Watts pulled to a stop at the next traffic light. "Sure, if it's quick."

Doubtful whether they had sufficient time for this particular topic, Roberts decided to go ahead and ask his question anyway. "It's about a lecture you gave at Stanford a while back, the one about science and religion."

Watts grinned. "Ah yes, one of my favorite subjects. I thought I spotted you in the audience. What's your question?"

"Are Christians expected to defend things in the Bible that science seems to contradict, like the Creation Story for example?"

The traffic light changed to green. Watts shifted through the gears and raised his voice to be heard above the smooth yet powerful engine. "As you probably recall from my lecture, I described a number of prominent scientists throughout history who had also been theologians. Despite their belief in God, these great men also cautioned against rigid interpretations of scripture in the face of contradictory scientific evidence." He downshifted to make the turn, accelerated again, and went on to explain. "So my short answer is that the Bible was not meant to be interpreted as a scientific textbook. Instead, it offers us a history of God's interaction with humankind. By reading it with an open mind, we learn how to find meaning in our lives through a relationship with Him."

Watts pulled back into the Spectrum parking lot and drove around to his former space. He revved the engine once more before shutting down the ignition. Then he turned to Roberts and gently patted him on the shoulder. "Let me end this brief discussion by stating that science may well reveal certain truths about God's creation, but it can never explain our reason for being here or what our lives mean."

They both climbed out and shut the doors. Roberts walked around to offer his hand. "Thanks Jeremy, I really appreciate your making this time for me."

Watts shook it warmly. "My pleasure, Brett. I'm sure you'll land yourself another position in short order."

Roberts drove back across the bridge without switching on his car stereo. His former CEO was comfortable with his beliefs. Roberts wished he felt the same way.

Friday, March 15th, 2002

Roberts took a deep breath and tore open the envelope. Inside was his formal a job offer from BioProbe, a rapidly growing biotechnology company that had pioneered a new technology for diagnosing infectious diseases based on their DNA signatures. It was called *molecular diagnostics*. The company had already passed $200 million dollars in annual revenue, having launched over a dozen tests for blood viruses and sexually transmitted diseases. Emboldened by this success, BioProbe's CEO had recently convinced the board to expand into the area of cancer diagnostics. And based in part on Jeremy Watts' recommendation, Roberts had been chosen to lead the effort.

As promised, Mudford was the first person who Roberts called after telling his wife. He practically shouted into the phone. "Hey Owen, I got the job! We're moving to San Diego!" It felt great to say it again out loud.

"Fantastic news, bud! When do you start?"

"April 1st. BioProbe will be renting me an apartment until my kids have finished out the school year. They'll be flying Ruth down in a few weeks so we can do some house hunting."

"Outstanding! Tell you what, how'd you like to join me out in the Anza Borrego desert for *Moon Howl?*"

Some things about Mudford never changed, apparently. "What's that? Some sort of *Burning Man* thing?"

"I guess you could say that, although this one's run by my extended family of uncles and cousins. It's just us guys so we can fart whenever we want. We pick a date each spring when there's a full moon, which this year happens to be fall over this coming weekend. Hope that's not too short notice. What do you think? Close buds are always welcome. You, my friend, would fit right in."

Roberts was sorely tempted. He could use a good blowout before starting his next job. "Let me ask Ruth and get back to you."

"She's a fabulous woman, Brett. Elsa keeps asking when the four of us can get back together."

"Let's definitely plan something for when Ruth comes down in May."

"Sounds like a plan. Let me know what she says about *Moon Howl.* Tell her I promise to get you back in one piece."

Roberts called downstairs after hanging up the phone, "Hey Ruth! I'm thinking about making reservations at the Blue Dolphin for dinner tonight. What do you think?" No answer. Realizing she'd already left to pick up the boys at school, he grabbed a basketball and went outside to shoot a few at his neighbor's curbside basketball hoop. After a few errant shots, he spotted Danny trudging up the sidewalk with a backpack full of books.

"Hi there Danny, hope you don't mind," said Roberts.

Danny grinned. "Hey Mister Roberts! No, I don't mind. Care for a game of HORSE?"

"So you can beat me like last time?" said Roberts. He liked Danny. "Okay, here goes." Roberts dribbled to the top of the key, which was actually a manhole cover, and hurled a shot that rolled around the rim before falling through the hoop.

"Nice one, Mister R," said Danny. He shrugged out of his backpack and Roberts tossed him the ball. Danny then dribbled to one side, turned and fired a swisher.

Roberts fired from the same spot and watched in disbelief as the ball missed the rim entirely.

Danny ran after the ball. "You've got an 'H' now, Mister R." He started dribbling, spun once on his way to the hoop and easily made a bank shot from under the rim with his left hand. "Okay, let's see if you can make that."

"No problem!" Roberts said with conviction, although his awkward attempt at mimicking Danny's move failed to produce the same result. "Oh well, three more misses to go. Hey Danny, would you mind watching our boys tonight? I've just accepted a job offer and would like to take my wife out to celebrate."

Danny grinned, "Hey that's great, Mister Roberts! Sure, I'd be glad to." He dribbled out to the corner of the key and spun around to fire another rimless swish.

Brett had finally earned an 'E' when Ruth pulled into their driveway with the boys. Thomas and Michael jumped out of the car and ran over.

"Daddy! Mom says we're moving to San Diego!" shouted Michael.

"Can we go to Sea World?" interrupted Thomas excitedly.

"Can we go to the zoo?" added Michael.

"Yes, boys. But we won't be moving until summer time."

"Aw!" shouted Thomas. "Aw!" mimicked Michael.

Ruth called to the boys, "Come on you two, we need to get started on your homework," which elicited another "Aw!" from each of them in rapid succession.

Brett said, "Let's go, guys." He took them by the hand, assisted with their backpacks and shepherded them toward the house. Passing Ruth, he whispered in her ear, "Danny's agreed to watch the boys tonight."

Ruth's eyes lit up. "Blue Dolphin?"

"Already on it," said Brett with equal enthusiasm. He loved those eyes, especially when she was smiling.

The Blue Dolphin Restaurant was a remodeled Victorian house on Main Street, originally owned by a patriarchal family back in the late 1800s. Downtown Pleasanton didn't quite live up to its name in those days, back when it was better known as "The Most Desperate Town in the West". All sorts of nefarious characters patronized its brothels and gambling halls. Chinese immigrants dug a network of tunnels beneath the street to smuggle goods and for paying customers to move back and forth after curfew.

Some of those old buildings were supposedly haunted, although many of them had been transformed into upscale boutique shops and restaurants by the early 1990's. Just a few of the original businesses remained. The Pleasanton Hotel had been restored to its original pristine condition and the rooms were always booked. Stepping inside was like a trip back in time. The Kolln Hardware Store hadn't changed much since the '40s. Roberts often wondered how they managed to keep it going with its endless shelves of oddball fixit items.

He offered Ruth an arm and they strolled down Main Street toward the restaurant. Its clapboard walls and vaulted gables featured dramatic contrasting colors of bright ocean blue trimmed in red rust. The former front yard was now a courtyard for outdoor dining, with adobe brick pavers interspersed with colorful blue and red tiles to match the building. Two mature oak trees remained to shade the white linen-draped tables and powder blue chairs during daytime hours. Strings of tiny white twinkle lights hung down from their branches, giving off just enough light for a romantic evening dinner. Colorful spotlights illuminated the exotic looking cacti and agave plants sprouting from tall Mexican ceramic pots placed artistically throughout the grounds. Shoulder-high amber streetlamps guided patrons up to the front porch reception station.

The hostess escorted them to a table near one of the twinkling oak trees and handed them each their menus. The place settings included colorful folded napkins and blue tinted glassware. "Perfect," said Brett as a busboy came over to help Ruth be seated. And, "No, Gracias." when the young man offered to do the same for him. Ruth gave Brett an amused look when the busboy turned away to assist another table of guests.

"You look like a kid on your first visit to Disneyland." Ruth said with a smile.

"Can't help it I guess. Aren't you excited about San Diego?"

"I've always loved it there, although the thought of selling and buying another house still terrifies me." Ruth picked up her dinner menu.

Brett studied the drink menu while Ruth browsed the entrees. After a moment, he said, "We'll take everything a step at a time."

"I know," she said. "Oh, this looks good."

When the waiter arrived, Ruth ordered the *pescado cathedral*, a sautéed mahi dish with roasted chile poblano and epazote sauce served over a bed of white rice with a side of cabbage salad. Brett requested the *camarones ala diabla*, a hot and spicy shrimp dish also served over white rice with a generous splashing of red chipotle sauce.

"And would you bring us a pitcher of your Blue Dolphin margaritas?" Brett glanced over to Ruth for her approval. She broke into a grin and nodded. When the pitcher arrived, Brett poured the glasses and Ruth took a substantial sip from hers before setting it down.

"Thanks, I needed that," she said.

Brett kept the conversation light over dinner. They talked about getting an annual membership to the San Diego Zoo, maybe also one for Sea World. Their older son Thomas had always been fond of dolphins. And Michael loved building with Legos. Legoland had recently opened in Carlsbad. So many adventures awaited them and the boys.

"We could also go to the beach whenever we wanted," said Brett. "By the way, Owen invited me to go camping with him out in the desert next weekend. It's an annual event that he and his uncles and cousins have been doing for years. Just guys, apparently. Would you mind if I drive down a bit early to join him?"

Ruth said, "That's fine, so long as you help me get the house ready to list before you go."

"That's a promise. And don't forget, I'll be flying home on weekends." Brett poured them each another glass of margaritas and waved the rest of the pitcher away. "It's nice out tonight," he said when they were alone again.

Ruth glanced up to a clear evening sky filled with stars. "Yes it is." Then returned her attention to Brett and recognized that pensive expression. "What's on your mind?"

"I was just thinking about something Jeremy Watts said last month on our way back from breakfast."

"That was nice of him to make time for that." Ruth took another sip from her glass, set it down and waited for Brett to continue.

Brett said, "I asked him what he thought of the creation story in the Bible, given everything we've learned about evolution. He said that it wasn't intended to be read like a scientific textbook and therefore should not be interpreted in the same way. Instead, Watts described the Bible as a history of God's interactions with humankind, a compilation of writings that instruct us how to find meaning in our lives through a relationship with Him."

"I like that," said Ruth. "Yet something about this supposed conflict between science and religion still bothers you, evidently."

Brett sighed. "I've been struggling with it lately, to be honest."

Ruth evened her gaze. "After you told me about Dr. Watt's lecture at Stanford, I found another quote from Blaise Pascal on the internet that really struck me." Calling it back from memory, she recited, "...*To those who wish to see, God gives sufficient light; to those who do not wish to see, He gives sufficient darkness.*"

She leaned forward. "How about you, Brett?"

"What do you mean?"

"You've been tagging along with me and the boys to church for years, but have you ever committed yourself to exploring your own spirituality?"

Brett felt put off by that at first, but changed his mind after a brief moment of self-reflection. Ruth was right. Why did he keep putting this off?

Ruth let the matter go, knowing her husband would eventually reach his own conclusion. They split an order of Mexican flan for dessert and enjoyed it with decaffeinated coffee.

After dinner, they walked hand in hand up the sidewalk and turned into the Towne Centre Bookstore. Ruth left Brett to browse the aisles while she perused the Book Club table.

Brett gravitated to the history section and soon found himself thumbing through a book about the Amazon Rainforest by Louis C. Barboza. Recalling his *yopo* experience, he decided to buy the book and tucked it under his arm.

His next stop was the religion section, where he encountered an overwhelming variety of books. So many different takes on spirituality. Some felt inspirational to him, and others quite dark. He almost gave up until one particular book happened to catch his eye. He pulled it from the shelf and started flipping through the pages, pausing again and again on passages that strangely spoke to him.   Although not quite yet ready for such ponderous reading, he returned *Autobiography of a Yogi* to its proper place on the shelf and went to check on Ruth.

CHAPTER FIFTEEN

"Howlers"

Saturday, March 23rd, 2002
Anza-Borrego Desert, California

Brett Roberts cranked up the stereo as he passed through Pine Valley. He was on his way out to the desert for his first Moon Howl experience. Most of the other *Howlers* had been out at the campsite since Thursday, his friend Mudford included. Unfortunately, Roberts had been asked to stop by BioProbe the day before to sign his employment documents. This explained his late departure, and also his solo attempt at navigating Mudford's photocopied map. Mudford had been a bit coy about what to expect. "All shall be revealed," was all he would say.

Roberts passed through Ocotillo, followed highway SR-2 out of town, and counted the mile markers until he spotted a dirt road turnoff. He pulled to the side of the road and consulted the route that Mudford had annotated for him. Yep, this must be the one, although the rugged dirt road looked like it hadn't been graded in quite some time. Mudford had strongly advised Roberts to reset his odometer before leaving the highway, and to follow his scribbled instructions to the tenth of a mile.

The winter rains had brought forth an abundance of wildflowers, although Roberts was now too preoccupied with the possibility of getting lost or stuck to enjoy the desert scenery. He constantly needed to wrestle with the steering wheel to avoid the ruts and boulders as he navigated the turns.

His trunk was filled with camping and hiking gear, along with a five gallon plastic jug of water, a small charcoal grill, and a twenty gallon cooler packed with food, beer and ice. He had also been asked to bring along a bottle of Don Julio tequila for his initiation into the Howlers. Quit worrying, he told himself. Plenty of provisions to survive out here for a few days if need be. Then he spotted the first landmark on the map, an old water tower standing next to a railroad track that looked like it hadn't been used for over 60 years. He killed the engine and stepped out into the dry desert heat to get his bearings, and he badly needed a beer to calm his nerves. The campsite was supposedly just beyond the Jacumba ridge. He shielded his eyes from the blinding sun and glanced around to find the spot where the rails had been covered over with gravel, where he could supposedly cross over.

Mudford had written 'take it slow' on the map in bold letters from there on. He was supposed to drive to a 'T' in the road and make a right and one final left toward *Dos Coyotes* canyon, so named for the two large rock formations rising up from either side of its entrance. They supposedly looked like howling coyotes when reflected in a certain way by the setting sun.

The final stretch turned out to an obstacle course of boulders poking their heads out of the sand with his hands deftly gripping the wheel to avoid them. But he presumed he was headed in the right direction when he spotted a pair of giant parabolic listening devices positioned near the canyon entrance. Nestled amidst the rocks and cacti stood a jumble of tents, camper trucks and other assorted vehicles with plastic tarps tethered between them. A flag pole in the center of camp had a banner with the silhouette of a coyote howling at the moon, flapping proudly in the breeze. The *Moon Howl* logo, apparently. Roberts grinned with relief. He had arrived.

Roberts pulled over next to a small clearing where he decided to pitch his tent. He incorrectly presumed the creosote bushes and desert willow surrounding that clearing might shelter his tent from the notorious wing gusts that often blew into the canyon after dusk.

Mudford spotted Robert's VW Jetta approaching and walked up with a beer in each hand. He handed one to Roberts as he stepped out of the car. "Gimme a hug, bubba!" Mudford wrapped his arms around Roberts and squeezed him tight. He'd gained about fifty pounds since prison but was still fit as a bear. "Great to have you with us, my brother."

Roberts took a full breath before answering. "You too, Owen. Think anyone would mind if I camped over there?"

Mudford nodded. "Camp anywhere you like. We've got the whole canyon to ourselves. My cousin Gerald got here early Thursday morning to stake our claim and I drove in later that afternoon with my cousin Jack. Most of the others have arrived by now. We've taken over man, no-one's gonna bother us."

Mudford helped Roberts put his tent up while describing the hike they had planned for later that afternoon. "Bring a day pack with two liters of water, a first aid kit if you have one, something to snack on, and extra sun screen for sure." Then he walked Roberts over to meet the rest of the *Howlers*. His cousin Jack Bradley wore a faded tie dye shirt with hippie beads and frayed denim shorts. Jack was recovering from a serious hangover and wouldn't be joining them on the hike. Instead, he and Marvin planned to drop a tab of acid and lounge in their hammocks beneath a plastic shelter that extended from the back of Jack's camper.

Marvin played fiddle in a blue grass band back in Ashville. He and Jack had closed down a bar one night and fast became drinking buddies. They'd also just sworn a blood oath not to leave those hammocks until they stopped tripping. The camp table between the hammocks supported a thoughtful assortment of kaleidoscopes, prisms and other such colorfully obscure items to keep them busy.

Jack emerged from the camper wearing a pair of circle rimmed sunglasses and a white Panama hat. He'd be channeling Hunter S. Thompson for this particular acid trip, apparently. "Okay Marvin, let's see if we can solve the world's problems over the next few hours, shall we?"

"You're on, buddy."

Jack's brother Gerald waited for the day trippers just outside the canyon entrance. Gerald was a commercial artist from San Diego who specialized in sea murals and marine life sculptures, a level-headed guy with an amazing capacity for maintaining that demeanor while under the influence of hallucinogenic substances. His son Lester was a professional BMX rider and had willingly volunteered to be Gerald's co-pilot for this afternoon's little foray through the desert. Jack's brother-in-law Andy was a retired veterinarian who also played guitar with a penchant for cowboy ballads. Everyone considered Andy *Moon Howl's* patriarch, having conceived the theme over twenty years before. This time he'd brought along his neighbor Harold, who like Roberts would also be experiencing his first *Moon Howl.* Other participants in this afternoon's adventure included Frank, a loyal member of Jack's production crew, and also Lorenzo, head chef at an upscale restaurant in San Diego's Little Italy neighborhood, one that Jack frequently patronized.

When they had all assembled, Gerald announced "Here you go," and produced a paper bag full of dried magic mushrooms and passed it around. Satisfied that everyone had taken a sufficient pinch of caps and stems, he then said, "Come on boys, eat up!"

Having tried mushrooms once before with Mudford, Roberts felt less trepidation this time. He knew that psilocybin, the active ingredient, has a chemical structure remarkably similar to that of DMT, yet for him the effect seemed quite different, more malleable and participatory.

Gerald waited until each of them had washed down their palmful of 'shrooms with a swig of water before doing the same. "Okay, now listen up. I want you all to buddy up in pairs. No one hikes alone, *comprende?*" He waited again before continuing. "Good. We'll be making our way across the desert floor toward that rock ridge over yonder." He pointed to a rising pile of rust colored boulders about two miles away. One particular cluster resembled an array of giant toes, hence their name in Spanish, *Piedras Grandes.* "I'll do my best to keep y'all together. If you need to stop for any reason, piss, trip out, whatever, just hold up your hand so I'll know. And remember, you must *not* lose sight of your buddy under any circumstances."

They started out single file and weaved their way through a seemingly endless maze of cholla cactus and creosote bushes. Stands of ocotillo were scattered about, with clusters of brilliant red plumage extending that drew the eye with lingering fascination. Gerald cautioned his charge of desert wanderers to steer clear of the cholla. "Watch out, men. Those spiny knobs can easily snap off and ride along with you through the desert. It's how they transplant themselves. Almost impossible to pluck out the needles without leaving the barb behind, real painful too."

The hallucinogenic effect of the 'shrooms began to kick in. With the desert now in full bloom, Roberts became increasingly distracted by the eye-popping blues and lavenders, pinks and yellows. Cactus buds were sprouting in fast-forward filmography, beavertail and barrel cactus and a variety of others that Roberts couldn't name. The desert had become alive!

"You okay buddy?" Roberts was relieved to see Mudford standing nearby, who was likewise absorbed in the desert flowers.

"Dude, these blossoms are freaking amazing!"

"I know." Mudford smiled and flashed his teeth.

Gerald wisely called a brief halt. "Ten minutes, guys."

Mudford wandered over to a stand of ocotillo and Roberts reflexively followed after him. These strange looking desert plants have tall, straight and spiny stalks angling outward from a central base, and can rise as high as 20 feet. Although leafless for most of the year, hundreds of tiny and narrow oval leaves had recently sprouted from their branches. Mudford drew near one of them and stood there with his arms outstretched.

Roberts picked another one and likewise extended his arms. While slowly breathing in and out, he began to sense a surprising connection with this majestic plant, its tiny leaves soaking up the sun's rays, processing carbon dioxide from the air into sugars... "Whoa! I can actually feel its energy. Dude, this plant is happy right now."

Mudford grinned and nodded in agreement. "Me too. These ocotillo come alive every spring."

Gerald shouted, "Times' up, Howlers. Take another swig of water and then follow me. We've got about a mile left to cover."

"Where's he taking us, Owen?" Roberts asked his best friend in the whole wide world.

"Freaking awesome place, you'll see."

The *Howlers* resumed their march with palpable enthusiasm. Most had been to the cave a number of times. Twenty minutes later, with the boulders now towering above them, Gerald led them to a crevice and waved them inside. One at a time, they squeezed through and entered a cave of surprising dimensions. Roberts estimated it to be about 10 feet wide by 14 feet deep, with enough head clearance to stand fully erect, and a rock chimney toward the back.

"Check it out, you guys," Lester pointed.

"Whoa!" said Roberts as noticed the Pictoglyphs. He stepped forward to examine the centuries-old drawings, rams and bison and people on horseback and crab-like animals and what looked like some kind of armadillo, and the sun with two rings surrounding it.... Water must have been plentiful back then, wild game as well. The indigenous people must have once thrived in this region, Roberts thought to himself.

It felt refreshingly cool inside the cave. They sat cross-legged on the crushed granite floor and absorbed its peaceful aura. Andy reached into his daypack and passed around a few musical instruments. He kept the thumb harp and began by plucking it softly, a soothing and rhythmic melody. Gerald joined in with a bamboo flute. Lester gently tapped rhythm on a Navajo hand drum. Roberts leaned back against the smooth stone wall and closed his eyes to listen. He envisioned the Kumeyaay people who once inhabited this cave, their brown-skinned women grinding maize in morteros outside the cave, their men hunting jack rabbits and big horn sheep in the canyons beyond. And the ancient ones who had come before them, never recorded and long since forgotten. He vaguely sensed them speaking, as he had done with the noble ocotillo. Their spirit lingered here.

The musicians gradually slowed the tempo and stopped on the same note. After a suitable moment of silence, Gerald said softly. "Gentlemen, are we ready to go?" Everyone seemed to feel it was time.

They squeezed back through the crevice and emerged into blinding sunlight. Thankfully, the hallucinogenic effects of the 'shrooms had abated by then. Thought processes and sequences of events gradually reconnected as the *Howlers* made their way back toward *Dos Coyotes* canyon. Roberts spotted Jack and Marvin manning the giant parabolic listening devices as they approached the entrance to the canyon. Passing between them, he overheard Jack cussing Marvin out in Pidgin English and laughing hysterically when Marvin replied in return.

"Let's leave them be," Gerald sagely advised.

The *Howlers* returned to camp and engaged in a game of musical camp chairs beneath the sun tarps and easy-ups to escape the late afternoon sun. With little shade left to squeeze into, Roberts spotted Andy and Harold sitting in the shade behind a badly oxidized Chevy panel van with a cooler between them.

"Have a seat," said Andy, still wearing his desert hat. "Plenty of room for one more." He reached into the cooler and handed up a beer.

"Thanks," said Roberts. He studied the letters on the side of the van before setting down his chair. It read *Misión de Esperanza*, still wavering and somewhat three-dimensional.

Andy resumed playing his thumb harp. Roberts found the soft and rhythmic chords a bit hypnotic. He shut his eyes again to listen. After a moment, he distinctly heard a whisper in the air. *You've got a strong spirit there, Brett.*

"What?" Roberts glanced toward Andy, who simply grinned. Roberts shook his head. "Whoa, I had no idea 'shrooms could have this effect."

Andy held Brett's gaze. *That wasn't the shrooms talking, Brett. It's me.*

Harold nodded in agreement.

Roberts felt certain that neither of them had spoken. "Hold on a second!" he exclaimed. "What's happening?"

Andy spoke his next words out loud. "Just a special gift some of us have. You have it too, apparently."

Roberts shuddered involuntarily when he recalled Vivian saying essentially the same thing to him years ago, the woman from Marin back in graduate school. In no shape to think this through, he decided to change the subject. "I presume that van is yours."

Andy said, "Yep. Harold and I started a mission school down in Guatemala about ten years ago."

"We'll be heading back down next month," Harold chimed in. "Care to join us?"

Roberts found this idea a bit intriguing, but then said, "Maybe after I retire. I'm starting a new job the beginning of April."

Andy pulled out a pen and notepad and handed them to Roberts. "Here, write down your email address and we'll add you to our newsletter."

The shade behind the mini-bus gradually lengthened until it merged with the rest of the darkening canyon as the sun began to sink beneath the craggy ridge. Mudford poked his head around and said, "Hey Brett, did you remember to bring the tequila?"

Roberts stood, polished off his beer and turned to thank his benefactor. "Thanks Andy."

Andy nodded sagely. *Don't mention it, Brett.*

Had he actually heard Andy speaking just then? He didn't think so. Roberts shrugged it off and turned to Mudford who evidently hadn't noticed. "Can you help me get my stuff from the car?"

Mudford grinned, "You bet."

Roberts opened the trunk and Mudford lifted out the cooler. Roberts grabbed his bottle of Don Julio Añejo and tried not to think about the cost. They returned to camp and Roberts ceremoniously presented the tequila to Lester.

"Aaooo!" Lester howled with glee. He ran to his tent and quickly changed into a Mexican Serape and sombrero. Popping back out, he shouted "Who's ready for margaritas?" Before anyone could answer, he darted over to Gerald's truck for a storage container that held his makeshift bar items. He plugged the blender into a power outlet on the back of Jack's camper, filled the pitcher with ice from a cooler and added a generous pour of tequila, Cointreau and lime juice.

Roberts took his first sip. "Damn, that's good."

"So glad you approve, Señor Brett!" Lester leaped around topping off glasses from the frosty pitcher and returned to make another batch.

Mudford leaned toward Roberts and muttered, "I wouldn't encourage Lester if I were you." Roberts understood after finishing off his glass, beginning to feel a bit buzzed already. He waved Lester off when he came back around.

Lorenzo poured charcoal into a Weber grill, added a generous squeeze of lighter fluid and lit it with a brilliant *'foom!'* Frank brought out a platter of cheese and crackers to tide everyone over. Gerald passed around a bowl of cocktail shrimp on ice. Someone fired up the first joint of the evening.

Mudford passed the joint over to Roberts. "We've got cleanup detail. It'll be worth it, you'll see." Meat began to sizzle on the grill and it smelled delicious already.

Jack and Marvin finally shuffled over. "How's everyone doing?" shouted Jack. Everyone howled with enthusiasm. "Well good." Jack asked for the joint, pinched it between his lips and took a long drag. Then noticing the margaritas, he asked Lester to whip up another batch. Lester didn't mind. He clearly enjoyed playing the role of Mexican desperado bartender.

Lorenzo set the tables with platters of lettuce and cheese, sour cream and guacamole, and refried beans with Spanish rice. He returned with two large steaming platters of fajitas and clay pots of warm tortillas. "Dinner is served, assholes!"

The food was polished off with a final shot of tequila. Roberts and Mudford stood and began clearing paper plates away while Lorenzo and the rest of the cooking crew settled back in their chairs and passed around another joint. The heat radiated quickly out of the porous granite soil as darkness began to fall, and a chilly breeze pressed into the canyon with its departure, the *Moon Howl* flag flapping urgently in reply. Most went for their jackets, except for Roberts and Mudford who were busily scrubbing the pots over tubs of hot dishwater.

Harold dragged over a portable fire pit and constructed a mini-volcano of sticks inside which he lit and blew to life while adding larger pieces of wood. A circle of Howlers pulled their chairs around to enjoy its warmth. As if on cue, the moon began to rise above the jagged rocks. It was full tonight, which explained why they had picked this particular weekend for *Moon Howl.* Andy went off to get his guitar and Marvin his fiddle.

Roberts finished drying the pots and pans, and then dumped the tubs of dishwater behind a cactus. Lorenzo hoisted himself out of the chair and went to inspect their work. "Good job, guys. I'll put all the dishes and cooking gear away, you go on ahead and join the others." Finally aware now of the evening chill, Roberts and Mudford returned to their tents for wool beanies and pullover sweaters before heading over to join the fire circle.

Jack passed the joint to Roberts. "You seem a lot more relaxed now, Brett. Good to have you with us."

"Thanks Jack, I haven't let go like this in quite a while." Jack patted Roberts firmly on the shoulder to acknowledge his approval. "You probably needed it, Brett. Now just settle back and enjoy."

Andy and Marvin took a good amount of time tuning their instruments. Finally ready, Andy strummed out a few chords and Marvin raised his fiddle to join in. These two men, one older one younger, they played together with intertwined musical ribbons of sound, a free-flowing jam fest with each musician anticipating the other's changes. It was mesmerizing to watch how they fed off each other and even more enjoyable to listen to. Roberts had the feeling he may never hear anything quite like this again. The tequila bottle came by but he passed it on without taking another sip. No, he was good. He settled back and studied to the jagged rock silhouettes of the canyon ridge with a radiant silver moon rising, about 30 degrees above the horizon now, casting long cacti shadows on the sandy ground. The dropping temperature caused wisps of crushed-eggshell cloud patterns to form in the nighttime sky, with a halo around the moon that made it look eerily majestic. For Roberts, it felt like one of those rare moments of extreme awareness… or maybe he was just stoned.

Andy started strumming a familiar cowboy ballad and everyone seemed to know the words. It was a song about a coyote calling up to the moon, the *Moon Howl* theme song apparently. *"Coyote… aaooh! Howl while you can, howl while you can…."*

Marvin launched into a solo and everyone paused to listen. He slowly bowed his final note, a perfect ending. Dry wood popped and crackled in the fire pit with sparks spitting skyward.

After a while, Jack stood and walked out to one of the giant parabolic listening devices. He turned it to face the desert floor and then hollered back toward camp to ask if anyone wanted to join him. Mudford encouraged Roberts to go, having already done this activity the previous night.

When Jack saw Roberts coming, he stepped away and motioned him toward the sound tube. "Here, have a listen." At first all Roberts heard were the amplified sounds of creosote branches rustling in the breeze, but then came the distinctive *"hoot-hoot!"* of a great horned owl. "Hear that?" Jack asked. Roberts heard it again and nodded. A snake slithered across the sand. A jack rabbit scurried out of its hole. The desert had come alive.

"Thanks Jack. This is awesome."

"Yes it is," Jack said with emphasis on each word.

Gerald had been using his wide-lens Nikon camera to photograph the nighttime sky. Lester handed out glow sticks and Marvin began waving his around in spiral-like patterns. Seeing that, Gerald snapped Marvin's picture with a 2 second exposure, thinking he might put it on next year's *Moon Howl* invitation.

With the fire logs almost fully consumed, the circle of *Howlers* stared silently into the dying embers. Gradually they surrendered to their sleeping bags. Roberts chose that moment to whisper over to Mudford, "Can you spare a few minutes? Somewhere away from the others, if you don't mind."

"Sure buddy," said Mudford. They picked up their chairs and carried them over to Brett's campsite with the bright moon illuminating their way.

"So, what do you think of *Moon Howl?*" asked Mudford.

"Probably just what I needed Owen, thanks for inviting me… but there's something I've been wanting to talk with you about."

Mudford leaned forward. "What's up?"

"It's about the time we tried *yopo* back in graduate school. I've been reluctant to bring it up again, considering what happened to you afterwards."

"Forget about that, Brett. It's all in the past."

"Yeah, I know. But that's not the part I wanted to talk about."

"Then I presume you're ready to talk about that *yopo* induced hallucination of yours. You sure it was Virtanen?"

"It was him, Owen. I'm sure of it, and he's been popping back into my head ever since."

"Whoa, buddy. That still sounds pretty out there."

"Maybe so. Although I met this lady up in Marin a few weeks after my first encounter who claimed that she too could talk to spirits. What do you make of that, Owen? Think there's life after death?"

"Couldn't really say. Guess I'm more of a philosopher, but I do believe in a higher power, if that's what you're asking."

"Well anyway, she said you need to have an earth guide whenever attempting to contact the spirit world, otherwise you might lose your way."

Mudford took a long breath, seeing where this was going. "So you think Virtanen may have accidently left his body after taking one of those compounds he'd been synthesizing in the lab?"

"Yeah, Owen. I really do."

"Well then, where'd that body disappear to?"

"Guess that's a good question… maybe got time-shifted somewhere? Even you seemed to think that was possible."

Mudford shook his head and yawned, "Well dude, I'm way too tired to discuss this any further. See you in the morning, okay?" He picked up his chair and crunched over to his own tent on the opposite side of the campground, isolated and well apart from the others. Mudford was a snorer. But he was a considerate snorer.

The wind had stopped and the air was cool and perfectly silent, at least for the moment. Roberts removed the rainfly on his tent so he could gaze up to the nighttime sky while lying atop his sleeping bag. The stars of the

Milky Way glistened above him like finely crushed diamonds....

Luisa nearly crossed the veil into Brett's mind that evening. *Soon*, she imagined.

Lorenzo had a large pot of coffee brewing the next morning. He also had Italian seasoned scrambled eggs and sausages simmering on the camp stove that smelled like heaven. Gerald seemed to be having a good time photographing everyone's hung over faces as they climbed out of their bags and stumbled over to grab a cup.

"Good morning, campers!" Jack shouted from his camper van. They all made a feeble attempt to howl, not a very convincing one this time. But by their second pot of coffee, and with warm food now settling in their bellies, the Howlers started showing a few signs of life. The sun's rays peeked above the rocky ridge and threatened some serious heat once it had resumed its proper place in the sky.

Jack walked over to shake Brett's hand. "Glad you could join us, Brett. You've got a nice spiritual energy about you." He seemed to mean it from the look in his eyes. Roberts took a moment to process that thought before thanking him. What was it about this family? And why was Mudford so blissfully immune?

"Who's ready for another Margarita?" shouted Lester with his usual wild-man enthusiasm. Roberts was relieved by the jeers of dissent that followed.

Gerald called everyone over for the group photo. They clustered together with arms around shoulders in front of the *Moon Howl* flag, Gerald set the timer to join them, and they all hollered like coyotes right before the shutter clicked.

Lester carried a cooler of beer around while they all broke camp, his way of saying goodbye. By the end of the hour, the campground had been restored to its usual pristine condition. Reloaded vehicles began to slowly head out.

Mudford had ridden in with one of his cousins, but rode back with Roberts to make sure he found his way out to the highway, and this time it took less than 20 minutes for the Jetta's wheels to return to solid pavement, leaving the bumps and jolts behind with a cloudy trail of dust.

Roberts said, "Thanks for riding back with me, Owen. Hey, think you might be ready to continue on with last night's discussion?"

Mudford rolled the window down and stuck his head out to feel the wind against his face. After settling back in his seat, he said "Hey, Brett, I need to take a piss. Can you pull over?" Roberts pulled over and they each found a different cactus to water. Then he popped the trunk to grab another couple beers. Mudford willingly accepted. "Thanks, bud." Leaning against the car they sipped their cold brews and gazed out to the desert, a bit less four dimensional today... but still just as beautiful. Mudford belched. "Okay man, let's head back to civilization."

Roberts rolled the windows back up, switched on the AC and accelerated onto Interstate 8. He selected a classic CD to pop in the deck, the *Hunky Dory* album by David Bowie. Mudford started tapping on the dashboard. "Guess I'm ready now, what's still on your mind?"

"Okay, here goes. A couple of years ago, I got involved in an experiment that showed a clear linkage between DMT levels in the brain and gene expression patterns right around the time of death. Remember that paper I published with Janet Feinstein?" Roberts described Calvin Schwarzkopf's accident, where two of those tissue samples had come from, and the results that were never published.

"No shit? Unbelievable!"

"Still have a hard time believing it myself. But there's more." He then described the new microarray prototype he'd been working on right before leaving Spectrum. "And according to that new data, Schwarzkopf's brain had been expressing abnormally high levels of a novel gene called SIGMAR-1. I'm pretty sure this gene codes for a novel membrane receptor, although its function hasn't yet been characterized. But here's the thing. Suppose there are mutations in this gene, ones that cause some people to respond differently to DMT than others, maybe even trigger brainwaves strong enough to break through to the spirit world."

"Hmm..." said Mudford. "Let's assume for a moment that Virtanen sampled *yopo* before coming to graduate school. Since his mother happened to be indigenous, he must have expected something spiritual to happen, and when it didn't... well, that may well explain all those DMT-related compounds he'd been working on. Must have believed one of them would eventually work for him."

"That's precisely what I was thinking," Roberts added, "although I still can't believe you sold Virtanen's lab notebooks to that kitchen chemist drug pusher. Sorry to bring that up again, but dude, really?"

Mudford waited for the song to end while deciding how to answer. *Dammit, here goes...* "I photocopied Virtanen's notebooks before handing them over. After seeing those drug fatalities on the evening news, I figured I'd better stash them away someplace safe. Never told the cops about it, and now you're the first to know."

"Well shit! I probably shouldn't have just told you what I did."

"Don't worry, I definitely learned my lesson the last time. But hey, wouldn't you like to see those photocopies?"

"Not a chance. Matter fact, we should probably forget about this whole discussion." They descended into El Cajon Valley and Roberts popped a Frank Black CD into the deck. Mudford cranked up the volume.

"Fine by me," he shouted above the noise. "Just let me know if you change your mind."

Roberts hoped he never would. Good thing he had a new job coming up to distract him.

CHAPTER SIXTEEN

"The mutation"

Early fall, 2002
La Jolla, California

BIOPROBE occupied a glass-walled building on Torrey Pines Mesa, a rapidly expanding biotech hub due to its close proximity to the Scripps Research Institute, UC San Diego, and the Salk Institute to the south. Built directly across the road from a world famous golf course, BioProbe's west-facing upper floor office windows looked out to a panoramic view of the Pacific Ocean.

The cancer diagnostics program was progressing nicely with Brett Roberts leading the effort. He and his team had recently developed a highly sensitive blood test for detecting the presence of cancer cells based on their genetic mutations. The assay was currently being tested with actual patient samples to demonstrate its potential for monitoring their response to chemotherapy. Positive results needed to be confirmed by targeted DNA sequencing, still considered the gold standard for identifying such mutations. BioProbe didn't own a DNA sequencer, although Bob Miller's lab down the road at Scripps still used one of the early automated models for studying human hereditary diseases such as cystic fibrosis. Roberts had negotiated a contract with Miller to run his samples whenever their lab schedule allowed.

Brian Sakow was the instrument's chief curator, a talented post-doctoral fellow who worked in Miller's lab. He had close-cropped brown hair, Slavic features, keen hazel eyes, and a look that told you he was probably a step ahead of whatever you might be thinking. He also happened to be an avid cyclist who didn't own a car. It didn't take long for Roberts to encounter Sakow during one of his early morning rides into work. He preferred it to driving in rush hour traffic since it was generally faster, and also a lot more fun. The route from Brett's house to work ran south along Torrey Pines State Beach and then up to the mesa. Sakow turned out to be a surprisingly strong rider despite his lean physique. Roberts found it difficult to keep up with him during their steep ascent up the Torrey Pines grade. Nevertheless, the two of them soon became regular cycling buddies.

Sakow's unbridled enthusiasm and disarming personality made it difficult to avoid his probing and sometimes unwelcome questions. One morning while riding in together, he asked Roberts about the paper he'd published two years earlier with Janet Feinstein. Roberts found himself discussing his DMT experiment, and eventually confided that he'd actually tried *yopo* once in graduate school.

Sakow wanted to hear every detail about that experience and wouldn't let it go. "Think you might have had some sort of spiritual encounter?"

There was that question again. *Oh well,* thought Roberts, he'd already stepped his toe into this one. "Seems hard to believe even now, but it definitely felt that way, at least to me. Although a buddy of mine also tried it and wasn't all that impressed. Evidently his experience was nowhere near like mine." Roberts would never mention Owen by name and he certainly had no intention of telling Sakow about Juan Virtanen.

Sakow waited until they'd reached the top of Torrey Pines hill before commenting, "I know what you mean."

This admission caught Roberts off guard. "Look Brian, I hope you're not just trying to patronize me…."

"No really, Brett. Our brains have been slowly accumulating genetic mutations over the millennia. Perhaps some of those mutations have attenuated our ability as humans to make spiritual connections, although there's a compelling amount of evidence to suggest that some still can — psychics, clairvoyants, healers, even water diviners. Most are probably quacks, just maybe not all of them."

"Sounds a bit farfetched Brian, even coming for you." Although Roberts had been struggling with the same idea.

Sakow waited until their next ride to prod further. "Hey Brett, think you might have a slightly different form of this SIGMAR-1 gene? I could sequence it for you, just need a blood sample is all. Come on, what have you got to lose? Or are you afraid to find out you're no different from the rest of us heathens?"

"I dunno, Brian. Let me think about it," said Roberts. Although compulsively intrigued, Roberts had never quite considered this possibility, to examine his own his own genetic instructions.

Roberts cycled west on Carmel Valley Road the following Wednesday morning. With a heavy mist in the air, the features of the lagoon were barely visible to his left. He peddled up the rise to the sound of waves crashing along the shore. Brian Sakow had been waiting at the traffic light per their usual schedule, and together they coasted single file over the bridge and down toward Torrey Pines State Beach. Roberts glanced right to inspect the waves as they peddled south above the granite seawall. About chest high today, with a pretty decent curl. Maybe he'd head out there with his board after work....

"Mornings have been kinda chilly lately," Sakow shouted.

"Yeah," Roberts acknowledged, now in tucked position to minimize his body's exposure to the frigid crosswind. "But I still prefer this time of year to the summer crowds. A lot more peaceful."

"I hear you. Hey, look out there!" Sakow pointed. Roberts spotted a school of black Pacific dolphins playfully surfing the waves and experienced a brief moment of unexpected joy. "You know Brian? I don't think I'll ever get tired of these morning rides along the ocean."

But Torrey Pines hill loomed just ahead, an imposing climb leading up to the mesa. An ancient pine tree dominated the top of bluff, its branches sculpted sideways by the constant updrafts.

Their breathing accelerated as they upshifted into the climb. Roberts struggled to maintain a respectable distance behind his riding partner, and found that he needed to rise up off his seat a few times during the steepest part of the ascent, although Sakow never left his saddle. They rounded a bend and then powered up the final slope. The bike lane widened from there and they rode side by side the rest of the way.

Sakow politely slowed at the top and waited for Roberts to catch his breath. "I've already ordered the sequencing primers for that experiment we talked about. Can you stop by my lab after work? All I need is your blood sample."

Roberts considered the implications before answering. "You sure we can keep this confidential?"

"My technician Amy is also a trained phlebotomist. I'll tell her you volunteered to be a normal healthy donor for one of my experiments. She'll never know which one. Look, I'll stay late tonight and process the sample myself. Don't worry, I brought my bike light."

Sakow's new Night Rider model lit up the road ahead like a beacon, although that wasn't what concerned Roberts just then.

Later that morning, Roberts sat with his team in BioProbe's second floor conference room. "Alright then. I think we have a good plan for the coming week. Any questions?"

One of his technicians asked in her heavy Russian accent, which hadn't improved much since coming to America, "How we can prove our test have valid results?"

Katya Belyakov's one-year sabbatical from the Russian Academy of Sciences in Novosibirsk was almost over, although she'd been hinting lately that she no longer wished to return to her native country. Katya was a Russian Jew, and despite the recent collapse of the Soviet Union, religious persecution continued to be endemic in her home country. She also reportedly had Romanian gypsy blood in her lineage.

Roberts pondered his response while studying Katya's startling green eyes. She'd volunteered to read his palm during a party the previous fall. How astonished her expression had been when he reluctantly complied. According to her reading, he possessed a strong spiritual energy but was also being tormented by a dark angel of some kind. She couldn't be more specific than that, probably a good thing. "We could send a random number of our samples over to the Miller lab for sequence verification. I'll stop by after work and ask when they can fit this into their schedule."

With less than an hour of daylight left, Roberts made his final rounds through the lab and decided it was now or never. He changed back into his cycling clothes and carried his bike down the stairway to the main lobby. "Have a good evening, Karen," he called over to the front desk receptionist.

Karen Perlman was the mother of BioProbe's CEO and founder, and considered them all part of her extended family. "You too, Brett, be safe!"

Roberts reached for the door and tugged his bike through, then turned around to wave back at Karen. He took the pedestrian walkway underneath Torrey Pines Road and clipped in to peddle the short distance down to the research wing of Scripps Medical Center, where the Miller lab was located on the second floor. Exiting the elevator, he walked his bike down the hall and knocked on lab door S-236. Sakow opened it almost immediately with a beaming smile.

"Hey Brett," he said. "Go ahead and walk your bike around to my back desk carrel."

Roberts leaned his bike against Sakow's and glanced out the window to Torrey Pines Golf Course, a much better view than what he had to look at back in graduate school.

"Brett, this is Amy," said Sakow. Roberts turned around to see a young woman in a white lab coat with short blond hair and dazzling green eyes.

Amy reached out to shake his hand. "Pleased to meet you, Dr. Roberts. So… are you ready?"

"I suppose so," Roberts answered. He followed her over to a phlebotomy station along the side wall. Amy cinched a rubber tourniquet above his elbow and quickly got to work. Roberts barely felt the needle stick. She handed the tube of blood over to Brian.

"Thanks, Amy," said Sakow. She smiled and politely left the lab, shutting the door behind her with a soft click.

Then Sakow said to Roberts, "I'll spin this down and extract the DNA right after you leave. The sequencing results should be ready by tomorrow morning."

Roberts suddenly began to have second thoughts. "Why are you doing this, exactly?"

"Look Brett, there's nothing to worry about." He held up the tube. "See? I've given your sample an anonymous barcode ID, so…."

Roberts persisted, "No really, Brian. I'd really like to know why are you seem so keen on helping me."

Sakow's face turned serious. "Okay, here goes. My twin brother and I used to communicate telepathically. There, you happy?"

This was the first time Sakow had ever spoken about his family. Roberts studied his eyes for any hint of bullshit. "Used to?"

"He died in a car crash two years ago."

"Oh man, I'm so sorry."

Sakow's eyes glistened. "Don't be. He still speaks with me once in a while."

Shortly after Roberts left, Sakow went over to the phlebotomy station and tied the rubber tourniquet around his own upper arm, using his teeth. Then with the aid of a syringe, he withdrew seven milliliters of his own blood and squirted it into a second barcoded sample tube.

Back on his bike, Roberts leaned over the handlebars to reduce his wind resistance while he accelerated down Torrey Pines hill. He glanced repeatedly at the odometer until it showed a top speed of just over 50 mph. Cars had slowed to a crawl down on Coast Highway. Motorists glanced enviously toward Roberts as he sped past them.

Reaching the bottom, he glanced left to admire the setting sun's rays reflecting on the water in millions of glistening tiny ripples. Parents sat on their blankets and watched it set while their children chased each other around playfully. Surfers were out in abundance, too many of them unfortunately. Roberts wished he'd gone out earlier. He continued peddling up the coastal bridge and made a right at the streetlight onto Carmel Valley Road to accelerate down and rejoin Los Peñasquitos Lagoon.

He rode along its northern perimeter while glancing intermittently to his right to study the meandering blue streams of salt brine cutting their way through vast fields of cord grass. One of those streams ran alongside the road and he looked down to admire the thin green fingers of fluttering eelgrass beneath its surface. A moment later he spotted a blue heron perched on one of the sand islands keenly eyeing the water for an evening meal to swim by.

Roberts enjoyed this peaceful stretch of his ride along the lagoon, a place where he somehow felt more alive. He crossed under the Interstate-5 overpass and checked his wristwatch before upshifting again to make the last gentle climb into the residential section of Carmel Valley. It was a golden late afternoon and he looked forward to getting home a bit earlier than usual. Ruth deserved a break. He thought about taking Thomas and Michael for a walk to the local market to buy some steaks to barbeque for dinner. A glass of red wine would go nicely with that, maybe open one of the bottles they'd bought down from Napa.

Roberts got a call from Sakow two days later while eating a sandwich at his desk.

"Hey Brett, can you stop by after work? I've got your SIGMAR-1 gene sequence right here in front of me on the computer screen. I'd like to show you how it lines up with the reference sequence from UC Santa Cruz."

"What did you find? Can you give me some idea over the phone?"

"You should probably come over and have a look for yourself."

Roberts left early that Friday afternoon and was relieved to find Sakow alone in the Miller lab when he got there. Sakow booted up the alignment program and keyed in the gene sequences on his computer screen.

"The reference sequence from UC Santa Cruz for the SIGMAR-1 gene is shown on top. Your sequence is the next one down." Sakow scrolled the tab left and right to show Roberts where the exon and intron boundaries were located. He zoomed in on one of the exons and pointed to the screen. "There you are," said Sakow.

Roberts moved closer and raised his eyebrows when he saw the mutation. "What does it mean?" he asked.

Sakow said, "Assuming we have the right gene, this mutation could help explain why you're so sensitive to the effects of DMT. The program predicts it would code for an entirely different amino acid, somewhere near the binding pocket I'm guessing."

Roberts pointed to the next row. "Yeah? Well, what's this sequence?"

Sakow smiled. "Mine, of course. Dude, we both harbor the same mutation! See if you can read my mind. Come on, I know you can."

"I don't know, Brian…." Roberts reflected on his ability to communicate telepathically with Andy at *Moon Howl* and it frightened him, not only because he couldn't read Brian's mind just then. The closer he got to an answer, the harder it was for him to believe. And each time that happened, he tried to let it go. But he couldn't. This whole thing had him bottled up inside. "Look, I gotta go."

Sakow handed him a thumb drive. "Well here, take this. We can talk about some another time. Still planning to ride in on Monday?"

"Yep, see you then. And thanks, by the way. Really appreciate your help with this, although I'm still finding it difficult to believe that a single genetic mutation could be responsible for what I've been experiencing."

Roberts tried desperately not to think about the thumb drive until the following Friday afternoon when he finally succumbed. "Shit!" Something still didn't make sense, and that something had to do with Virtanen's disappearance. He took it out of the drawer and started twirling it around by the key ring, knowing that it contained his SIGMAR-1 gene sequence in FAST-A format, a standard file that could be opened and read by most bioinformatics programs. After a brief moment of indecision, he fumbled in his wallet for Mudford's cell phone number.

"Brett! You're the first person besides Elsa to try calling me on this phone. How the heck are you, my friend?"

"Doing well, Owen. How's the new baby?"

"Charlie? Oh man, he's great. Really loves the beach, just like his parents. Although Elsa's been talking a lot about daycare lately. Seems she's eager to get back to work."

"Yeah, well good luck with that. Listen Owen, I've been thinking about that lab notebook of Virtanen's, the one you photocopied? How'd you like to take a quick road trip with me up to the Bay Area to have a look at it?"

"Um, I thought we'd agreed to leave that one alone...."

Roberts explained in detail what he wanted to do. Mudford responded, "No way! Dude, you might be even crazier than me. But okay, you can count me in. When do we go?"

"I was thinking about heading up tomorrow morning. Think Elsa would be okay with that?"

"Yeah, she probably won't mind. But what about Ruth? Have you told her about this DMT obsession of yours?"

"Some, but not all. I've never quite gotten the nerve to tell her everything."

"And you two have been married all these years? Unbelievable. Well look Brett, if we do go through with this, I really think you should."

Roberts felt duly embarrassed. "You're right. I've been putting this off for some reason. Look, I'll tell her the rest tonight."

"Good luck with that," said Mudford

Brett dialed Ruth right afterward. "Hi Dear! Just got off the phone with Owen… yeah, he sounds good, Charlie's sure keeping him busy… anyway, we just discussed making a short trip up to San Francisco this weekend to visit Patrick. Would you mind?"

Although spur of the moment, Ruth answered, "I suppose not. You and Owen haven't done much together in a while. But what's this about?"

"I'll explain tonight." And Brett actually meant it this time. With that out of the way, he flipped through Rolodex to find O'Reilly's new number.

"Patrick O'Reilly," he answered.

"Hey Patrick, sorry I haven't called in a while. …Good, thanks. How about you? …Great to hear. Well look, here's the reason I called. I've been studying a novel gene that appears to be implicated in neurological disorders. …Yeah, I have the primary sequence. Seems to be related to the serotonin family. Think you'd be willing to run it through one of your structure prediction algorithms?"

O'Reilly replied, "Sounds interesting. How many amino acids does it code for? …Okay, I suppose I could give it a try."

Roberts said, "Great. But listen Patrick, this project is highly confidential. I'd rather meet with you in person. Matter of fact, I was thinking about driving up tomorrow. Would Sunday work for you? Sorry about the short notice."

O'Reilly glanced wistfully out his bayside office window to the white caps down below. "There's a windsurfing group I usually sail with on Sunday mornings, but the place where we meet isn't that far from my office. Sure you can't stay over?"

Roberts said, "Wish I could, but I really need to be back at work on Monday. Oh, by the way, Owen will be making the drive up with me. I've already filled him in on this project, but it's just between us."

O'Reilly puzzled over what this might be about, but decided not to ask. "That sounds great. Can you meet me at the Oyster Point parking lot, say around noon?"

"We'll be there. Looking forward to it, Patrick."

"Me too Brett, drive safe."

Roberts arranged a Presto log in the fireplace and lit it shortly after the boys had gone to bed. He popped open a bottle of merlot, poured two glasses, and joined Ruth on the sofa.

Ruth took her first sip. "Good choice. Okay, so why this sudden trip up to the Bay Area to see Patrick?"

Brett took a sip as well while trying to compose his thoughts. Finally he began, "Remember that dream I told you about when we were still in graduate school, the one with Juan Virtanen? I know I promised to mention if it ever happened again."

Ruth leveled her eyes. "Go on."

"Well yes, I have had a few more dreams like that, most recently a couple of years ago while attending the GSAC meeting in Miami. I'm sorry Ruth, I didn't want to worry you."

"So why now?"

Brett continued, "Well, I've just learned something that might help explain what triggered those dreams."

Ruth briefly shook her head. "Wait, what does this have to do with Patrick?"

"I'll get to that. Hear me out, please."

Ruth listened intently, asking simple 'yes' or 'no' questions while Brett told her about the envelope, his experience with *yopo*, and more about the visions of Virtanen that followed.

"Brett, I can't believe you've never told me this before."

"Honestly Ruth, I've been trying for years to convince myself it wasn't real, that I'd simply imagined those visions. But there's more." He described how Calvin Schwarzkopf's tissue samples had been collected and walked her through the details of his unpublished experiments. "The data showed a strong association between DMT levels in the brain and a novel membrane receptor called SIGMAR-1. The gene shares a fair amount of sequence similarity with another well-known gene that codes for the serotonin receptor. Which is why I want to visit Patrick. His computer programs should help determine whether or not this SIGMAR-1 receptor actually binds DMT."

Ruth put down her wine glass and pushed it away. "Alright, but you conducted those experiments over a year ago. So let me ask you again, why now?"

The Presto log was almost spent by the time Brett had finished telling Ruth about Brian Sakow and their DNA sequencing endeavor.

Ruth waited for the flames to flicker out, took a cleansing breath, and then said, "Let's see if I've got this. You've identified a novel brain receptor, one that supposedly binds dimethyltryptamine. Correct?"

"Yes, that's right. I…."

She interrupted, "And since you have a mutation in some gene that you think might be responsible for DMT's effects on the brain, you now believe it could help explain your *yopo* experience, and these nightmares you've been having?"

Brett said, "I know it's a stretch, Ruth, but for some reason, I feel compelled to find out."

Knowing her husband, Ruth presumed it would do no good to object. She loved Brett, although he could be a real bonehead at times. And Ruth was angry because he had kept this from her for so many years. But scientifically, she knew that a trip to see Patrick was in order. She sighed, and then said, "Well it's a good experiment, so you should probably go. But you're going to owe me later." She finished off her wine and gave her husband a quick peck on the cheek before carrying the empty glasses back to the kitchen.

That night, right before falling asleep, Ruth said a special prayer for God to help her husband. It was the only way she knew how to help him herself.

CHAPTER SEVENTEEN

"A quest for answers"

THE DRIVE UP INTERSTATE 5 seemed endless, especially that long stretch through the Central Valley, also known as America's produce basket, practically nothing but farmland. Roberts wished he'd remembered to bring along more CDs. *Frampton Comes Alive* could not be listened to more than once, and the FM dial mostly offered an assortment Country & Western and Mexican Mariachi stations. He found a Christian rock station and made an effort to listen until Mudford protested. "How can you listen to that stuff, man?"

Eventually they stumbled onto an alternative rock station after descending into the Livermore Valley. The song *Los Angeles* by the band X came on. The lyrics written by John Doe and Exene Cervenka set the perfect mood. Mudford tapped away on the dashboard in time to the music. Almost there.

They proceeded north on I-580 and made their way toward Oakland. Roberts handed a buck fifty to the tollgate attendant and drove onto the first span of the Bay Bridge. It was a crystal clear day with sailboats tacking and reaching back and forth on the water below. They passed through Treasure Island and then crested the second bridge span with the downtown city skyline rapidly approaching.

"Aaa-woo!" howled Mudford.

Roberts grinned. He'd made reservations at The Stanyan Hotel, a converted old Victorian office building at the corner of Stanyan and Waller Streets, figuring it might be nice to return to their old stomping grounds. "How about we have dinner tonight at Cha-Cha-Cha's on Haight Street?"

"Now you're talking!" said Mudford enthusiastically.

They took the Fell Street exit and headed west toward the Panhandle. "We've got a little over an hour of daylight left. You thinking what I'm thinking?" said Roberts

"You're on!" Mudford agreed.

After patrolling around multiple blocks without any luck, they finally spotted a parking space on Beulah Street that Roberts managed to wiggle his car into. He wondered if he'd be able to waggle it back out the next morning.

It was a crisp and sunny late-afternoon. Fifteen minutes after checking into the hotel, Mudford and Roberts strode out to their favorite meadow in Golden Gate Park and started tossing a Frisbee back and forth. They found their rhythm after a few errant tosses. With the familiar sound of drums pounding in the distance, it felt like they'd never left.

They returned to the hotel and then walked up to Cha-Cha-Cha's on the corner of Haight Street and Shrader. Roberts gave his name to the hostess and was told it would be about a 45 minute wait, so they walked back to Amoeba Records and began to browse the seemingly endless aisles of Vinyl albums and CDs. Indie music played from a turntable behind the counter of the converted former bowling alley.

"Hey Owen, I just realized something," Roberts said while flipping through a bargain bin of 80s-era new wave bands. "What's that, my mutant friend?"

Roberts grimaced. "That safety deposit box you mentioned, aren't banks supposed to be closed on Sundays?"

"I never said it was a bank," said Mudford. "How about Dim Sum tomorrow?" He wouldn't say more just then. Roberts wondered what the connection might be, although Dim Sum did sound like a good plan.

A table didn't free up at Cha-Cha-Cha's until after 8 PM. The hostess ushered Roberts and Mudford to a window table and suggested they start with a pitcher of Sangria. The Caribbean voodoo theme seemed a bit tacky, although certainly not out of character for Haight Street. They ordered tapas of jerk chicken, Cajun shrimp, Seafood paella and dirty rice, which came quickly and went magically well with the Sangria. They were working on their second pitcher around 9 o'clock when the waitress returned with the check. A light rain began splattering against the window.

Now that felt familiar, Roberts thought to himself.

The thought of finding a parking space in China Town tomorrow also disturbed him. "How about we leave the car here in the morning and take a streetcar downtown?" said Roberts. "We should have plenty of time."

Mudford polished off his glass of Sangria and grinned. "Why not? And we can catch a Cable Car up to China Town from the Powell Street stop. I never did manage to ride one of those things when we lived here before."

The cable car loading station had a long queue of tourists when they arrived the next morning. After a good half hour, Roberts and Mudford finally stepped up and grabbed hold of the rail with the bench seats already full. Their ample-bellied cable operator sported a bushy grey beard and wore a striped denim shirt, a brown leather vest and matching beret with the MUNI logo, dapperly tilted to one side. "Everybody hold on!" he shouted. Without further ado, he ratcheted the lever down and the overloaded car lurched forward up the 30-degree grade with the wheels whining in protest. He released the lever at the top of the block and waited just long enough for a few passengers to squeeze on or off before yanking it back down. Women gasped and men laughed when the cable car jerked forward up the next surprisingly steep grade. The cable operator tugged repeatedly on the bell rope between stops while hollering out amusing bits of trivia, and some of his jokes would have been considered a bit racy in other parts of the country. But this was San Francisco. At the 10th stop, he shouted "Washington Street, China Town!" Roberts and Mudford were more than happy to step off onto the solid unmovable pavement.

They weaved their way through busy sidewalks of tourists and street vendors until Mudford turned unexpectedly into the Grand China Herb Company. Roberts glanced quickly about the shop, wondering why they had stopped there. The shelves were stocked with odd shaped glass bottles of Chinese medicines, although most of the characters were gibberish to Roberts. An aging Chinese gentleman behind the counter looked up from his newspaper and nodded toward Mudford with an expectant look. Then he fixed his eyes on Roberts and studied him carefully. The old guy seemed to know him.

Mudford whispered a few words to the store's proprietor. He grunted, turned and shuffled to a back room, and returned a moment later with a shoebox size container that he ceremoniously handed over to Mudford, along with another grunt for good measure. Roberts thought he recognized the Chinese Characters scrawled across the top, the same ones on the envelope that Virtanen had supposedly left for him back in graduate school.

He watched with nervous anticipation as Mudford lifted the lid and withdrew a thick scroll of paper. Mudford untied the cord and unfurled the pages to reveal unmistakable photocopies of chemical reaction schemes with wild scribbling in Virtanen's handwriting.

"I don't get it, Owen, why'd you stash this here?" Roberts whispered.

"Seemed like a safe enough place," Mudford answered nonchalantly. "Come on, let's go get Dim Sum."

Mudford offered the old man some money for his troubles but he refused. He gave Roberts a sage nod as they were leaving the shop. Once outside, Roberts said, "That old guy seemed to know me, Owen. What's up with that? I've never set foot inside his shop before."

"Honestly Brett, I was just as surprised as you were. The first time I went to see him myself was shortly after you showed me the envelope, the one you found on your chair back in graduate school, wanted to make sure I'd interpreted the characters correctly."

"Did he say where it might have come from?"

"Nah, the old guy seemed very discrete. That's why I figured it would be a good place to stash these photocopies. Crazy thing though. He accepted them without any questions, didn't even want to take any money for the service. And well, you know what happened to me afterwards."

Roberts followed Mudford up the stairs to the second floor of the Golden Dragon Restaurant. The circular tables were crowded with Asian families enjoying a Sunday meal together, chatting away animatedly as they reached forward to stab at various dishes on the service wheel with their chopsticks. Mudford managed to convince the waiter to find them a single table along the back wall.

A greying Chinese woman wheeled over a cart loaded with stacks of circular steamer baskets. She spoke in rapid Cantonese with a harried expression. Mudford pointed to various dishes that were quickly transferred to their table. Before Roberts could thank her she was gone. A waiter rushed over with a pot of hot green tea and two table settings of cups, napkins and chopsticks.

"Whoa, that was fast," said Roberts.

"Yeah, this is their busiest time of the week," said Mudford. "Man, I've missed these pork dumplings," he mumbled between chews.

"Me too," said Roberts, after a taking a bite of his Siu Mai and washing it down with a sip of tea. "So, I still can't believe you thought about making copies of Virtanen's notebooks, but now that we have it, what's next?"

"Let's eat first."

Roberts glanced around when their plates were being cleared and noticed that the morning rush was almost over. Their server returned with the check and asked in halting English whether they wanted more tea? Mudford held up his hand for 'no' and waited for her to leave. Diners pushed back from their tables and the place soon got a lot quieter. "We should be left alone for a while," said Mudford. He pulled the stack of photocopies from his backpack, thumb-flipped to the last few pages, and arranged them carefully on the table. "Here, take a look at this," he pointed.

Roberts studied the reaction scheme and then quickly read through Virtanen's scribbled notes, with his initials and date at the bottom of the page. The chemical structure was nearly identical to DMT except for a longer sidechain between the ring system and the dimethyl-amino group. He inhaled and slowly exhaled. "That's about what I was expecting."

"Yeah, I know," said Mudford.

It was close to noon when they made it back to The Stanyan Hotel. They quickly packed up their things and checked out. Mudford made hand signals from the sidewalk while Roberts inched his car out of the parking space. They drove south on 19th Avenue and then headed over to Hillside Boulevard, which would take them straight on down to Oyster Point according to Brett's map.

They drove up to a picnic table near the water and exited the car to a surprisingly powerful wind gust that slammed the doors back shut behind them.

"That must be Patrick out there!" Roberts pointed with his finger to a dozen or more windsurfers zipping back and forth a few hundred yards out. The riders were all tethered to their booms and leaning backward at seemingly impossible angles to trim their Mylar sails while speeding forward in excess of thirty knots. They launched over whitecaps and splashed back down throwing huge sprays of water behind them.

"Yeah, but I'm not standing out *here* much longer!"

"Hang on, I think they're beginning to return to shore."

One by one, the windsurfers whooshed toward the beach and let go of their booms with a splash. O'Reilly was the last one in.

"Hey Brett, Owen! Great to see you guys." He shook the water from his wrist before shaking their hands. "Have you been waiting here long?"

Roberts answered, "Just got here." He ignored the sopping wetsuit and gave his former roommate a hug.

Mudford hugged him right afterwards. "How's it going Patrick?"

O'Reilly stepped back, not quite used to all this hugging. "Good. Glad you two were able to find me. Sure you can't stay the night? You'd be welcome at my place."

Roberts said, "Wish we could, but as I said over the phone, I really need to be back at work tomorrow. We've got some investors coming in for a lunch meeting."

"Okay, give me a chance to hitch up my board and change into some dry clothes." O'Reilly went over to say goodbye to his windsurfing buddies. After the board was re-secured atop O'Reilly's Subaru Legacy, he lifted the rear hatch and pulled out a pair of two-gallon jugs of water from his Styrofoam cooler. Steam rose while O'Reilly used them for his makeshift shower. Hot water… pretty clever, thought Roberts.

O'Reilly toweled off and left it tied around his waist while tugging off his swim trunks to change into a dry pair of jeans. Then he unwrapped the towel, pulled on a sweatshirt and used the side mirror to brush his hair.

"You guys ready?" said O'Reilly.

"You sure your hair looks okay?" teased Mudford.

They followed O'Reilly's Legacy south for about a half mile until they reached Genome Drive, where he made a left and headed back toward the water. Digital Drug Design was a two-story, diamond-shaped, silver glass-walled structure on the point overlooking the bay. O'Reilly used his card key then led them up the stairs to the computer graphics facility. They entered a darkened room filled with high-definition monitors and humming tower computers.

"Can I see the thumb drive?" asked O'Reilly. Roberts retrieved it from his pocket and handed it over with growing anticipation. This was it, he realized. Would his suspicion about the binding pocket be correct?

O'Reilly opened several windows on his computer screen and started typing in commands.

"Since you mentioned the serotonin receptor, I presume this must have something to do with that paper you published on DMT?"

"Yes, but I need you to keep this confidential. I think I've identified a membrane receptor that binds DMT, and might even be responsible for its effects on the brain. I'm hoping your structure prediction software can confirm my hypothesis."

"Okay… but I thought you were working on clinical diagnostic tests these days."

"It could be related to schizophrenia, but that's all I can tell you."

O'Reilly shrugged and kept on typing. The software automatically translated the FAST-A file into the gene's corresponding amino acid sequence. "Here are the peptide regions that share homology with the serotonin receptor, so I'll cut those segments out and move them over to align with the serotonin structure. On the screen, the serotonin receptor was represented as a blue folded ribbon of bends, twists and turns that illustrated how the amino acid chain folded upon itself into three-dimensional protein. The entire structure could be rotated around on the screen by typing in a command and using the mouse. Alternatively, the ribbons could be pixilated to show what the individual atoms might look like. It was also possible to zoom the protein in and out of the screen to view internal cross-sections of protein structure.

Whenever Roberts thought about the DNA-to-RNA-to-Protein discoveries, it always amazed him how strings of amino acids could fold into a three-dimensional protein. They had to fold in a predictable and reproducible way, otherwise the protein wouldn't be able to do its assigned job inside the cell. Fortunately for proteins, strings of amino acids had some kind of intrinsic structural memory. It was a bit like dropping a hose from a second story window and watching it form the exact same three-dimensional pile every time on the pavement below. The precise arrangement of kinks and bends in that hose would always be the same, no matter how many times you dropped it onto the pavement.

"Okay, so now I'm going to reconnect the loops that would be predicted to extend above and below the cell membrane," O'Reilly continued. Such hydrophilic loops would interact with aqueous environments inside or outside of the cell. Roberts was mostly interested in the outside loops, since those were the regions where DMT might bind.

O'Reilly leaned back in his chair while tapping his fingers on the table in front of him. "We've still got a fair amount of unassignable structure here."

"Try focusing on this particular loop region right here," Roberts pointed. It was the region where his own gene had a mutation. It also happened to be one of the loops that should be pointing *outside* the cell, at least according to the model on the screen. Roberts had a bit of trouble containing his growing excitement. "Can you energy-minimize it?"

Roberts was referring to a folding program that one of O'Reilly's computer scientists had written. It could predict the most likely structure for an unknown string of amino acids, based on similar structures that had already been solved, although it was less reliable for strings greater than 25 amino acids. It did tend to work better for peptide loop segments, since the ends were known to be closer together in space.

"It looks like the loop you're interested in has about 40 amino acids. The program might not be able to fold it, but I can try…" O'Reilly said while typing away. "There," he hit return. Gradually, the loop began collapsing into a three-dimensional structure.

O'Reilly said, "Hmm, looks like it worked."

Roberts leaned forward and studied it closely. "That sure looks like a binding site," he pointed.

O'Reilly rubbed his chin while expanding the structure and then zooming in and out. "Yes, it sure does. Okay, let's bring up the structure for DMT and see if we can drive it in into that pocket." He typed a few commands and the DMT molecule appeared on the screen, with green spheres for the carbon atoms, blue spheres for nitrogen, and smaller white half-domes for the hydrogens. He clicked on it with his mouse and tried docking it into the energy-minimized loop structure.

"Congratulations," said O'Reilly. The contours of the binding pocket wrapped perfectly around the DMT molecule. But what excited Roberts even more was the amino acid nearest the dimethyl-amino moiety of DMT. His *mutation* would have coded or this particular amino acid. Assuming his mutation was somewhat rare, that would suggest that most people had a *different* amino acid at this position, one that would *not* be expected to bind DMT quite as snugly.

So, Virtanen had managed to correct the flaw in his own gene by synthesizing a DMT analog with a longer side chain!

Roberts could tell from the expression on Mudford's face that he'd already reached the same conclusion. He nudged Mudford's shoulder and subtly shook his head to preempt Mudford from saying anything.

"What?" O'Reilly had obviously noticed the gesture.

"Nothing," said Roberts. "Look Patrick, I hope you won't mind keeping this confidential."

O'Reilly said, "I've got no reason not to do otherwise. These results aren't conclusive enough to publish anyway. Sorry about that, by the way."

Roberts said, "Pretty much what I expected, but encouraging nonetheless."

They returned to the car and stood there awkwardly. Roberts felt bad about leaving so soon. "Thanks for meeting us on such short notice, O'Reilly. Let's plan to get together next Thanksgiving. Ruth and I would be happy to host if you and Lisa don't mind driving down."

"You could meet my new son Charlie," added Mudford.

O'Reilly's face brightened. "Now that's something I definitely can't miss. Drive safe, you guys." He waved as they turned out of the parking lot.

Roberts took the San Mateo Bridge across the Bay and cut through Hayward to merge onto I-580 headed east. Neither of them spoke, or even thought to pop in one of their recently purchased CDs, until they began descending into the Livermore Valley.

Mudford finally broke the silence. "Hey Brett, didn't you used to live out this way?"

"Yeah," Roberts answered.

"Must have been one heck of a daily commute."

"That it was," said Roberts.

"Since we're talking again, do you mind if I ask you something?"

"Shoot," said Roberts.

"Okay, here goes. Considering what we just learned about this mutant DMT receptor of yours, do you have psychic abilities or what?"

"Not quite sure, to be honest," said Roberts. "The encounters I've had with Virtanen over the years sure felt real enough. Although thinking about them now scares the shit out of me."

"Why's that?" asked Mudford.

"Virtanen has been trying to reach me for a reason. I can feel it. But I have no idea what that reason could be.'

Mudford taunted, "So you now believe in the supernatural, huh?"

Roberts caught a lump in his throat. "Look, Owen. I consider myself a person of faith. And I do believe in God. But I can't comprehend how one particular brain receptor could be the gatekeeper to spiritual awareness."

They descended into the Central Valley and rejoined Interstate-5 headed south. With nothing much left to look forward to but farmland and cattle, Mudford stretched out his arms and yawned. "Think I'll catch up on some shuteye. Wake me in a couple hours and I'll take over at the wheel." He ratcheted the seat back and was out within seconds.

Roberts inserted a Tears for Fears CD into the deck and it seemed to fit his present mood. He adjusted the knob to find a suitable volume that masked Mudford's snoring without disturbing his sleep. As he tapped his steering wheel to the music, Roberts mused about what they'd learned so far. A critical piece to the puzzle had just been found, and firmly pressed down into place. Which left one question still unanswered: *what was he supposed to do with this new information?* Roberts shook his head, once again determined to let it go. But could he?

Over three hours later, they started up the Grapevine grade and left the Central Valley behind, both of them relieved to be nearing civilization again. Mudford was at the wheel now. "You know Brett, I've been thinking."

Roberts braced for what might be coming next. "Nothing to do with Virtanen's notebooks, I hope?"

"Well yeah, in a roundabout way, because I finally realized something. There must be hundreds if not thousands of other unpredictable genetic mutations in our brains yet to be discovered. Sure could help explain all the crazy people in the world."

The knots in Brett's shoulders began to unwind, and he let out a breath. "That's not what I expected you to say, and also quite a relief. So, you're not planning on re-synthesizing any of those compounds?"

"*Hell no!* Gonna burn these photocopies just as soon as I get home, probably on the beach in one of those fire pits. Want to attend the ceremony?"

"Can't believe I'm saying this Owen, but I trust you. So — it's over then?"

"That's for sure. I much prefer mushrooms anyway. Speaking of which, you planning on heading out with us again to Moon Howl next spring?"

CHAPTER EIGHTEEN

"Shifting sands"

Sunday, September 11TH, 2011
La Jolla, California

THE SALK INSTITUTE was perched atop a bluff overlooking the Pacific Ocean, with a neighboring glider port to the north and a pristine beach beneath that was known for its "clothing optional" sunbathers. With the last two attributes aside, Salk's primary charter was to explore basic questions of human biology.

The Nobel Laureate Jonas Salk, famously known for his discovery of the polio vaccine, established the institute in the 1960s. He tasked a world-renowned architect named Louis Kahn to design the buildings using simple materials that would last for generations with minimal maintenance. Kahn used poured-in-place concrete with tall leaded-glass windows to let in as much natural sunlight as possible, along with teak trim panels on the westward facing walls. Built around a three-sided courtyard of travertine marble, almost every laboratory had a relatively unobstructed view of the ocean.

Dr. Janet Feinstein had decided to leave Stanford two years before and join the Salk as a Research Fellow. This now afforded her the luxury of focusing full-time on her research. It was a sunny Sunday afternoon, and most of the other scientists who occupied this facility had succumbed to the constant allure of the ocean by venturing outside. Yet today was no different from any other day as far as Dr. Janet Feinstein was concerned. She ignored the view like always from her second floor office window.

Her computer monitor suddenly went to blue screen and the following letters appeared in quarter-second intervals:

h-e-l-l-o--d-o-c-t-o-r--f-e-i-n-s-t-e-i-n…

Startled at first, her innate curiosity quickly took over. She hit return on the keyboard and a blinking cursor appeared next to the letters Z:\ROBERTSLAB. *How strange…* she thought, until she remembered the Zip drive that Spectrum Genomics had sent to her shortly after closing down the microarray facility, which contained the data files from each of her microarray experiments along an invoice for final payment. She'd uploaded the drive to her server at the Salk Institute and forgotten about it, until now.

She hit return again and a table appeared with the dates, descriptions and filenames of each experiment that had been billed to her account. She recalled most of them quite clearly, except the very last one. *Huh…* that last experiment didn't appear to be one she'd authorized. Presuming it must have been mistakenly copied along with the others, she right-clicked on the filename and read through the synopsis. So… Brett Roberts had evidently performed another microarray experiment using Schwarzkopf's brain biopsy samples. Clearly he'd lied about there not being enough material for a second run.

Feinstein fumbled around in her messy desk drawer until she located the viewer software. She popped the CD into her computer and used it to open the file. Okay, now she was angry. A new brain microarray prototype had been fabricated, *also without informing her!* But keen to learn what Roberts may have discovered, she used the software to compare the mRNA expression levels in the pre- and post-death samples. The cluster analysis pointed to a novel membrane receptor gene that she hadn't heard of before, something called SIGMAR-1. She launched UniProt Online and typed in the name. *How interesting…* SIGMAR-1 shared a considerable amount of sequence homology with another more well-known serotonin receptor.

The screen flickered again and the word *ACCESSING…* appeared next to another blinking cursor. Feinstein hit return again. Nothing happened. She was about to reboot the computer when another table appeared with the heading "Amy Rosen Blood Draws for DNA Sequencing: Miller Lab – 2002". *Hmm,* thought Feinstein. Amy must have errantly uploaded this particular notebook log after joining her research group at the Salk. She'd chosen to leave Miller's group when he accepted another position back East. Amy was a surfer.…

Feinstein spotted quite a number of entries drawn on behalf of an investigator named Brian Sakow, with his initials and dates next to the donor IDs. That name struck a bell, a scientist-entrepreneur she'd recently met at a local investor conference. Sakow had mentioned once working as a post-doc in Bob Miller's group at Scripps, which allowed her to deduce that he must have overlapped with Amy. He'd also mentioned knowing Brett Roberts, a co-author on one of her most widely cited *Nature* articles. Apparently they'd been cycling buddies around that time. Her eyes narrowed when she spotted an entry with the donor ID "BR" next to it. Could this 'BR' have been Brett Roberts? And if so, for what reason had Roberts donated his blood sample? Could it have had something to do with his interest in this SIGMAR-1 gene? She almost picked up the phone right then to call Sakow and ask herself.

But she stopped herself from dialing. No, it would be unethical to reveal the name of an anonymous donor. She wasn't willing to push Brian Sakow quite that hard just yet. And Brett Roberts… well, the two of them hadn't spoken in over ten years. He'd never mentioned the microarray experiment that her computer had just mysteriously revealed to her. And although she also suspected who the donor had been for this particular experiment, she didn't really expect Roberts to be candid with her about it now. There must be another way for her to get her hands on this SIGMAR-1 gene sequence, assuming that was what Roberts was after. As Janet Feinstein tapped her nail-bitten fingers against her desk, a third possibility came to her.

She flipped through her rolodex to locate Barry Hammond's number. Barry was Managing Director for BioBeach Ventures – a local group of angel investors focused on biotech start-ups. She knew Hammond had made an initial investment in Sakow's new company. And could probably use the assistance of a respected molecular biologist to focus them toward breakthrough product applications. That would be her, obviously.

"Barry? Feinstein here. I remember you mentioning a startup investment here in La Jolla, the company developing some sort of next-generation sequencing platform? Might you be looking for someone to head their scientific advisory board? …great, then I'm interested. Let's have lunch to discuss. Would Friday work for you? Wonderful, see you then. Ciao!"

Calvin Schwarzkopf had once commented about Brett's issues with DMT, which may have been why he'd asked her to draw a sample of his cerebral spinal fluid that fateful Sunday afternoon. Perhaps he and Roberts even hatched this experiment together, although Roberts had feigned surprise when she brought Cal's tissue samples to his office the following morning. Well, if SIGMAR-1 actually did turn out to be the gene responsible for the effects of DMT in the brain, Brett's discovery would soon be hers to exploit.

MONDAY, January 30TH, 2012

Bolstered by their initial round of funding from BioBeach Ventures, SnapGen had grown to 8 full-time employees. They occupied 2500 square feet of leased incubator space in a derelict office building of Spanish architecture, just south of downtown La Jolla and a block away from the ocean. Yet none of them cared much to look out the windows. Time was money, and theirs was rapidly being depleted. Hammond wanted to see real progress before making a larger investment.

Janet Feinstein now had remote access to SnapGen's sequence files and servers, having reached a separate agreement with Hammond to chair their scientific advisory board. She sat in her office at the Salk, reviewing the results from last week's run at SnapGen. *Getting closer,* she thought to herself, *an entire yeast genome this time, sequence quality looks good....*

She dialed Sakow's office number. "Brian, I think you're about ready to test your machine with human DNA. I do have a few suggestions."

Sakow pressed the speaker button and leaned back in his chair with his fingers clasped behind his head, gazing at nothing in particular. The view of the ocean from his cluttered little second-floor office mattered even less to him than it did to Feinstein. "Okay, shoot."

"Our study should probably have something to do with population genomics, comparing DNA sequences from multiple individuals. That would really demonstrate the power of your instrument."

"Yes, of course." Sakow tried his best to sound confident over the phone. He didn't mention that he'd already tried sequencing a sample of his own DNA. Unfortunately, the sequence quality still wasn't quite good enough.

Just then, Alfredo Ruiz poked his head into her office, a visiting scientist in her lab on sabbatical from Brazil. Which gave her another idea. Feinstein waved him away, uncovered the phone, and continued, "We should target an indigenous population to begin with, preferably living in a remote area protected from outsiders. The Amazon, perhaps."

Sakow found that prospect intriguing and immediately thought of Roberts, just as Feinstein had hoped. "I guess that makes sense," he ventured.

"We'll also need to find a local donor to use as a control, someone who would be willing to donate another sample if needed, but preferably no one directly employed by SnapGen."

Sakow rubbed his scruffy chin, with shaving no longer a priority. "Think I know someone who might be interested."

Feinstein said, "I thought you might. There's just one more thing. As you know, the Sanger method is still considered the gold standard for sequencing quality, although it's only capable of sequencing one gene at a time. So pick a gene of interest and have it sequenced from your donor by both methods for comparison. Preferably something related to brain biology, since that's my area of expertise." Yes, that sounded right. She'd rehearsed this part.

"Any particular gene you have in mind?"

Well then, she mused. If Sakow knew that she knew, he'd certainly not let on. "I'm sure you'll think of something interesting. Just let me know when you think you're ready." And with that, Feinstein clicked off the call.

WEDNESDAY, February 1ST, 2012

Brett Roberts sat brooding at his desk, and for good reason. BioProbe's cancer program still hadn't turned a profit after almost ten years of R&D investment. For one thing, it had taken considerably longer than originally projected to get their innovative blood tests approved by the FDA. To make matters worse, cancer genomes were now known to be highly unstable, meaning that additional mutations could arise with every new cell division. One would need to detect hundreds if not thousands of such mutations in order to comprehensively diagnose a given cancer patient. BioProbe's diagnostic instruments simply weren't up to the task....

When her knocking didn't work, Katya stepped in anyway. "Have you forgotten about group meeting? ...Brett, you seem lost in other world these days." Her Slavic accent hadn't changed much over the years.

Roberts glanced at his watch. "Damn! Sorry Katya, I'll be right there." He joined his few remaining team members in the conference room. Most had already been assigned to other projects despite his objections. Yet he found it difficult to focus on the data being presented….

He'd been musing about a new type of DNA sequencing technology that had recently been introduced to the research community. It was called "next-generation sequencing", capable of performing hundreds of thousands of sequencing reactions simultaneously on a biochip about the size of a quarter. The first wave of commercial instruments were still somewhat cumbersome and expensive, although the pace of innovation had been accelerating exponentially. Several new startup companies were already claiming that their radically improved instrument designs could bring the cost down below $1000 per genome. One of them happened to be in La Jolla. SnapGen, Brian Sakow's new company….

After returning to his office, Roberts Googled the name and clicked the link to launch SnapGen's website. The site was taking a while to load… *hmm, content must reside on Sakow's hard drive… startups… there, finally.* He clicked the **Technology** button and read through the blurb that followed… hmm, it looked promising; and then clicked **Clinical Applications** … yep, the usual suspects: neonatal screening, hereditary disorders, and *cancer diagnostics*. He clicked **Contacts** and jotted down the phone number.

"Hey Brian! It's Brett. Sorry we haven't managed to get together in a while."

"No worries, Brett. Been pretty busy myself. But it's actually good timing that you called considering I was just about ready to call you myself. How are things at BioProbe these days?"

"I've had a good run here Brian, although it's probably about time for me to make another move."

"Not surprised to hear that, unfortunately. I met that new CEO of yours at an investor conference last month. He didn't even mention your oncology program."

"Yeah, the vast majority of our revenue still comes from diagnostic tests designed to detect infectious diseases like HIV and gonorrhea."

"Well then, I presume you've called to inquire about opportunities at BioProbe?"

Roberts didn't want to sound too presumptive. "I see from your website that your company's interested in cancer applications...."

Sakow interrupted, "Sorry Brett, we can't afford to bring on another full-time employee just yet. Our seed funding will only cover us for about six months. BioBeach Ventures wants proof that our instrument is actually capable of sequencing an entire genome before making a larger investment."

Roberts persisted, "I figured that... but hey, maybe I could consult for you guys in my spare time? I'd even be willing to do it *pro bono* until you manage to secure another round of funding. Most of my team at BioProbe was recently assigned to other projects, so I'm no longer all that busy. Frankly, I could use the distraction."

Sakow waited a beat, just to mess with his friend. "Sold! In that case, I've got an idea for a pilot study I'd like to bounce off you. Could you come by SnapGen to discuss? I'd love to show you our new prototype instrument."

"I'd like that. Okay, how about I stop by this Friday after work?"

"That would be great! You still cycling into work these days?" asked Sakow.

"Don't I always?"

Sakow glanced over to admire his newly purchased Cannondale road bike. "Great! Then let's plan on riding home together."

That Friday morning, Roberts got a call on his office phone from Judith Walton's extension, BioProbe's vice-president of human resources.

"Happy Friday, Judith! What can I do for you?"

"Hello Brett. Can you please stop by my office? Westfield suggested I speak with you." Roberts suspected bad news from the sound of her voice. BioProbe's board had recently hired Karl Shipman to replace their out-going CEO Kenneth Pearlman, who supposedly left 'to pursue other opportunities'. Roberts knocked on Walton's open door jam and she waved him in. "Have a seat, Brett."

Sure enough, the news wasn't good. Shipman wanted to shutter BioProbe's cancer program. Roberts was offered a generous severance package if he agreed to leave immediately. A security guard would escort him back into the building on Saturday to retrieve his personal items.

Roberts wasn't all that surprised by Shipman's decision, although it still felt like a punch in the gut. He returned to his office, changed into cycling clothes, and carried his road bike down the stairs for the very last time.

Karen called over to him from across the reception desk. "Leaving so soon, Brett?"

"I couldn't resist, Karen. It's such a beautiful day outside."

Karen pressed her lips together, sensing something amiss. Roberts never left the office before noon. Despite his strained attempt to smile, she could see it in his eyes, another one gone. Things hadn't been the same here at BioProbe since her son Kenneth's departure. She removed her headset and came around to give him a hug goodbye. "Enjoy your ride, Brett." Roberts smiled again, this time for real. "Take care, Karen." Roberts walked his bike out BioProbe's front entrance and clipped in. Karen grabbed a tissue and dabbed her eyes as he rode away.

Ruth volunteered in the church office on Fridays, and Sakow wasn't expecting Roberts to drop by SnapGen until after 4 pm. With plenty of time to kill, he rode north and made his usual right on Carmel Valley Road, but this time took another turn into the state beach parking lot. Roberts desperately needed a walk on the beach to process his recent separation from BioProbe.

After using a six foot cable lock to secure his precious road bike to the rack outside, he went into the men's restroom to change into a spare pair of gym shorts and flip flops that he kept in his backpack for such occasions. He dabbed on a bit of sunscreen before exiting out the back and followed the sound of crashing waves.

Emerging from the pedestrian underpass, Roberts spotted a colony of seagulls perched on the sand nearby, keenly eyeing the water for schools of smelt to venture into the shallows. One started squawking and the rest noisily joined in. Eventually they settled down, only to repeat the process after too brief an interlude. Better to head north, Roberts concluded, thinking there should be less car noise that way under the bluff's protection. He concealed his backpack behind a rock near the bluff, stepped out of his flip flops, and trotted down to greet the surf. White foam tickled his toes as he watched the sand fleas quickly burrowing back under the sand every time the water receded.

A train approached from the north, its rumble getting louder as it traveled down the tracks until it passed along the bluff directly behind where he was standing. …CUH-CLACK!-CUH-CLACK!-CUH-CLACK! …CUH-CLACK!-CUH-CLACK!-CUH-CLACK! …CUH-CLACK!-CUH-CLACK!-CUH-CLACK! Then it disappeared beneath the bridge and continued south over the lagoon and into Sorrento Valley. Quiet at last.

He started walking but deliberately stayed close to the water, allowing the frothy surf to wash over his ankles again and again. The icy chill reminded him he was alive. About a mile up he took a few steps back, then settled onto the dry sand and hugged his knees. A tear rolled down his cheek as he pondered his next move. He had to admit that he'd seen this coming. A black dolphin leapt up from the water about forty yards out, and re-entered nose first with hardly any splash. Now that felt like a good omen, maybe things would be okay after all. Roberts couldn't help but grin while watching several more dolphins repeat the same maneuver.

Feeling a bit better, Roberts started reasoning that he'd just been given a rare opportunity to re-assess his priorities. Having mastered a variety of coping skills to accommodate his autistic spectrum disorder, Thomas was now a freshman at Oregon State, majoring in computer science no less. Michael was in his junior year of high school, and would soon be heading off to college as well. Brett and Ruth would soon be empty nesters, at least for a few years anyway.

Not a bad time to reassess his priorities, thought Roberts. He simply needed to catch another thermal, find something new that spoke to him.

Checking his watch, Roberts saw that it was already after 2 pm. "Best get going, Brett," he muttered to himself, estimating that it would probably take a good forty minutes of hard riding to make it down to Sakow's leased incubator space in La Jolla.

First he stopped by the Carmel Valley Market to get something to eat for lunch. He grabbed a couple of Clif bars and brought them to the counter. "How's it going Yerem?" Roberts called over to the swarthy young proprietor. Yerem seemed quite bored despite the stunning view outside, which extended across the lagoon to the blue Pacific Ocean. The shelves behind him were fully stocked to the ceiling with colorful liquor bottles of various shapes and sizes. They glistened in the afternoon sunlight. Roberts noted that some of them were quite large. He shuddered to think what might happen if there were ever an earthquake.

With the sun now beaming directly through the storefront panel window, Yerem squinted as he rang up the cash register. "It's well for me today, Mister Brett. Beautiful day outside, no?"

"Sure is. Looks like you'll soon have another one of your beautiful sunsets to enjoy."

Yerem shielded his eyes. "Yes, I am looking forward to that. But tell me, Mister Brett, how is it that you are here at this hour?"

Roberts hesitated before answering. "Guess I couldn't resist such beautiful weather."

"Good for you, my friend. Wish I could do such a thing. I work here late again tonight myself."

"Well enjoy your view, Yerem."

Yerem grinned. "I shall, Mister Brett. Enjoy your ride!"

Roberts wolfed down one of the Clif bars as he peddled south along Coast Highway and shoved the empty wrapper into the back pouch of his cycling jersey before peddling up the Torrey Pines grade for his second time that day. He kept his eyes focused straight ahead while riding past the BioProbe building and then made a right at the fork just beyond the Scripps Research Institute to continue southward toward downtown La Jolla. He noticed several hang gliders riding the updrafts along the bluff near the Salk Institute. *Janet Feinstein worked there now… should he stop by briefly to say hello? Nah.*

After passing the UCSD campus to his left, he made another right at La Jolla Shores Drive and coasted down the winding steep grade, leaning over the handlebars to reduce his wind resistance as he plummeted downhill.

There was a storm drain just beyond the final turn that had a metal grate protecting it, one with vertical bars spaced an unfortunate distance apart. An errant road bike tire could slip between them if the cyclist weren't paying attention. Brett's bike did just that when he rounded the bend. He flew over the handlebars and tumbled to a stop about twenty yards down, cracking his helmet against the asphalt. Remarkably unhurt, he stumbled back up the hill to inspect his bike, also undamaged. Unbelievable. He waited a moment for his adrenaline rush to subside, then straddled his bike and continued downhill with his hands clutching the brakes, passing the Scripps Institute of Oceanography at a much more conservative speed. *Must have a guardian angel up there,* he thought to himself.

Passing Scripps Pier to his right, he headed down to the boardwalk and decided to walk his bike for a while. Pale-looking tourists were enjoying the beach on that breezy February afternoon. He stopped briefly at a restroom to check himself out in the mirror. Other than a pair of badly scuffed riding gloves, the rest of him appeared to be relatively unscathed. He fished from his backpack the broken pieces of his riding helmet and tossed them in the trash.

Back on the bike, he made a left at the end of the boardwalk, peddled back up to Torrey Pines Road, and continued southward toward the Village, making a final right on Prospect Street. He coasted down to the Cove and briefly watched long distance swimmers braving the frigid ocean water. The stench of sea lions soured his nostrils so he re-mounted his bike and rode on past Ellen Browning Scripps Park, which offered a spectacular view of the ocean and coastline to the north. He made a left on Coast Boulevard, braked to a stop in front of a Spanish style office building, and checked the address to make sure it was the right one. Pretty unusual place for a biotech incubator, and only a block away from the ocean, certainly not what he was expecting. He scanned the ring buttons for SnapGen and pressed it firmly.

"Yes?" came a voice from the speaker.

"Sakow, it's me. Can you let me in?"

"Dude, you're early! Open the door when you hear the buzzer. I'm on the second floor, up the stairs and third door to your right."

Janet Feinstein stepped out of Brian's office and spotted Roberts walking his bike up the hallway, his bike shoes clopping noisily against the asbestos tiles. Damn, she'd hoped to be gone before he arrived. She cleared her throat. "Brett! Good to see you again."

Roberts took a moment to recover from bumping into her so unexpectedly. Feinstein's frizzy hair had greyed considerably, still clipped loosely behind her neck with a wide plastic barrette. And her eyeglasses seemed a bit thicker than he remembered, probably from staring at her computer screen for so many years. Yet she'd been talking to Sakow just now. What was that about?

"Hi, Janet. I heard about you joining to the Salk Institute. Sorry we haven't managed to touch base yet." Roberts intentionally used her first name this time, mostly to annoy her.

"Yes, although I expect you've come to speak with Brian. Don't let me keep you. Perhaps we should have lunch together sometime."

"Sure, Janet. That would be great. Good to see you, by the way." He waited for her to disappear into the stairwell before rapping on Brian's door.

Sakow quickly opened it and heartily shook Brett's hand. "How the heck are you, Roberts? What's it been, almost a year now?"

"Yeah, I guess it has."

Brett looks a bit more somber than usual, even for him, Sakow thought. "So!" he said with a brisk hand-clap, "you must have bumped into Janet Feinstein on her way out. Hammond asked her to chair our scientific advisory board."

"Yeah, I think she just invited me to lunch," said Roberts.

"You don't sound too excited about that," said Brian. "Thought you two were close."

"Not really," Roberts replied. "Guess I've always found her a bit too egocentric."

Sakow nodded. "Can't blame you there… anyway, welcome to SnapGen my friend!" He slapped Brett's shoulder. "Hope you don't mind the mess inside my office. You can leave your bike out here in the hall. Everyone else has already left for the day."

Roberts took the chair recently occupied by Janet Feinstein and noticed Brian's new Cannondale road bike, hanging from a rack on the side wall. "Apparently you've upgraded."

"Pretty sweet, huh?"

Roberts stared vacantly out the window without commenting.

"Dude, you look like someone just ran over your dog. What's up?"

Roberts sighed. "Well, apart from a nasty spill I took while riding down here, I also got canned from BioProbe this morning. Our new CEO decided to shut down our cancer program, offered me a six-month severance package if I agreed to leave immediately."

While relieved to see that Roberts was unhurt, Sakow also considered this good news. "Whoa. That's too bad, buddy. But what I just learned might cheer you up. Feinstein's now head of our scientific advisory board. She just informed me that BioBeach Ventures is willing to invest another

$15 million, provided we can demonstrate that our instrument is capable of sequencing an entire human genome in less than 24 hours. We were just discussing a feasibility study that ought to be publishable if it all works out."

There was no escaping Janet Feinstein, apparently. "What's she have in mind?"

"Something in the area of population genomics."

Roberts crossed his arms. "I have a bad feeling about where this might be going."

"Come on Brett, at least hear me out. Her idea is to send someone down to the Amazon to collect DNA samples from the indigenous tribes. That's where you come in."

Roberts couldn't believe his ears, although quite intrigued by the idea. "Okay, I'm listening."

"Her scientific rationale is to screen for mutations that help inform their migratory patterns over the millennia. But between you and me, this could also be an opportunity to learn more about this SIGMAR-1 gene obsession of yours."

Roberts reflected on the hallucinogenic extracts used by these tribes for their religious ceremonies. Including *yopo*.... "Dammit Sakow, now you know I'm hooked. So, how close are you to achieving this technical milestone of yours?" Roberts understood all too well the 'smoke and mirrors' game of biotech startups.

"Tell you what. Let's go to the lab and I'll show you how it works."

Sitting on a platform table in the dimly lit lab was a 'breadboard instrument', essentially the working guts of the machine mounted onto a three-by-four foot aluminum base plate. It was a jumble of microfluidic tubing and peristaltic pumps, lasers and fiber optic cables connected to a tiny square chamber at its center, where Sakow's revolutionary biochip was housed. There was also a powerful CCD camera mounted directly over the chamber with its cables connected to a custom-built tower computer.

Sakow walked Roberts over to a schematic on the side wall and pointed to the various steps of the sequencing process. "First, we break the genome apart into millions of tiny fragments and load them onto the biochip. There are fifty million micro-wells, each one capable of simultaneously sequencing a different DNA fragment. The CCD camera records each base addition as tiny flashes of light."

"What's the read length?" asked Roberts.

"Up to 500 bases." Sakow waited for Roberts to run the calculations in his head, that his new machine should actually be capable of sequencing an entire human genome in a single run.

Roberts asked, "How does the camera identify which base has been added?"

"That's the innovative part," Sakow explained. "Each base is labeled with a different fluorescent probe – red, yellow, green or blue."

Roberts thought he had it now. "Alright, but does this thing actually work?"

Sakow grinned. "We sequenced an entire yeast genome last week. The sequence quality was over 99.8% percent accurate when compared to the published reference sequence."

"What about human DNA?"

"Tried it a couple times already. The accuracy wasn't quite as good but we'll get there soon, probably within the next week or so. Still tweaking the fluidics."

They returned to Sakow's office to discuss the logistics. Roberts would travel to Brazil and attempt to collect DNA samples from as many of the indigenous tribes as he could locate. He'd record the name of each tribe on the collection tube along with their GPS coordinates.

"Sounds tempting, Brian, but what I really should be doing right now is looking for another full time job."

"Come on, Brett. I could give you a $125,000 stipend in advance and the same amount when you return with the samples. SnapGen would also cover your travel expenses, including the customary government bribes if necessary, provided they're not too unreasonable. And assuming our next funding round comes through, I could then bring you on full time, just like you wanted. So. Are you in?" Sakow fixed his eyes on Roberts with just the hint of a smile.

"Like I said earlier, you know I'm hooked. But I need to talk this over with Ruth."

Sakow slapped his knee, "Fair enough. You ready to ride?"

Roberts had just finished telling Ruth about his job termination. They were seated outside on the back patio with a nearly full moon on the rise, sipping glasses of cabernet from a moderately expensive bottle that he'd just opened.

Ruth said, "Oh Brett, I'm not sure I can handle moving again. We've got roots here now."

"Perhaps we won't have to," Roberts continued. "Brian Sakow just offered me a part-time consulting gig with his new company. It's just a start up, but they may have a full time position for me if things go well."

Ruth set down her glass and folded her hands on the table. "Now that's a name I haven't heard in a while. Didn't Brian move back east after finishing his post-doc?"

"Until about a year ago, when he decided to move back to San Diego and become an entrepreneur. Before that he was working at the Broad Institute, which was where he got the idea for his new company. It's called SnapGen, and they're working on a…"

Ruth interrupted, "Brett, let's discuss this tomorrow. You've had more time to process it than I have." Ruth wasn't quite sure she liked the idea of Brian and her husband working together. She took another sip of wine and then finished it off. "Think I need to go upstairs and read for a while."

"Sure dear. I'll be up in a minute."

Roberts poured himself another half glass of wine and rehearsed in his mind how best to tell Ruth about Sakow's proposal. He eventually decided to make online dinner reservations at Las Mareas for the following evening, and chose a time right before sunset. Las Mareas was located directly across the highway from Cardiff State Beach. And with its innovative Puerto Vallarta style menu of Mexican seafood dishes and generous selection of custom crafted margaritas, the restaurant evoked fond memories of the Blue Dolphin restaurant back in Pleasanton, an earlier touch point in their lives.

A tall and attractive hostess with a volleyball player build escorted them to their table. Roberts ordered a pitcher of margaritas which came within minutes along with a bowl of fresh salsa and tortilla chips. They quietly sipped their drinks while watching a spectacular sunset. "That was beautiful," said Ruth. "Okay, I'm ready now. Tell me about Brian's new company."

"They're working on a new kind of technology called next-generation sequencing. This could be a real game changer for cancer diagnostics."

Ruth nodded, admiringly. "And that's why they need you?"

"Tell you what, let's order first." Brett motioned for a waitress to take their orders, a Baja style mixed seafood taco platter for Brett and a sea bass Veracruz dish for Ruth.

He was almost finished describing the workings of Sakow's new instrument when a server appeared with two steaming dinner platters. "*Cuidado*," said the man while setting them down with hand towels to protect his fingers. "Plates are hot!"

"*Gracias*," said Brett, his accent having improved somewhat since returning to Southern California. The server politely replied "*de nada*", and left them to enjoy their food.

The mood was perfect and Brett didn't want to spoil it. So he poured them each another glass from the pitcher of Margaritas and changed the subject to more pleasant dinner conversation. Ruth eventually began to suspect he was stalling. "So what does Brian want you to do, exactly?"

"Care for a walk on the beach? I'd rather not discuss this part with other people around."

"Sure," said Ruth evenly, suspecting where this may be going.

Brett beckoned their waitress over who promptly cleared their plates away and returned with the check, thanking them both before excusing herself to take another order. Brett paid with cash and left a generous tip.

Ruth went back to the car for her sweater and they left their shoes near the seawall to walk barefoot along the water's edge, taking care to avoid the wintery surf as it washed toward them and then receded.

"Brian wants me to help him conduct a pilot study designed to demonstrate the performance of their new instrument, preferably something that could be published in a peer-reviewed scientific journal. His idea is for me to travel to the Amazon and collect DNA samples from the indigenous tribes."

Ruth stopped right there in the sand. "You have got to be kidding."

"These people represent a uniquely undisturbed population going back thousands of years. The official rationale is to screen for mutations that can help trace their ancestral lineage."

"But why you? You've never done something like this before, and if

I'm understanding you correctly, the study won't have anything to do with cancer genomics."

"True, but this could be a great opportunity to study the SIGMAR-1 gene in native populations. The vast majority of these tribes use plant extracts for their religious ceremonies containing high concentrations of DMT."

"*I knew it!* Brett, I thought you decided to let this go after your last trip to see Patrick."

"We might also be able to identify other gene mutations responsible for spiritual awareness."

Ruth sighed heavily, and Brett put an arm around his wife to shelter her from the wind while they continued walking. "Look Ruth, if you think it's a bad idea, I can call Brian tomorrow and tell him I won't do it."

Ruth nuzzled against her husband, mostly because the breeze blowing in from the ocean had been picking up. "Brett, if this is something you strongly feel you must do, then now is a probably a good time. I'll support you like I always have. But promise me you'll plan this trip very carefully, and make sure you have an experienced guide with you at all times."

"Of course, Dear. Safety will be my top priority."

They reached the inlet to the lagoon and quickening the pace back to the spot where they'd left their shoes. Brett started the car and turned on the heater before backing out of their space.

Ruth seemed distant on the drive home, and Brett wisely decided to give her time to process. He'd given her a lot to think about, and he desperately needed her reassurance. He pulled into the garage and shut off the engine. "I love you, sweetheart. Thanks for listening to me."

"I love you too, Brett." Ruth turned to open the car door.

Brett gently touched her shoulder. "Wait. Anything else you'd like to say about what we discussed back on the beach?"

Ruth sighed. Her husband needed to hear this. "Well yes, there is. *Before* you go, I want you to spend more time contemplating what it means to be a spiritual person. I've read a considerable number of books about spirituality over the years, and there's one thing they all seem to have in common. People come to God through faith, Brett. Not drugs."

Brett admired her for that. Ruth typically gave up her beloved romance novels over Lent and dedicated that time to reading books on spirituality.

"I will dear, I promise."

Ruth smiled and gently touched his cheek. "And promise me you'll pray about this."

"I have been, believe me." Brett answered.

"Well good. Keep it up."

Roberts got up early the next morning to make breakfast and see the boys off to school. He smiled when Ruth entered the kitchen, a bit sleepy-eyed. "Good morning, sweetheart! Sleep well?"

"Thanks, dear. I don't often get a chance to sleep in like that." Ruth poured herself a cup of coffee and then rubbed Brett's shoulders reassuringly before seating herself at the table, facing her husband. She rested her chin in her hands, "So, what's next?"

"First order of business is to negotiate a consulting agreement."

"I think that would be wise, even if Brian is your friend. And while you're planning this trip, if anything doesn't feel right to you, or to me for that matter, we should be able to call the whole thing off. Make sure to get that in writing."

"I will, I promise. Thanks for believing in me, Ruth."

Ruth nodded with just the hint of a smile. "I always have, I suppose. Guess that's *my* special gift."

Ruth volunteered at a downtown food bank on Mondays. And after she had left, Brett carried a second cup of coffee up to his home office and switched on the computer.

CHAPTER NINETEEN

"Dominoes"

THE INDIGENOUS TRIBES of the Amazon Rainforests were estimated to have once been somewhere between seven and ten million in number before the first European explorers arrived. Archeological evidence dated the earliest human settlements in the region at 32,000 - 39,000 years B.C. These were mainly agrarian societies, unlike their more urban Mayan and Aztec counterparts in the Andes to the west. Their villages were originally concentrated along major waterways, but the invading Europeans of the 1600's brought with them diseases that decimated over 90 percent of their total population. Most of those that survived were driven further into the rainforest to continue living as they had for thousands of years.

They remained relatively undisturbed after that until the 1840s when a process for vulcanizing rubber was developed. This roughly coincided with the discovery that the Amazon rainforest grew some of the finest rubber sap producing trees in the world, which resulted in an aggressive wave of expansion into the Amazon interior that continues to this day. Mining and logging quickly followed. When the indigenous people proved to be too difficult a labor force to work the rubber plantations, peasants were brought in from the surrounding regions to displace them. This drove the remaining tribes to ever more remote regions.

In the early 20th century, a man named Cândido Rondon was assigned to bring telegraph communications into the Amazon interior, and he worked hard to gain the trust of the tribes and to promote a peaceful coexistence with them. Rondon played an influential role in convincing the Brazilian government to legislate new policies intended to protect the indigenous tribes. In 1910, he helped found the Serviço de Proteção aos Índios (Service for the Protection of Indians) or SPI. But the SPI was later handed down to bureaucrats and military officers who leveraged this authority to suit their own means. By the 1960s, it had become known that the SPI was extremely corrupt and abusive to the indigenous peoples, even subjecting them to slavery, sexual abuse, torture and mass murder. It was little wonder those tribes that remained were extremely reluctant to engage outsiders.

And then the Fundação Nacional do Índio (National Indian Foundation), or FUNAI was established in 1987 with the charter of protecting the interests, cultures, and rights of the Brazilian indigenous populations. It had become recognized that unessential contact with these tribes spread illness and promoted social disintegration. The FUNAI therefore dedicated itself to preserving the remaining uncontacted tribes, estimated at that time to be less than 70 in number. Their policy was to leave them mostly undisturbed, except for an occasional check-in to evaluate their health and verify their numbers.

Roberts recognized that he would need FUNAI's permission before visiting the protected reserves. He narrowed his focus to the Amazonas province, where the vast majority of the remaining tribes were located. This region still covered a large area with an estimated 26 uncontacted tribes. It didn't escape him that Manaus happened to be the capital of Amazonas, the city where Juan Virtanen was from. Neither did it escape him that the Yanomami tribes happened to be concentrated in the northern part of Amazonas....

The ringing of his cell phone snapped him back to the present. "Brett Roberts here." He had given this number out to a few recruiters.

"Hey Brett!" It was Sakow. "I presume you've had a chance to talk things over with Ruth. So, what did she say?"

"She's willing to support it, with a couple of conditions. You and I should probably discuss them in person, although I can't leave my home office just now. I'm expecting a recruiter to call back later this morning."

"Tell you what. I have my bike here with me in the office. How about you ride down after lunch and we can both ride home together."

"Okay, see you in a bit." Roberts hung up before he could change his mind. He still had intentions of paying a visit to the downtown library, but he probably wouldn't have time to do that today.

Roberts used a hand towel to mop his face and neck as he sat in Sakow's office two hours later. "So here's what I know so far. There's a government organization called FUNAI that's responsible for protecting the indigenous tribes, and there's an application form I need to fill out to get their permission. Also, Ruth wants me to plan everything out carefully and share it with her before she gives her final approval."

"Sure Brett, I understand. Safety first. What else?"

"Well, I think we should draft a formal consulting agreement with staged deliverables and clear go/no-go decision points."

Sakow stroked his chin. "Yeah, I can see why Ruth would want that, and it's probably a good idea. But I'll have to run the agreement by Barry Hammond for his approval, since it's still his money. Alright, any more conditions?"

"The sample collection process, I want to make sure that's something I can actually do out there in the rainforest."

Sakow smiled. Roberts was definitely interested, as he knew he would be. "Funny you should mention that. I've already ordered the collection devices. Let's go to the lab and I'll show you how simple the procedure is."

They entered the lab and Sakow opened a white paper box filled with individually-wrapped, tube-like plastic containers with special toggle caps that couldn't be reopened a second time without a special tool. Each tube contained about an inch of a clear foamy liquid at the bottom. The pouch also contained separately-wrapped cotton swabs with long wooden handles. Sakow tore one open and removed the swab.

"Okay, open your mouth," he said.

With a tinge of apprehension, Roberts complied and allowed Sakow to rub the swab against the inside of his cheek a few times. He watched Sakow insert the swab into the collection tube and snap the cap back down.

"There. We've just transferred a few hundred of your cheek cells to the collection device. You probably didn't even feel the swab removing them. Your cheeks produce these cells continuously to replace the ones lost every time you chew and swallow. This special detergent buffer will lyse the cells and stabilize the DNA. The conditions of the rainforest shouldn't be any problem."

Sakow handed over an unopened, 50-unit box of collection devices, about the size of a kid's lunchbox. "See? It doesn't even weigh that much. You should probably plan on carrying two of these boxes in your backpack, just in case."

"Looks like it shouldn't be a problem," said Roberts. "What happens after I return them to the lab?"

"We use that robotic workstation over there." Sakow activated the robotic pipetting arm and demonstrated how the samples were processed through the various stages of preparation for DNA sequencing. He'd already pocketed Brett's cheek swab sample but Roberts had been too engrossed in Sakow's explanation to notice.

Sakow said, "I think that covers about everything. Still interested in riding home together? We should still be able to catch the sunset if we leave right away."

Roberts realized that he was already committed emotionally. He shook his head and smiled. "When can you have the consulting agreement ready?"

"I should be able to get it drafted and ready for your signature by next Tuesday at the latest."

Roberts nodded. "Fair enough, let's ride."

Brett Roberts logged onto the FUNAI website from his home computer to find it almost entirely in Portuguese. He used Google Translator to navigate the tabs and eventually found the appropriate department for submitting his research proposal. Clicking the link, he composed an email describing the study along with the potential role it could play in assessing their overall health risks based on genetic disease predispositions. His request seemed simple enough.

An email reply came two days later from Fernando Delgado, FUNAI's director of research programs. It surprised Roberts to receive such a rapid response, although it too was in Portuguese. He re-launched Google Translator and pasted Delgado's email into the left-hand text box. After several seconds, an imperfect but understandable translation appeared on the right. FUNAI would perhaps be willing to support his proposal; however they wanted to see a detailed research plan no later than Friday, February 17th, less than 8 days away given the time difference. No reason was given for this particular deadline.

Roberts leaned back in his chair with his fingers clasped behind his neck. He'd have to work quickly. He called Brian Sakow to give him the news.

"This is Brian Sakow, President of SnapGen, how may I help you?" It amused Roberts to hear how 'official' his friend sounded over the phone.

"Hey Brian, this is Brett. Listen, I just got an email reply from a guy at FUNAI, Brazil's National Indian Foundation."

"Whoa, wait a minute. I thought you needed more time to figure this whole thing out. You telling you've already decided?"

"Not quite yet, but I wanted to alert FUNAI in case they had any major objections. The reply suggested that they'd be willing to assist us, although we need to get them a detailed research proposal by next Friday at the latest. I'm guessing they only do their tribal surveys maybe once or twice a year. So, what do you think?"

"Hmm," Sakow considered. "I can have your consulting agreement ready by tomorrow. But getting such a detailed research plan together that quickly will require some pretty long hours over the next seven days."

Roberts interjected, "Better make that six. We should probably get it translated into Portuguese before submitting to FUNAI."

Sakow had a quick answer for that. "I know a guy at the Salk Institute who can help. His name is Alfredo Ruiz, an MD/PhD neuroscientist from Brazil who's currently here on sabbatical from the University of São Paulo. I'll give him a call as soon as we hang up."

Roberts was back in Sakow's untidy office the next morning, carefully flipping through his 14-page consulting agreement.

"Take your time, Brett, although we've got a tight deadline here."

Roberts grimaced. "What's this part about my consenting to be included as a subject in the study?"

"Oh that? It's nothing really. It just means we'd be using your DNA as reference material, to control for sequence quality. But between you and me, and strictly off the record, it also means you'd be able to compare your genome sequence to the Yanomami, assuming that's one of the tribes you're planning to visit."

Roberts slowly nodded. "Okay, but the official study will focus exclusively on the migratory patterns and hereditary risks of the indigenous

Amazon tribes, correct?" Sakow jumped in, "Absolutely. There'd be nothing in the final publication that could possibly link any of the data to you. Your genome identity would never be disclosed to anyone outside this room. Look, it's all there in writing."

"Alright, then," said Roberts. He flipped to the final page of the agreement and asked for a pen.

"Great!" said Sakow as soon as Roberts had added his signature. He rubbed his hands together. "So, let's get started. I'll work on the overall research plan, including justification, sample size and biostatistics, with a brief description of the sequencing methodology we'll be using. You decide which tribes you want to visit and put together a detailed trip proposal. We can exchange working documents via email, but let's plan to meet back here no later than Wednesday afternoon to pull it all together. How's all that sound?"

Roberts reached out to shake Brian's hand. "Sounds good. Guess you won't be joining me on the ride home today."

"Sorry Brett, no time for that in this case. Enjoy the sunset."

Sakow speed-dialed Janet Feinstein shortly after Roberts had left. "Janet, great news. Roberts actually agreed to your idea. I'll fill you in on the details later." He pondered Feinstein's response after hanging up the phone. She hadn't seemed all that surprised.

For the past few days, Roberts had been camping out in the anthropology section of San Diego's downtown library. This reminded him of the many long hours he would spend in the library back in graduate school. From the look of the dusty shelves, knowing one's way around a library had evidently become a lost art. Most of the scientific articles he needed for work these days were readily accessible over the internet. He chuckled to himself, wondering if he should have also brought along a slide rule.

Nevertheless, his plan was coming together nicely.

First he wanted to visit the Matsés tribes of the Javari River Valley, along the Peruvian border with Brazil. The word Matsés actually meant "people" in their native language. Their origin was largely unknown, although they were living along the Huallaga River in Peru when Jesuit Missionaries first made contact in the 18th Century. The disease epidemics that followed quickly devastated their numbers. Those that survived were now living in one of the first government-protected Indian reserves, although their current population was estimated to be less than 3000. One reason why Roberts wanted to start with the Matsés was that they reportedly spoke Spanish as well as Portuguese. Roberts also spoke a bit of Spanish and thought it might come in handy.

The Tikuna tribes were next on his list, reportedly one of the first tribes to be contacted by the Spanish Conquistadores. With an estimated population of over 36,000 residing within the Brazilian Amazon, and with much smaller numbers in neighboring Columbia and Peru, the Tikuna were considered one of the most prosperous tribes in the region. And yet even after 400 years of contact with outsiders, they had somehow managed to preserve their native language, their religious practices and rituals, and most of their cultural art forms. Roberts was interested in an area called Alto Silomones, where many of these tribes were living now, just south of the Rio Solimoes River. It should be reachable by boat, along with a relatively short hike into the protected interior, perhaps less than a day. The Tikuna were also known for their prodigious art, including ceremonial masks and clothing, basket weaving, and the famous Tikuna dolls. They were the only people within the Amazon region that painted simply for the sake of painting. Roberts found that intriguing.

The Banawá Indigenous Territory was a considerable distance to the south of any of the major tributaries, hence they would probably be one of the most difficult tribes to access. However it was their reclusive nature that Roberts found most intriguing. They had lived mostly in isolation for thousands of years, one of the least known of all the indigenous peoples in Brazil. Roberts found it interesting to read about how, unlike many of the other tribes, the Banawá reportedly buried their dead in gravesites close to the village. They would typically 'feed' the graves with ceremonial offerings for several days until the 'soul' had left the physical body. Shamanism was a key to Banawá culture, and the shamans were expected to live in complete isolation for a time, to purify their souls before beginning their official duties. The main village was supposedly located near the upper course of Banawá creek, over 100 miles to the south of the town of Coari on the Rio Solimoes. Roberts presumed that region ought to be accessible by helicopter. He made a note to inquire about this possibility in his research proposal to FUNAI.

From there, Roberts wanted to travel to the capital city of Manaus. There was a highway leading northward out of the city that could probably take him within hiking distance of the Waimiri-Atroari reservation, in the northernmost section of Amazonas. The Waimiri-Atroari proved to be fierce warriors and were greatly feared when first contacted by Europeans back in 1732. But their numbers had dwindled to less than 950 souls after centuries of such conflict. In 1999, the Brazilian government instituted Programa Atroari to offer them protection, education, and healthcare services for battling their epidemics of measles, malaria, and influenza. A side benefit of Programa Atroari had been rescuing the Waimiri-Atroari's cultural practices from near extinction. It became a model for other such programs throughout the Amazon region.

Of course, Roberts also wished to visit the Yanomami, and intended to visit them last. He learned that it was possible to charter a small plane upon returning to Manaus and fly up the Rio Negro to a much smaller riverfront town called São Gabriel da Cachoeira. From there he could take a jeep northward to a location within hiking distance of the Yanomami's protected territory.

Roberts estimated the trip would probably take about a month and a half to complete. No small commitment, to be sure, but in his mind, he was already there.

Sakow pushed away from his computer screen and rubbed his eyes, thinking he should probably give Feinstein another call. "Hey Janet, Roberts agreed to serve as a control subject for our Amazon Project. Hoping that's okay with you…. Yeah, we used one of our cheek swab collection kits like we're planning to use for the indigenous tribes…. Uh huh. Sequence quality looks quite good, actually. You can view it right now on your own computer if you'd like." Sakow reasoned that Roberts would ultimately agree to this once FUNAI had accepted their proposal. And he needed Feinstein's endorsement to convince Hammond they were making good progress.

"That's wonderful, Brian. What about that control gene we talked about? Have you picked one yet and had it sequenced by the Sanger method for comparison?"

Sakow took a moment before answering. "That's right, you wanted something related to brain biochemistry. Sorry Janet, I almost forgot. I do have a particular gene in mind, and I can probably get someone over at Scripps to run it for me. But I'll need to have Roberts come back in and give a blood sample. His cheek swab wouldn't have provided enough DNA for the Sanger method anyway. Should have the results in about a week. That okay with you?" He heard a click, and then a dial tone.

Sakow returned the receiver to its cradle and began to rub his temples. No way would Roberts submit to another blood draw without wanting to know the reason in precise detail. And he probably wouldn't agree to release his SIGMAR-1 gene sequence to Feinstein in any case. *Or would he?* There was still a remote possibility that Roberts may have mentioned something to Feinstein about his microarray discovery. *Probably not,* Sakow concluded. Roberts didn't even like Janet Feinstein. Sakow toyed with the idea of sending a sample of his own blood over to Scripps, knowing that he too possessed the exact same gene sequence. But in the end, he decided to wait until the end of the week and then send her Brett's original SIGMAR-1 gene sequence file from years before. What difference did it make?

The buzzer startled him and he immediately flipped a switch to answer. "Roberts, is that you?"

"Hey Brian, I've brought along a summary of the tribes I want to visit."

"Come on up." He pressed another button to open the downstairs door.

Roberts booted up his laptop, and for the next several hours they edited and merged their respective documents into a final research proposal. Sakow finally held his hand up and said, "Dude I'm famished. Care to take a break and go get some dinner?"

They took a relatively short walk up Coast Boulevard to Las Palomas, a touristy restaurant on the point overlooking La Jolla Cove. This being a weeknight, the place was almost empty. Roberts and Sakow were sitting in a back booth, still working on their pitcher of Dos Equis lager after polishing off a platter of fish tacos.

Roberts asked, "You think this guy you know will be able to translate our research proposal into Portuguese by Friday morning? FUNAI's headquarters in Brasilia is 5 hours ahead of us, and I'm afraid they might reject it if we don't meet the deadline."

"The translator program he uses can't handle the technical jargon, but he promised to make the necessary corrections himself if we get it to him by tomorrow morning."

"Guess we'll just need to go with what we have then. Perhaps you should send it to him tonight when we get back." Roberts leaned forward while nervously stroking his moustache, one he had worn most of his adult life.

Fernando Delgado, FUNAI's director of research programs, had always been a busy man. However, keeping an eye out for scientists who wanted to go poking around inside the protected areas was part of his job. Delgado thought he'd called this Brett Roberts fellow's bluff, and was surprised to see the email reply when he arrived at his desk that Monday morning. He opened the file and scrolled down while reading the document. It had been translated into Portuguese, a show of respect. He was impressed, but as he read further down it became clear that such a study would be out of the question.

Just then he got a call on his outside line, a number from America. It would be an impertinent move on Roberts's part to be calling so soon. He picked up anyway.

"Fernando, how are you my friend? It's Alfredo Ruiz, remember me from medical school?" They had both attended university together in São Paulo. Delgado remembered that Ruiz was on sabbatical at the Salk Institute in Southern California. This Brett Roberts was also from San Diego. Strange that Ruiz should be calling him just now.

"Ruiz, you old *merda*! I'm doing fine, but I'm surprised to hear from you. I didn't think you would be coming back home until next fall."

"*Boa*, I will get right to the point. I understand that you recently received a research proposal from a Dr. Brett Roberts, on behalf of a genomic sequencing company called SnapGen, *Como no?*"

This seemed like more than just a coincidence. Delgado measured his response, "I have… and it has also been translated into Portuguese. I'm guessing you had something to do with that, considering you happen to be living close by?"

Ruiz went on to explain that yes, SnapGen had indeed asked him to translate this proposal, although he was against the idea of exporting DNA samples from the indigenous tribes to America. He did think the study had scientific merit, however. He went on to explain how genomic profiling could potentially help elucidate their genetic risk factors and disease predispositions.

Ruiz had an unspoken reason for endorsing this study, knowing Janet Feinstein's affiliation with SnapGen. They'd had numerous discussions on the topic of genetic variation and the human mind. Thus, he presumed she must have an ulterior motive for endorsing this research proposal.

Delgado rubbed his bald head while considering. Knowing Alfredo, he suspected that Ruiz may have an ulterior motive. "So, you're proposing we allow this Brett Roberts into our protected regions, shepherd him around so he can collect DNA samples from the indigenous tribes, and then what?"

"Those samples must never leave Brazil." Alfredo Ruiz went on to explain his plan to ensure this. The samples would be confiscated and shipped instead to his laboratory in São Paulo, where they would reside in a -70°C freezer until his return. A sizable donation from Ruiz to FUNAI was also discussed. This was of course how the wheels were greased in their native country.

Roberts was absently staring at the computer screen several weeks later when Ruth suddenly plopped a fat 9 x 12 inch manila envelope onto his desk. "The return address says it's from the Fundação Nacional do Índio in Brasília. You think this might be junk mail?" she teased.

He tore it open to find a 21 page agreement for him to sign, a number of other forms to be filled out, including a medical checklist with the required vaccinations, and a brochure covering the 'dos and don'ts' of traveling inside Brazil. It would be necessary to wait for the rainy season to abate before traveling into the protected reservations. FUNAI would sponsor his visa and any necessary permits, however a FUNAI representative must accompany him at all times when visiting the indigenous territories.

SnapGen was of course expected to compensate FUNAI for their assistance. Good so far, Sakow had already promised to cover that. ...And based on Roberts' proposed itinerary, an additional "kind donation" to FUNAI was requested in the amount of $50,000, with half the amount to be received within 10 business days as a show of good faith. Roberts certainly hoped SnapGen would be willing to cover this "kind donation". If this trip turned out to be a failure, his future employment at SnapGen seemed doubtful.

Yet the cover letter had been signed by Fernando Delgado himself. Assuming Dr. Roberts agreed to their terms, he would be met in Iquitos Peru to follow the trip itinerary outlined in his proposal. It was suggested that they target the second week in May.

"They've accepted my proposal!"

"I can see that." Ruth had been reading the agreement over his shoulder while Brett flipped through the pages. "Looks like you've got some planning to do. That's less than two months away. And don't forget that other promise you made to me."

Brett stood to give his wife a hug and kissed her on the cheek for good measure. "I won't."

After Ruth left, Brett called Sakow to give him the news.

"Excellent!" Sakow said. "Come by any time on Monday and I'll have a check advance waiting for you."

"Thanks for suggesting this, Brian. I'm already beginning to feel excited about it."

"I know." Sakow hoped he was doing the right thing by sharing Brett's SIGMAR-1 gene sequence with Feinstein. Roberts was a good guy. But then again, this was science after all.

While Roberts was researching his first trip south of the equator, Janet Feinstein got busy planning her next experiment. The reference gene that Sakow had chosen was precisely the one she expected. *And now she had it!* Although the sample ID in the annotations had a much earlier date, again no surprise. She recognized this date as the one Amy had recorded in her blood draw logbook prior to leaving the Scripps Research Institute, the one with initials 'BR'. Always a stickler for detail, Feinstein resaved the file.

She quickly spotted the mutation in this gene sequence from Roberts. It explained a lot about his evasive actions in the past, for example not telling her about his second microarray experiment with the remnants of

Schwarzkopf's brain samples. He must have been curious about what this gene's function might be, even to the point of having his own DNA sequenced. Which of course meant that Roberts suspected he may be different.

The potential implications from this discovery could be far reaching. Feinstein had been on the right track when conceiving the Amazon study. But for the moment, she had a more practical experiment in mind. To transform cultured neurons with a mutated version of this SIGMAR-1 gene, and to measure their response under the stimulation of DMT. To accomplish this, she would try out a new technique invented by a former colleague at UC Berkeley. The method was called Clustered Regularly Interspaced Short Palindromic Repeat, or CRISPR. It was a way of cutting out the normal gene and splicing a mutated version in its place. Her colleague claimed that CRISPR would one day revolutionize the field of gene therapy, to edit out hereditary mutations in patients with beta-thalassemia or hereditary hemochromatosis, for example. But the process was supposedly laborious and difficult to perform. Along with that, the gene insertions were not always precise, meaning they could occasionally be inserted elsewhere in the genome accidentally, sometimes with unintended consequences. It would take decades for CRISPR to be ready for testing in humans. Or so Feinstein had thought at the time.

The first task was to clone the mutated SIGMAR-1 gene into a bacterial plasmid vector. A company called Invitrogen was marketing a kit that she could use to perform those steps herself. She would do the work late at night when no one else was around. But then she wanted to use this new CRISPR procedure to transfer the genetic material into the chromosome of a neuronal stem cell. For that she would need to work with someone highly skilled in cloning techniques.

Feinstein was about to call her friend at UC Berkeley when Alfredo Ruiz stepped into her office. "Hey Alfredo, have you read about this new CRISPR technique?"

"Of course, Janet. I have been eager to attempt the protocol."

"Then have a seat, Alfredo. Let's talk."

Alfredo Ruiz had long been obsessed with research pursuits intended to unlock the mysteries of the human mind. Janet Feinstein's landmark paper on gene expression patterns in the brain around the time of death had immediately captured his attention. When she left Stanford to join the Salk Institute in La Jolla, he figured she must be onto something important. This was the main reason he'd applied to work in her lab during his sabbatical leave.

So, Feinstein wanted him to clone some novel gene into neuronal stem cells and culture them in a petri dish, although she wouldn't tell him which one it was. Her plan was to test their response to the different neurotransmitters, including DMT. When he asked her why, she confided about her unpublished observations with DMT, and went on to explain how the experiment had been conducted. But she immediately regretted having shared this bit of information with Ruiz and swore him to secrecy.

Ruiz found what he'd just been asked to do quite intriguing, for reasons he would never share with anyone, regardless of his promise to Janet. Perhaps the little genetically modified neurons might even be capable of generating electromagnetic waves strong enough to interact with external forces. Why he suspected this had much to do with tortured past. But if his suspicion turned out to be correct, he would steal the clones and have this DMT gene sequenced by an outside laboratory. Ruiz could then study it further after returning to São Paulo.

Hmm… he mused, and the more he thought about it, the more convinced he became. A person with such a gene could possibly read minds, move metal objects with their thoughts, perhaps even see into the future. Much as his parents had done.

Few people had known about his parents' innate psychic abilities. They were a product of an inter-breeding experiment conducted by the Nazis back in the 1930s. Der Führer had proclaimed the Amazonian interior to be Germany's Wild West, an undeveloped land to be settled much as the Americans had done in their continent to the north. When reports came back about the indigenous tribes and their apparently unique ability to communicate with the spirit world, trusted experts in paranormal psychology were then dispatched to join the colonization effort.

Ruiz's parents tormented him as a child with arduous mental tasks intended to unlock his own paranormal abilities, although he disappointed them time and again, to their increasing consternation. They sent him away to an exclusive secondary school in São Paulo to further educate his mind.

There he first met Juan Virtanen, a like-minded student who evidently suffered from parental anxieties of his own. Virtanen had been unwilling to talk about them, so Ruiz committed himself to besting the young fool academically instead.

Ruiz had also hoped his academic achievements would impress his parents. But they resumed their testing when he returned home that summer, and the summer after that, and on and on into early adulthood. It ultimately drove him to a state of madness.

Which was why he killed them.

CHAPTER TWENTY

"Delgado"

Thursday, May 10TH, 2012

25,000 Feet over the Rainforests of Peru

AFTER ALMOST TWO MONTHS of nerve-wracking preparation, packing and repacking, exchanging out the heavier gear for lighter but more expensive brands, testing and retesting the weight distribution inside his new Kelty 5100cu backpack, Brett Roberts was on the last flight leg of his journey to Iquitos Peru. He sat in a window seat over the wing of an incredibly noisy Brazilia turboprop and was glad he had accepted earplugs from the flight steward when climbing on board. His scratched and hazy window still presented him a 180 degree view of a vivid green canopy down below, extending out to the horizon in every direction. The hum of the propellers increased in pitch as the plane made its final approach. He watched the winding Yarapa River getting wider by the second until the airstrip appeared with the sundrenched city of Iquitos in the background. The sprawling city was much larger than he had imagined it to be, now a major port on a tributary feeding directly into the Rio Amazonas, which his U.S. map referred to as the Amazon.

The wheels screeched down onto the tarmac and the plane taxied over the bumpy concrete to a terminal named 'Coronel FAP Francisco Secada Vignetta', with the English words 'International Airport' painted beneath it in smaller letters. Roberts immediately felt the searing heat and oppressive humidity when he climbed down the stairs and waited by the plane for his backpack. He thrust an arm through one of the straps and followed the queue of passengers. His shirt was already drenched in sweat when he entered the terminal, and the air-conditioned blast shocked his system even more. Wondering which way he should go, he spotted a man holding up a card with his name printed in large capital letters.

"Fernando Delgado," the man announced proudly with an outstretched hand. The sage Latin gentleman had a balding pate with a rim of jet-black curly hair, a matching full beard, and intelligent looking eyes behind those circular wire-rimmed glasses. So, Delgado himself had come to meet Roberts. This was unexpected.

"Senhor Delgado," Roberts reached out and received the firmest handshake he'd ever experienced. He flexed his fingers afterwards to make sure they still functioned. "I wasn't expecting to meet you personally."

Delgado's smile was more genuine this time, revealing a bright and even set of teeth that had obviously seen good dental care. "Yes, Senhor Roberts. As it turns out, I myself have taken an interest in your research study. So, here I am!" He clapped his hands together and smiled once more.

Delgado shepherded his charge through security after flashing his credentials to the functionary and exchanging a few words with him in Spanish. Roberts' passport was summarily stamped, and before his sweat glands had fully recovered, they stepped back out into the searing jungle heat. Delgado led them across the access road to a parking lot where his Jeep waited with a soft canopy roof and no side windows. Roberts pursed his lips when he realized that the vehicle had no air-conditioning, but the breeze whipping around the windshield soon gave a welcome relief once they'd gotten underway. Delgado took the main road and followed it into town.

They pulled over in front of a two-story whitewashed colonial style hotel with powder blue trim facing the river along Antonio Raimondi Road. A young man had been waiting at the curb and promptly accepted the keys from Senhor Delgado with a deferential nod.

"We will not be needing this Jeep where we are going," Senhor Delgado explained, and motioned for the other man to get Brett's backpack. "My gear is already inside. Come, let us get you checked in. You must be tired. I suggest you have a two-hour siesta before we go out and enjoy an evening meal together. Okay, as you Americans like to say?"

Senhor Delgado's English was far better than Roberts might have expected. "A nap does sound good about now. Thanks again for meeting me here in Iquitos, Senhor Delgado."

"Please, you may call me Fernando."

Brett's room turned out to be small but clean with a view of the river, and thankfully the air-conditioning unit had been on for a while. He fell back onto the single bed with his feet still touching the floor, thinking maybe he'd just shut his eyes for a few minutes… and was rudely awakened two hours later by the phone on the nightstand. Checking his watch, he saw it was already past 6 PM.

"Doctor Roberts, Brett, are you ready to come down for dinner?" It was Fernando, as he recalled, although Roberts still wasn't comfortable calling him by his first name. The man had an officious air about him.

Roberts cleared his throat before answering. "Yes, hello Doctor Delgado." He knew the man had a medical degree, having checked him out online before departing on this trip. "Guess you were right, I must have really needed that nap. But I am pretty hungry. I can meet you downstairs in, say about 15 minutes?"

"Of course, Senhor Brett."

Roberts changed into a new pair of cargo pants with a loose fitting cotton shirt and Teva sandals. Noticing the price tag still attached to one of the belt loops, he snapped it off then slapped his cheeks a few times as he checked himself out in the mirror.

"Okay, here goes," he said to himself.

He descended the stairs and noted that Fernando Delgado had changed into a pair of designer jeans with a tan cowboy-style shirt trimmed in braided brocade.

"I have a reservation for us at one of my favorite restaurants here in Iquitos. It is just a short walk from here."

Roberts did his best to keep up with Senhor Delgado as they walked down Antonio Raimondi, lined with jumbles of industrial shops, markets and business establishments all packed together like sardines, to the Plaza de Armas, a pleasant little grassy square featuring palm and magnolia trees, park benches and a water fountain with an obelisk monument in its center. The locals were lounging on park benches while enjoying the cool evening breeze blowing in from the water.

They made a left at the square and headed toward a boardwalk that ran along the river, with curios shops for the browsers and sidewalk cafes for dining when the weather allowed. The Amazon Café was about a block up and had an outside table waiting for them with Senhor Delgado's name written on the little white card. A waiter rushed out when he saw Senhor Delgado approaching and graciously pulled out their chairs. Delgado spoke quickly to the man in Spanish. The twinkle in his eyes hinted that he was pleased to see his old friend.

"Hello Luis, I'd like to introduce you to my colleague Doctor Roberts." Senhor Delgado had kindly returned to English, a relief to Roberts since he was having trouble keeping up.

"Very pleased meet you, Doctor Roberts!" Luis said enthusiastically while reaching over to shake Brett's hand.

Senhor Delgado ordered for both of them, again to Roberts' relief, and Luis went back inside the restaurant to give the chef their orders. No sooner had he left when a busboy came out with two bottles of cold beer and a large bottle of sparkling water along with a pair of empty glasses. They turned their chairs to face the water and settled back to enjoy the cooling evening breeze. A fishing boat motored by on its way back to the harbor while a pair of deckhands busily tugged at the nets and prepared for docking. "A beautiful country, yes?"

Roberts took a deep breath and leaned back. The humidity must be dropping, he realized. "It certainly is, Senhor Delgado. Excuse me, I mean Fernando." He glanced over to catch Delgado grinning back at him. The beer had apparently loosened him up a bit.

Luis returned with a platter of steamed fish for the table, a variety that Roberts didn't recognize, along with bowls of dirty rice and assorted green vegetables that likewise looked a bit odd to him. But it all was quite delicious, to his pleasant surprise, especially when washed down with another swallow of this malty local beer.

Luis came back outside to clear the plates away and returned once more with two small ceramic cups of strong Brazilian coffee. "There is no rush," he said. "Please, stay as long as you like."

Over the next half hour, Roberts made an effort to explain his scientific rationale for the study while avoiding technical jargon as much as possible. Senhor Delgado nodded attentively and asked a few astute questions along the way to feign his interest.

"Thank you for agreeing to do this Senhor... I mean, Fernando."

Delgado nodded with his lips firmly pressed together. "I hope you still wish to thank me at the completion of our journey, Senhor Brett. There will be difficulties along the way, of that I am certain, and perhaps some dangers as well."

"I feel confident that we will be successful, Senhor Fernando." 'Senhor Fernando' seemed like a reasonable compromise.

A full moon on the rise reflected its silver light on the water and cast the densely packed trees on the opposite bank in dark silhouette. Roberts finished off his second beer and enjoyed the peaceful quietude.

"I see you are still tired, Senhor Brett, and we will have an early start tomorrow."

They returned to the hotel with the moon lighting their way.

Early the next morning, they crammed inside a motorcycle cab with their backpacks piled over their thighs and tried not to breathe as it putt-putted them down to the docks. After extricating themselves, Senhor Fernando led them over to a 1950s-era cabin cruiser that looked to be about a 40-footer. He introduced Senhor Brett to Captain Senhor Jorge, a sage-looking and well-muscled mestizo in his late-forties with a broad moustache and a firm handshake. Then Roberts was introduced to the first mate Jaime, about ten years younger and considerably rounder of belly but equally strong and agile.

Senhor Brett and Senhor Fernando were each shown to their separate cabins after climbing on board. These small but comfortable wood-paneled rooms had a small closet, latched dresser drawers and a pull-down bunk built into the interior wall, a bolted-down table and chair beneath the portals and a small metallic sink in the corner with a hand pump and stainless-steel vanity mirror. Roberts angled his backpack into the closet and was relieved to find out that it actually fit. He had been told not to unpack since they would be arriving in Genarro Herrera before nightfall.

Roberts took a bench seat along the bulwarks just as Jaime was casting off. Captain Jorge motored the boat out toward open water and made a right to follow the Rio Amazonas upriver in a southwesterly direction. Seeing him sitting in shorts and a T-shirt, Senhor Fernando explained that sunburns could happen quickly out on the water. He advised Roberts to return to his cabin and change into a long-sleeved shirt and pants despite the rising temperature, and also to wear the wide-brimmed hat that he had been instructed to bring along. Roberts figured now was not the time to be disagreeable. His life was in Senhor Delgado's hands for the foreseeable future. He came back out and cinched the chinstrap to keep his hat from flying away in the wind.

Senhor Fernando settled onto the bench seat next to Roberts. "It should take us about eight hours to reach Genaro Herrera," he said. "Enjoy the scenery, but please remember to drink plenty of water today." He settled back and cracked open a book, evidently a mystery novel by its cover, although the title was in Portuguese.

The water level along this stretch of the Rio Amazonas had receded considerably over the past several weeks, although the trees along the banks were still partially submerged. Senhor Fernando explained that it would remain like this for another month or so. The banks would then dry out for a time until the rains returned two short months later. Roberts spotted an overwhelming variety of trees and knew but a few of their names, although he consoled himself with the factoid that scientists had only managed to characterize about 227 of the over 16,000 tree species estimated to be living in the rainforest, a mere 1.4% of them. Furthermore, they had learned through failed attempts at managed forestation that such natural diversity actually protected the trees from species-susceptible pathogens that could otherwise spread rapidly from one to the next. Plantations demanded the use of toxic chemicals to fend off such infestations. But such a thing was still considered unacceptable in the old-growth rainforest, itself a delicately balanced ecosystem.

The two men eventually shifted from the bulwarks to the back of the boat where they found it easier to read while passing the time. Jaime could be heard clanking away down in the galley, busily preparing their mid-day meal of steamed rice, beans, and shredded pork.

"The Amazon is truly amazing," Roberts commented while scraping the last of the food from his metal plate.

"You will get bored with it soon enough," said Delgado. He was right. By mid-afternoon Roberts decided to head down to his cabin and try lying in his bunk, but found it difficult to sleep under the sweltering heat, even after stripping down to his skivvies. So he put back on his clothes and hat and returned to his bench seat along the bulwarks where the breeze eventually revived him. The air was still hot and sticky, about as good as things would get until nightfall.

They took a left at a fork in the river and followed the winding and narrowing Ucayali upriver for another three and a half hours. It was almost sunset when they reached the quiet little town of Genaro Herrera where they tied up alongside its floating wooden dock. The dwellings near the river all had thatched roofs, whereas most of the ones on higher ground had roofs constructed from tin sheets or tile. After retrieving their packs, Delgado and Roberts said their goodbyes to Captain Jorge and his first mate Jaime, who quickly climbed back aboard and cast off for their return trip to Iquitos. They wouldn't make it back to Iquitos until well after midnight, an extremely long day for them, thought Roberts. He didn't know that they routinely made this trip during the dry season.

Roberts couldn't see anything that looked like an inn in this village. He wondered if the villagers would mind if they made camp nearby. Noticing Brett's concern, Delgado explained that a colleague of his would be sharing his home with them that evening.

Hector was a stout and unmarried mestizo in his late thirties, a man who evidently had no interest in being tied down. He was also a registered guide for FUNAI and well versed in the Matzes dialects, which would prove essential over the next stage of their journey. He led them up the hill to his modest little two room house and offered them a quick meal of beans, rice and pork that had been stewing on a small gas stove in the front room. Roberts sat and flipped through a guidebook while Hector and Delgado gossiped together in Portuguese. Hector then escorted his two guests to a back room where a pair of rolled out foam mattresses waited for them on the hard packed dirt floor.

Roberts awoke the next morning to the sound of raindrops pinging against the tin roof overhead. Gradually, the rain stopped. He glanced to his right to see if Delgado was awake. Delgado flexed his cheeks and opened his eyes. He stretched his arms and said, "Are you ready, Senhor Brett?" "As ready as I'll ever be," Roberts answered. "Boa, vamos!" said Delgado with an enthusiastic grin.

They cinched up their packs and ventured outside to find Hector bent over the engine of his old and rusty Jeep. "She burns a little oil," he explained before slamming the hood back down. After loading up their gear, Roberts took the back bench seat with Delgado riding shotgun.

Hector cranked the starter and the engine rumbled to life with a puff of billowing black smoke coming out the exhaust pipe. He ground the transmission into gear and they were off.

They headed southeast through the rainforest along a bumpy dirt road that connected with the town of Angamos. Their destination was located on the Peruvian side of the Rio Javari, a winding river that served as a natural border with neighboring Brazil. Trees towered above them as they rumbled along, their upper boughs networked into a dense canopy that blocked out most of the sunlight, and it was difficult to communicate above the whine of the Jeep tires. It took the better part of the day to cover that 100-kilometer distance, a dark and monotonous drive.

When they finally arrived at the quiet little river town, Hector pulled over in front of a dilapidated-looking open air market and mercifully shut off the engine. He escorted them to the man behind the counter and introduced his friend Jesús, who happened to own a 25-foot flat boat with a red tin roof canopy. Their next passage would be by river, Delgado explained. After depositing them at their next destination, Jesús would remain with the boat while the three of them hiked into the rainforest. It would take them about three days to visit the first Matses tribe and return to the boat. There were still other tribes living deeper in the rainforest, but Jesús was unwilling to wait any longer than that.

Jesús led them up the hill to the house he shared with his wife and five children, quite similar in construction to Hector's. They enjoyed another meal of stewed pork with beans and rice and fresh corn tortillas that Jesús's wife kept bringing out from the kitchen until Roberts finally caught on and pushed back from the table. That night, they slept on woven straw mats in the main room.

The children ran out to say goodbye the next morning, having already grown quite fond of the tall white American. Roberts gave them each a piece of hard candy from a side pouch of his pack. He smiled to himself, pleased to have anticipated this contingency.

They loaded their packs and provisions onto the boat and cast off to begin the next leg of their upriver journey, which according to Brett's map would be in a south by southwesterly direction. The Rio Javari was less than 100 meters across with frequent and unpredictable bends and turns, and proved to be slow going with the flatboat's little two-stroke outboard motor. Jesús carefully navigated around seemingly endless obstacles of dead tree trunks, partially submerged cypress, walking palm and rubber trees. After several hours of such meanderings, Hector instructed Jesús to reduce the throttle and waved him toward a narrow cove on the Peruvian side of the river, the place where Jesús would tie up and wait for them during their first foray into the rainforest.

Roberts had only just cinched his backpack and was rechecking the weight distribution when he noticed Senhor Delgado and Hector disappearing into the trees. He shuffled quickly to catch up. Due to the absence of daylight beneath the canopy, the ground between its pole-like trunks turned out to be relatively clear of vegetation, thus it was not difficult for Roberts to follow their lead once his eyes had adjusted to the dimness. His first impression of the rainforest was its smell – thick and earthy, like being inside a well-planted greenhouse but fifty times more intense. He wished he could zip off his pant legs and roll up his sleeves, but the insects discouraged such foolishness. As he hiked on behind Senhor Delgado, Roberts studied the lower growth vegetation and vines that somehow managed to eke out their existence beneath the canopy. He spotted an occasional parrot or macaw nestled in among them, each bird a bright flash of color against the surrounding gloom. These were quick to take flight whenever Roberts happened to make even the slightest gesture toward them. Senhor Delgado smiled to himself whenever this happened. Ah, to be re-experiencing such surprises of the rainforest through a novice's eyes.

Every so often they encountered a stream from which they could pump water through their purifiers. Hector suggested they make camp once it had become almost too dark to see. He removed a small gas lantern from his pack, lit it with a match and held it up while Delgado and Roberts strung their hammocks from the trees, then Delgado held the lantern while Hector did the same. Roberts produced a Jet Boil stove and demonstrated how it could be used to boil water for their dehydrated meals. After dinner, Roberts arranged his sleeping bag in one of the hammocks and climbed aboard, somewhat clumsily at first, but eventually he settled in. The cacophony of distant animal and bird noises made it difficult to fall asleep at first, but gradually Brett's tense muscles began to relax. His next memory was one of being shaken awake in the murky dawn. Thankfully, his dreams had not been disturbed that night.

They headed eastward for much of the next day. Hector held up a hand for them to stop around mid-afternoon. He whispered a few words in Portuguese to Delgado. "He says that we are nearing the village," Delgado whispered back to Roberts. "He wants us to wait here while he goes to make introductions."

Delgado shared a few things about the Matses culture while they waited. These people preferred to live communally, and traditionally practiced polygamy and animism. They also engaged in various odd rituals of accepting "energy" from one person to another, such as enduring whippings or being stung by ants or injected with frog venom. If the recipient endured the challenge, they would become a more resilient and productive contributor to the tribe.

Hector returned about fifteen minutes later. Delgado relayed his message with a hint of relief. "They are willing to meet with us. But please Senhor Brett, do not say anything until one of us motions for you to do so. The Matses are still quite wary of white men."

"Should we bring our packs along with us?" Roberts asked.

"Yes. If they accept us we will camp nearby."

As they exited the trees, Roberts caught his first glimpse of a large rectangular log structure surrounded by a few smaller thatched huts a good distance away. "What are the smaller huts for?" whispered Roberts. "They are sometimes used by social outcasts. The Matses are known to have their disagreements. If they offer one to us, we must refuse."

Hector advised them to remain at the perimeter of the village until one of the elders came out to address them. After a short while, although it seemed much longer, a little brown-skinned man exited the hut and stepped toward them. The unkempt grey hair gave him an ominous look, although his officious manner suggested he may be of some importance, perhaps even the tribal chief. He stood eyeing them warily, then returned to the hut where several others were now awaiting his decision with spears in hand. This was a tense moment, at least for Roberts, but thankfully the little man waved them forward.

Roberts then received his first opportunity to view the indigenous people up close. Most of them were less than five feet tall. The men all wore woven breech cloths to cover their loins, and strings of carved wooden beads with animal teeth around their necks. One had a small curved rib bone hanging from his nose, and several others wore straight wooden pegs pierced through their lower lips. They spoke to Hector and eyed the other two white men when he answered. Roberts found it a bit amusing to watch the pegs bobbing up and down while they spoke in their halting dialect. After a few such rounds of questioning with Hector translating, they nodded and grunted their agreement. Hector announced, "They are satisfied. We shall be welcome in their village."

Women now began exiting the log hut. Most were startlingly naked except for the red painted designs on their faces, arms, breasts and torsos. Many of them had narrow sticks pierced through their nostrils, which explained why outsiders referred to Matses as the "Cat People", and some also wore colorful bands of bird feathers around their heads, presumably to indicate their importance to the tribe.

The younger boys came out and began engaging in a vigorous type of wrestling game over near the fire pits. After a while, a few of the women came to shoo them away. Younger girls were then escorted out from the log house to assist with preparing the evening meal.

Older men remained by the log hut, squatting in a circle while passing around a long pipe with the pungent smell of wild tobacco smoke in the air. Hector, Roberts and Delgado were encouraged to join them. "Do we have to smoke that stuff?" Roberts asked, coughing already. "It is not expected," answered Delgado. "Just squat here next to me and say nothing until I ask you a question." Roberts noticed Delgado making notes in his field journal while Hector relayed their greetings. Such notes would be typed into a report when he returned to FUNAI headquarters.

The chief spoke briefly with Hector, who relayed his question directly to Roberts. "He wants to know why you are here."

Roberts considered a moment but then got an idea, one he thought might actually work. "Tell them we have come to share our spiritual energy."

Delgado gave him a hard look but then shrugged his shoulders in complicit agreement. This was Senhor Robert's problem to solve, not his. Hector relayed Brett's request back to the elders who responded with quizzical looks on their faces, being unfamiliar with the customs of these foreigners. The chief spoke again with Hector and grunted for him to translate. "They ask how this can be done."

"I will demonstrate for them." Roberts went over to rummage inside his pack for one of the sample collection boxes. He fingered out one of the packets and tore it open to remove the swab. He opened his mouth and turned his head to make it appear as though he had just inserted it directly inside his mouth. Then he directed the swab toward one of the elders and nodded that it was now his turn. Surprisingly, the little man obliged by opening his mouth and pointing with his finger to indicate his approval. Roberts carefully inserted the swab and rubbed it up and down three times against the man's cheek. Then he ceremoniously withdrew the swab and transferred it to the plastic cartridge, maintaining eye contact the entire time. The man seemed wary at first, but then broke into a grin and motioned for his tribesmen to do likewise. It surprised Roberts how easy this had been. Soon he had collected ten samples, his intended quota for this particular tribe. He returned the box to his backpack and made a mental note to label them all later.

The men then reassembled by the fire pit to be fed by the women. Several steaming pots were now hanging from a long pole suspended over the campfire. Senhor Fernando indicated with an encouraging nod that it would be safe for them to eat, a stew of wild animal meat with tubers and other vegetables. There would also be plantains for desert, still individually wrapped in palm leaves and roasting in the fire's embers. The people ate with carved wooden spoons and later used their fingers when the pots of stew were passed around a second time. After the communal meal was over, the children were instructed to return to the main hut, presumably for bedtime.

More wood was added to the fire and a few hand drums appeared with hands pounding softly. The Matses encouraged Roberts and his colleagues to join in on the chanting. Roberts found their simple, celebratory spirit contagious and asked to borrow one of the hand drums. He attempted to match the rhythm of the others, much to their amusement.

As the embers died down in the fire pit, the Matses people began returning to their log hut. Taking the hint, Hector, Delgado and Roberts returned to the trees and strung their hammocks. Brett Roberts slept soundly again that night, momentarily at peace with himself and this strange new world where he could breathe deeply.

He felt a spring in his stride as they hiked back out of the rainforest the next day. They returned to the place where Jesús had moored the flatboat to find him sound asleep beneath the canopy. Delgado hollered over to him, "*Acorda, você vagabundo preguiçoso!*" Which meant essentially 'get up, you lazy bum'. Jesús jumped out of the boat and came over to welcome them back, obviously eager to get going. His disappointment was just as evident when Delgado announced his intentions to make camp. Getting darker by the minute, it would have been perilous to navigate the Rio Javari after nightfall. While they were stringing up their hammocks, Delgado explained that they would be heading northeastward and downriver the next morning. It would take them at least two days to reach Leticia, where they would spend the night and then rejoin the Rio Amazonas to continue downriver. Glancing over to the flatboat, Roberts now understood what those extra 5-gallon drums of gasoline strapped to the back were for.

CHAPTER TWENTY ONE

"Amazonas"

Thursday, May 17ᵗʰ, 2012

IT WAS ALMOST DARK when they motored into the multi-cultural port city of Leticia, located at a nexus of borders separating Columbia from Brazil, with Peru just across the river to the south. The following day they'd be traveling downriver along the Rio Amazonas into the Brazilian interior. But for now, Brett Roberts desperately wanted to stretch his legs again on solid ground.

They pulled up to a dock at the end of Calle 3 and said their goodbyes to Hector and Jesús, who were planning to stay overnight at the pier's bunkhouse and leave bright and early for their return trip to Angamos. Roberts and Delgado both shouldered their heavy backpacks and hiked up Calle 3 to a hostel that Delgado had reserved for the night. Delgado nodded to indicate that it was Brett's turn to pay. Spotting the prices on the wall, Roberts retrieved the money belt from his pack and counted out 20 Reals of Brazilian currency. He handed the notes over to the wrinkled brown-skinned man behind the counter, who nodded with a toothless smile and handed them each a badly worn hand towel and a used bar of soap along with their room keys.

"Could you please ask him where I could make a phone call to America?" Roberts asked Delgado. Delgado exchanged a few words with the desk clerk in Portuguese and relayed his answer, "He says you can use his phone to make a three minute call for 15 Reals."

Roberts handed the money over and asked for a notepad to write down the number. The man picked up the receiver, gave instructions to the operator, and handed the phone over to Roberts. Seeing the number had gone through, Delgado decided to head up to his room.

"Hi dear, it's me!" said Roberts.

"Brett! Where are you?" Ruth replied through the static.

"In a town called Leticia. We'll be headed downriver into the Brazilian State of Amazonas tomorrow."

"Well thanks for calling. I was just beginning to get worried."

"Sorry Ruth, this was my first opportunity to use a pay phone since we left Iquitos Peru."

"That's alright. Any problems so far?"

"Things have gone pretty much according to plan so far, although I'm starting to appreciate all those shots I had to get before coming on this trip. Spent the night in a Matses village which was quite an experience. Wish I had time to describe it for you, although I've probably got less than two minutes left on this call." After another hurried exchange, Roberts heard the operator say *"tempo de quase-se"*. "Sorry dear, gotta go."

"Be safe, Brett. Please call me again when you can."

"I will, sweetheart." He heard a *click!* Evidently his time was up.

Roberts handed the phone back to the man and said "Gracias", which elicited another toothless smile. Roberts shouldered his pack and clambered up the creaky stairway to unlock the door to his room, which reeked of Lysol and badly needed a coat of paint.

They ate street tacos for dinner and retired early with expectations of getting a full night's sleep. Brett's tiny bed squeaked so badly every time he shifted that he eventually decided to pull the mattress to the floor.

He was awakened at dawn the next morning by an abrupt knocking at the door. "Time to get ready, Senhor Brett! Jorge and Jaime are waiting for us down on the dock."

After braving one of the musty shower stalls at the end of the hallway, Roberts repacked his things and carefully made his way back downstairs. He found himself in better spirits after stepping outside, even more so when they had reached the end of the dock. They would be returning to the larger boat, the one that had taken them from Iquitos to Genaro Herrera, also the one with separate cabins and bunks for the passengers. Despite the rising temperature that had already caused his pores to glisten, he resolved to nap later in his cabin once they had gotten underway.

They hefted their packs up to Jorge and climbed aboard. Roberts got his first whiff of breakfast aromas from the galley and was delighted when

Jaime handed him a steaming plate of scrambled eggs with spicy beans and rice. He devoured it within minutes as they cast off and motored eastward along the Rio Solimões. The sun's rays reflected dully on the rippling brown water, laden with sediment.

Roberts carried the empty plates back to the galley and went below to his cabin where he unpacked his things for a longer stay on the boat. As Delgado had explained shortly after coming back on board, their next stop would be São Paulo de Olivença, a community of about 35,000 people located at the mouth of a narrow tributary leading southward into the Tikuna territory. From São Paulo de Olivença they would travel eastward another three days along the Rio Solimões to the municipality of Coari, where they would make their next side trip south to visit the Banawá tribes, this time by helicopter as Roberts had originally presumed. Their final river leg would be another two days eastward to the capital city of Manaus. Roberts intended to leave a few of his clothes and other non-essentials behind on the boat between stops, it would lighten his load considerably while hiking through the rainforest.

It was close to mid-afternoon when the municipality of São Paulo de Olivença first came into view. Jorge angled the boat over to one the longer wooden docks, threw the engines in reverse, and then tossed the mooring lines down to Jaime. Roberts glanced up to a smart-looking church of Rococo style architecture at the top of the hill. It seemed out of place with the jumble of wooden stilt structures below it, their corrugated tin roofs badly oxidized, although a number of them were brightly painted in complementary colors of turquoise, avocado green, mustard yellow and crimson. Roberts was still taking in this seemingly isolated vestige of humanity from his bench seat along the bulwark when Delgado broke in, "So, are you ready for another overnight in the rainforest?" Roberts couldn't suppress his disappointment. "I presumed we'd be staying here in town tonight." "No," replied Delgado, thinly amused, "Jaime has arranged another boat for us to borrow, this one much smaller I'm afraid. We should reach the Tikuna protected area before nightfall."

Captain Jaime had already disembarked with a hefty backpack of his own. "Jaime and I have visited the Tikuna village many times before," Delgado explained. Roberts went back below and hastily repacked what he thought he would need. Jorge wished them well as they stepped down to the dock. He'd be staying on the boat, apparently.

Jaime led them around to the back side of the dock where an 18-foot aluminum hull boat was waiting. Roberts glanced skeptically at its rusting 45 HP Yamaha outboard as they lowered their gear. "No worry, Senhor Brett. Boat runs good. I have used many times," said Jaime in broken English, although it took him a number of rope pulls to yank the smoking outboard to life.

The Rio Jandaituba was a winding and narrow snake of a river, less than 50 meters across over its narrowest stretches. Even more laden with sediment than the Rio Solimões, its opaque brown water made a stark contrast to the vivid green landscape it slithered through. The densely packed vegetation alongside the banks looked almost impenetrable, and it didn't take long for Roberts to realize that he was lucky to be traveling by boat despite its sputtering engine and the constant stench of gasoline.

Dusk had fallen when Jaime spotted a clearing along the left-hand bank and pointed the boat in that direction. Delgado explained that they would be making camp there tonight. Although it was within walking distance of the villages, the Tikuna should only be approached in daylight.

They ate a quick breakfast the next morning and hiked through the rainforest to an open clearing just beyond the trees. Jaime volunteered to go on ahead into the village and make introductions. After a few minutes, he returned and spoke in Portuguese to Delgado. "The men have already left the village to hunt for game," Delgado explained. "He spoke with one of the elders who requested that we remain here until the men have returned." Following Delgado's lead, they carted their packs over to a grouping of trees and sat beneath them while reading or making notes in their journals. Around mid-afternoon, a withered old man came over to announce that the Tikuna were ready to meet with them. Delgado suggested they leave their packs where they were against the trees, although Roberts unclipped his daypack to bring along just in case. He had thought to zip one of the collection boxes inside before leaving the boat.

A large thatched structure with a triangle roof stood in the center of the village, apparently of some communal or religious importance, with family sized huts surrounding it and a few quite tiny huts set well apart from the others. Noticing Senhor Brett's quizzical expression, Delgado explained their purpose. "Those are reserved for girls entering their time of ripening, Senhor Brett. Only their mothers are permitted to visit them during this time, and afterwards there will be dancing and celebration to commemorate her entry into adult life."

The three outsiders were introduced to the elders who eyed each one of them closely and responded with eventual nods. But unlike the Matses tribe they had visited several days earlier, the Tikuna seemed more accustomed to outsiders. They turned out to be surprisingly friendly and many of them spoke at least a few words of Portuguese, which made it possible for Delgado to converse with them along with Jaime who also spoke their native language. They wore intricately woven clothing with brightly painted patterns and seemed eager to show their art work to the tall white man. Their ceremonial masks were fascinating to view up close, however Roberts found the Tikuna dolls to be the most engaging, to think that these tribespeople would place such importance in the toys of children.

"Do they expect us to buy these?" Roberts asked Delgado.

"I cannot allow it," said Delgado. FUNAI strongly discouraged commerce with the indigenous tribes. Roberts handed it back to the woman and made a slight bow with his hands pressed together in thanks. The woman found this gesture a bit odd but smiled back graciously anyway.

The Tikuna freely shared their evening meal and then encouraged Roberts, Jaime, and eventually Delgado to join in on their dancing around the evening fire. They seemed amused by the awkward and clumsy movements of their guests. Later, they good-naturedly participated in Roberts's cheek swab ceremony.

That done, and with Delgado's gentle urging, Jaime thanked the villagers and the three of them hiked back to their previous campsite. Roberts wisely chose not to ask why. He waited until they had re-strung their hammocks before commenting to Delgado, "It surprised me how welcoming the Tikuna were."

"Yes, we have made excellent progress earning their trust."

"But we must not overstep ourselves," Roberts concluded.

"Indeed, that is the point of our returning here to camp, Senhor Brett. It is the trusting nature of the Tikuna that makes them most vulnerable.

This is why we so carefully regulate access from outsiders."

"Solimões" was the word used by Brazilian Portuguese speakers to describe the upstream portion of the Amazon River extending westward from the city of Manaus to the Peruvian border, where for some reason it became known again as the "Rio Amazonas". Over a kilometer wide over most of this stretch, the muddy brown water flowed through an expansive flood plain of over 80 kilometers top to bottom. The city of Coari was about 1000 kilometers downriver, another two days until they could set foot again on dry land. Despite the oppressive heat, the men still wore long clothing to protect themselves from the blistering sun, although Roberts wrestled constantly with the inclination to strip them off. However it was much too unpleasant to be below deck during the heat of the day.

Jaime produced a guitar and started strumming. Soon, the three Brazilians began singing a medley of popular Portuguese ballads. The best Roberts could do was clap and try to hum along. It definitely helped pass the time.

They frequently encountered other boats coming upriver. An exotic looking fish jumped from the surface every now and then, and occasionally a rainforest dolphin or two breached out of the water. A keen eye could spot a great variety of birds along the banks, such as the Amazon Kingfisher, the Yellow headed Caraca, and the Jabiru Stork, so much more colorful than their North American counterparts. Sometimes one or two of them would swoop out over the water and glide near its surface while hunting for fish. Roberts asked if they might stop for a brief swim but Jorge warned there could be piranha in the waters. He may have been teasing, but Roberts wasn't taking any chances.

With a brilliant sunset gracing the sky, they pulled into a shallow cove and dropped anchor for the night. Jaime went below to prepare platters of cured meats, cheeses and some fresh fruit that he had purchased in Leticia. He also brought up a loaf of fresh bread and sliced it on a cutting board for them to help themselves. Then he went back to the galley and returned with two six packs of Brazilian beer that he'd kept cold on an ice block in the galley cooler. The cans of frosty brew were gratefully received by all as Jaime passed them around. When everyone had eaten their fill and grabbed another beer, Jaime took the leftovers below and returned again with his guitar. He strummed another few ballads but eventually ran out of steam and hummed the final chorus. Delgado released a satisfying yawn and patted Roberts on the shoulder. "Sleep well, Senhor Brett."

"*Dorma bem*", said Roberts to Jaime and Jorge, a line he'd memorized from his guide book. "I'll be down in a few minutes," to Delgado. He breathed in the cool evening air, looked up to the Southern Cross and accessed his mental jukebox, a song by Crosby, Stills and Nash. A perfect day.

Back in his cabin, the gentle rocking of the boat had a hypnotic effect. The Brazilians were snoring loudly already, he could hear them through the walls, and Roberts soon fell fast asleep as well.

The second day on the Rio Solimões seemed pretty much the same as the first, monotonous but beautiful. Roberts felt re-energized when the bustling city of Coari came into view and they motored into its shallow harbor, and even more excited when Delgado announced that they'd be staying the night in one of Coari's finest hotels. The four of them carried their bags up the dock. When they had all showered and changed, they walked up the hill to an outside café near the town's main cathedral, the Catedral de Sant'Ana e São Sebastião.

While they enjoyed their plates of Moqueca, a spicy fish stew generously ladled onto a plate of rice, Delgado described his plan for the coming two days. The dinner and hotel accommodations that night had obviously been quite a treat for Jorge and Jaime, who would return to the boat the next morning and remain there until Senhor Delgado and Senhor Brett had returned from their visit to the Banawá. Having pulled a few strings, Delgado had procured a military helicopter to ferry the two of them to a drop site near the largest of the four Banawá villages. Delgado had also arranged for a local guide named Eneas to join them, a passionate young man who had been working to earn the trust of the Banawá people over the past several seasons. It would not have been possible to visit the Banawá without Eneas, Delgado explained. Roberts was reminded to bring along one of the envelopes of Brazilian Reals that he'd been instructed to carry for such men.

"This view is fantastic!" Roberts shouted above the rotor noise while looking down through the helicopter's partially opened side door to the bright green canopy below. "Yes, I never get tired of it!" Delgado shouted back with a wide grin and a nod. He was strapped into one of the bench seats opposite Roberts. Eneas, likewise strapped in and seated next to Delgado, had a queasy look on his face and appeared as though he may be sick at any moment.

Less than twenty minutes later, the co-pilot turned and shouted back to Delgado in Portuguese, who relayed the news to his colleagues. "Time to get ready, my friends! We are nearing the drop site. Unfortunately, the ground will be too wet for the helicopter to land. Our pilot will hover just above the surface and let us out."

A small clearing came into view and the noisy helicopter dropped precipitously. It hovered less than a meter above the marshy turf. Delgado unclipped his harness and jumped down, then shouted for Roberts to unclip and hand their packs down to him.

"Now jump and bend your knees as soon as your feet hit the ground!" shouted Delgado. Roberts complied as his boots sank into the soggy earth. After Roberts had regained his balance, Delgado motioned for him to carry their packs over to the edge of the clearing where the ground was firmer. He then reached back to help Eneas down with his own gear. Once the two of them had stepped away from the still hovering helicopter, it climbed back into the sky. The 'thwop-thwopping' of the rotor blades quickly faded as it disappeared from view. Delgado pulled out a contour map from his side pouch, unfolded it and used his finger to show Eneas their location. Eneas mustered a bleak smile and nodded that he was ready to go.

Their young guide proved to be quite energetic once he had located the trail that would take them to the Banawá village. Although slight of build, he shouldered his pack and marched into the canopy at a quickened pace. Roberts found it a challenge to keep up with him.

They hiked westward for about an hour until they reached a narrow creek where the trail split in two directions. Without hesitation, Eneas took the left-hand fork and the others followed his lead. After several minutes, he slowed and held up a hand for them to stop. He whispered in Portuguese to Delgado, who relayed the news back to Roberts. "He says the village is not far. He suggests we allow him to do the talking."

"Fine with me," said Roberts, who now understood the drill.

The village consisted of two rows of stilt huts facing each other, about 10 meters apart. Eneas approached the largest hut and called up in a Carib dialect that Roberts found unfathomable. The chief climbed down and patted Eneas emphatically on the shoulder, obviously pleased to see him. He wore a Nike T-shirt and Bermuda shorts, although barefoot, with a barrel chest and a formidable appearance despite his diminutive stature. Remembering the child-play that Roberts had witnessed while visiting the Matses tribe, he had no desire to wrestle this little man.

The chief barked a few commands and the villagers climbed down from their huts to greet the new visitors, most of them women and children. They all wore western style clothing, which surprised Roberts considering the tribe's remote location. The children seemed eager to touch the tall white man, presumably to see if he was real. The women clearly disapproved and snatched them back.

Eneas made introductions in the Banawá language. After a brief exchange, he relayed the chief's answer. "The chief has accepted our presence on behalf of the tribe, but we must remain outside the village until the men return."

Delgado explained, "Most are hunting or fishing at the moment."

The chief grunted and motioned that they should follow. He led them through the trees to an adjacent clearing, long and narrow, with a clapboard cottage at one end that looked remarkably out of place. Beyond the house appeared to be a runway suitable for small aircraft to land, although badly overgrown. Delgado explained that the house had been formerly occupied by missionaries until the government rescinded their permit two years before. Now Roberts understood where the villager's clothing had come from. Unfortunately the door was securely locked. Delgado relayed through Eneas that they would be happy to make camp nearby. The chief seemed disappointed, although he eventually nodded and left them to settle in.

Roberts peered through the hazy glass window and spotted a ham radio along the back wall. The furniture had all been covered with dusty linen sheets.

"A new team of missionaries has petitioned to return," said Delgado.

"Will the government allow it?" asked Roberts.

"A difficult question," said Delgado. It was evident that he preferred the Banawá be left alone.

Delgado and Roberts sought shelter on the covered front porch from the blazing afternoon sun, nibbling dried rations and sipping from their water bottles. Eneas grabbed a fishing kit from his pack and ventured down to the creek to try his luck. Delgado began making notes in his journal, and Roberts tried flipping through a mystery novel but it held little interest. He wished he'd thought to bring along a field book describing the plants and animals in this region.

Late in the afternoon, Roberts finally heard the sound of men returning to the village. Delgado preempted him from rising. "We shall not disturb the Banawá until after they have finished eating, Senhor Brett." Eneas made little effort to conceal his disappointment, having returned empty-handed. Roberts pulled out his backpacking stove and proceeded to boil water for yet another dehydrated meal.

The sunlight began to fade in advancing shades of darkness. "Have they forgotten us?" asked Roberts. "Be patient, Senhor Brett." Just then the chief returned to lead them back into the village. The Banawá had apparently just finished their communal evening meal and were stoking the fire with fresh wood. The chief introduced the men to a half-circle of elders near the fire who encouraged them to sit. He invited Eneas to speak and they exchanged a few words in the Banawá language before Eneas relayed the information back to Delgado in Portuguese

"He says the Banawá are pleased to have us visit them," said Delgado. "They thank us for being respectful. I suggest you do not attempt to collect your cheek swab samples at this time. Better to wait until tomorrow when we are ready to leave. They may be receptive then, but if they resist, well, at least we will be on our way."

To Brett's surprise, the Banawá sang a song for him in heavily accented English, although they seemed to have little idea what the words meant. Roberts gamely sang along, which delighted the tribespeople. Delgado even joined in at the second verse.

The following morning, Roberts decided to give his cheek swab ceremony another try. Delgado caught on and asked Eneas to explain how this worked. Surprisingly, the tribespeople complied. Roberts returned the box to his backpack and the three men then said their goodbye. They hiked back through the rainforest to the spot where they had been deposited the day before. Delgado produced a Sat phone from his backpack and made the call. This was the first time Roberts had seen it, and he felt much better afterwards.

"The helicopter should arrive in about an hour," said Delgado.

The three men returned to the protection of the trees while they awaited the helicopter's return. Roberts rested against a broad trunk and closed his eyes, having not slept well the previous night.

With the sound of rotor blades approaching, Roberts reflexively patted his clothes and found them soaked to the skin. A light rain must have fallen, he realized. He glanced over to Delgado and Eneas, amused to see them in similar condition.

When the helicopter touched down back in Coari, Senhor Delgado reminded Roberts to give Eneas one of the envelopes of his Brazilian currency. Being a government official, Roberts presumed it unacceptable for Delgado to pass money directly, especially to a person who wasn't his close friend or relative. Eneas graciously accepted and thanked him in Portuguese. Roberts nodded and shook Eneas' hand to show that he understood.

Delgado and Roberts checked back into the same hotel and picked up their laundry from two days earlier. They showered and changed back into clean clothes. Rejoining Delgado downstairs, Roberts looked forward to another freshly prepared meal. He followed Delgado back to the same restaurant they'd eaten at two nights before. The proprietors of these establishments must be friends of Delgado, he presumed. Delgado encouraged Roberts to try the Feijoada, a hearty Brazilian stew of black beans with marinated pork and sausages. He also ordered a round of Cachaças, a fermented sugarcane beverage with a fiery kick.

The next day seemed endless on the broad and winding Rio Solimões. Delgado was reluctant to engage in much conversation, and except for the occasional approaching watercraft, there was little to draw the eye. The constant drone of the diesel engine was hypnotic, and Brett's thoughts were eventually drawn inward. Images began flashing by inside his mind

– the surprised look on the faces of Jesús's children right after their first taste of hard candy – an elder from the Matses tribe, his brown face wrinkled with wisdom – the smiling eyes of a Tikuna woman with straight and long whisker sticks extending from her nostrils – and the piercing eyes of the Banawá chief while making his decision whether to receive them on behalf of the tribe. Their pure sincerity astounded him and he yearned for more, wondering what the next day would bring.

The busy docks of Manaus finally came into view after twelve long hours on the water, a bustling city of impressive size with densely packed buildings extending to the distant hillsides. Roberts repacked his gear and reemerged above deck shortly after Jaime had finished tying up at the dock.

Delgado urged Roberts to hand another envelope of Real notes to Captain Jorge before they disembarked. It would be considered an important show of gratitude, although Jorge had already been well paid for his services. Jorge feigned surprise but quickly pocketed the envelope and then gave Roberts a hearty embrace with a firm pat on the back. "Vá com Deus, Senhor Roberts." Jaime climbed back up and did the same. They would remain on the boat and prepare for their return trip to Agamos early the next morning.

Roberts followed Delgado up Rua Solimões to a hotel within walking distance of the docks, one of the few establishments still open at this hour. He felt a bit disappointed not to be staying near the City Center. They approached the desk clerk and Delgado indicated again that Roberts should pay. "Our guide to the Waimiri-Atroari will pick us up tomorrow at 10 o'clock, Senhor Brett. I encourage you to get a good night's sleep. It will be another long day tomorrow." After confirming that room service was still available, Delgado said good evening and headed toward the stairs. Brett's backpack felt much heavier as he trudged up after him.

Brett Roberts awoke shortly before dawn and found himself unable to fall back asleep. With several hours to kill before their scheduled departure, he decided to venture down to the waterfront and stretch his legs. After enjoying a nice hot shower, he repacked his things and laced up his hiking boots. The sun was just beginning to peek above the horizon when he reached the dock and looked out to observe the Meeting of Waters, the point where the dark waters of the Rio Negro collide with the silt-laden Rio Solimões and gradually mix together to become one mighty river, the Amazon. The sun began its ascent and he could already feel the temperature rising. Today would be another hot one, he mused.

Then Roberts remembered and kicked himself for not calling Ruth the previous evening. With the 4 hour time difference, she may still be in bed. On his way back to the hotel, he passed an internet café and decided to send her an email. He stepped inside and gave the man behind the counter a 20 Real note for 15 minutes at one of the workstations. With five minutes to spare, he launched the Brazilian version of Google and typed in Virtanen + Manaus and got only three hits, two of them historical records of the Virtanen family when they had prospered during the rubber boom era, and a more recent article about a used bookstore having once been owned by a Generro Virtanen. Roberts presumed this must have been Juan Virtanen's father. He scribbled the address and made a mental note to stop by the bookstore after he had finished with Delgado.

Delgado had already checked out and was waiting at the curb, leaning against a mud splattered Toyota Land Cruiser when Roberts returned to the hotel. "I thought you might have overslept, Senhor Brett. I tried your room phone but there was no answer."

"Sorry, Senhor Delgado. I woke early and decided to have a look around."

"Well then, I'd like to introduce you to my friend Pablo, our new guide.

Pablo reached out from the driver's seat to shake Brett's hand. "It's a pleasure to meet you, Doctor Roberts!" he announced in surprisingly fluent English.

"Please, call me Brett." Pablo simply nodded, apparently more comfortable with formalities.

Delgado checked his watch. "Are you ready to go, Senhor Brett?"

"Sure, just let me get my pack," said Roberts. He handed the front desk clerk his room key and thanked him with an "*Obrigado*." The man slid the bill across and only smiled after receiving his payment.

They exited the city and headed northward on Estrada 174, a paved highway through one of the longest and densest stretches of rainforest that Roberts had yet experienced. He eventually nodded off in the back seat. Fortunately, Delgado had been watching the odometer closely. If not for his vigilance, they may have missed the trailhead about 30 km south of

Rorainópolis, a bustling logging town that had recently been carved out of the Amazon Rainforest. Pablo pulled over and shut off the engine.

Delgado turned around and gently shook Roberts awake. "*Boa*, now we walk." He seemed eager to get going.

Roberts rubbed his sore neck and tried to focus. "How far?"

"We shall hike until dusk," Delgado answered. He intended to put a good amount of distance between them and the logging town before nightfall.

They shouldered their packs and Pablo took the lead. Roberts felt grateful to have an experienced guide to lead them, imagining the boldness of the earliest European explorers to venture into this region. As promised, Delgado called a halt with twilight descending. They followed their usual routine of stringing up hammocks and making camp, although this time Delgado had brought along fresh provisions for preparing his own version of Feijoada. It tasted even more delicious than the meal they had eaten back in Coari.

While Roberts washed the dishes, Delgado prepared a steaming pot of lemongrass tea. They sat cross-legged around a gas lantern sipping the tart and soothing beverage. "Thank you, Senhor Fernando," said Roberts. "I have enjoyed our journey so far."

Delgado broke into an earnest grin. "And I as well, Senhor Brett." Indeed, he enjoyed being back in the field.

The three men retired to their hammocks and rocked to the distant sounds of tree frogs, crickets, and the occasional birdsong. The noises eventually quieted down along with the cooling temperature, and soon they were all fast asleep.

Delgado had a fresh pot of coffee brewing when Roberts awoke the next morning. Coffee had never smelled so good. After a quick breakfast, they cinched up their packs and returned to the trail. Pablo again took the lead, being well-known among the Waimiri-Atroari tribes. His presence was necessary, as Roberts would soon find out. These people were notoriously wary of outsiders.

Pablo held up a hand after three drudging hours of hiking through sauna-like conditions. As before, Roberts and Delgado remained behind while Pablo made introductions with the Waimiri-Atroari. This time, it took well over an hour before he returned.

Pablo relayed the news. "The elders will welcome our visit, however we must not stay long." They followed Pablo into a clearing where an enormous conical dwelling came into view. The thatched structure must have been over twenty feet high, with evenly spaced poles around the open air perimeter. As they ducked inside, Delgado commented that the tribe lived communally. Like the Banawá, many of the villagers wore western style shorts or swim trunks, although most of the women wore nothing above them. Several clusters of these women were busily weaving baskets while their children played close by. The men sat apart and gossiped amongst themselves while sharpening their long wooden poles, presumably used for hunting. Their heavily tattooed bodies had zig-zag patterns made from some kind of charcoal-colored pigment. Roberts estimated close to 200 villagers, although Delgado later counted 221 in all, including the children.

Pablo stayed close to his charges while they mingled amongst the various clusters of tribespeople. Few of them seemed willing to make direct eye contact with the outsiders. Roberts sensed it may be difficult to collect DNA samples from these people, but then got an idea and whispered it to Delgado. Delgado clearly didn't like this idea, but he relayed it to Pablo who knelt down and softly spoke with one of the groups of women in their native language. He relayed their answer to Delgado in Portuguese, expecting him to make the final decision. Delgado eventually nodded.

"As you asked, Pablo informed the women that you have treats for the children and would like to play a little game with them. Loosely translated, they would be more than happy to have you distract these children for a while."

With Pablo remaining close by, Roberts cautiously approached the children and made hand gestures to indicate that he wanted them to join him outside for a game. The women nodded in agreement and promptly shooed them off. Roberts walked the children over to the perimeter of the clearing where they had left their backpacks and knelt there while they gathered around. He reached into a side pouch and opened his hand to show them the colorful hard candies. This gesture elicited beaming smiles from the children. Then he reached into his pack to remove one of the swab pouches, tore off its wrapper and showed them how he could rub it up and down against the inside of his cheek. He pulled out the swab with one hand and popped one of the candies into his mouth with the other, then handed a fresh swab to one of the little boys. The other children were eager to do the same after seeing him get his candy. Roberts collected ten swab samples and then continued handing out candy to the rest of the children. He wasn't quite sure how to end the game when one of the women hollered out and the children promptly rushed back to their mothers.

Pablo whispered something to Delgado, who shared his concern. "Pablo thinks we shouldn't press our luck, Senhor Brett, and frankly I agree. We must leave immediately."

The three men walked back to the dwelling and waved their goodbyes. The children waved back energetically and a number of the women did so as well, although with much less enthusiasm. The men mostly ignored the outsiders, although several grunted their acknowledgement, obviously glad to see them go.

When they reached the Land Cruiser, Delgado pulled out his Sat phone and, unbeknownst to Roberts, pretended to make another call. This had been Alfredo Ruiz's idea. He asked several questions into the phone with a growing look of concern.

Roberts couldn't wait to ask, "Something wrong, Senhor Fernando?"

"I am sorry, Senhor Brett. There has been an urgent change of plan. I must return to FUNAI headquarters immediately."

"What about the Yanomami tribe? Look, you approved my proposal, so you know I need to collect samples from at least five different tribes for this study to be successful. Anything less than that won't have sufficient statistical power for our analysis. And you've already been paid handsomely for your services, I might add."

"Again I apologize, Senhor Brett, but you must understand. This is Brazil. Things do not always go according to plan."

"But what am I supposed to *do*? My flight home isn't scheduled until a week from Monday."

"Then might I suggest you reschedule your flight, or perhaps do some sight-seeing. Either way, I can no longer help you."

Roberts brooded in the back of the Land Cruiser while Pablo and Delgado took turns driving. They drove all night and made it back to

Manaus with the sun just beginning to rise. Pablo pulled over to the curb at Eduardo Gomes International Airport and shut off the engine.

Delgado opened the door, went around to retrieve his pack, and came back to say goodbye. Roberts rolled down the window, still extremely upset.

"Take care, Brett Roberts." With that, Delgado hoisted his backpack and turned to enter the terminal.

"I too am sorry for your disappointment," said Pablo. "Where would you like me to take you?" Roberts had no idea. Sensing his confusion, Pablo continued, "I know just the place."

Pablo drove to the historical district and stopped in front of one of the city's finest hotels. "The first night is on Senhor Delgado. Enjoy your stay, Senhor Roberts."

Roberts handed Pablo his last envelope of money before exiting the vehicle. Pablo dispensed with formalities and broke into a smile. "I have greatly enjoyed your acquaintance, Senhor Brett. Adios!" Then he fired up the engine, shifted into drive and slowly drove away.

Roberts then realized that he would need to find a bank and withdraw more local currency. *Crap!* Now what was he supposed to do? Then he remembered something. He unzipped his travel wallet and found the slip of paper on which he'd written the bookstore address. He showed it to the desk clerk who unfolded a walking map and outlined the way with a felt tip pen. The wall clock reminded him that it was still too early to call Ruth.

Roberts opened the door to his room and saw that it featured a breathtaking view of the Grand Opera House. Feeling a bit better about his prospects, he took a long hot shower and changed into street clothes.

With the aid of his map, he navigated the downtown district until he spotted the street name. He continued up a side street to a narrow three-story building matching the address, although the downstairs establishment was no longer a bookstore. Finding a café there instead, although now quite discouraged, he decided to go inside for a cup of coffee and maybe breakfast.

Roberts spoke slowly when a pretty young Brazilian waitress approached his table, hoping she might know a few words of English. To his surprise, she answered with a flawless American accent.

"Yes, this *was* once a bookstore," she said. "But no longer, as you can see." She studied him a moment. An American, she had guessed that correctly. But the poor man hadn't slept well, seeing the bags under his eyes. "Is there something I can get for you?"

Roberts figured he might as well ask. "I was hoping to locate a member of the Virtanen family."

"They used to live upstairs, although Senhor Virtanen passed away over thirty years ago."

"Oh, I see. Are any members of his family still living in Manaus?" Roberts feared the answer may be no.

The woman pursed her lips and considered before answering. "Just the daughter. But why this interest?"

"Do you know where she lives?" Roberts asked hopefully, while ignoring her question.

She glanced around to see if anyone might be listening before angling her head toward him. "Maria became a nun after her father died. She's living now in a convent behind the Cathedral of Immaculate Conception. It's not very far, actually."

Roberts unfolded his walking map and spread it out on the table. "Can you please show me?" She took out a pen, circled the neighborhood he should head toward, and marked the location of the cathedral with an 'X'. Without a final word, she went to take another order. Roberts left a 5 Real note on the table before stepping back outside.

Roberts had begun to suspect the waitress may have misled him when he finally spotted the cathedral. It was beautiful. After a brief moment of indecision, he entered through the main door and paused a moment in the narthex to collect his thoughts. Streams of colored light reflected on the travertine tile floor beneath his feet. He turned around and glanced upward to admire the arched stain glass window with a circular white dove design near the top, a universal Christian symbol for the Holy Spirit.

Overcome with an urge to enter the sanctuary, he slowly approached the altar and ducked into a pew to pray for his first time in many days. He felt his body slowly relax as he said his silent prayer, this time sensing that God might actually be listening.

Roberts opened his eyes to find a young priest standing next to him in the pew. The padre spoke first in Portuguese and then switched to English when he noticed that Roberts had not understood. "Peace to you this day. I am Father João. What brings you here, friend? Are you troubled?" He looked to be in his early thirties, clean shaven with ginger curly locks and compassionate eyes.

"No, not really." Although thinking about it, Roberts felt obliged to admit, "I guess I'm searching for something."

"Then you have come to the right place," the priest said with a smile. His eyes widened with recognition. "You have come at last… well then, I expect you wish to see Sister Maria."

Roberts found the priest's words a bit unsettling. How could Juan's sister Maria have known he was coming? "I'm sorry, Father João… perhaps you've got me mistaken for someone else?"

"Sister Maria once told me that a man meeting your description might come to us one day. This was shortly after Father Ernesto's retirement, my predecessor here at the parish. I doubted her then. And yet, here you are."

Roberts felt a sudden wave of uneasiness. "Did she say why?"

The priest's eyes narrowed and he gently shook his head, "I can introduce you to her now, if you wish."

Roberts nodded and followed the priest out a side door and into a back courtyard, where a plain looking two-story building stood at the opposite end. "Please wait a moment while I go to fetch her," said Father João.

Several long minutes later, the priest returned with a resigned looking nun following close behind, who abruptly put a hand to her mouth when she beheld Roberts for the first time in the flesh. She wore a black habit with a cream colored coif and wimple with only her face visible. Juan's sister would not be much older than himself, thought Roberts, perhaps in her late-fifties, although the careworn lines on her face made her look much older. The priest stepped aside and excused himself.

Sister Maria motioned Roberts toward a bench seat facing a circular garden. "Please." He sat first and she settled next to him a respectable distance away.

After a moment of internal reflection, she said, "We meet at last, Brett Roberts."

Roberts felt the familiar goosebumps returning.

"And how would you know my name? I've never been anywhere near this region of the world before."

She gently touched his arm. "From my mother, of course."

"But didn't she die years ago?"

"She still speaks with me occasionally. And since you are here now, I presume that my brother Juan must have sent you." The look in Brett's eyes showed confusion mixed with fear. There was hope for him yet.

After a moment to collect himself, Roberts ventured, "I'm not quite sure, to be honest. You see...."

"Yes, Senhor Roberts, I know that already. My mother informed me that my brother Juan has also departed this earth. I was hoping you might be able to tell me how that happened."

Brett's fingers rested on his moustache and he reminded himself to breathe. "I think it might have had something with the medicinal compounds he was studying. But I have no idea how or why."

Maria nodded and reached over to gently touch his arm for reassurance, sensing how distraught he was. Perhaps she should explain. "Our mother Luisa was born in a Yanomami village, once located in the northernmost part of our country. She left to rejoin that village when Juan and I were still very young."

Maria pulled her hand away and studied the flowers for encouragement before continuing. "Juan ventured into the rainforest to find her years later. He seemed so disappointed to learn that our mother had died. But the next morning he sounded hopeful again. He had conceived a new plan, one that compelled him to return to America and become a scientist."

She turned to face Senhor Roberts again. "God gave me a premonition that it would lead to my brother's destruction. I tried to warn him but he was most unwilling to listen. You see, Juan did not inherit my mother's gift of spiritual resonance, as I did. And now he is gone." She studied Brett's eyes, and then said, "Well then, do you still wish to visit the Yanomami?"

Roberts shuddered involuntarily but recovered quickly. "Yes, Sister. Can you help me?"

Sister Maria looked up to Father João, who had conveniently returned a moment before. The priest nodded in agreement. Then turning back to face Senhor Roberts, she simply stated, "Father João can take you to them."

Roberts glanced up to Father João, wondering how much he'd heard of Sister Maria's narrative. "When?"

Father João replied, "Meet me here Tuesday morning at seven o'clock. Plan for at least five overnights in the rainforest. You have a backpack, yes?"

"I do, although I've almost exhausted my provisions. Is there a store here in Manaus where I can purchase such items?"

"There is no need, Senhor Roberts. I shall have everything ready when you return." Father João clapped Roberts on the shoulder and returned to the sanctuary.

Roberts twisted back to face Sister Maria. "Thank you, Sister." Maria averted her gaze. "I shall pray for your safe return. Please excuse me, Senhor Roberts."

Back in her cell, Sister Maria said the Rosary seven times and then crossed herself before summoning Luisa. *"You were right, Mother...."*

With exhaustion kicking in, Roberts rallied after returning to his hotel room and picked up the phone to dial Ruth. Heartened by the sound of her voice, he brought her up to date but omitted parts of what Sister Maria had recently told him. Such things would best be discussed with his wife after he got home, Roberts reasoned. And anyway, he hadn't yet had time to process them.

Although relieved that he'd finally called, Ruth heard her husband out with growing unease. "Brett, I've been reading about the Yanomami since you left. You're not planning on trying *yopo* again, are you?"

"I'm not quite sure, Ruth. But I might. Does that bother you?"

"Do I really need to answer?"

Roberts wished he could promise Ruth otherwise. But he'd never lied to his wife, and he wasn't about to start now. "Sweetheart, I can't really explain how I'm feeling right now. I'm so tired I can barely think."

Ruth sighed. "Please be careful, Brett."

"I will, dear. You know I love you."

"I love you too."

They ended the call, and with that out of the way, Roberts stripped down to his boxers. But before nodding off, he called downstairs to arrange a wakeup call. The historical district of Manaus awaited. Two hours should be enough….

The phone's loud ringing practically levitated him out of bed. He changed into a pair of shorts, sandals and a light cotton shirt, and remembered to bring along his bank card.

Under a late afternoon sun, Roberts strolled along Avenida Eduardo Ribeiro and admired the Teatro Amazonas, a neo-classical opera house of Italian design. The 'rubber barons' of the late 1800s had commissioned this building to showcase their prosperity. With its rose colored walls, white trim and colonnades, and magnificent dome decorated in green and yellow tiles, the grand old building still glistened with charm. And down that way was a cultural museum that he'd probably check out tomorrow.

Approaching the corner, he crossed to the other side and headed toward a verdant public square with colorful outdoor restaurants surrounding it, the Espaço Cultural Largo de São Sebastião. In the mood for people watching, he located an empty outside table and ordered an early dinner. He guessed at the menu and later wished he'd thought to write down the name of his entrée. Ruth would have loved this dish. Perhaps they'd come here together one day. Somehow he knew they would, and the thought of it made him smile.

Before heading up to his room, Roberts asked whether it would be possible to reserve the same room for the following weekend and check a bag while he was gone. With that agreed, he repacked what he would need for his final trek into the rainforest. Finally surrendering to fatigue, he nestled into an amazingly comfortable feather pillow and fell fast asleep.

Juan Virtanen made his final visit that night in dream state.

"Virtanen! What do you want?" shouted Roberts from inside his dream.

You're the one who summoned me this time.

"What?" thought Roberts?

It's why I came to you initially, this supposed gift you have.

"I have no idea what you mean."

You've met my sister, yes?

"She explained to me about your mother. I'm sorry Juan, but I have no idea how to help you."

It is no matter. I have chosen another to replace you, one even more brilliant and motivated to assist, which is fitting, considering we once were rivals.

"But I still don't understand!"

Farewell, my friend.

"I am not your friend!" Roberts shouted himself awake and found his room as before, with nothing out of the ordinary. He rose to fetch a drink of water and studied his face in the bathroom mirror. "You've got this," he muttered to himself. He hoped he was right.

CHAPTER TWENTY TWO

"Mutant neurons"

Sunday afternoon, May 27TH, 2012
The Salk Institute, La Jolla, CA

A FREAK SUMMER RAINSTORM blew in from the Pacific Ocean and pelted urgently against the windows of Professor Feinstein's laboratory, loud and ominous like a snare drum roll right before a firing squad. She paid it no heed while perched on a lab stool facing her work bench, running through her mental checklist again to make sure everything was ready.

With Ruiz's assistance, it had taken a little over two months to clone the mutant version of the SIGMAR-1 gene into a neuronal stem cell host. The transformed cell line now grew inside a three-dimensional matrix containing the necessary growth stimulants to promote their differentiation into morphologically distinct neurons. Feinstein had just finished inspecting the integrity of their tiny synapses through a phase contrast microscope. Their long and rambling tendrils had indeed formed tight junctions that ought to be capable of supporting biochemical signal transmission.

She transferred the dish to a chamber that had been specially designed to measure any electrochemical responses that resulted following neurochemical stimulation. A special EMT detector mounted directly overhead would record any such readings, the same design perfected by her engineers back at Stanford. Other custom equipment was distributed along the lab bench as well, all of it connected to a specially dedicated computer workstation that had been programmed by one of her post-doctoral students to process and analyze the signals.

Any instruments she might want to use for probing these tiny little neurons had to be sterilized first immediately prior to use. Feinstein had just ignited a Bunsen burner for that very purpose, its blue flame glowing just an arm's reach away as she prepared to manipulate the neuron chamber. Next to it was an Erlenmeyer flask containing about two fingers of 100% ethanol. She would reuse her stainless steel probes by first dipping them into the ethanol and then use the Bunsen burner to ignite the solvent with a tiny flash. This was a simple and effective method of sterilization, one she had been using for years. Most of her students preferred the individually wrapped disposable variety, although they were a bit more expensive. And besides, Janet Feinstein was old school.

Her car was the only one still left in the faculty parking lot outside that day. Everyone else had either stayed at home due to the weather or left early instead to avoid the worst of the pounding rain. Had she known about the dire weather prediction, she wouldn't have cared. She hadn't felt this excited in years. This experiment had required months of preparation, and at long last, she was ready to begin.

Feinstein switched on the electromagnetic wave detector and snapped on a fresh pair of latex gloves. She exhaled slowly, then quickly sterilized one of the stainless-steel applicators, carefully unscrewed a tiny vial containing a solution of N,N-dimethyltryptamine in buffered saline, and dipped it into the vial. With the aid of a wide angle microscope, she gently touched a tiny droplet of the DMT solution onto the plate where one of the synapses were located, then turned her attention to the EMT detector. The pen wiggled on the chart recorder and then returned to baseline. Yes! A classic waveform. Her left eyelid began to twitch but she barely noticed.

Emboldened by this initial observation, she re-sterilized the applicator and applied more DMT to several other distinct clusters of neurons. As anticipated, this produced a complex waveform on the chart recorder. Her experiment was a success!

Feinstein failed to anticipate what effect these electromagnetic pulses might have on her own brain, but she couldn't ignore the brief hemifacial spasm that followed. She removed her gloves and gently massaged her right cheek and eye socket until it went away. Better now. Perhaps it had been just her imagination. "Must be tired, old girl," she muttered to herself.

Undeterred, she pulled on a fresh pair of gloves and used a pipette to withdraw another aliquot of DMT from the vial, curious to learn what might happen after stimulating multiple nerve clusters at the same time.

The pen began to waggle violently from side to side, maxing out the response of the chart recorder. Feinstein's body started convulsing right along with it, accompanied by a shrill and discordant shriek that only she could hear. Her pulse rate quickened once she realized what must be happening, an electrical resonance of these mutant neurons with her own brain. Yes, she could feel it! How fascinating… but elation turned to panic as a massive shock of pain penetrated her skull and wouldn't let her go.

Doctor Feinstein's eyes rolled back in her head and foamy spit started dribbling down her chin. In a final effort to steady herself, she reached for the bench and inadvertently knocked over the flask of ethanol. The ethanol vapors were ignited by the Bunsen burner and a wall of flame spread quickly down the lab bench, reaching a four-liter bottle of xylene that promptly exploded and spat its flaming contents throughout the laboratory.

With the temperature continuing to rise, the walls and shelves caught fire and the electrical wiring soon melted as well, a seemingly endless cascade of combustion until the entire laboratory was consumed by the flames.

The identity of Doctor Feinstein's charred remains could not be confirmed until three days afterwards, from her dental records.

CHAPTER TWENTY THREE

"The second man"

Tuesday, May 29TH, 2012
Manaus, Brazil

THE PHONE RANG NOISILY on the night-stand inside Brett Robert's hotel room. It was 6 AM, his pre-arranged wake-up call. He showered and changed back into his bush clothes, then groggily carried his backpack down the stairs. He left his key and a bag containing the rest of his things with the desk clerk before stepping out into the emerging daylight.

Father João had been waiting patiently outside the church for Roberts to arrive. He was similarly dressed in cargo pants with a loose fitting long-sleeved shirt and a wide brimmed hat, and with his own backpack leaning against the portico wall. "Good morning, Doctor Roberts!"

"Thanks again, Father." Roberts felt more trepidation about his next foray into the rainforest for some reason. What would the Yanomami actually be like?

"A pleasure, my new friend. And thank you for being on time. I now see our ride approaches." A battered-looking Volkswagen minibus with the words "Missões Católicas de Manaus" painted on the sides pulled up to the end of the narrow street below. The brakes squeaked loudly as it came a stop, then a balding old man with an unkempt beard stuck his head out the window and waved to Father João with a beaming smile. He slowly climbed out to greet them as they approached with their backpacks. The old man had crinkling eyes and his bushy eyebrows seemed a good match for his beard.

Father João made introductions. "Senhor Roberts, I present to you Father Ernesto, my predecessor here at the parish." Father Ernesto stepped forward and gave Roberts a surprisingly firm handshake. The old priest seemed familiar, somehow.

"An honor to meet you, Father Ernesto. And please, you can call me Brett if you wish."

Father Ernesto smiled and went over to struggle with the van's sliding side door, then motioned for the two of them to climb aboard. When they were all seated he fired up the engine and the van rumbled forward. They crossed back over the bridge, made a left turn and followed the signs to the airport just outside of town.

Father Ernesto called back once they'd gotten underway, "You were a friend of Juan Virtanen, yes?" He wanted to be certain that this was the man. Roberts answered, "We studied together in graduate school, although Juan was not exactly a friend."

They followed Avenida Santos Dumont to a commuter terminal behind the tarmac and screeched to a stop. "I need to speak a moment with Father Ernesto," said Father João. "Please fetch our backpacks."

Roberts waited patiently while the two priests conversed together in Portuguese. He noticed the older priest hand over a small leather bound journal to Father João before they both climbed out of the van.

"Father João knows the way to the Yanomami territory," explained Father Ernesto. "I just gave him the last known location of a tribe I once visited. Where I took your friend, years ago." He cleared his throat. "I would take you there myself, but my missionary days are behind me, I'm afraid. It is here now that I am needed. The favelas are overflowing with indigenous refugees in need of our assistance."

Father Ernesto studied them both with glistening eyes, then smiled and heartily shook their hands. "May God be with you both," he said. Then he returned to the van, fired up the noisy four-cylinder engine, ground the shifter knob into gear, and drove slowly away.

"Yes, may God be with us," said Father João. He studied Senhor Brett to make sure he was ready. Satisfied, he clapped the American's shoulder and said, "*Vamos!*"

Father João led Roberts into the commuter terminal and introduced him to their pilot, a hunched over grey-haired mestizo with a surprisingly hearty handshake who spoke little English.

Roberts glanced toward Father João and whispered, "Can he still fly?"

Father João replied confidently, "Of course, Senhor Brett. Have no fear. God will protect us." His eyes twinkled when he grinned.

They followed the old guy out the back door toward a staging area where a mustard yellow bush plane shimmered under the blazing sun. The pilot's movements became more energized as he approached his *bebê*, a plane he had proudly flown for over 40 years. He showed them where to stow their backpacks and offered them each a set of earplugs. Father João accepted and suggested that Roberts do likewise.

Roberts admired the broad and winding Rio Negro as they flew directly above. It shimmered like obsidian glass, such a striking contrast to the vibrant green landscape. With the Super Cub's cruising speed of 155 km/h, he estimated that it would take about three hours to reach São Gabriel da Cachoeira, hopefully enough time for him to sort through his thoughts, with a looming conundrum now top of mind. If Virtanen truly had left him, why then did Roberts still feel compelled to visit the Yanomami? It bothered him as a scientist not to be able to come up with a reasonable hypothesis.

He had progressed no further by the time the plane touched down on a narrow grass landing strip outside the little town of São Gabriel da Cachoeira. The pilot taxied over to a hanger and shut off the engine. Roberts and Father João retrieved their backpacks from a side compartment while the pilot began to refuel his plane for the return trip to Manaus. The priest instructed the pilot to return next Saturday morning and wait for their return.

Father João led Roberts around the hangar to a back parking lot where a weathered looking hard-topped Jeep was waiting. He rested his backpack against the bumper and un-cinched the top straps to remove a pair of deli-wrapped Bauru sandwiches, one of which he handed to Roberts. "Would you mind driving, Senhor Brett? I prefer to use the time to review Father Ernesto's notes."

They tossed their packs into the back of the Jeep and Roberts climbed into the driver's seat and twisted a rusting key on the dashboard to start the engine. Father João slammed the passenger door shut and pointed to a road sign directing them to Estrada 307, now a paved two-lane highway following the same general route that Juan Virtanen had taken with Father Ernesto nearly 35 years before, but now extended all the way to the Venezuelan border. "We should reach the trailhead in less than two hours, a distance that would have once been a three-day journey by foot. We shall also be travelling by a more convenient route than Father Ernesto used to take to visit the Yanomami. I disapprove of such modern intrusions into the rainforest, but there are certain benefits."

Father João ate quickly, crumpled the wrapping paper and tossed it in the back. He took a swallow from his canteen and handed it to Roberts. "Splendid highway, no?"

"Yeah, although the sudden dips and rises are kind of hard to get used to."

The priest clapped Roberts on the shoulder with an amused grin. "Welcome to Brazil, Senhor Brett. Our government engineers are not so well paid as yours." He cracked open Father Ernesto's journal and began flipping through the pages.

Roberts pointed the Jeep straight down the bumpy highway through a seemingly endless stretch of rainforest, with towering trees blocking nearly all the sunlight. Father João's 'less than two hours' seemed much longer than that, but eventually the trees thinned out and a mountain ridge came into view. They followed the highway around its left hand side to reveal an even taller ridge in the distance. Father João checked the contours of his map. "The trail runs along a river that we should be seeing in a moment... yes, there it is, the Rio Demitri. Pull over to that clearing, Senhor Brett."

They laced up their hiking boots, and shouldered their packs. "We should cover as much distance as possible before nightfall," said Father João while tightening his straps. He took off down the trail at a strident pace. Roberts found it difficult keeping up, being about 25 years Father João's senior. "Hold up, Father!" he shouted at last after admitting defeat. Realizing his error, the priest turned around and waited for Senhor Brett to catch up.

"What's the hurry?" asked Roberts.

"The people of this area are not friendly to outsiders, Senhor Brett."

Roberts nodded and indicated that he was ready to go after taking a moment to catch his breath. Father João proceeded down the trail at a more measured pace. Roberts settled into the rhythm of his gait, although he found himself frequently glancing upward left and right to either ridge as they hiked along through the narrow gorge. They stopped after an hour, pumped water from the stream, and nibbled from a loaf of *pau de queijo*, a hardy cheese bread. Feeling re-energized, Roberts said "okay, Father, let's make tracks." Father João responded with a quizzical look. "Never mind, let's go." Father João smiled and nodded. "*Sim, vamos lá.*"

They neared the opposite end of the gorge with dusk falling rapidly, which made it increasingly difficult to see the trail ahead of them. Father João called a halt and clicked on a penlight. After a bit of exploring, he was able to locate a secluded patch of ground nearby behind a large boulder. "A good place to stop for the night, Senhor Brett. We should be safe here."

Later in his sleeping bag, Roberts gazed up to the stars and listened to the sounds of the rainforest, but found it difficult to quiet his active mind. He called over to Father João in a low voice, "are you still awake, Father?"

"Yes, Senhor Brett. What is it?"

"Father, how can we truly know God?"

Father João pondered a moment. "That is not an easy question. God is eternal, you see. And with that in mind, I do not see how it is possible to ever 'truly know' Him. This would require infinite knowledge, which only God has. On the other hand, it *is* possible to experience God's grace, as I believe. Which is as close to knowing Him as we mortals can get. To do this, we must first learn to open our hearts."

"Some find that easier to do than others," said Roberts.

"I suppose so, Senhor Brett. Prayer and meditation are essential to reach this point of openness, but sometimes we must endure suffering as well. Such times offer moments when we abandon our usual thoughts of selfishness and ask the ultimate question, why?"

Roberts felt convicted by Father João's words, but also grateful. "Thank you for sharing that, Father. And thanks also for your willingness to take me to the Yanomami."

"I could not have said no, Senhor Brett. Sister Maria encouraged me to do this, although I too am curious to see what may happen."

Roberts awoke the next morning to the pleasant smell of strong Brazilian coffee brewing on Father João's tiny kerosene backpacking stove. "Crack of dawn!" the priest cheerfully commented while handing over a tiny porcelain cup of the thick and heavily caffeinated beverage. Father João apparently enjoyed such American expressions, having learned a few of them from his brief assignment to a parish in Florida.

They ate a light breakfast of stewed beans and rice with a sprinkling of powdered goat cheese. After breaking camp, Father João unfolded his topographical map and described the next leg while tracing the route with his finger. "We shall hike southeast through this canyon, until we reached its end. From there, we bear northeast and begin the climb upward toward this taller range of mountains. As you can see, it runs along the border with Venezuela."

"That looks like quite a distance," Roberts commented dispiritedly.

"We shall not travel that far today. The village I remember is located right about here," he pointed, "although it is not the village we seek. We shall visit them and camp nearby tonight."

"I hope to learn from them the location of Father Ernesto's tribe. He believes they may have migrated further northward, perhaps as far as Pico da Neblina." Father João pointed to a peak roughly 3000 meters tall. Roberts nodded. "Do not worry, Senhor Brett. I shall set a manageable pace today."

The trail gradually steepened and became more unpredictable, tough going with the humid air and rising temperature. Remembering his charge, Father João stopped repeatedly and urged Roberts to drink plenty of water. While pausing to replenish their containers, Father João drenched his bandana in the cool spring water and tied it around his head, encouraging Roberts to do likewise. This brief respite motivated them to continue.

After two long hours of arduous uphill hiking, they crested the ridge and descended into a neighboring valley where they got their first glimpse of the Rio Cauaburi, a fast water river fed by mountain streams. They followed it northward toward a large clearing where the trees had been hacked away and sent downriver. Father João put a finger to his lips and pointed to a mining outpost that appeared to still be in operation. Roberts spotted a landing strip just beyond it and whispered, "Couldn't we have just flown here?" Father João whispered back that they were reputedly quite secretive about their operations and most unfriendly to outsiders.

They followed the tree line around its eastern perimeter and then re-accessed the trail, continuing in a northeasterly direction. From there the trail got steeper for their second round of strenuous uphill hiking. After a long thirty minutes, Roberts paused and rested his hands against his knees.

He called up to Father João between sucking gulps of air, "How much farther to the Yanomami village?"

To Brett's relief, Father João looked similarly fatigued when he turned around to answer. "It is not far. According to my map, we should find the village in a shallow valley just beyond the next ridge." He unbuckled his waist belt. "Tell you what. Let's rest a while. There are some things about the Yanomami that you should know before we meet this tribe."

They propped their packs against each other and found a rock ledge wide enough for both of them to sit while gazing down to the valley below. Father João began, "The Yanomami suffered much during the Gold Rush of the 1980s, when more than 40,000 Brazilian gold miners illegally invaded their land. Too many corrupt politicians turned a blind eye. The constant flights of supply planes overhead combined with the noisy generators and pumps being used for their mining operations frightened many of the animals away. High pressure hoses washed away river banks and filled the rivers with silt, destroying fish spawning grounds as well. To make matters worse, the mercury they used to separate gold from soil and rock also spilled into the rivers, further disrupting the food chain by poisoning birds and fish.

"This was a terrible time for the Yanomami people, many of them threatened with near starvation," said Father João. "The miners murdered some who refused to work and tortured many others. Many people died."

Father João went on to describe more recent efforts made by the government to expel the miners and protect the Yanomami from further outside intrusions. The Yanomami Territory was officially demarcated and ratified by the Brazilian government in 1992; however the government did not consistently keep its commitments to protect their land.

"Our missionary operations throughout this region were restricted as well," said Father João. "In truth, some of our earliest efforts were not well received, despite our best intentions as Christians. It is fair to say that we too have contributed to this Yanomami disruption.

"Today, the Yanomami are struggling to recapture their social and cultural identity. Outsiders are no longer permitted to enter the Yanomami Territory without written permission from the government, and our missionaries respect those restrictions. I am one of the few who still have discretionary permission to enter. It is solely for the purpose of checking on the Yanomami from time to time, and reporting back to FUNAI regarding their overall health and well-being. But these days, most of our efforts are directed toward helping the displaced indigenous peoples who regularly enter our urban slums, our favelas.

"I tell you these things, Senhor Brett, because the place we are about to visit is a relatively new settlement that passionately believes they are living according to the old Yanomami ways, yet they lack the knowledge and wisdom of their ancestors. Most have escaped from other villages that no longer exist. There are no elders living in this village, yet they are stubborn in their thinking, and most wary of outsiders. We will not be staying long in this village, Senhor Brett."

"Then why are we stopping there in the first place?" Roberts asked.

Father João answered, "There will be men in this village who should know the whereabouts of another Yanomani tribe that Father Ernesto instructed me to find, the same tribe he led Sister Maria's brother to over 30 years ago." Roberts felt a sudden chill despite the oppressive heat. He could feel it down to his sinews. Yes, this was the tribe he had been driven to find.

Father João stood up and stretched his back. After checking his compass to be certain of his bearings, he reached down to help Roberts up. "We have less than 500 meters to go. Come."

True to his word, they reached the top of the ridge less than twenty minutes later. Father João pointed down to a curious looking donut-like structure. "There it is!" Roberts estimated it to be about 60 feet in diameter. Open to an internal dirt courtyard and supported by tall wooden poles, the thatched roof angled downward to a perimeter wall of woven vines and branches. He noticed tiny brown people milling about in the courtyard. "The Yanomami call this communal building a *shabono*," explained Father João. "Our missionaries once had these structures torn down, believing them to be unhealthy places that encouraged sexual promiscuity. We no longer impose our dogma in such a way…. Come. Let us see if they are willing to meet with us."

A band of women were just leaving the shabono when Roberts and Father João reached the edge of the clearing. "The men have already returned from their hunt," Father João explained. "It is time for the women to go out and gather additional items for the evening meal, fruit and vegetables from the garden over there, for example." He pointed to an adjacent clearing where Roberts spotted plantain and cassava plants growing in rows along with a variety of other low-lying plants. "They also forage for nuts and grubs in the forest nearby."

They cautiously entered the shabono and made their way to the inner courtyard. Men sat around in small groups chattering amongst themselves in a halting and abruptly punctuated singsong language. The men wore nothing more than leather straps tied around their waist that girded their loins. Their faces were painted with tar-like pigments, many with bold stripes above the brow and across the cheek bones. Some of the men had blackened their faces entirely except for just around the eyes. Three such men wore white feather crowns, evidently of some importance to the tribe.

Father João walked toward this circle of men with his right hand touching his chest to indicate he was unarmed and came in peace. One of the men motioned for Father João to approach and he carefully moved closer, squatting down a respectful distance away. To Robert's surprise, he then began speaking with them in their native Carib language. His words were slow and deliberate, pausing often to make sure they were understood.

Feeling unwelcome at the moment, Roberts looked to his left and noticed a mob of young boys crouched around a dead armadillo, poking it with sticks and giggling with excitement. He presumed the ugly looking beast would be dinner later on. One of little boys handed him a stick and nodded for him to join in on their game.

Roberts crouched down and gave the carcass a tentative poke, which elicited a round of hysterical giggles. Hmmm… could he pull it off again? Good thing he'd remembered to unclip his day pack and bring it along with him into the shabono. Father João would not have approved had he noticed, although still engaged in a lively discussion with the men.

The boys seemed to enjoy the tall white man's new game but soon lost interest and resumed their dead armadillo poking. Roberts stashed the swab collection box back inside his day pack and glanced over to see that Father João had now joined the circle of men with a pipe of wild tobacco being passed around. Father João's uncontrollable coughing fit seemed to amuse the tribal leaders.

Noticing that Roberts had been watching, the priest beckoned him over. Slowly and evenly, he approached the circle of elders and waited for permission to sit. When one of the feathered men nodded, he crouched down and tried to feel at ease, although he had no intention of accepting the pipe if it were passed to him.

Father João brought him up to date. "We are not welcome to stay the night, as I suspected. However, they invited us to join them in their evening meal." Roberts attempted to show his gratitude, although still a bit concerned about the dead armadillo. One of the younger men then stood and spoke briefly to Father João.

"He wishes to show you around," said the priest. He smiled thinly to suggest it would be a good idea to go.

Inside the shabono, Roberts studied how the wooden poles had been positioned to support the roof while also segmenting the structure into family-sized living quarters, each one with vertically stacked hammocks strung between them near the back wall. The roof was an intricate network of sticks and vines tightly woven with palm fronds and leaves. The flooring consisted of hard-packed dirt and straw with animal skins tossed here and there. There were few other adornments except for freshly cut bunches of plantains hanging in the stalls to ripen.

Two groups of older women sat crouched on their heels while weaving baskets from dried roots and slivers of bark. The baskets came in various shapes and sizes, larger ones to strap on their backs for carrying food back to the shabono, and smaller ones used to store roasted seeds, roots, nuts and other wild foodstuffs. Most of the older women wore a woven cloth to cover their loins, each one decorated with bright red pigment from a berry known as *onoto*. Juice from the *onoto* berry was also used to decorate the baskets once the weavers had finished.

Young girls sitting among them labored over little basket projects of their own. They would wear no clothing at all until reaching their stage of menstruation. Gaggles of small children played close by, as Roberts had observed in the Tikuna village.

Roberts returned to the courtyard to find the younger men now engaging in a vigorous sort of wrestling competition. From the dejected expressions on the faces of the losers, he deduced this must be some means of determining their pecking order in the tribe. Father João advised Roberts to keep well enough away. This was no game. Roberts crouched next to the priest and remained silent while this was going on.

Father João finally spoke as the games were wrapping up. "I have obtained the information for which we came, however we must accept their invitation to remain for dinner. It would be impolite to refuse."

The fertile women began returning to the shabono as the wrestling match wound down, each one now bearing a heavy basket of food strapped to their back. The men mostly ignored them as they lowered their baskets and proceeded to re-stoke the fire pits with fresh wood.

"It is the women's job to prepare the meal," Father João explained. "This is expected. The men would beat them if they did not comply."

Roberts watched while a team of women proceeded to skin and butcher the armadillo. They proved to be remarkably efficient in their duties. The entrails and waste were quickly carried out to be buried and later used as fertilizer for the gardens. Strips of meat were soon hanging from poles above the fire.

Noticing the men growing restless, two women rushed into the shabono and returned carrying gourd jugs filled with a pungently sweet-smelling fermented drink that the men readily accepted, however the alcohol soon made them even more unruly. They grew increasingly impatient and started barking orders for the women to hurry with the meal.

The women complied and carried their prepared dishes over to serve the men. Seeing these women up close for the first time, Roberts found many of them strikingly beautiful with prominent cheekbones and alluring almond eyes, although they also betrayed a hint of sadness. Their petite brown bodies were tattooed in sweeping designs around the breasts, arms and torsos. Like the Matses, they also wore long narrow sticks pierced through their nostrils and cheeks. The victor of the wrestling competition grunted when a particularly attractive woman approached. Father João put a hand to Brett's shoulder not to interfere the first time this happened, however it was fairly obvious what had just taken place. The victor had chosen this woman to lie with him for the night. It was the Yanomami way of ensuring the strength of the tribe.

After the men had been served, the women returned to their cooking fires and ate together with the children. They spoke softly amongst themselves, careful not to disturb the men.

When the meal was over and the bowls had been carried away, one of the men went into the shabono and returned with an intricately decorated blow tube and a gourd bowl containing the tribe's own version of *yopo*. Father João leaned toward Roberts and spoke softly, "I suggest we prepare to leave. There is no shaman in this village and these men have little understanding of the ritual."

"Can't we stay just a bit longer?" Roberts asked, curious to observe such a ceremony for the first time. Father João struggled with his decision but eventually acquiesced. "You shall soon see why I warned you, I'm afraid. We must leave immediately when that happens."

A pair of men accepted the ceremonial items and initiated their sharing of 'energy'. Like the other men, they each wore breechcloths and had red tattoos crisscrossing their chests. While Roberts watched, the first man removed a pinch of powder from the bowl and tamped it into one end of the blow tube. He directed the other end to the second man's nostril and quickly puffed a blast of *yopo* up the second man's nose. Then he frog-walked over and reached out to steady the second man while he experienced his first wave of the powerful hallucinogen. He seemed to enjoy it at first, but the second man started to moan and soon began emitting shrieks every few seconds. A bad trip, apparently.

Father João put a hand to Brett's shoulder and sternly warned him to remain seated. "You may find what happens next quite disturbing, Senhor Brett, however you must not interfere."

The second man's body began to writhe uncontrollably, as though he might be experiencing some sort of brain seizure. The first man grasped him with both arms and slowly rocked the second man back and forth in an effort to sooth him. This calmed the second man for a moment, but he then broke into another round of convulsions and started screaming in a most horrifying way.

Father João grabbed Brett's arm urgently. "We must go, Senhor Brett. Now." Without objection, Roberts followed Father João's lead out of the shabono, and back through the trees to the place where they had left their packs. The screaming grew fainter and eventually stopped.

"Now that did not look pleasant," said Roberts as they re-accessed the trail. He guessed they had about an hour left of daylight with the sun beginning to set.

"No, Senhor Brett, indeed it did not."

Father João guided them back over the ridge, and paused a moment to study the terrain. "So, where to next?" Roberts asked. "As I suspected, the tribe we seek now lives on a secluded bluff just beneath the summit of Pico da Neblina." Father João pointed to a mountain peak off in the distance. "It is about 20 kilometers north from here." He unfolded his topographical map and traced the route with his finger. "We shall follow the trail over the next rise and make camp at this creek. It is about three kilometers away. Tomorrow we shall continue upward through this narrow ravine."

Roberts forced himself not to think about what might be happening back at the village. "Lead on, Father." They shouldered their packs and began the next climb. Dusk had fallen when they finally stumbled upon the creek. Father João made tea while Roberts strung up their hammocks. He looked forward to using them again after sleeping on the hard ground the night before.

They rocked back and forth in the gentle rustling breeze, but Roberts couldn't stop thinking about the *yopo* ceremony. "You still awake, Father?"

"What now, my friend?"

"Why were we in such a rush to leave the village?"

"To be honest, Senhor Brett, this was also my first time witnessing the *yopo* practice. Father Ernesto shared his personal observations with me before I took over his duties. Most of his impressions were highly unfavorable, especially without a shaman in attendance to perform the ritual. This was why I thought we should leave, before…."

"What?"

"Never mind, Senhor Brett. Go to sleep."

Roberts found sleep elusive that evening despite his exhaustion, although eventually he began to dream. And in this dream, he and Ruth were walking on the beach with a golden sun justd touching on the horizon, its radiance almost blinding.

Do you believe in God? She asked, her amber hair fluttering with the ocean breeze.

"Come on Ruth, we've been worshiping together for years. Of course I do."

Yes, I know. But do you <u>truly</u> believe?

CHAPTER TWENTY FOUR

"From the ashes"

Wednesday, May 30th, 2012
La Jolla, California

THE RISING SUN made shimmering reflections on the surface of the ocean, with the sandy beach below the bluff still cast in shadow. Above stood a world famous glider port, presently shuttered and quiet this early hour. A sun-bleached VW bus with a surf rack on top stood alone in the dirt parking lot nearby, its former hold of barefoot dawn patrol surfers now making their way down the steep and treacherous path to Blacks Beach. They'd have it all to themselves until the inevitable clothing optional sunbathers began to arrive. Another bright and sunny day would soon be enjoyed by all.

Hard to imagine how much rain had fallen three days before, except perhaps for one glaring detail at the Salk Research Institute. The recent downpour had mostly spared the southern wing from near certain destruction by fire, despite the cavernous blackened square up on the second floor where Janet Feinstein's laboratory had previously been located. Working alone in the laboratory was against Salk policy, yet so like her to have done such a thing. Her charred remains were still being examined at the coroner's lab downtown.

Forensic scientists had been sorting through the charred debris for the past 24 hours. Alfredo Ruiz had willingly volunteered to assist with the layout of the former lab. Although unable to salvage anything of biological value, it was he who spotted the Bunsen burner lying among the ashes, he who first suggested to the possible cause of the fire, a hypothesis later confirmed to be the most likely scenario.

The detective in charge made a final entry on his checklist and handed the clipboard to an associate. "You look exhausted, Dr. Ruiz. Why don't you go home? We're about to wrap things up."

Ruiz mustered a cordial smile. "Thank you detective. Indeed, I do have an overdue appointment with my bed. Would you mind if I take one last look around before you seal off the laboratory? There could still be a few salvageable items. I come from a country where laboratory equipment is fixed and reused until it has become unfixable."

"Suit yourself, Doctor. I'll give you another five minutes before we board over the doorframe." The detective stepped out into the hallway.

Ruiz kicked through piles of blackened metal and melted plastic until he spotted what he had been looking for — a charred hard drive, hopefully from the lab bench computer that Feinstein had used to control her sophisticated instruments. He picked it up and stashed it away inside his jacket after glancing around to make sure no one was watching.

The detective poked his head back in, close to losing his patience. "Find anything?" he asked. "No, not really," said Ruiz as he exited into the hallway.

"Okay men, let's seal it off." Two men held up a sheet of plywood while a third man nailed it over the charred rectangle that used to have a door.

Ruiz sluggishly made his way downstairs to the faculty lot where his dented Subaru sedan had been waiting since yesterday. He opened the door with a rusty squeak and tossed the hard drive onto the passenger seat before inserting his key into the ignition. The badly worn starter motor eventually ignited the engine, although it took a while for all four cylinders to fire evenly. Ruiz felt the same. He gingerly gave it some gas to coax his protesting vehicle out of the parking lot, stopped and looked both ways at Torrey Pines Road with weary concerted effort, and made a right to continue southward.

He needed to slap his face a few times to stay alert while driving the short distance to his apartment just beyond the UCSD campus. Pulling into the complex, he clicked a button for the gate to the underground parking garage, successfully made it into his assigned parking space, and exhaled heavily with relief.

While fumbling with the keys to his apartment he realized that he desperately needed a nap before tackling the hard drive, even though he'd been tinkering with such computer hardware for years.

Ruiz awoke to darkness beginning to fall outside his bedroom window. He pushed himself up off the bed and shuffled over to his desk to initiate the hard drive's delicate resurrection. His plan was to recover Feinstein's DNA sequence files, even though the mutated clones themselves had been destroyed in the fire. He disassembled the drive to carefully clean the disk and replace the motor, then soldered on a new cable connection and plugged it into the back of his tower workstation. At first nothing happened. *"Merda!"* he muttered to himself.

He tried unplugging the cable and plugging it back in, which turned out to be a surprisingly effective solution. The hard drive hummed to life and lines of machine code began spilling continuously down his computer screen. *"Droga!"* he cussed in frustration. One thing left to try. He hit the Ctrl+Alt+Delete keys, hoping this procedure might reboot his computer and install the drive. After a barely endurable long moment with both drives whirring and clicking away, his usual Windows interface reappeared. Okay so far. He clicked the Windows Explorer icon and smiled, pleased to see that the hard drive had now been added to his directory as 'FEINSTEIN-5 (E:)'. Then he clicked to open the file tree and sorted by date to May 27th, Janet Feinstein's' last day alive.

"Bueno Senhora, let us see if we can find out exactly what you were up to."

He clicked open the folder and saw only three documents – a data file, presumably from the EMT recorder; an image file, probably a picture of the tiny neurons taken through her microscope; and a Word document. He opened it and quickly scanned through Feinstein's notes until he spotted the name of the gene sequence he must have cloned. She had simply labeled it 'ROBERTS-07262002'.

Of course! Why hadn't he made this connection before? Feinstein hadn't mentioned much about her involvement with SnapGen, although Ruiz had a pretty good idea now what that was about. Roberts had been a co-author on her *Nature* paper, the one showing spikes in gene expression patterns shortly after the time of death. The two of them may have continued such experiments, which suggested that this gene sequence must indeed be special. Could this be the gene variant that he had long been seeking, one that he unfortunately did not possess? Roberts must possess this variant, he realized. And suppose the indigenous tribes back in his home country also possessed this variant? *That* would explain SnapGen's research proposal, the one he had translated for them into Portuguese. He leaned back and reflected on the brilliance of his idea to bribe his former colleague, Fernando Delgado. Roberts be damned! Those cheek swab samples would soon be his.

The hard drive whirred briefly and a login window appeared, followed by a sequence of typed commands.

The spirit of Juan Virtanen had once again penetrated the boundaries of his spiritual confinement, still a massive exertion of his ethereal will, but well worth the effort. Of that he felt certain. Alfredo Ruiz had just become his new pawn in a nefarious game plan to free himself.

Ruiz's could scarcely believe his eyes as the phantom accessed the Salk Institute server and opened a FASTA sequence file from Janet Feinstein's directory, one simply labeled 'ROBERTS07262002'. Relieved to find his mouse now working again, Ruiz right-clicked on the sequence file and saved it onto his personal hard drive. At precisely that moment, the external drive from Feinstein's laboratory emitted a puff of smoke and died with a loud clunk.

But Ruiz no longer cared. He hadn't managed to steal the physical genetic material from Feinstein's lab before it caught fire, yet he now possessed the digital sequence of this most intriguing gene. . . . He couldn't wait to return to São Paulo and study it further. His cross-breed parents had presumably inherited their psychic abilities from the indigenous tribes. . . .

A grand new experiment began to crystallize inside his mind, one that was not actually his own, and would ultimately end Alfredo Ruiz's life while conceiving another.

CHAPTER TWENTY FIVE

"Revelation"

Thursday, May 31ˢᵗ, 2012
Pico da Neblina, Northern Brazil

THE TORTUROUS AND TWISTING uphill trail made it tough going for a 56 year old man with a full backpack, with plenty of roots and boulders to hobble the wayward boot step. Roberts stopped a moment to wipe a thick sheen of perspiration from his brow and noticed that the sun had reached its zenith.

He called ahead to Father João. "How much farther?"

The priest stopped and glanced around to check his bearings, then nodded. "We should reach the village in by mid-afternoon, Senhor Brett. Tell you what, let's stop and rest a moment."

Roberts felt light as a feather without his backpack. A handful of dried fruit and nuts mixed with chocolate and a few swigs of water quickly revived him.

Continuing on, they eventually summited the ridge. Roberts glanced upward from there and caught his first glimpse of Pico da Neblina, a craggy molar of a mountain rising up from the shimmering green earth. Father João commented, "Beautiful, isn't it? Come, the route we shall take runs down to this meadow and then back upward in that direction," he pointed.

After they had crossed through the meadow, the trail began to steepen and wind its way upward through dense vegetation. Roberts found it easier to lean forward and raise each knee a bit higher before taking his next step. The trees gradually thinned out as they gained altitude, until Roberts felt the sun's hot sting against the back of his neck despite the noticeably cooler air. He reached around to adjust his bandana.

The last half hour of uphill trekking consumed Brett's entire focus. He accidentally bumped into Father João when the priest abruptly stopped at the top of the rise. After regaining his footing, Roberts asked, "See anything?"

Father João took a step sideways, and said, "Stand here next to me and see for yourself, Senhor Brett."

Roberts trained his eyes on where the priest had been pointing. He spotted a tiny grouping of thatched huts nestled near the bottom of a steep and narrow gorge, so unlike the shabono they'd left behind the day before. "Is that the village?" "Yes, Senhor Brett, I believe it is. Follow me, and remember to wait while I make introductions."

Father João called a halt within 100 meters of the huts. Roberts looked beyond them and noticed crops growing further up the rise, similar to those from the previous village along with a patch of sugarcane and a few jagged rows of corn. Naked women were working the fields while a group of men smoked wild tobacco around a smoldering camp fire down below.

"What do we do now?" Roberts asked.

"We wait, Senhor Brett."

Moments later, a little man walked down to confront the intruders. Roberts noticed streaks of grey in the man's bowl cut hairstyle. He also noted the embroidered Hobie insignia on his frayed board shorts. To Brett's further surprise, the little man began speaking with Father João in rusty Portuguese. Father João appeared to be having some difficulty understanding him, however. Evidently the man hadn't spoken this language in many years. Father João switched to Carib and then translated for Roberts.

"He says the elders have been expecting us," said Father João. Then noting Brett's confusion, he added, "I was as surprised by this as you are now. Come, he asks us to follow him."

The little man led them up to the village, held up his skinny arm for them to wait, and went over to speak with the elders. Most appeared to be well past middle age.

Board Shorts relayed the elder's response back to Father João. Turning to Roberts, Father João translated, "He says they know my chief. I think he meant Father Ernesto. They invite us to stay with them tonight."

"But how could they have known we were coming?"

"We must be patient, Senhor Brett. If these men trusted Father Ernesto, they are unlikely to harm us. Smile, my friend." Roberts did his best to comply. As they approached the circle of elders, he held a clenched fist to his chest as a show of respect. The men broke into smiles with gleaming white teeth, clearly amused by this gesture.

Board Shorts motioned for Father João and Roberts to join their circle. He then reached over and gave Roberts gentle pat on the back to reassure him that they were welcome. Roberts squatted there and tried his best to feel at ease.

Not long afterward, the women returned and set about preparing the evening meal. Cast iron pots began to simmer above the fire pit, presumably bartered (or stolen) from illegal gold miners who continually invaded this area. When the meal was ready, all were welcomed to join the expanding circle. Roberts exchanged glances with Father João to express his surprise. The priest grinned, and whispered, "I too find this tribe to be a bit more enlightened, Senhor Brett."

Roberts had only picked at his food from the previous village, especially after his first taste of barbequed armadillo, however the steaming bowl of stew he now held in his lap smelled truly delicious. And indeed it was, from his very first tentative sip onwards. The savory broth had a hint of lemon grass. Although it contained no meat, he found the perfectly cooked tubers, vegetables and wild nuts to have an excellent mouth feel.

When the bowls had been cleared away, a large gourd jug of fermented cassava juice was produced and passed around the circle. Still feeling a bit anxious, Roberts took a greedy gulp and realized right away that it must be quite potent. He soon experienced a warm sensation in his belly with his arms resting comfortably in his lap. Glancing about, he noticed something different about this tribe. Most of the men had lost the firmness of youth, the women all beyond the age of child bearing. "Where are the children?

Father João answered softly. "About ten years ago, according to Father Ernesto's notes, the younger and stronger men of this village were forced into slavery to work the gold mines. Many escaped with anger in their hearts. Those men set off to establish a tribe of their own, rather than return to their former villages in disgrace, although they raided villages like this one from time to time to capture their younger women and children. As you see here, none remain."

Roberts had a pretty good idea where some of those people might be living now. While studying the resilient faces around the circle, he noticed a blackened face elder who had been staring at him intently. The elder nodded when their eyes met. He motioned for Board Shorts and spoke with him briefly. Board Shorts walked back around the circle and relayed his question to Father João.

"He asks if you have come to see the shaman."

Roberts touched Father João's shoulder, "What should I do?"

"It is not for me to say, Senhor Brett. Although I sense that you have already made your decision."

Roberts blushed at being so obvious, however he turned to Board Shorts and nodded yes.

Board Shorts skurried over to a hut near the perimeter of the village and returned with a much older man shuffling behind him, bone thin and wrinkled with age, with a blackened face and unkempt mane of pure white hair, and a large palm frond tattoo across his chest. He wore a leather strap girding his loins and an intricate bone necklace draped around his neck, nothing more. Something felt familiar about this little man despite his somewhat frightening appearance.

Standing there on wobbly legs with Roberts still seated, the shaman's eyes bore into him with fierce intensity. Then something unusual happened. The shaman communicated a message using his mind, not exactly with words, but the meaning was clear.

It is you.

"How is it that you know me?" Roberts surprised himself by his ability to communicate with the shaman in a similar manner. The shaman made a serious and somber nod.

Follow me.

Roberts rose with no conscious effort of his own and followed the little man back to his hut. Ducking inside, he spotted a tallow candle piercing the darkness from the shaman's makeshift altar, and something like Cedro incense filled his nostrils.

The shaman guided his new charge toward an animal skin near the side wall.

Sit, Brett Roberts.

This came as a relief to Roberts, being unable to stand fully erect anyway, although surprised to 'hear' his own name. He awkwardly lowered himself down, crossed his legs, and rested his arms on his thighs.

Good, now quiet your thoughts.

The shaman squatted before him on the earthen floor and waited for Brett's eyes to close and his breathing to slow. Satisfied, he started chanting softly with a soothing melody, one of age and wisdom. Roberts had no idea what the words meant, hearing them this time out loud, but their rhythm soon lured him into a state of deep relaxation, almost like being hypnotized.... He then felt a sharp and tingling blast penetrating his sinuses. Recognizing it to be *yopo*, Roberts focused on his breathing until the first wave of anxiety had passed. He willed himself forward as the drug began to take hold of his mind, still aware of the shaman's chanting, his warm hands now resting gently on Brett's shoulders.

He suddenly experienced an indescribable weightlessness. No longer confined to his physical body, Roberts levitated above the hut and hovered there, with his perspective expanding outward in all directions. He watched an elder relight his tobacco pipe and pass it around the circle of men, Father João politely handing it to the man next to him without partaking, the women now rinsing out their pots in a nearby spring, all of this happening at once. Every living thing began to glow – the inward flow of sap in the plants and trees, their roots now visible beneath the transparent soil, animals scurrying about through the tall grass, and tribespeople themselves now radiant. Phantom spirits began to emerge, those who had died unable to escape the earthly plane. He spotted them walking around, sitting amongst the circle of men, working the crops, residing in the huts, all of them completely ignored by the living.

A shimmering light appeared in the sky and commanded Brett's attention. It wavered back and forth and then floated down to meet him. Roberts feared this could be Juan Virtanen's spirit returning to vex him and immediately regretted his decision to try *yopo* once more. *"What have I done?!"*

But then a radiant angel emerged from the ball of light… a woman with Yanomami features, but taller… and piercingly radiant blue eyes… could this be…?

We meet at last, Brett Roberts.

"Luisa Virtanen?"

Yes, Juan was my son. He has left you now, I see….

"So he told me, although I never understood his pestering."

It saddened Luisa to learn that she would not be able to reach her son in such a way, although *yopo* had indeed allowed her to probe inside the mind of this Brett Roberts. And having done so at last, she now understood Juan's intentions as well. There was only one way to save them both.

I too have watched over you for many years, Brett Roberts, hoping for a chance to make this connection. And now that I have done so, I must say goodbye.

"I don't understand. Where are you going?"

To a former time. But before I do, there is something I must show you. Come. Take my hand.

Luisa pulled them upward and Roberts watched the circumferential horizon collapse into a spherical planet he recognized as Earth. Having read Brett's thoughts, Luisa sensed that he would appreciate such a moment.

"It's so beautiful…."

Yes, Brett Roberts, and precious as well. However, we are not yet there.

She reached again for his hand and they rocketed out of the solar system through a rippling tunnel of light. Stars whizzed by, then galaxies, then a supercluster of galaxies as the ethereal beam drew them ever onward to its Eternal Source….

Roberts entered a realm of shimmering light and experienced an overwhelming euphoria. With Luisa nowhere nearby, he looked down to see his spirit now clothed in a loose fitting gown of pure white linen. The luminous fabric rippled and flowed, as though from a gentle wind. He became aware of the sound of distant trumpets and turned in that direction to behold the 'I Am' seated on a golden throne. Clad in a radiant purple robe, His long hair and beard like radiant clouds. His face shone like a thousand suns, and His eyes glistened like diamonds. Choirs of angels filled Brett's heart with joy as he approached, getting louder and louder, until… he was nearly there when the vision began to fade….

Breath returned to his lungs. Regaining the sensation of his physical body, Roberts then experienced an overwhelming disappointment. Had this all been some figment of his imagination? A *yopo* induced hallucination?

Roberts opened his eyes and saw the shaman hovering there before him, with his hands still resting gently on Brett's shoulders. He watched the shaman lower one leg down to the floor, and then the other. Recognizing that the shaman too had been levitating, Roberts now realized that his *yopo* experience had been no mere hallucination. The shaman nodded with the hint of a smile. A tear of joy ran down Brett Roberts' cheek. He savored this moment. *"Thank you,"* he uttered at last. Had he just done this with his mind?

You are welcome, Brett Roberts. The one who came before you eventually lost his way. Take care that you not do likewise.

The shaman urged Brett Roberts to stand and reached for his hand to steady him. The strength of this little man surprised Roberts. He followed the shaman out through the low cut door. It took a moment for his pupils to adjust to the waning daylight.

Father João had been waiting patiently and greeted them when they finally emerged. His eyes glistened with relief once he saw that Senhor Roberts was okay. "I see you have survived the *yopo* ritual." Before Senhor Brett could explain, he held out his hand. "You must be tired, my friend, and we have a long hike down the mountain tomorrow. Come, we have been given a hut for the night. We can discuss this tomorrow."

Darkness had fallen by that time, and it was utterly quiet. Father João began snoring softly from the hammock above, although Roberts still found sleep elusive. Why hadn't Juan's spirit bothered to reveal itself during his *yopo* experience? According to the shaman's telepathic words, Juan's spirit must have lost its way. He shuddered.

Then he reflected on what Luisa had shared with him. Roberts felt changed somehow, but for what purpose? He folded his hands and started to pray, mindful of the need to open his heart as well as his mind. He began with the "Our Father" and focused on the words as he said them silently. Sensing a turning point in his life, he then asked God for guidance. A profound peace fell upon him as he continued breathing in and out, one unlike anything he'd experienced before.

The downhill trek took less than two days. Roberts and Father João engaged in rich conversation along the way. The priest's probing questions drew Roberts back to his discovery of the envelope. It surprised Roberts to find the priest so open-minded. Yet in the end, Father João seemed convinced that Brett had been on a spiritual quest, not a scientific one.

"What I saw felt so real, Father João, as though I'd just been given my first glimpse of Heaven. It was truly wonderful."

"Of course it was, Senhor Brett, although I myself would prefer to wait until my Father calls me."

Roberts reflected on that. "Perhaps you're right. I almost wish I hadn't seen it yet."

"And why is that?"

"I have this sense that more will be expected of me now. It's a little bit scary."

"Indeed, this is how God works, my friend. What you experienced was a gift, and with this gift comes great responsibility. But you need not worry, so long as you remain open to where God may be leading you."

They returned the Jeep by late afternoon on Saturday. Father João made note of the setting sun and then shook his head. "We won't make it back to São Gabriel da Cachoeira before nightfall, I'm afraid. The air strip closes at sunset, but not to worry. I know an innkeeper in town."

"Fine with me, Father." Roberts was more than happy to let Father João take the wheel this time, although the priest had an ulterior motive for letting him drive.

"Now Senhor Brett, let us talk about what God might have in store for you…."

Father João pulled to a stop in front of Hotel Deus Me Deu a little after 9 PM and shut off the engine. "I must go inform the pilot of our return. Give Eduardo my name and ask for a couple of rooms. We shall leave for Manaus at first light."

Sunday, June 3rd, 2012
Eduardo Gomes International Airport. Manaus, Brazil

The Super Cub touched down with a screech onto the sundrenched concrete runway. As they taxied over to a hangar, Brett Roberts sensed that a huge weight had been lifted from his shoulders. Father João's reminder was key to that realization: *have faith.*

They stepped down to the tarmac and accepted their backpacks from the pilot. Roberts offered to pay the man for his services but he politely refused.

"The priest and I have an understanding," the pilot explained. "I take him where he wishes to go, and he remembers to pray for me in church on Sundays."

Father João thanked the pilot and shouldered his pack. "I do not expect we will be needing these much longer, Senhor Brett." Roberts broke into a wide grin. "Thank God for that." The priest nodded with a wink. "Which reminds me that I must now resume to my former duties. Come, Senhor Brett."

The taxi deposited them a few blocks away from the church and they hiked up to the cathedral square along a cracked and littered sidewalk. Roberts offered his hand when they reached the church. Father João pulled him into a hearty embrace instead.

"Thank you, Father. For everything. I shall never forget your kindness."

"Nor I your friendship, Senhor Brett. By the way, I expect Sister Maria will be waiting for you in the courtyard. I must take my leave now, Mass will soon begin."

Roberts entered the sanctuary and paused a moment before a rack of candles next to a side chapel. He studied the dancing flames, imagined their prayers being lifted up to Heaven, and bowed his head to utter a silent prayer of his own.

"Welcome back, Senhor Roberts!" whispered Sister Maria. How long had she been standing there?

"Sister Maria! I was just about to go looking for you. Father João had mentioned you'd be waiting in the courtyard." She appeared a bit anxious to speak with him.

"Follow me, Senhor Roberts."

"Please, Sister. Feel welcome to call me Brett, if you like."

"No, Senhor Roberts. It is unacceptable for a nun to speak to a man with such familiarity. Come." She led him out to the courtyard and they resumed their positions on the now familiar bench seat where they had spoken before.

Sister Maria took a moment to admire the Hibiscus, Camelia Rosa, and Cattleya plants that surrounded a cast cement statue of the Virgin Mary. The yellow-orange, brilliant pink, and deep purple blossoms of these plants seemed in perfect balance, as if divinely inspired. "This is one of my favorite places," she said.

"Yes, I can see why. It's good to see you again, Sister."

"And you, Senhor Roberts." After another brief moment, she added, "My mother once told me you have a bright spirit. I could feel that as well, from the first moment I saw you. Which was why I decided to fulfill her request."

"So wait… my visit to the Yanomami was your mother's idea?"

"In a roundabout way, I suppose." She turned to face him. "My mother first learned about the connection you share with my brother from a medium who used to summon her. And she has watched over you ever since that moment. You see, Senhor Roberts, my mother believed she could reach her son by channeling through you."

Roberts now felt like a pawn on some spiritual chessboard with players he barely recognized. "We failed, Sister." He glanced toward Maria and felt stricken by her deep blue eyes, so much like her mother's. "You don't look disappointed."

"Oh no, Senhor Roberts. It means my brother has left you." Maria paused a moment to collect herself, briefly taken aback by the awareness that three days had passed since her mother last communicated with her directly.

Roberts understood this now. And something else, as well. "Your mother led me to someplace wonderful, a glimpse of heaven, I believe."

Sister Maria's eyes brightened. "Then my mother was right about you after all. You too can see beyond the spiritual veil, once you focus your mind to do so. This time it was with the shaman's assistance. You no longer need such help, drugs or otherwise, as you will soon come to learn. You have achieved an awakening, Senhor Roberts. But you must also understand something. God expects more from people like us."

"Father João told me essentially the same thing."

She smiled, "Of course he did."

They sat together in silence enjoying the colorful blossoms and breathing in their perfumes. After a while, Roberts sensed the moment had passed. "Well Sister, I really should be going. I could probably use a hot shower about now, and I think I just heard mass begin."

"I will go in a moment. Tell me, Senhor Roberts. Your plane leaves tomorrow, correct?"

"Yes Sister." Had it been a week already?

"Then return to your family, Senhor Roberts. Hold them tightly."

"I will, Sister, and thank you again, for everything."

"Go with God."

Tower bells announced the beginning of mass and Sister Maria left abruptly to join a queue of nuns entering the sanctuary. Roberts walked around to the front of the church and quietly entered to retrieve his backpack from where he'd left it before, propped against the wall next to the side chapel. Father João had changed into a priest's robe and was now standing before the altar. Roberts instinctively crossed himself along with the congregation, and said a silent prayer of thanks before stepping back out into the sunlight.

While making his way back to the hotel where he'd stayed previously, Roberts got a sudden urge to visit one of the favelas before leaving Brazil, see for himself the conditions of such places of last resort for the indigenous poor.

The front desk clerk acknowledged his return with an ominous nod. "We expected you yesterday, Senhor Roberts."

Roberts unzipped his money wallet and started counting out the bills. "Sorry about that. Here. This should cover two nights lodging... and another 50 Real note for your troubles. I'll be checking out tomorrow."

The rail thin mestizo broke into a smile. "In that case, I have the same room for you again, Senhor."

"Thanks. Would you please also hand me another one of those street maps?"

Roberts unlocked the door and set down his pack, thankful to find his extra bag of clothing already there in the room. He immediately picked up the phone to dial Ruth.

"You made it!" she practically shouted into the phone from over 4,000 miles away. "So how was your visit to the Yanomami?"

"Tell you all about it when I get home." Roberts gave her his flight itinerary, and then added, "Ruth, I owe everything I've experienced to your encouragement."

She wondered what that might be about after the call had ended.

Roberts left his backpack in the room but decided not to change. He exited the hotel, hailed a cab and gave the man directions. The heavyset driver briefly shook his head disapprovingly, then shrugged and shifted into drive without comment. He deposited Roberts at a busy corner Mercado with a final word of warning, "Cuidado!"

Roberts purchased a Fanta and began walking along the main road of the lower district, but avoided the rutted dirt alleys leading upward to hillsides, sensing them unsafe places for a foreigner to venture. The hills above were crowded with shanties pieced together from discarded scraps of wood, corrugated tin and particleboard. He approached an indigenous woman sitting on the hard dirt sidewalk, dressed in rags with two filthy children playing close by. Her destitute and careworn expression tugged heavily on his heart, so he handed her his last 100 Real note, then realized he had only one 50 Real note left and hoped it would be enough for cab fare back to the hotel. Her fleetingly hopeful nod almost made him cry. Roberts reached down to grasp her thickly calloused hands and said a silent prayer for the mother and her children.

Roberts continued down the road until he heard the unmistakable sound of gunfire, which caused him to turn around and head back at a brisk clip. He approached the corner where the cab driver had dropped him off earlier. A young indigenous girl was sitting there now, begging on the sidewalk with a badly worn blanket wrapped around her. She looked to be no more than twelve or thirteen.

Peace be with you, traveler.

Wait, had the young girl just spoken with him telepathically? Roberts realized that her lips hadn't moved. He hearkened back to his first such experience many years before in the California desert. At the time, he'd attributed this auditory hallucination to a residual effect of the mushrooms. But now… had *yopo* triggered this, and might it be permanent? The young girl reminded him of the shaman, an enlightened spirit within an earthly body. Then he noticed her eyes. They were blue, like Sister Marias. "Do I know you?"

Perhaps.

He reflexively reached into his money pouch and handed her his last 50 Real note.

She accepted the note, gave Roberts a vague look of recognition, and then nodded toward a vehicle parked nearby.

Your ride awaits.

"Senhor Roberts!" Roberts glanced in that direction to find a remarkably familiar VW minibus, with Father Ernesto leaning out the driver's side window and waving to him excitedly.

Roberts rushed up to meet him. "Father Ernesto! Seems I forgot to bring along enough money for cab fare back. Could I ride with you?"

"Of course! Climb aboard." The retired priest ground the shifter knob into gear and gently released the clutch with an inevitable lurch forward. He navigated the pot holes, quickly accelerated onto a slightly better maintained road, and continued on with no hint of slowing down. "What on earth brought you to this favela, Senhor Roberts?"

Roberts struggled to remain calm despite Father Ernesto's fearful driving, grateful for the ride back into town. "Not sure exactly. I just had this compulsion to see it for myself. Guess it wasn't such a good idea. But I sure was lucky to encounter you back there!"

"It must have been God's providence, although I also happened to be delivering used clothing to the poor." He made a hard right to avoid a stopped truck and sped through the alley. Roberts held his breath until the priest turned back onto a main road. Recognizing its name, he gave Father Ernesto directions and inwardly rejoiced when the mini-bus finally pulled to a merciful stop in front of the hotel.

"Blessings to you, Senhor Roberts. I imagine we'll be meeting again one day."

"I'd like that, Father Ernesto, although I'm looking forward to going home just now. I pray the Lord continues to bless your ministry."

The priest patted Brett's shoulder affectionately. "I shall pray for you as well, my son. Go with God."

Roberts stepped down to the sidewalk and waved as Father Ernesto putted away. The front desk clerk smiled when he entered the lobby.

"Would you like a wakeup call in the morning, Senhor Roberts?"

Roberts had a long flight home in the morning. "Yes, I think that would be a good idea. 7 AM, please."

After washing up, Roberts decided to head back out for an early dinner and call it a night. He handed the desk clerk his key and fortunately remembered he was out of cash. "Would it be possible to withdraw 200 Reals from your register and charge it to my credit card?"

"Of course, Senhor Roberts. Enjoy the rest of your stay."

Roberts had been wise to check out early the next morning. The line through security crept along at a snail's pace, and it took over 90 minutes of mindless of shuffling for Roberts to reach the security checkpoint. Just as Roberts was handing over his passport, a swarthy looking military guard stepped over and tapped his agent on the shoulder. After listening to the guard's whispered words, the agent said, "Excuse me sir. Please follow this man."

Roberts was taken to a private room and instructed to unpack his backpack and spread everything out on a table for inspection.

"What is this?" said the military guard, holding up one of the paper boxes suspiciously.

"Those are medical specimens from the indigenous tribes. FUNAI has approved them. See? Here's the authorization letter...." The guard snatched the envelope and read through the letter quickly. "I must verify, please excuse." He returned a few minutes later with an ominous expression. "I am sorry, I must confiscate these boxes."

"What do you mean? I have all the appropriate paperwork, and...."

"According to my superiors, you have violated the agreement by entering the Yanomami territory without an escort." He handed the boxes over to another guard who briskly took them away.

"Wait! Father João Rivera was my escort, from the Cathedral of Immaculate Conception here in Manaus. He has authorization from FUNAI to enter these territories."

The guard held up his hand preemptively. "Inaceitável! I see nothing in this letter about a Father Rivera. You may repack the rest of your things and go. Safe travels." The guard made a yellow-toothed sneer.

Roberts headed for the gate in a powerfully conflicted mood, struggling between two opposing emotions: outrage, and relief. How could they *do that?!* What would Brian say when he returned to the States empty-handed? Then again, sequencing those samples no longer struck Roberts as such a good idea. In fact, something about it felt disturbingly wrong ....

CHAPTER TWENTY SIX

"A new beginning"

Tuesday, June 5th, 2012
Lindberg Field, San Diego California, 10:35 AM

THE GENTLE COASTAL BREEZE felt delightful against his sweat encrusted face. After over 18 hours of air travel, with stopovers in São Paulo and Atlanta, Brett Roberts was finally home. He waited at the curb outside baggage claim, anxious to see his wife again after their longest time apart. He glanced to his left and spotted a familiar VW Jetta just turning the corner to join the throng of vehicles simultaneously making their way toward the passenger pickup zone. Five long minutes later, Ruth successfully navigated across two lanes of traffic, stopped at the curb and powered down the window.

"Hi there, stranger!"

Roberts wanted to pull Ruth out of the car and hug her right there. "Hello, dear! How's my beautiful wife?

Ruth popped the trunk. "Hurry up and get in. Traffic's backed up."

Roberts loaded his backpack, climbed into the passenger's seat and leaned over to give her a kiss.

"Blech! You taste salty!"

"Sorry. Air conditioning was out inside the Manaus terminal and it took over two hours to make it through security. Then my next flight from São Paulo up to Atlanta was overbooked and I wound up in a middle seat, sandwiched between two large Americans who probably wished I hadn't boarded the plane."

Ruth found a gap and pulled into a lane that was moving. "Sounds like a pretty rough trip back."

"That wasn't the worst part. A customs agent confiscated my cheek swab specimens right before I left Brazil, citing some bogus technicality."

"Oh Brett, you mean after all that effort you return empty handed? I'm so sorry! I know how much that study meant to you."

"Yeah, well I'd better call Brian to let him know. Maybe his investors can pull a few strings with customs. Did you remember to bring my smart phone?"

"It's in the glove compartment."

Roberts thumbed his phone on and waited for the screen to load while composing in his head what to say to Brian. He noticed a handful of text messages and tapped the app to preview them. The top one was from Sakow and he tapped again to open it:

> Brett – bad news. SnapGen lost its funding. Can't talk today.
> Give me a call tomorrow. Welcome home, by the way.

With a rush of anxiety, Roberts tapped the *Finance* app next to check on BioProbe's stock price. *Holy cow*! He swiped right and quickly read the recent investor blogs about his former company. *Well, I'll be…*.

"Brian just texted to let me know his investors have decided to pull the plug. He wants me to call him in the morning."

Cars began to separate ahead of them and gradually speed up. Ruth shifted into second, and then third. "Doesn't sound like you'll be getting another consulting check," she muttered almost to herself.

"Probably not. But I think we're going to be okay."

Ruth exited onto Harbor Drive. "What do you mean?"

Brett couldn't take his eyes off the sailboats out on the bay. "BioProbe gave me six months to exercise my stock options after signing my severance agreement, although most of them were under water before I left for Brazil."

Ruth made a left onto Laurel. "So how's that supposed to help us?"

"I just checked BioProbe's stock price. It got a 30% bump right after the market opened this morning, still rising it looks like. Apparently they just announced a deal with a major national reference lab for their entire infectious disease portfolio."

After passing under the freeway, she made another left on India Street and then took the ramp up to Interstate 5 headed north. Brett noticed how nervously she gripped the wheel after reaching cruising speed. "Ruth, my BioProbe stock options are now worth over two million dollars."

Ruth struggled to regain her composure. "Should we head home then, so that you can use the computer?"

Brett tapped another app on his smartphone to access his investment account. "Looks like the price has leveled off now… there. I just exercised a third of them. I'll check again tomorrow, maybe exercise some more."

"What a whirlwind!"

"My thoughts exactly."

"Would you like to go out to lunch somewhere and celebrate? Or are you too tired?"

"Heck yes! How about the Poseidon in Del Mar?"

Ruth sped up and merged into the HOV lane. "I hope you won't mind driving home from the restaurant. I could use a margarita about now."

Brett accepted the ticket from the parking valet and finally managed to give Ruth a quick hug before escorting her into restaurant. The hostess led them to a table on the back patio, right on the beach. Multitudes of teenagers on summer break were out sunbathing or tossing footballs and Frisbees around while volleyball players engaged in mixed doubles matches on the sand courts nearby.

"This is exactly where I wanted to be."

She smiled easily. "Me too. It's good to have you home."

There it was, that spark he'd fallen in love with. "So, you ready to hear about my adventures in the rainforest?"

"Get on with it, big guy."

He ordered their drinks, just ice water for him, and then glanced down to the menu. "Let's start with appetizers. This could take a while."

Brett recounted the events of his journey over lunch. Ruth delighted in his descriptions of the rainforest and the indigenous tribes, and asked plenty of questions about things he hadn't even considered. The waitress came back to clear the plates away just as he was describing his first visit with Sister Maria. "Would you two like dessert?"

Ruth shook her head, eager for her husband to continue. The waitress smiled with a nod and flipped her order pad shut.

"Wait!" said Brett. "Could I please have an espresso? And how about you Ruth, perhaps a decaf cappuccino?"

Ruth raised her eyebrows, but then nodded yes. "Of course," said the waitress. "I'll bring those right out."

Brett continued. "I got addicted to strong coffee down in Brazil.

Don't worry, I'll cut back now that I'm home. Anyway, like I was saying, it seemed I was destined to find Sister Maria…."

Ruth leaned forward with sharpened interest when Brett got to the second Yanomami village and described his introduction to the shaman. Brett expected Ruth to be skeptical, but what she did next surprised him.

She reached over to take his hand. "You know, Brett, what you've just described sounds a lot like other spiritual encounters I've read about. How did it make you feel?"

"I'm not sure. It changed my perspective somehow."

"What do you mean?"

"I see things differently now, things I used to ignore or take for granted. And I witnessed so much poverty in Brazil, especially in the favelas. People are suffering and dying from curable diseases, simply because they lack access to basic healthcare. Father João thought I might be destined to improve their situation in some way, considering my scientific background."

"Well sweetheart, I think you've now been given an opportunity to do just that."

"Good point." Brett sighed and looked out to the water.

Ruth followed his lead and leaned back. "I'd like to meet this Father João one day."

Roberts called Brian Sakow the next morning. "Hey, Brett. Sorry for my cryptic text message yesterday. Figured it best to tell you directly over the phone. Before we get to that, how was Brazil?" "A hugely rewarding experience Brian, until the very last moment." "Why? What happened?" "I managed to collect a total of 50 cheek swab samples from five different tribes. Things were going great until a customs officer at the airport tapped me for secondary screening. He confiscated the boxes on some technicality, even after I showed him the permission letter. I'm really sorry, Brian. Do you think we can do anything to get them back, hire a customs lawyer maybe?"

"SnapGen can't use them now, unfortunately. Photon Biosciences filed a patent interference against us, about a week after you left for Brazil. Rather than fight it in the courts, Hammond's investment firm decided to pull the plug on our funding. *It is what it is.*"

The veiled sarcasm in Sakow's last comment was obvious. Roberts knew how much he hated that expression.

"Janet Feinstein's untimely demise didn't help either."

"What?" said Roberts incredulously? Sakow explained and Roberts shook his head in disbelief. "Wow. What a terrible way to go."

"Yeah, I thought so too," said Brian. "But whatever. I'd like to tell you about another new opportunity I've been working on...."

Roberts politely listened while Sakow described his new idea, a consumer genomics company. People would pay to have their genomes sequenced and then be given access to an online web portal where they could learn about their hereditary risk factors. The value proposition was to help them make better life choices. Photon even offered to fund Sakow's new company as part of the settlement, along with the proviso that he use their DNA sequencers exclusively. "So, what do you think?"

Roberts paused for what he hoped had been an appropriate amount of time. "I'm not sure I'm ready for that."

"You've got no other options at the moment... do you?"

"No, but I just got back. I need more time to figure things out."

"I thought you'd jump at this opportunity. You've always been so driven. Guess I was wrong."

"Sorry Brian, let's keep in touch." Roberts regretted not being more definitive, although Sakow had already hung up. Such rude gestures no longer bothered him, however.

Remembering that Ruth had Bible study that morning and must have already left, Brett powered down his computer and went upstairs to change into his cycling clothes. It looked like another beautiful day outside, perfect weather for a ride up the coast.

Approaching the seaside town of Encinitas, he got a sudden urge to check out the waves and turned into the upper parking lot for Swami's, a popular local surfing beach. He dismounted, walked his bike to the rail fence near the bluff, and gazed down to about knee high waves. Just a few long-boarders out there surfing the boneyards this morning, but what an incredible view! Something felt spiritual about this place... and then he remembered. With swelling curiosity, he re-straddled his bike and peddled one block northward to Swami's namesake, the Self Realization Fellowship Temple.

He coasted to a stop near a gated entrance on the right-hand side of the complex and dismounted. As he approached, a docent held up a card up that read SILENCE. Noticing a bike rack just beyond the gate, Roberts politely whispered, "May I lock my bike over there?" "Of course," the man whispered back. "But no need to lock it. I shall keep an eye on it for you. Our Meditation Gardens are to your right. Please enjoy."

Roberts removed his helmet, and also his cycling shoes to prevent their clopping against the pavement, and left them by his bike. He walked bare-footed over to the stairway and began the meditation walk.

An old man clad in a simple ochre robe made a 'yodaesque' nod when Roberts passed by. This would be his only acknowledgment while on the path. Two flights of stone steps led him to the first meditation nook, where a woman sat in lotus position atop a white stone bench, surrounded by exotic flowering plants of different varieties. Her eyes were shut, her serene expression impossible to ignore. Roberts wondered if she might sense his presence… apparently not. He proceeded around to another nook where he encountered a long-haired young man in similar pose, his breathing slow and even. What might these people be experiencing, he wondered?

Drawn to the sound of a gurgling stream, Roberts crossed over a small foot bridge and descended to a secluded Koi pond teaming with colorful fish, swimming slowly and gracefully around. Flowering lily pads floated above them. From there the trail led upward to an ornately tiled swimming pool, long since emptied due to its close proximity to the eroding bluff. Behind it was a crushed brick path lined with marble benches where people could sit and gaze out to the ocean. He chose one to sit on, closed his eyes, and savored the gentle breeze against his face while breathing slowly in and out. Yes, this was exactly what he needed.

After a while, he resumed the garden path and paused briefly at an unoccupied meditation nook but changed his mind. No, Roberts didn't feel quite ready, unsure where his mind may lead him. Ruth was right, he realized. Roberts needed to devote more time to exploring his own spirituality. Yet he felt the need for further guidance before embarking on this next adventure.

The docent awaited Roberts at the bottom. "Would you like to see the Hermitage?" he calmly whispered.

"Yes please, if you wouldn't mind," Roberts whispered back.

"Follow me."

He led Roberts up a path to a building overlooking the ocean, where they entered and took a flight of stairs to a sitting room filled with antique furniture dating back to the early 20th century. A row of portraits had been hung along the back wall. Noticing Brett's interest in these great men, the docent whispered as he pointed to each one. "On the right is Paramahansa Yogananda, the founder of our fellowship. And there next to him is Sri Yukteswar, his former mentor."

An unmistakable portrait of Jesus Christ was also featured prominently. "I thought this was a Hindu fellowship," Roberts whispered.

"Swamiji Yogananda embraced all religions," the docent explained. "He revered Jesus Christ as a spiritual saint of highest prominence."

Roberts remembered something that sparked his interest. Yes of course, from the Towne Center Bookstore back in Pleasanton. "Wasn't he also the man who wrote that book, *An Autobiography of a Yogi?*"

"Yes, of course. May I now take you to his study?" The docent led Roberts down the hall and entered a room with a large picture window facing the ocean. Streams of sunlight filled the room, which gave it an ethereal radiance. The docent pointed to an antique oak desk, likewise facing the ocean. "This is where he wrote it."

Roberts imagined the yogi gazing out to this magnificent view while writing his remembrances. "Where can I buy his book?" he asked.

"Let me show you," said the docent. He led Roberts back outside and pointed, "We have a bookstore just outside the main entrance. I hope you have enjoyed your visit." He offered his hand and Roberts took it warmly.

"Indeed I have. Thank you so much for time."

Roberts walked back to retrieve his bike and took a final look at the gardens before exiting through the gate.

Roberts perused Yogananda's book over the next several days from his home office, during breaks from his online search to learn more about world health issues. He wondered whether Yogananda's writings had actually been meant to be taken literally. Many of his descriptions seemed beyond incredible, although clearly he'd written them in the form of an autobiography. But eventually he began to find meaning behind the words.

What impressed him most were the yogi's accounts of his spiritual journeys beyond the physical body, and also the way he described miracles, with Einsteinian principles blended with spiritual phenomena into an ultimate reality.

He was just finishing the final chapter when Ruth stuck her head in. "Brett, you've been holed up inside this office for days now. Don't you think you could use a change of scenery?"

Roberts glanced out the window and got an idea. "Hey Ruth, would you mind lending me your keys to the sanctuary? I've always wanted to experience rainbow time." This was how their pastor described the sanctuary during the late afternoon, her favorite time of day, when sunbeams penetrated the stained glass windows. He also knew Ruth had the keys, since she worked in the church office.

"If you see Pastor, tell her I considered you trustworthy. And would you mind picking up something to barbeque on your way home?"

"Sure Ruth."

Ruth handed her husband the keys and wondered if he'd remember. Probably not. She took out a frozen casserole just in case.

Roberts unlocked the doors to the church and passed through the narthex. Pastor was right, he realized. A rainbow of colors reflected on the floor, pews and walls, a dazzling display of light. He pulled down a kneeler, took a deep breath, and quieted his mind.

"What would you have me to do?"

His body slowly relaxed, and with each cleansing breath, Roberts felt a renewed sense of purpose building inside him. "Thank you, Lord," he whispered out loud, his silent communion with God now concluded. He couldn't wait to get home.

Ruth's casserole had been terrific, as always. Roberts took a final sip of wine. "You know, Ruth, spending time in Brazil made me realize how misplaced my priorities have been. People in developing countries are dying from curable diseases, simply because they lack basic healthcare."

Ruth nodded, "You haven't spoken much since returning home. So, are you ready to discuss what's on your mind?"

"Well, I was thinking about applying for a grant from the Gates foundation, yet I haven't the faintest idea where to begin."

"Perhaps you should try some volunteering first," said Ruth. Brett looked puzzled. "Hey, I have an idea. Let's go to your office and do some web searching."

She took the keyboard and typed in the names of a few world relief organizations she had heard about, eventually landing on one that their church supported. "This looks like your best option. Our pastor would be happy to write a letter of recommendation. And you know what? I may just join you once Thomas heads off to college."

Brett's face brightened as he clicked through the various ministries they supported, pausing on one located in Africa. They read through it together. "This feels right to me. How about you, sweetheart?"

Ruth's eyes crinkled, "I think we'd make a great team. By the way, you should try reading this one next." She handed him a book entitled *Everyday Saints and Other Stories*, by Archimandrite Tikhon, a collection of remembrances and teachings from the many great men who had inspired him along his ministry. Perhaps not surprisingly, which must have been Ruth's reason for lending this book, Brett found Tikhon's descriptions of seemingly miraculous events to be remarkably similar to those recorded by Paramahansa Yogananda.

CHAPTER TWENTY SEVEN

"Confirmation"

Monday, February 11TH, 2013
São Paulo, Brazil

THE SPRAWLING CITY OF SÃO PAULO had grown to become one of the largest urban centers in the world, now with close to 20 million people living within its metropolitan hub. Located a short distance from the southeastern coastline of Brazil, it could be an intimidating experience for the first-time traveler, a complex sprawl of modern architecture and sky scrapers with green spaces seemingly few and far between. But for those brave enough to endure its constantly crowded streets, it featured world-class museums and restaurants, vibrant neighborhoods representing different ethnic groups from around the world, and over 15,000 bars and nightclubs. Numerous historical places of interest had been preserved, such as the Pátio do Colégio, a colonial-style cathedral built in 1554 by Jesuit priests who also founded the city, and the Mosteiro Depaulo Bento, a monastery of neo-Gothic architecture built in 1598 where Gregorian chants could still be heard on Sunday mornings.

Residents here all proudly called themselves *Paulistanos*, and although some might complain about the persistent smog and traffic, few would ever seriously consider relocating. Alfredo Ruiz was happy to be back. La Jolla had been a nice place to live temporarily during his sabbatical, but São Paulo would always be his home.

Ruiz began his career as an assistant professor at the university after receiving his Medical Degree along with a Ph.D. in neurological sciences. His lab soon achieved world recognition for their pioneering work in hereditary neurological disorders. Alzheimer's was their current focus, although a much more difficult research area than Ruiz had originally anticipated. Their most recent grant application had not received funding.

Because of this, Ruiz would be spending more of his time at the medical center across town, his "second career" as he often referred to it, but only while he was at the university.

But his first stop upon returning to São Paulo was of course the laboratory. The boxes that had been confiscated from Dr. Roberts now safely resided in one of his -70°C freezers. For this he paid Delgado the agreed upon sum of $50,000 dollars in U.S. cash, all of it from his own personal funds. Ruiz hoped this would prove a worthwhile investment.

He was about to find out. Ruiz verified the contents of the boxes, returned them to the freezer and locked it with a key.

Despite their increasingly strapped budget, his team here in at the university had recently acquired a new MegaSeq 2100 next-generation sequencer from Radiant Bio, one of the first companies to successfully commercialize this new technology. Radiant Bio also happened to be headquartered in San Diego, which gave Ruiz numerous opportunities to interact with their scientists and engineers. By doing so, Ruiz had gained invaluable hands-on experience with this new instrument during his sabbatical leave, and was confident now that he could conduct most of the procedural steps independently.

He would come back the following night and begin the work of extracting DNA from each of these indigenous cheek swab samples.

Wednesday, February 27th, 2013

After over a week of late nights in his laboratory, most of them spent working alone, the sequencing results were finally available. The protocol that Ruiz had chosen to use only targeted the protein expressing regions of the genome, which allowed him to sequence up to 8 samples at a time on the instrument. This particular version included protein domains whose functions had not yet been fully characterized.

A total of 51 cheek swab samples had been processed in all, 10 from each of five different indigenous tribes, and a final tube labeled "BR". Ruiz had a pretty good idea from whom that particular sample had come.

From inside his cluttered office, Ruiz allowed himself a moment to lean back in his chair and gaze out the window to admire the sunset. The rowing team was just wrapping up their afternoon practice down on the Raia Olímpica, a man-made strip of water adjacent to the Rio Pinheiros.

His senior lab technician Humberto poked his head in to announce that he was about to head home. Humberto had received the boxes while Ruiz was away, and had assisted his boss in recent evenings with the actual sequencing runs on the instrument. "Working late again Professor Ruiz?"

"Always, Humberto. But don't mind me. Go home to your pretty wife and kids," he teased with a wave of his hand. Ruiz knew this comment would make his most trusted technician feel guilty, a subtle method of keeping him in line.

"I can come in early tomorrow if you need me, Professor."

"Indeed I may, Humberto. Please plan to arrive by 8 o'clock sharp. Depending on these results, I just might have a little cloning side project for you."

"Very good," Humberto replied with suppressed disappointment. This was considered an atrociously early hour for a Brazilian to report to work. "Would you like your door closed, Professor?"

"Yes, that would be wise. And Humberto, please consider our work here confidential." Ruiz turned back to his computer screen and waited for the click of the door latch.

Returning to his keyboard, he typed a few commands to launch the alignment editor.

The sequence analysis software displayed a graphical representation of all 52 sequence alignments (including his own), each of them mapped to their corresponding gene locations on the chromosomes, with little red dots to indicate where a mutation had been detected relative to the registry sequence from UC Santa Cruz. A total of 496 unique mutations had been detected in all, the majority of them distributed throughout the genome, although none of them mapped to known genes involved in brain biochemistry, except perhaps for one. By zooming in and comparing the sequence with the one he had on file, he confirmed that it was identical to the one he'd resurrected from Feinstein's scorched hard drive. He launched the SwissProt search engine to find out what this particular gene's function might be. Its name was SIGMAR-1, and just as he'd suspected, it was now known to code for a neuronal membrane receptor.

Perhaps not coincidentally, Brett Roberts possessed a mutation in this SIGMAR-1 gene, one that was also present in 11 of the 51 indigenous samples. Ruiz was not entirely surprised to learn that he did not possess this mutation. He actually found the knowledge reassuring, comforting even. Although still traumatized by the memory of his parents, Ruiz began to feel better about himself. Because at long last, he believed he'd finally found an explanation.

Tomorrow, he would direct Humberto to order the necessary reagents for cloning this SIGMAR-1 gene, along with the mutation that he'd just identified.

CHAPTER TWENTY EIGHT

"Missionaries"

Friday, September 11TH, 2015
East Kalamatan, Indonesia

KUTAI MARTADIPURA was one of the earliest Hindu civilizations ever discovered in Indonesia, a 4th-century kingdom located about 15 kilometers upriver from the Makaham delta. Although much of the area had already been consumed by the more modern city of Samarinda, an occasional Yupa stone could still be found in the depths of the rainforest nearby. The first such plinth now resided in the National Museum of Indonesia in Jakarta, bearing the dedication "to all Brahma priests" in an ancient form of the Pallava script.

Eddie Jensen was a third year archeology student from Mercyhurst University whose team had decided to delay their return for the fall semester to make one final go at a find. The monsoons had abated after a longer than usual rainy season, and the students were determined to make their first discovery. He noticed something poking out of the soggy ground, a rock of some kind, could those be toes? He hacked the foliage away with his machete and stood back in shock. "Holy shit!"

"What?!" His buddy Jimmy came running over. "No fucking way! Looks like some sort of ancient wax figure. Where do you think it came from?"

"Beats the shit out of me. The facial features don't seem to match any of the indigenous tribes we've studied." Eddie gently tapped the figure with his shovel and was surprised by how easily it chipped, as though it had been sculpted from pumice stone.

"Better call Professor Thomson," said Jimmy.

Doctor Blake Thomson, a leading expert on indigenous peoples throughout the world, had already reasoned that something must be amiss.

The facial features and those red tattoo markings reminded him of a Yanomami tribe he'd once visited in the rainforests of Brazil. This didn't seem possible, yet the more time he spent studying the little man, the more certain he became. But perhaps he should get a colleague's opinion before reporting this find to the local authorities. Brett Roberts immediately came to mind. Thompson had bumped into Roberts a while back at the Jakarta airport. Yes, now he remembered. Roberts had come to Indonesia to demonstrate some new diagnostic test he was working on. If anyone could verify Thomson's hypothesis about this finding, it would be Roberts. He pulled out his smart phone and dialed the number.

Brett Roberts sat on a wooden crate with several members of his medical staff standing nearby, and a long line of villagers waiting to be tested. True to his plan, Roberts had secured funding from the Gates Foundation to create a new diagnostic device requiring no external power source, one capable of producing a test result in less than fifteen minutes from a single finger stick of blood. The single-use test cartridge was constructed from laminated paper, about the size of credit card. It gave a visual colorimetric readout and could be incinerated after use to prevent contamination. This was their first field test, and expectations were high. The hope was to detect malaria outbreaks before they spread across the region.

He was about to transmit some data via his smart phone when it actually rang. "Brett Roberts."

"Hello, Brett! Blake Thomson here. You still in Indonesia?"

"I happen to be on Java at the moment. What's up?"

"I'd like to get your opinion about a new find. I'm looking at it right now. Can your phone receive image files?"

"Yes, please go ahead."

"It's coming your way."

Brett's eyes widened when he received the photo on his smart phone display. "Looks Yanomami to me, Blake."

"That's precisely what I thought. How could something like this wind up over here on the opposite side of the world?"

"No idea. Where are you now?" Roberts asked.

"On expedition outside of Samarinda, near the Kutai ruins."

"I can be there in two days."

Roberts could scarcely believe his eyes when he inspected the figure in person. "I think you're right, Blake. Definitely appears to be of Yanomami origin." Goosebumps began to form on his forearms as he studied it further, the first time this had happened in years. It bore a remarkable resemblance to the Yanomami man he'd observed with Father João three years ago, the one from the first village they'd visited. The markings were the same, the horrified expression unmistakable. How could this be? Imagining what might possibly explain such a phenomenon, he began to see a connection with Juan Virtanen's mysterious disappearance. A wave of disparate thoughts suddenly coalesced inside his mind: *damn, was I lucky*!

Tuesday, November 10th, 2015
Batrovci, Serbia

The grand exodus of Syrian refugees was now in its fifth year. Desperate families risked everything to escape into Europe, traveling with little more than the clothes on their backs, and sometimes a little money that was never enough.

Mohammed's family was among them. For generations, they had been farmers in the fertile Euphrates River valley near the city of Ar-Raqqah. But now this region was under the control of the Islamic State of Iraq and the Levant, more commonly known as ISIS in the western world, although the American president still preferred to refer to them as ISIL. They seized Mohammed's land, and there were no longer any jobs to be found in the city. Had he been willing to stay and fight for their militia, ISIS was promising free housing and a monthly stipend in US dollars, enough to support his family. Most of his neighbors and friends had already chosen this path with no other option but to flee. But Mohammed was a proud man, and for him the prospect of fighting and dying for this unlawful and detestable "caliphate" was unthinkable.

The hardest part thus far had been the sea crossing from Turkey to Greece, with large waves crashing over the boat's gunwales which had drenched their clothing again and again. They had no choice but to wrap the children in wet blankets and hold them tightly while they shivered. It had taken another three days to make their way through Greece and Macedonia. The buses had been unreliable. Occasionally they managed to catch a ride from some local resident, although most of their journey had been covered by foot.

They arrived at this Serbian border crossing with high hopes, only to find over five hundred of their fellow tribesmen encamped nearby, all of them waiting for permission to pass. Many had never slept outside before, and the nights were getting colder. They used cardboard boxes or whatever other scraps they could find to shelter themselves from the light rain that persistently fell from a grey and dreary sky. Now they were being told they could not pass into Croatia without 'official' bus transport. But Mohammed had seen no such buses since he arrived three days before. Many of his countrymen had been stranded there for over two weeks. Dozens more arrived daily.

Mohammed hadn't decided yet on a final destination, probably Germany or Sweden. His brother in law escaped six months before and managed to find work in a factory warehouse on the outskirts of Berlin. Ahmed had sent them money to make this trip. Without his assistance and willingness to sponsor them, they could not have come this far. Yet Mohammed continued to struggle with many doubts, and also many worries, such as how he would manage to learn the local language. He'd be more than happy to work as a cook, a cleaner, anything. But right now, what Mohammed needed most was medicine for his children. Both of them suffered from head colds and were burning with fever. His wife was exhausted, and his situation was getting more desperate by the hour.

He weaved his way through the makeshift campsites to ask again about the buses. The morning drizzle was heavy and damp with the conflicting scents of wet pine trees and diesel exhaust. Upon exiting the soccer field, he saw that aid workers had finally arrived. They had strung plastic tarps over two rows of tables and were handing out boxes of food and dry clothing. A van was parked nearby, American apparently. Its marking read Hope World Relief, although Mohammed was unable to read the sign. He hurriedly joined one of the shorter queues and shuffled along.

When Mohammed arrived at the table, a tall American man standing behind it asked, "How many in your family?" He had a white moustache and wore a powder blue ball cap pulled down over his greying hair. The man held up two fingers, then four, then five, each time nodding quizzically to see if Mohammed knew what he was asking. When Mohammed realized what the man wished to know, he held up four fingers. The American smiled and began to load a box with food for the man's family. He then raised and lowered his arm, trying to determine how tall Mohammed's children were. Catching on now, Mohammed used his right hand to indicate the heights of his son and daughter, pausing each time to make sure the American had understood.

The American called back to an aid worker behind him and then promptly added the items of clothing to Mohammed's box as well. Mohammed felt a sudden grip of emotion. He sensed compassion in the white man's eyes, something he feared might no longer exist, at least on this earth.

Then the American did something miraculous that Mohammed would long remember. He communicated a message with his mind. *May God's peace be upon you, weary traveler.*

"Tawdi sagi," said Mohammed in reply. This was 'thank you' in his native language.

The American spoke this time out loud. "You are most welcome."

Mohammed shook his head in disbelief and was about to turn away when a woman standing next to the man spoke up, "Please wait a moment." She reached down for a hand-sewn quilt and held it out for him to inspect. When Mohammed nodded, she carefully folded it and placed it on top of the box. "For your children," she said. The warmth of her smile filled him with hope.

Mohammed hummed softly to himself as he carried the box back to his family. Human kindness was contagious, after all. His wife opened the quilt to admire it when a rolled up washcloth dropped to the ground. She untied it to find toiletries and a bottle of cold medicine inside. *"How had the woman known?"* He wondered.

Sensing movement at the tollgates, Mohammed walked back over to inquire again about the bus schedule. The customs agent simply nodded and pointed to a convoy of empty buses on the opposite side of the border, having just arrived. He trotted happily back to give his people the news.

Brett glanced over to his wife. "I sensed he too may have the gift and tried communicating telepathically. This doesn't seem to work too often, although it did with him. Do you think Mohammed's family will be okay?"

Ruth answered with certainty, "God definitely has a plan for them."

CHAPTER TWENTY NINE

"Playing God"

Monday, September 14TH, 2015
Cidade de Deus, on the northern fringes of Manaus, Brazil

THE BROWN SKINNED INDIGENOUS GIRL clutched her frayed blanket and waited patiently for dawn. Concealed in the darkness of an abandoned storefront, she replayed the dream that had awoken her a moment before. Her brain possessed no actual memories of her spirit's former life, that of Luisa Virtanen, although the vision that had come to her felt real enough. And it had left her with a clear awareness of what needed to be done. All along she knew she was different, and now she understood why.

When the sun finally peeked above the horizon, she gathered her meager belongings and readied herself for the long journey ahead. She would take a city bus to the downtown station, and from there a much longer bus ride southeast to São Paulo, a two-day journey.

Although childless, the young woman with an old soul whispered to herself while making her way down to the corner bus stop, "If you can hear me, my son, I am going now."

Hospital Israelita Albert Einstein, Morumbi district
São Paulo, Brazil

The Albert Einstein Hospital was founded in 1958 by Jewish community leaders with the vision of bringing a world class medical center to their adopted city. Built on donated land in the southeastern section of São Paulo, it had grown to become one of Latin America's leading hospitals. Despite its presence, the Morumbi district was a place of many contrasts, being in close proximity to the Paraisópolis favela, the city's second-largest urban slum.

Alfredo Ruiz's second office at the medical center looked out to a pretty little park with the winding Rio Pinheiros in the distance. He'd been staring at a paper clip on his desk for the past five minutes. *Wait, had it just moved a little? No, apparently not.* He flicked it away in disgust and then shoved a stack of journal articles off his desk for good measure, which fell to the floor in a heap. Ignoring this, he gazed out the window to calm his nerves while sipping from an unwashed cup of highly caffeinated coffee.

He preferred his office here to the smaller one across town at the University. This was where he displayed his diplomas, awards, and other such memorabilia, including his Brazilian Medal of Science, which hung prominently in a gilded frame. Hanging beneath those items in a much smaller frame was a photograph of Ruiz as a young boy with his parents standing behind him. Unlike Alfredo, who looked more like a mestizo, they both had sandy blond hair and a curious blend of indigenous and Aryan features. They'd been given the name Ruiz by the Germans to conceal their true lineage. Alfredo kept this photo as a reminder that he was nothing like they were.

He could never quite shake his parent's disappointment with him, even after they were gone. Not unlike Juan Virtanen, such painful memories fueled his desire to become a scientist, and dedicate his career to finding out why. Why he couldn't read other people's minds the way they had done. Or perceive the future. Or move metal objects with his mind. *Caramba!*

After decades of laborious research, he just might have found an answer. One that he, now a man of sixty who had never married, could still perhaps pass on to his offspring.

The first key to this discovery had been his sabbatical leave in Janet Feinstein's laboratory, and the events that followed despite her unfortunate demise. From this he knew about the mutant form of the SIGMAR-1 gene and its relatively high abundance in the indigenous tribes throughout the Amazon rainforest.

The second key had been his appointment a few years before to head the hospital's genetic advisory board. Under Ruiz's leadership, and working in conjunction with his own sequencing laboratory over at the University of São Paulo, they had developed a revolutionary technique for screening human embryos prior to implantation. This method was now being used to help couples wanting to conceive who happened to have a parent or sibling with a disabling hereditary disorder.

Once the in-vitro fertilized embryo had divided into eight cells, it was possible to pluck out a single cell and test its DNA for genetic mutations that might be associated with the disorder. Provided such mutations were not present, the remaining 7-cell embryo could be cultured and then implanted into the woman's uterus. Over 12 healthy babies had already been delivered at the hospital using this new procedure.

Of course, the success of this program had also provided a reliable revenue stream for his laboratory to continue their research efforts.

Not incidentally, the final key had come to Ruiz the previous spring. As a peer reviewer for the journal *Nature*, he had received a manuscript from a group of scientific investigators in China. For the first time in history, the team led by Junjiu Huang had used CRISPR to modify non-viable human embryos. They chose to study the β-thallessemia gene, which contained a single mutation associated with a disabling hereditary hemophilia disorder. These embryos had been given two sperm injections instead of the usual one, and therefore had an extra set of chromosomes. This had been done as a precaution to ensure that the genetically edited embryos would never survive implantation and thus could never result in a live birth. Regardless, the editor of *Nature* had ultimately decided not to publish the article on the grounds that the work had crossed an ethical barrier that required further attention, arguing that such germline genetic manipulations could have unpredictable effects on future generations. The National Academies of Science would be hosting a summit later that year in Washington DC to address the scientific and ethical issues posed by gene editing in humans.

But none of this had deterred Alfredo Ruiz from moving ahead with his grand experiment. He was about to proceed with the final phase, one that would likely bend the rules of human ethics well past their breaking point if he were ever discovered.

Ruiz glanced at his watch and saw that he was late for another one of his lab meetings across town.

"Lando, I'm not sure you have sufficient data to make that conclusion." Ruiz had recently tasked his second year post-doctoral scientist with a genomic profiling study of children with autism.

"But Professor…"

"No Lando, your linkage disequilibrium analysis is simply not strong enough. We must recruit more families." Ruiz stared down his post-doc until the proud young man bowed his head in submission.

"Yes Professor."

"Good. That is all everyone." Then Ruiz added as they were rising from the table, "Humberto, could you please come back to my office for a moment?"

Ruiz motioned for Humberto to take his badly worn but perfectly serviceable reading chair. Ruiz would never replace it for something new. He had conceived many successful research projects while sitting in that chair.

"Do you think the hospital's ethics committee will approve this procedure, Professor?" Humberto presumed the project they had been working on must have something to do with Alzheimer's disease.

"Of course, Humberto. The couple has already signed the consent forms. They traveled all the way from America to have this procedure. Both their parents died from Alzheimer's at an early age."

"But they probably won't live long enough to learn whether it has truly benefited their child."

Ruiz nodded. "Indeed, Humberto. But as you already know, these parents are driven more by hope than the reality of realizing their dreams for their children. Anyway, I'd like to go over the next steps in the procedure one more time, if you don't mind."

Humberto understood that this was his mentor's way of redirecting him. They had gone through this procedure numerous times already.

"Well, Doctor Ruiz," he began. "As you have demonstrated already, the CRISPR method is very precise. However its insertion efficiency is only about 18%. That means that we will must transfect at least 8 cells to ensure that one of them has acquired the resistance gene."

"An entire 8-cell embryo…" Ruiz spoke the words slowly.

"Yes. We must destroy the embryo in order to conduct the experiment."

"But assuming we are successful transfecting one of these cells, can it then be encouraged to divide?"

"Yes, Doctor Ruiz. I think so. At least according to the manuscript from China that you shared with me. It should be possible to singulate the embryo into eight individual cells and inject each one with the CRISPR gene editing materials. The cells would then be given growth factors to divide, each one becoming its own a unique 8-cell daughter embryo. We could pluck a single cell from each of them for genetic analysis as we usually do. Assuming the resistance gene had been inserted correctly, we would then culture that daughter embryo for implantation."

Ruiz pretended to reflect on his senior lab technician's analysis. "Yes, Humberto, I think this will work...." He turned away and gazed out his office window to see several students walking leisurely across the quad together. The attractive girl in the middle caught his eye, had she been in one of his classes?

"And...?" Humberto asked.

"Nothing, Humberto, I will let you know when we are ready to proceed."

What Ruiz hadn't told Humberto was that no such couple existed. Instead, he was planning to kidnap a Yanomami woman for the procedure, using sperm donated from himself, of course. His cheek swab data had identified a few other unique mutations in the Yanomami tribesmen that could possibly be of some synergistic importance to the SIGMAR-1 gene.

"That is all, Humberto. You may go now." The next bus back to the medical center would be departing in fifteen minutes.

She had kept mostly to herself while riding in the back row of the noisy and crowded bus. After two long days of monotonous road travel without air conditioning, it finally pulled to a stop and disgorged her along with the other passengers onto the bustling downtown streets of São Paulo. A poorly dressed indigenous woman was not welcome in this part of town, and before long a policeman pulled over and "generously" offered to give her a ride to the nearest favela.

She watched the policeman drive away and then glanced about to behold a neighborhood very much like the one she had left behind in Manaus. Driven by a subconscious motivation that she calmly yielded to, she clutched her bag of meager belongings and began walking down the badly littered and crumbling sidewalk toward what appeared to be a city park, hopefully a place where she could rest undisturbed. She passed a stray dog tugging at a flattened and barely recognizable sparrow, a desiccated snack some random car had recently smashed against the pavement.

A small group of well-dressed people waited patiently at the corner for a local city bus to arrive. She couldn't help noticing the man in a grey overcoat who stood apart from the others, of medium height and build, with dark curly hair and a carefully groomed beard.

Ruiz felt a similar tug on his awareness when he spotted the young indigenous woman coming his way in her tattered brown canvas dress. She held his gaze. This could not be happening, and yet....

On some deep level, she felt drawn toward him. There was no hesitation.

The wretched girl approaching had tattered clothes and unkempt jet black hair. Then he noticed her penetrating blue eyes. So unexpected for an indigenous, and apparently of Yanomami descent from the shape of her brow and prominent cheek bones. His heart rate quickened. *Yes*, he thought. This young woman would be perfect for his experiment. Ruiz struggled to contain his excitement.

The bus stopped briefly to accept new passengers and motored on, with just the two of them left standing there.

"Are you lost?" Ruiz ventured.

She struggled to accept the man's resemblance to the vision from her dream, the one she had come here to find. She took a tentative step forward.

Ruiz didn't dare risk squandering such a perfect opportunity. He reached into his pocket and coaxed the ring onto his finger, one with a tiny needle protruding less than a millimeter from its silver band. Then he took her hand and waited for the needle to do its job, catching her before she could fall to the pavement. He draped her limp arm over his shoulder and put his own arm around her waist to march her over to the faculty parking lot two blocks away, where he kept his Opal sedan, one that he rarely used except on weekends. Today, he would make an exception.

The Ruiz plantation was located approximately fifty kilometers west by northwest of downtown São Paulo. Nestled within a narrow valley, and only accessible from an unmarked winding and bumpy dirt road, it went largely unnoticed despite its relatively close proximity to state highway SP-280. Ruiz's parents had purchased this land for their private retreat over fifty years before. Although the banana groves went largely unattended after their deaths, Ruiz continued to maintain the farmhouse as an escape from the city. This was where he had chosen to construct his clandestine fertility suite.

Ruiz had spent hundreds of hours assisting other doctors to familiarize himself with the procedure he was about to perform. The medical equipment and surgical instruments had all been systematically "borrowed" from the medical center over the past six months of careful planning. Endowment money needed to be spent to satisfy the hospital board, hence the stockpile of surplus items that he had managed to find in storage. They would never be missed.

The ultrasound machine told him that artificial stimulation would not be necessary. The young indigenous woman had already reached her monthly time of ovulation. He checked his watch. The sedative should have worn off about now.

She slowly opened her eyes to find herself strapped down to a hospital bed with a bright surgical lamp illuminating the lower half of her naked body. The walls and ceiling were painted a glossy white enamel, the type of surface that could easily be cleaned. There was a catheter taped to her arm with tubing extending upward to a metal rack she couldn't see. She also noticed a rack of medical equipment to her right and a tray of surgical instruments to her left. Padded leg stirrups swung out from either side of the bed. *Where had he taken her?!*

A door opened and her breathing accelerated as the footsteps approached. She looked up to his unyielding and crazily determined eyes, the face of a man she had once thought she could trust. "Welcome back," said Ruiz glibly.

"What have you *done* to me?" she blurted out, most willing to play this game.

"Let me ask you a question first. Your features appear to be Yanomami, and yet your eyes…."

"I do not know who my father was," she interrupted angrily.

"I see. And how is it that you learned to speak English?"

"I was taken to an orphanage after my mother died."

"But your mother was Yanomami, yes?"

"Yes. Why have you brought me here?!" she asked a second time.

Ruiz leaned down and whispered in her ear, "You're the one who came to me, dear girl." He reached over and injected a ketamine solution into her cannula. The powerful anesthetic would render his subject unconscious for five to six hours, plenty of time for him to harvest oocytes from her womb.

He strapped her legs into the stirrups and pulled the lower half of her specially designed bed away. Then he used the ultrasound machine again to guide his trans-vaginally inserted needle to the proper regions of her ovaries where oocytes could be extracted.

He aspirated a total of nine oocytes and carefully lowered the collection tube into a Dewar flask of liquid nitrogen. Then he removed the young girl's legs from the stirrups and reassembled her bed. He switched out her IV bag for a diluted solution of Demerol, one that should maintain his recent donor in a dull state of awareness after the ketamine wore off.

After checking on his patient, Ruiz left early the next morning to return to his laboratory in São Paulo. He handed the Dewar flask over to Humberto, who immediately realized what needed to be done. Humberto carried the flask over to a sterile tissue culture hood and snapped on a fresh pair of latex gloves. Using a pair of metal tongs, he pulled out the frozen collection tube and waited for it to return to room temperature. Then he carefully pipetted the oocytes onto a plastic petri dish and used a high-powered microscope to examine them.

"Yes, they appear to be viable," announced Humberto. He used a micromanipulator to separate the oocytes into individual micro-wells for in-vitro fertilization.

Ruiz then handed Humberto another tube labeled 'OPA001'. This one supposedly contained the husband's recent sperm donation.

Humberto accepted the tube and nodded. "I should have embryos ready for you in about eight hours."

"Boa, Humberto. Then please singulate the embryos and proceed with the CRISPR procedure as well. I shall come back tomorrow afternoon to assist you with genetic analysis of the daughter embryos."

Ruiz knew this would keep Humberto busy most of the night, so he made a strained effort to smile. After exiting the lab, he stopped by his office and listened to his phone messages before heading back down the stairs. Time to head back and check on his patient.

Two days later, Ruiz implanted three of the genetically engineered embryos into the captive Yanomami girl. That evening, before removing her IV, he gave her a final injection of midazolam. This would help her sleep through the night. Tomorrow, he'd unbind her and move her to an adjacent cell, where he would begin her rehabilitation. This should not be a problem, he reasoned. Indigenous women were used to being dominated.

The following morning after breakfast, Ruiz decided to catch up on a few emails before heading down to check on his patient. His gabled upstairs office looked out to an untended banana grove. The broad leaves swayed gracefully to the accompaniment of a gentle breeze pressing into the valley. He paid them little heed as he tapped away on his keyboard.

The bookshelf to his right held his parent's meticulously kept journals along with other volumes on paranormal psychology. He'd pored through those journals many times. And hanging on the wall above was a black and white photo featuring three indigenous tribesmen standing alongside a wooden grave cross. The cross had a swastika at the hilt, presumably a Nazi of some importance. The crossbar contained his name and the date when he died: *JOSEPH GREINER * STARB HIER AM 2-1-36.* His parents must have kept this photo as a memoir from the aborted Nazi colonization of the Amazon interior.

Ruiz had buried his parents behind that banana grove. He'd adorned their graves with similar such crosses, and soon would have another grave to dig next to them. For the Yanomami girl, after she had given birth to his child.

She awoke that same morning to find herself naked and strapped to an operating bed. And another realization startled her even more, a warmth inside her belly that she hadn't sensed before. Anxiety led to outrage as she imagined what this man may have done to her. She had felt certain that he was the one, his face exactly the same as the vision from her dream. But it wasn't supposed to happen like this! How could he?

She glanced right and spotted a tray of surgical instruments, which gave her an idea. Employing a skill that she mysteriously possessed, she focused her concentration… harder… until one of the instruments began to wiggle, just a little.

Then she heard the click of a latch, followed by an ominous squeak.

Ruiz entered the room and saw that she was awake. "Are you able to speak?" he asked gratuitously. Her eyes followed his movements with fierce intensity. Something about her unsettled him.

"What have you done to me?" she asked in a hoarse and urgent voice.

"There, there, do not upset yourself. You were dehydrated and malnourished when I found you on the streets of São Paulo. You don't remember collapsing into my arms? I was unable to revive you, and so I brought you here. It was I who nursed you back to health. Surely you must remember… no? Well, you should be grateful. But no matter. How are you feeling, better I hope?"

"What have you _done_ to me? I will not ask this question again." But she already knew the answer. A man who would have sex with an unconscious woman, she had heard of men like this. She also knew such men could be easily angered. "I am sorry," she said. "Please forgive me. I was frightened unnecessarily. Come closer, it is still difficult for me to speak. I have something to share with you, about a dream I just remembered."

The pretty young thing had such fearful and captivating eyes. Ruiz sat down on the mattress and turned to her slowly. He actually wanted to hear what she had to say.

"Can you at least unbind me?" she pleaded.

"Of course, my dear." Ruiz loosened the strap to her right arm. Sensing her chance to escape, the woman's eyes widened with rage. She turned toward the tray of surgical instruments, a scalpel flew into her hand, and with a rapid sweeping motion she slit Ruiz's throat from ear to ear.

Alfredo Ruiz fell backward in a pool of his own blood. His final thought was that he had grossly underestimated this young indigenous girl. But there was no regret, for he would leave a child behind.

She waited for his final gurgling breath before unbinding the rest of her limbs. After taking a few deep breaths to steady her nerves, she prepared herself to stand. Her legs felt a bit wobbly at first, but she willed them to support her weight as she stepped around the dead man's body and made her way to the door.

The knob turned without resistance, for Ruiz had forgotten to re-lock it after entering. Still naked, the Yanomami woman climbed the stairway leading up to ground level and tried the upper door, finding it unlocked as well. Morning sunlight caressed her face as she peered out into the hallway. She spotted the kitchen and realized she was desperately hungry. She walked there slowly and deliberately on unsteady legs.

The sun's rays streamed in from a back picture window onto a breakfast table made from rich and dark-stained hard woods. Her eyes were drawn to the half-eaten loaf of pão francês, a coffee cup beside it with a few cold sips remaining, and a newspaper section folded over to the crossword puzzle. Just another morning for that horrible man, she thought to herself. Well, it had been his last. She decided to leave things just as they were to torment his ghost.

Instead, she opened the refrigerator and spied a bottle of milk which she nearly emptied before stopping herself. Then finding an apple in the crisper, she took small bites and chewed them slowly. This was not her first encounter with food after a period of near starvation.

Time to think about her next move. She needed clothes, obviously.

She climbed another stairway to the top floor of the house, hoping to find the sleeping quarters. First she tried the front bedroom where a man's dirty laundry lay sprawled across the floor. No, she had no intention of wearing the clothes of a man she had just killed. The side room had been converted into an office so she bypassed that one, although it did look out to a bright green field of banana trees, a stunning view she had no time to enjoy.

The larger back bedroom had two hazy windows drizzling in sunlight. Nothing appeared to have been touched in years. Thick layers of dust covered the nightstands and matching dresser bureaus. She boldly entered the room and began to look around. A photo of a young family in a silver frame caught her eye, a handsome young couple with a determined looking little boy standing between them. They must have been his parents, she realized, seeing how each one rested a hand on the little boy's shoulders.

She went to investigate the clothes closets along the back wall. The first one contained a man's clothing, the style decades old. She took a deep breath and opened the second one. A woman's clothing this time, probably his mother's, and nearly her size.

She selected a pair of khaki pants and a dark pullover blouse, dressed quickly and pulled on a pair of the woman's hiking boots, then emptied a leather bag in the back of the closet and used it to stow a few additional items of clothing, adding a pair of running shoes at the last moment before zipping it closed. With hunger pangs returning, she tried to think. What else? She went to the woman's dresser and cracked open her jewelry box to find a roll of Brazilian currency tucked away inside, more than enough for her return trip to Manaus.

A transit bus had left São Paulo's downtown station earlier that morning. Forty minutes into the trip, an elderly woman made her way up the aisle while struggling to maintain her balance, and politely informed the driver that she urgently needed to use the toilet. Remembering that the one in back had been unusable for weeks, the driver reluctantly pulled over. The dirty peasant woman could go find a tree to squat behind for all he cared. He kept the diesel engine running and waited while she went off to do her business. When he heard her rapping to be let back in, he turned his head to see a much younger woman climbing up the steps behind her. This one appeared to be much better dressed, although indigenous as well. "The fare?" the woman asked expectantly in Portuguese. "Two hundred Reals," the driver answered. She reached into her pocket and counted out three 100 Real notes. "For your trouble," she added.

The driver made an effort to smile after pocketing the banknotes. "Welcome aboard," he said. Their transaction thus concluded, he shifted into gear and pulled back onto the highway, without even waiting for these two women to find their seats.

The victimized Yanomami woman returned to Manaus and was back on the streets six weeks later, having depleted most of her cash and passed along the rest to a friend who needed it even more. A new vision came to her that night in her state of near wakefulness. And strangely familiar. The image of a young man with long dark hair parted down the middle, his circular glasses perched mid-way down an aquiline nose. Gradually, his face came into focus.

Hello again, mother.

Humberto Aponte was overcome with worry the following Tuesday morning, having heard nothing from Doctor Ruiz in over a week. He borrowed a car and drove out to the farmhouse, sensing that something must be wrong. Discovering his former mentor's body in the basement, and equally astonished to observe the medical suite surrounding him, Aponte suddenly realized that he had been an unwitting accomplice in something much more devious than a routine procedure sanctioned by Hospital Israelita.

Humberto left quietly and returned later that afternoon with a rented van and a hand truck, having already disposed of the research items back in the lab. He carted the medical equipment up the stairs, wiped the walls, light switch and doorknob clean, and took one final look at his former mentor. As he drove away, leaving the farmhouse behind for the last time, Aponte made a promise to God. For him, there would be no more cloning.

CHAPTER THIRTY

"Homecoming"

Saturday, September 11TH, 2021
Brasília, Brazil

THE NECESSITY of returning to the office on a Saturday morning was becoming increasingly burdensome for Fernando Delgado, although it had been this way ever since he agreed to chair the FUNAI organization. He glared at the stack of applications for entry into the indigenous territories, applications that his lower functionaries could not approve themselves due to various anomalies. After taking another sip of his preferred Brazilian coffee, Delgado heaved a heavy sigh and selected another application from the stack to peruse. This particular applicant had committed a customs violation on a previous visit to Brazil, according to the yellow sticky note. Delgado read the cover letter with growing unease… yes, the same Brett Roberts he'd shepherded into the indigenous territories nine years before.

Alfredo Ruiz had made a sizable donation to FUNAI immediately following that 'customs violation'. He obviously suspected Roberts would find another way to visit the Yanomami without FUNAI's assistance. Roberts technically violated his agreement, and that was too bad. Then again, if not for Ruiz's generous offer, Delgado would likely have denied Roberts's original application, and none of this would have ever happened.

Ruiz had died tragically a few years after returning to Brazil. His body was discovered in an advanced stage of deterioration, which made the precise cause of death difficult to determine, although they found a scalpel still clenched in his bony hand. Delgado grimaced at the remembrance. Well, perhaps this particular "customs anomaly" was no longer of any importance. He flipped the cover page over and began reading through the rest of the application.

He noted that Roberts had secured a new sponsor for this proposal, a well-known priest who had assisted FUNAI with productive surveillance efforts in the past. Unlike most other missionaries, Father João contented himself with serving as an observer of the indigenous peoples, bringing back valuable information as to their whereabouts and general health.

Father João was an honorable man, and Delgado concluded that Roberts must be as well. He now felt a bit guilty about that "unfortunate" customs seizure. *Bem.* Delgado reached over to select the appropriate hand stamp, tamped it briefly onto an ink pad, and struck firmly near the bottom of the application, "APPROVADO."

Amazon Rainforest, 34 km southwest of Pico da Neblina

Brett Roberts couldn't believe his eyes as the helicopter descended into the valley. This whole area had been a vibrant green rainforest the last time he visited… how could it all have changed so quickly?

The international climate accord reached in Paris had given him hope, made him believe things like this could be prevented, although many of the initiatives were postponed or ignored due to budgetary reasons. Since the 1970s, an unabated network of highways continued to penetrate the Amazon interior, exposing more and more of the previously untouched regions to logging and mining. Small farming and cattle ranching followed in rapid succession. Around the time of the Paris agreement, it was estimated that about 20 percent of the Amazon rainforest had already been destroyed. Logging rates actually declined a little from 2010 to 2013. But then, with global terrorism on the rise, political focus turned to more urgent matters.

Current estimates indicated that an additional 15 percent of the rainforest was now gone forever. Selective logging of hardwoods further upset the balance of the remaining canopies, putting other plant and animal species increasingly at risk. Such adverse effects on the ecosystem were now impossible to deny. Climate patterns were shifting to longer dry seasons with significant reductions in annual rainfall. Wildfires (intentionally set or otherwise) were also becoming increasingly common.

Those few indigenous tribes who still inhabited this region were barely surviving. This was largely ignored by the international media, and Brett Roberts intended to change that, although his application for reentry had been held up for some reason, hence the six week delay. Ever since joining the Hope World Relief organization, and later receiving a grant from the Gates Foundation to develop his diagnostic test cartridge, he had passionately communicated the needs of the desperate through his photographs, blogs, news articles, and documentaries. HWR considered this an invaluable tool for fund-raising, but for him it was more of a compulsion, to connect with the downtrodden and let them know that people still cared, that love still existed in the world.

They hovered over an area of recent logging activity covering a swath of over two hundred acres, the ground beneath them littered with uprooted tree stumps and shredded branches. Roberts focused his camera out the window and snapped a few pictures while they descended. This entire area, extending to the distant hillsides, had been completely denuded except for the occasional Brazil nut tree standing defiantly alone.

Roberts spotted a familiar face jogging forward to greet them once the helicopter had settled onto the dry brush with the rotor blades still winding down. He shoved open the side door and immediately jumped down to embrace the man. "Thank you so much for meeting me here, Father João."

"I would not have missed this for the world, old friend. Although most people now call me Monsignor Rivera, I prefer you to use my former name." Father João returned Bret's warm embrace with a firm pat on the back. Still trim and athletic, although now closer to middle age, Father João's smile quickly faded once their eyes reconnected. "Unfortunately, I wish our reunion had come under better circumstances." His face brightened again while surveying his friend. "You look quite fit for a man of such advancing years!"

Roberts responded with a smirk. "Come on, Father, I only just turned sixty five."

Father João gave Roberts another pat on the shoulder. "And still as solid as ever, I see. So, are we ready?"

"You bet!" Roberts accepted his backpack from the copilot and the two men stepped away to allow the helicopter to return to the sky.

They shouldered their backpacks and began making their way slowly northward. "Take care to avoid the tree stumps," said Father João. "Many are hidden beneath the brush. How is your lovely wife, by the way?"

"Ruth's doing great, although I haven't seen her in over six weeks. She took another assignment while I was waiting for my FUNAI application to be approved. Right now she's working in the Castrovirreyna-Huancavelica province of Peru, teaching people of the highland villages how to handle and prepare their food safely. Dysentery and poor nutrition continue to be major problems for such communities. But you should get a chance to meet her after we finish this survey expedition. She's planning to meet me in Manaus."

Father João's face brightened. "I cannot wait to meet this faithful woman."

"She's been keeping me in line," Brett replied, then winked with a grin.

Their passage through the canyon had actually become much easier due to the lack of trees. Roberts paused a number of times to photograph the devastated areas. They reached the old mining encampment along the Rio Cauaburi just before dusk, obviously now deserted. "What happened here?"

"This mine closed about five years ago," explained Father João. Roberts nodded while surveying the surrounding area with not a tree in sight. They'd obviously plundered this region until nothing of value was left. He noticed a dirt road running south from the complex. "Do you know where that road leads to?"

"No, Senhor Brett, I am seeing it now for the first time myself." Roberts raised his camera and was about to take a picture when Father João reached over to stop him. Then he removed a small journal from his side pouch and scribbled a few notes to document this observation. "I must handle this delicately, Senhor Brett. You do understand, yes?" Roberts surmised this meant trouble down the road, literally.

Glancing around, and with dusk beginning to fall, Roberts realized that they would not be able to use the hammocks. Father João sensed his disappointment.

"Yes, Senhor Brett. We shall sleep on the ground tonight, but there is no reason to worry. Sadly, there are no longer any large animals in this region."

After rolling out their bags and removing what they needed from their packs, Father João set about heating up a can of Brazilian black bean stew. Roberts noticed his new Jet Boil stove. "Where'd you get that?"

Father João replied, "I bought it online from REI Sporting Goods."

Roberts grinned. Of course he had.

Though the banks of the Rio Cauaburi were now completely denuded of trees, they found plenty of tinder nearby to build a small campfire. Father João made coffee after dinner while Roberts stoked the fire again to life. The two of them sat together in silence while sipping their coffee. After a while, Father João decided it was time to ask his burning question. "Senhor Brett. I trust you are not planning on trying *yopo* again?"

Roberts was taken aback, but then he realized it was a fair question. "No, Father João. I no longer feel that compulsion."

Father João tossed out the rest of his coffee, added a splash of water and wiped his cup methodically with a hand towel to conceal his relief. "I sense there is something else you wish to tell me."

Indeed, Roberts was eager to continue. "The last *yopo* experience must have freed me somehow. I felt such conflict within myself up to that moment, rational thought struggling with a willingness to believe. Now I'm free from such doubts."

Father João leaned forward "And how is that, Senhor Brett?"

"I now recognize that science can never prove or disprove the infiniteness of God. And you know what? I'm okay with that. To know God is to be open to God's presence. We all have this ability, although some of us may find it a bit easier than others."

Father João found that remarkable. Here before him sat the same man, if not a bit older, yet this version of Senhor Roberts held a serenity that had been lacking before. Almost like... Sister Maria's. "So, you are now at peace?"

"Oh yes, Father, most definitely yes."

Father João decided to test his faith, just a little. "I assume this is because you have seen God."

"Much more than that," Roberts replied. "I now walk in His presence, each and every single day."

Father João's face beamed from across the embers. "Then Senhor Brett, you have been blessed with an immeasurable gift."

"It feeds me like never before."

"In the priesthood, we refer to that as a calling, Senhor Brett."

They sat a while in silence before deciding to turn in.

The two of them headed northward toward Pico da Neblina the

following day. Now a national park, and one of the few protected areas remaining in this region, the lush green landscape looked much the same as the last time they made this arduous climb together. Unwilling to admit he was older, Roberts surreptitiously paused a number of times to take pictures of the landscape. How much longer would this area continue to look this way? He felt compelled to preserve it through his photographs.

It was late afternoon when they crested the ridge and looked down to the valley below. Roberts immediately pulled out his camera again.

The first Yanomami village now stood in ruins.

Father João was equally shocked by this. His monsignor duties had kept him from returning for several years. His shoulders slumped, and he let out a sigh. "For the Yanomami to have abandoned this once prosperous area is not a good sign."

"Now what?" Roberts asked.

"We document what we can find. Come," said Father João. They shouldered their packs and began the descent.

Over the next hour, they pored through the remains of the collapsed *shabono* while Roberts took more photographs and Father João took notes. Cooking pots, tools and spears, everything scattered about as though a zephyr had landed. The villagers had simply left it all behind.

Roberts knelt down to photograph a hand-woven child's doll sprawled in the dry grass. Noticing that it was getting dark, Father João put a hand to his shoulder. "It is time for us to go, Senhor Brett."

They climbed up the opposite ridge and continued onward into the trees, this time looking for a good place to string up their hammocks. Father João heated up their last can of soup. "Dried rations tomorrow, I'm afraid, although we should still be able to find plenty of water."

After they had settled into their hammocks, Roberts asked, "Do you think the next Yanomami village will also be deserted?"

Father João sucked in a long breath and released it slowly. "It is indeed possible."

"But surely we must go to find out."

The priest replied, "Yes, my friend. That we must."

The sun had long since passed its zenith the next day when they crested the final rise. Both nearly exhausted, it took a while to absorb what they were seeing. Although still a jumble of huts, the second Yanomami village had obviously expanded since he'd last laid eyes on it. Roberts used a zoom lens to capture his first picture. Turning to Father João, "This is good, isn't it?"

"We shall see, Senhor Brett. But please follow down close behind me."

Father João held up a hand for Roberts to wait when they neared the village. A small group of men in their mid- to late-teens sat in a circle while sharpening their wooden spears. Father João slowly approached them and knelt down to speak. After a brief exchange, one of young men directed Father João to a nearby hut. Father João ducked inside for a longer moment than Roberts would have liked.

When he finally stepped back out into the late afternoon sunlight, Roberts immediately recognized the little fellow climbing out after him, the same man who had escorted them into the village nine years before. His hair looked much grayer now. The little man walked over and shook Roberts's hand with a crinkling smile, obviously pleased to see the tall white man again.

"He says we are welcome to stay for dinner," said Father João. "But please keep your camera hidden. I do not expect they would approve of being photographed."

The women returned with baskets of fruits, legumes, corn, plantains and a variety of tubers. Roberts guessed they must be somewhere in their late thirties now, possibly older. One of the young men of the circle proudly presented a small speared tapir for them to prepare.

The evening meal turned out to be even more delicious than Roberts remembered, with everything freely shared. While he chewed, Roberts looked around and wondered why older men seemed scarce in this village. He noticed the younger males glancing toward him, apparently pleased to see the tall white man again. This caused him to study the women more closely as well ... none of them particularly pretty.

Father João had just finished speaking with their former interpreter, who evidently no longer wished to speak Portuguese. "Our friend here has just explained why you recognize these people, Senhor Brett. They came here from the lower village, the one we once visited and yesterday found in ruins. Game animals became scarce down below, but the men were much too proud to leave. One day, a group of miners came and offered the men food and other luxuries in exchange for their labor down by the river. They eventually returned to fetch the women and children they had fathered. Those left behind chose to move to higher ground."

Darkness fell and stars began to appear in the nighttime sky. Roberts took it all in for a while, but then realized someone from this village was missing. "What happened to the shaman?"

Father João turned to their interpreter and asked this question. "He says he can take you now to see him." The little man pulled a flaming stick from the fire and beckoned Roberts to come with him.

Roberts rose and followed his diminutive guide down a darkening and narrow path, feeling a bit dubious but also hopeful. The Yanomami stopped suddenly and held out his makeshift torch, beckoning Roberts to come forward. Roberts looked down to a gravesite mound illuminated by the flame, decorated with colorful pebbles in the manner of a tattoo he remembered. Such a custom would be highly unusual for the Yanomami. He also spotted a familiar bone necklace hanging from a wooden stake behind the mound, one he immediately recognized to be the shaman's. The little man standing next to him began chanting softly. Roberts closed his eyes to listen.

He immediately recognized the bright dancing spirit inside his mind. The shaman was obviously pleased that Roberts had come to his final earthly resting place.

You have found your new path.

"*Yes, I believe that to be true,*" thought Roberts in reply.

And returned to learn the plight of my people.

"*Indeed I have, honored one.*"

Thank you for your openness, Brett Roberts.

"*I have you to thank for that…*"

Roberts wanted to share more with the shaman, although the vision had already begun to fade.

Eduardo Gomes International Airport, Manaus, Brazil

Ruth Roberts watched her husband exiting the helicopter and waved to him from behind the security fence. Brett broke into a grin when he spotted her and jogged toward the exit gate. Remembering Roberts from his recent departure, the uniformed security guard waved him through.

"Hello again, stranger."

Brett pulled his wife into a warm embrace and held her for a long, blissful moment. "I didn't expect you until later this afternoon."

"Couldn't wait to see Manaus so I took and earlier flight."

Brett feigned a hurtful look.

"And you, silly."

"Ahem," interjected Father João, who had been waiting there patiently.

"Oh, please excuse me," said Roberts. "Ruth, I'd like you to meet Father João."

"It is my great pleasure to meet you at last, Senhora Roberts. Or I should say, Doctor Roberts. You are even more beautiful than I imagined." He bowed and extended his hand.

Ruth knew how much this man meant to her husband. She stepped forward and gave the priest a friendly embrace. "Thank you Father, for bringing my husband back safely once again."

Father João blushed for a moment, then nodded. "Senhor Brett's work is most important to us here in Brazil. I am always honored to assist him. By the way, how has your ministry been progressing?"

"Quite well, thank you. Our work in Peru is almost finished."

Father João studied the handsome couple a moment. So lovely together. He felt happy for them. Then, as if the thought had just occurred to him, he asked, "Might I invite you to our humble cathedral on Sunday? I will be saying mass at eleven o'clock...."

Ruth quickly answered. "We'll look forward to it."

The two men shouldered their packs and followed Ruth into the terminal to retrieve her luggage from baggage claim. Brett fastened his belt strap before bending down to pick up his wife's two heavy duffels. "Ooof!" he teased.

"Oh here, let me take one of those," said Ruth. Brett glanced around to see Father João waiting outside already. Then he saw a familiar looking VW bus pull up to the curb. It was Father Ernesto, much greyer, but definitely the same man.

Brett said, "Hey Ruth, there's someone else I'd like you to meet!"

Later that evening, Brett Roberts and his wife sat across from each other at an outdoor table overlooking the Espaço Cultural Largo de São

Sebastião, and chatted quietly while digesting their dinner. The waiter had just taken their plates away, although a few splashes remained in their bottle of Obrigado Cabernet.

"How much longer do you think your Peru assignment will last?"

"We were just wrapping things up when I left. In fact, I've already changed my flights. I'll be returning home with you on Monday."

Brett chuckled to himself. This explained her extra bag. "That's wonderful, Ruth! You have no idea how much I've missed you. And we could both use a bit of down time." He paused to dole out the last of the wine, but no longer felt like drinking his.

Ruth could tell that her husband was beginning to fade. She walked around the table and reached for his hand. "Come on big guy, let's get you back to the hotel. I've missed you too, by the way."

"Lead on, sweetheart." He fingered a 200 Real note from his wallet and left it on the table.

The bell tower rang cheerfully that bright Sunday morning while the two of them walked briskly toward the front steps of the cathedral. Ruth's face brightened as they made their way inside, such a pretty sanctuary with its stained glass windows and gilded alcoves supporting painted statues of Jesus and the Holy Family. They settled into a pew and barely had time to catch their breath when organ music started playing from the back balcony. Everyone rose and turned to face the center aisle. Now dressed in a white linen robe with a green pastoral stole, Monsignor João processed up the center aisle with two young altar boys in tow, holding up a large gilded bible for all to see as he slowly approached the altar. He made a slight nod with a suppressed grin while passing the Roberts couple, delighted to see them again.

The service was in Portuguese, although the liturgy was essentially the same as in all catholic churches worldwide. Brett and Ruth sang along to the familiar hymns in muted English. When it came time to share the peace, their surrounding neighbors greeted them with "a paz esteja contigo". An old man seated beside them had been wondering why this couple seemed so familiar. Now grasping the hands of these two kind people, he sensed his connection with them to be spiritual, not physical.

When mass had ended, Brett touched Ruth's arm and whispered,

"Let's wait a while." When it was quieter, he flipped down the kneeler and began to pray. Ruth came forward to join him. They prayed together in silence. When Brett finally opened his eyes, he noticed that Father João had once again been waiting there patiently.

"Sister Maria wishes to see you now," the priest whispered.

They followed Father João out of the sanctuary and into the courtyard, where they found Sister Maria seated on a bench beneath a Brazilian pepper tree, fondly admiring the flower garden with a joyful look of serenity. A fountain gurgled nearby. She looked a bit older now, but even more beautiful than Brett remembered despite the extra wrinkles. Sister Maria smiled when she heard their footsteps approaching. "It is good to see you again, Senhor Brett. And this must be Ruth. I have so looked forward to meeting you, my dear."

"It's a pleasure meeting you as well, Sister Maria. My husband has told me so much about you."

Sister Maria nodded with a disarmingly impish grin. "Mostly good things, I trust." Then her deep azure eyes connected with Brett's, and after studying him closely, she broke into a smile. "Senhor Roberts, I sense that your spiritual doubts have been resolved."

"Yes, Sister. I have learned that one must be present with God, accept His grace, and share this gift with others."

"These three things are all that God asks."

She turned her attention back to Ruth. "And you, my dear. Monsignor Rivera has told me much about your missionary work together. Your faith has been a blessing to us all."

Ruth blushed. "Thank you, Sister."

Sister Maria feigned a moment of inspiration, and then said, "We will be handing out bags of food to the homeless of Cidade de Deus this afternoon, one of our poorest favelas in the northern part of the city. Would you like to join us?"

Brett's heart skipped a beat when he recalled his previous encounter in that neighborhood. "Would there be time for us to change into more suitable clothing?"

"Unfortunately not. In fact, we are late already. Come." She led them around to the front of the church where a rumbling church mini-bus waited down below, with Father João riding shotgun and Father Ernesto in the driver's seat. "Bem vindo a bordo!" the older priest called up to them with a beaming smile.

They climbed aboard and scarcely had time to fasten their seatbelts. Once again, Father Ernesto's driving reminded Brett of Mister Toad's Wild Ride at Disneyland. Somehow they made it out of the Central District without colliding with another vehicle. He relaxed a little when they merged onto BR-174 and settled in behind a flatbed truck loaded with used tires. They headed northward out of the city and this time made a right just before the entrance to the airport.

Cidade de Deus came into view about 15 minutes later. Brett and Ruth had visited other favelas over the years while working with Hope World Relief, although this one seemed a bit more desperate than most. Ravines of raw sewage ran between the densely packed clusters of dilapidated looking stilt houses, many of them listing to one side. Father Ernesto navigated around the potholes without much success as they wound their way through the narrow and dirty streets, finally pulling over next to a heavily tagged block wall building with boarded up windows. The amateur spray can artists had apparently drawn inspiration from El Dia de los Muertos.

A seemingly endless line of the favela's homeless awaited them. It saddened Brett to see their broken indigenous faces, although he understood why they had relocated here, having seen the devastation of their former territories with his own eyes.

Father João climbed down and pulled out a sun shade that was welded onto the side of the mini-bus. Then he shoved open the side door and instructed Roberts to get the folding tables while the rest of them readied the food bags to be handed out.

They had settled into their routine when Brett thought he overheard Sister Maria call over to one of the recipients: *"Hello Mother."*

With a side glance meant only for Senhor Roberts, she whispered, "She came back for my brother."

Shocked by this realization, Brett glanced down to a careworn woman with distinct Yanomami features, and striking blue eyes. Had he seen her before? Yes, he remembered. But younger then. From the last time he was in this favela.

Brett made an attempt to converse with this woman with his mind, although somewhat wary of what her response might be.

"Hello Luisa."

With her lips pressed firmly together, the woman nodded warily.

When Brett turned his attention to the young child holding her hand, he felt a sudden chill. The little boy was dirty and his jet black hair hadn't been combed in weeks, but clearly this was not his mother's fault. His eyes were brown, unlike his mother's, and they conveyed a certain wildness.

"Hello Juan," Brett murmured out loud. Never again would he allow that disconsolate spirit to enter his mind

The reincarnated little boy made a barely perceptible nod and quickly yanked his mother out of the line. Before Brett could say another word, they were gone.

AFTERWORD

When I first began writing this book, I had no idea how difficult it would be to bridge the seemingly disparate subjects of science and spirituality. What compelled me to persevere still eludes me. But one thing I do know with certainty. I could never have finished this project without the help of two exceptionally talented editors. They also happen to be my wife Laure and brother Jeff. To both of you, thanks for patiently reading through my numerous revisions with a critical eye, and each time with such positivity.

As a scientist myself, I must admit certain aspects of the storyline were indeed influenced by my own life experiences, although many of them were just figments of my imagination. And as for the drug DMT, forgive me if I failed to adequately describe an experience in some way you were expecting. I read numerous accounts of DMT hallucinations from other people who have tried it and did my best to portray them.

The concepts I've explored in this book may seem a bit preposterous, although scientific discovery is often like that at the beginning. Take *entanglement* for example. Just last year, there was an article published in the prestigious journal *Nature* demonstrating that quantum entanglement could be measured over a substantial distance. Scientists at Delft University of Technology in the Netherlands were actually able to accomplish this by engineering a tiny spin trap inside a diamond, in this case one that could accommodate a single electron. They positioned two such spin traps at opposing sides of their campus, a distance of 1.3 kilometers, and used independent pulses of microwave and laser energy to entangle them. According to their recorded data, one such particle had indeed exchanged information with the other one. This observation disproved a fundamental principle of physics known as "locality", a precept that Einstein himself staunchly defended, which stated that an object could only be influenced by its immediate surroundings.

So might there be something special about human biology that enables us to perceive the supernatural, a *spiritual entanglement* if you will? If so, then I think it must also have something to do with prayer, when our minds are open and we permit this to happen. And having come full circle now, I find myself more grateful than ever to have been blessed with Faith. Because I do not believe this to be impossible.